STEER BY THE STARS

STEER BY THE STARS

BY

OLIVIA FITZROY

ILLUSTRATED BY ANNE BULLEN

Published by Fidra Books, 2007

First Published 1944 by Collins Publishers

Text © Estate of Olivia FitzRoy
Preface © Barbara Ormrod

British Library Cataloguing in Publication Data
A catalogue record for this book is available from the British Library

Printed and Bound by Biddles, Kings Lynn

ISBN-13 978 1906 12300 0

Published by Fidra Books Ltd
60 Craigcrook Road
Edinburgh
EH4 3PJ

www.fidrabooks.com

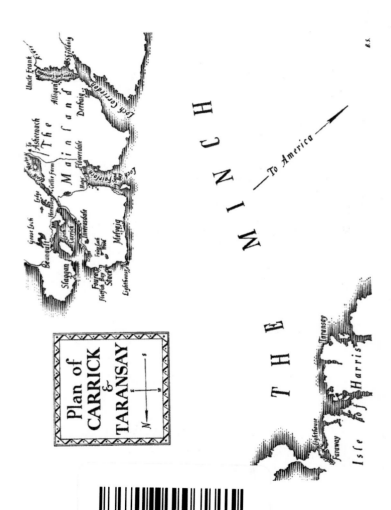

Plan of
CARRICK
&
TARANSAY

Olivia FitzRoy – her childhood

By her sister, Barbara Ormrod

Before the Second World War, my mother and father lived at 112 Sloane Street in London, in a house that they bought in 1930. My father was in the Navy, almost continuously at sea and except for an occasional two weeks' leave we saw very little of him. In those days no provision was made for Naval families so if my mother wanted to see him we were sent to stay either with my grandmother, Lady Manners, who lived in Sussex near Midhurst or with my great-aunt at Rockingham Castle in Northamptonshire.

My father Captain R O FitzRoy, RN was the eldest son of Captain The Right Hon E A FitzRoy who was the Speaker of the House of Commons from 1928 to 1943 where he and my grandmother lived in Speaker's House. When my grandfather died just before the end of the War, he was posthumously created Viscount Daventry (his constituency). My grandmother cleverly had herself made a Viscountess in her own right and so my father didn't become 2nd Viscount Daventry until she died. As my father had five daughters and no sons, the title passed to his brother who had two sons. My mother was Grace Zoë Guinness and she married my father in September 1916.

I was one of five sisters. The eldest three were

Mary (born in 1919), Olivia (1921), Katherine (1924), myself (Barbara, 1928) and Amelia (1930). The older sisters were mainly looked after by a governess whilst Amelia and I had a nanny and a nursery maid.

Every summer our aunt, Nancy FitzRoy, used to rent a cottage in Scotland, seldom the same one, and invite her nieces and nephews to stay. Up until the War, Amelia and I were considered too young and went to the seaside with Nanny, whilst Mary, Olivia and Katherine went to Scotland. The cottages were small and fairly primitive and all housework and cooking were done by the guests and my aunt. At the time this was very exciting as we never did anything like that at home! The cottages were also near the sea and the days were spent fishing in the sea, rivers, burns and lochs with much exploring and picnicking.

1939 was the first year that Amelia and I went and, when in early September most people went south and war was inevitable, my father sent a message "Don't move, stay where you are, you will be safer." He was sure that Hitler would invade. Mary and Kathy had already gone, so Olivia aged 18, and Amelia and I aged 9 and 10 stayed behind. It was very challenging for Olivia, a Debutante who had just finished her first Season, now without telephone, electricity, or even a wireless! How she managed from the very minimal village shop I can't think. In September she walked up to the 'Big House' to hear the news, leaving Amelia and I in bed. She heard war declared and brought the news back to us. At our age war was exciting so we were thrilled and sure that we would find enemy submarines hiding in the loch. Fairly soon my mother and sister Mary came back to Inverewe. Kathy had insisted on going to boarding school.

My father was Captain of the 1st Minesweeping Flotilla and his was the first ship to come into Loch Ewe. He was spotted by Amelia and I when we were on our way to take up the lobster pots and set the long line. Eventually, the whole Northern Fleet came in – Repulse, Renown, Prince of Wales, Ark Royal and so on and we had a ready market for our lobsters and fish! We lived in The Lodge, the gate lodge to the big Inverewe House, now all incorporated into the National Trust garden. It was a little black and white bungalow that will be familiar to visitors to Inverewe gardens and not at all like the Lodge in Olivia's books about the Stewart family! We had no staff so did everything ourselves.

Living in such remote area during the war shopping opportunities were limited and we soon ran out of reading matter so Olivia wrote *Orders to Poach* to entertain Amelia and I. Our tastes in books were, I suspect, typical of our time – *Swallows and Amazons*, Violet Needham, Sapper, Leslie Charteris, Baroness Orczy, Dennis Wheatley, R L Stevenson, Charles Kingsley, J M Barrie, Georgette Heyer and many others. Books were always favourite presents.

Orders to Poach was published by Collins. I think that they were the first publishers to see the book as Billy Collins lived near Rockingham and was a friend of the family. Olivia later moved to Jonathan Cape.

After one and a half years at Inverewe we moved to Strontian near Fort William to a house owned by our father's brother – large, freezing cold, again no electricity, miles down an unmade road in a bus. We spent a year there and Olivia kept us alive by stalking hinds in the winter. She wrote her second book, *Steer by the Stars* whilst living there.

My mother hated it. She was very talented - a very good artist, she also wrote well, was musical and extremely amusing, original and wise. Although totally impractical, she was a wonderful mother, grandmother and surrogate grandmother to many. She never got up until lunchtime and never went to bed before 3am! My maternal grandmother came up to visit us and spent her time picking sphagnum moss from the bogs and drying it to send south for wound dressings!

My father left the Navy when the war ended. He was a Captain and commanded the battleship Rodney. They bought an old rectory in Rutland – still without electricity! He became a Governor of Uppingham School, a county councillor and a head of the Red Cross.

Our rather nomadic life meant that we did not have many friends beyond ourselves. I think it was not a person who had the most influence on our lives, but the places where we lived – Rockingham was the most wonderful place to be brought up: steeped in history with huge gardens and a ruined keep. Sussex, quite different, had the South Downs to roam over and all these places came into Olivia's books and poems.

We were all musical, artistic and literate, Olivia being the best at writing. Mary went to school at

Owlestone Croft, Cambridge when she was about 15. Prior to that she was taught, like all of us, by various governesses and local tutors. Olivia had too many animals – ducks, pigeons, rabbits, dogs and ponies – to go away to school. She was very intelligent and masters from Uppingham School came to Rockingham Castle to coach her in Mathematics, History, Literature and English. Katherine was determined to be conventional and went to boarding school during the War where she was very good at games and music. Amelia and I had various local teachers – we also went to the village school in Strontian, the next place in Scotland that we lived after Inverewe. Here we learned the Lord's Prayer in Gaelic! We also went to various small schools in Sussex, which usually entailed bicycling miles.

My mother was not in favour of formal education which explains our idiosyncratic schooling. However, I think that if Olivia had had to conform to school rules, her writing might have lost its originality.

Barbara Ormrod, 2006.

STEER BY THE STARS

DEDICATED

TO

THE CREW

OF THE REAL

Fauna

CONTENTS

Illustrations

WHO GOES WITH FERGUS?

Who will go with Fergus now,
And pierce the deep wood's woven shade,
And dance upon the level shore?
Young man, lift up your russet brow,
And lift your tender eyelids, maid,
And brood on hopes and fears no more.

And no more turn aside and brood
Upon Love's bitter mystery;
For Fergus rides the brazen cars,
And rules the shadows of the wood,
And the white breast of the dim sea,
And all dishevelled wandering stars.

W. B. YEATS.

CHAPTER I

AUGUST EVENING, CARRICK
Thursday, 5th August

"*GOSH*!" said Fiona, for the twentieth time, "isn't the train ever coming in?"

"Och, it'll be in in a wee while," said the porter reassuringly, but Fiona did not believe him.

"It's five minutes late already," she insisted. "There's probably been a breakdown or something. Oh! Botheration! Why must it happen to this one train?"

"Seeing that it's the only one to-day," said Ninian, pushing a penny into an empty chocolate machine and picking it up as it fell through, "it's hardly surprising that if anything was going to happen it would happen to that one."

"Bother the train," said Fiona. She looked up at the big station clock. Surprisingly enough the hands had moved on only a minute since she looked last. She stared both ways down the lines. There was nothing to be seen but the long narrowing track of metals and the rolling purple and green hills. Beyond, in a series of blue peaks, rose the Corriedon Mountains, shimmering in the heat of an August afternoon.

Fiona and Ninian Stewart were waiting on Asheenach platform for the London train that was bringing Hugh Murray and their cousin Sandy Stewart from the south. They had arrived too soon, just in case the train was early, and that by some awful chance they should miss a minute or two of each other's company.

They had inspected every inch of the station; every crate and bundle; every pile of newspapers and each haunch of venison. They had talked to the porter, the man in the ticket office, and the station-master. They had had a drink of beer in the hotel. There was nothing else left to do.

"If the train doesn't come in soon," grumbled Ninian, "the Ford'll melt." Certainly the sun was very hot. The sky was cloudless; there was no wind. There were a couple of red-brown spots on the hill opposite that looked very much like deer. Some sheep were feeding near the station palings, and a black spaniel ran in and out, panting and lolling out his pink tongue.

Ninian left Fiona sitting on a wooden bench chewing a Crunchie bar, and wandered off to the edge of the platform. For the hundredth time he gazed down the lines.

Suddenly he gave a wild yell.

"It's coming, Fiona!" he shouted. His sister sprang up, and together they raced over the iron bridge and down on to the platform the other side. The train, with its curl of white smoke, came panting up the glen very much out of breath after the long climb up from Dingwall.

It stopped with a jerk and the steam came hissing and pouring from the engine. Doors were thrown open and mail-bags, trunks, crates and parcels came hurtling out.

Fiona and Ninian walked down the train, peering eagerly into every carriage. Just ahead of them a door was pushed open and Sandy jumped out, his arms full of fishing rods and gun cases. He looked just the same as ever, with his broad grin and untidy head, but he seemed to have grown even larger, and was easily as tall as Ninian. His wrists had left his coat sleeves some way behind, and his trousers were a bit short too, but being Sandy, he had not noticed and if he had he did not care.

Hugh jumped down behind him with a beaming face.

"Oh!" said Fiona, staring. "You've grown a moustache!"

"D'you think it's an improvement?" he asked.

"Definitely not," said Fiona; but Ninian looked at it enviously, and tentatively rubbed a finger along his upper lip.

The last of the luggage was hauled out before the little train went puffing on into the hills.

JAMIE WENT FISHING

"Well!" said Hugh, stretching himself and gazing appreciatively across to Corriedon. "Gosh ! It's good to be back!"

"Umn!" said Sandy, as they clattered back over the bridge. "I thought I should burst in the train. Seeing all the hills flashing past and having to stick on in that boiling furnace!"

The porter was carrying their things across the lines, and helped to stow them into the Ford.

"Where are the twins?" asked Hugh, as they wedged two suitcases on to the carrier.

"Jean was offered a day's fishing," said Ninian, "and Jamie went with her. There wouldn't have been room for them anyway."

"Is Drake still at Carrick?" asked Sandy.

"No, he left in a huff, thank goodness," said Fiona. "It's been taken by some friends of father's — Brown, they're called. He was in the army. They don't come up till next week, so they said we could fish until they arrived."

"Sounds a bit better than Drake," said Hugh, climbing into the back seat. "No more poaching?"

"No, and it's been hopeless for fishing too," said Ninian, as they jolted out of the yard. "It's too bright to-day, really, but Jean said she couldn't bear it any longer, and just went."

"What have you been doing then?" asked Hugh, leaning forward so that he could talk more easily with Ninian and Fiona in front.

"Just lazing about," said Fiona. "And then, of course, we haven't told you *the thing*."

"What thing?" asked Sandy.

"We promised not to say until the twins were there too," said Ninian. "But it's something really good!"

"Oh, this is too much!" groaned Hugh. "What sort of a thing?"

But the others refused to give even the smallest hint.

However, there was plenty to talk about, for they had not all four been together since last summer. Hugh had come up to Carrick for the hind shooting, and Sandy had come for Easter. Fiona had been to England for part of the summer and had seen a good deal of Hugh, who was at Pirbright, and Ninian, who was at Sandhurst.

But there was masses to say; masses to discuss and plan; and plenty of reminiscences.

They stopped for a minute at the top of the hill and looked down across the long blue length of Loch Marba, with its pine-wooded islands and bank of sheer hills.

Ninian let the car run down the glen with the engine off. The hood was down and as they glided along the smell of heather came pouring down the purple hills on each side of them.

Hugh sniffed hungrily. Last time he had been down Ninian had had the chains on, and even then they had slipped on the ice; and instead of purple the hills had all been white.

The engine came on again with a roar as they reached the bottom at Kinlochcarrick. Ninian stopped here to send a telegram he had forgotten to do at the station, and also bought some chocolate. Then they were off again, through the cool green birch wood, and out into the glare of Slatterdale and the tumbling waters of the Kerry.

"Not much longer now," said Sandy, as they climbed up into Fairloch. "Thank goodness, because I can't bear to wait for this tremendous secret much longer."

Ninian and Fiona looked at each other.

"Perhaps he won't like it?" she suggested.

"Probably not. In fact I should think it is the last thing in the world he'd like."

"Oh, can't you give me one little hint?" cried Sandy. "This is so tantalising!" But his cousins only laughed and drove on even faster.

At last they swung down the hill into Carrick, crossed the bridge, and started jolting up the track by the river to the lodge.

There were shrieks of delight as each well-remembered pool was passed, each fold of the wood, every crofter's house. The air rang with "D'you remember when —?" which continued right up to the lodge door.

As Hugh got out he realised that everything was just as it had been on the day he had first driven up the track, and looked out across Hernsary and the sea. There was old Maggie too, beaming in the doorway. Then she was pushed aside as the twins rushed past her and flung themselves on him.

It took half an hour for every one to get sorted out and the things put in their appointed places. Then there was tea, a lengthy business, because Maggie's teas were not things to be taken lightly, they were much too large and too good.

When at last it was finished and they were all sitting in a row on the grass outside, Sandy leant forward.

"Now tell me!" he said.

"Yes, come on!" said Hugh.

The others looked at Ninian. "You tell!" they said.

Maddeningly, Ninian took out his pipe, filled it and lit it. Then, when it was going properly, he spat out a small piece of tobacco and began.

THE TWINS

"To start with," he said, "I'd better warn you it's got nothing to do with fishing or stalking!"

Sandy looked disappointed at this, and Hugh wrinkled up his forehead.

"Guess it," said Jean.

"I couldn't possibly."

"Well, just try."

"Has it got anything to do with ponies?" asked Hugh.

"No, nothing!"

"Walking?" said Sandy gloomily, with visions of long hot hikes across the hills.

"No," cried the others.

"Sailing then?"

"We must tell him!" cried Jamie, and Ninian began again:

"We've been lent a boat by the Danvers of Loch Bruisch. It's a cabin cruiser really, about fifteen tons. Four bunks, a sink and a lavatory. We cook on a Primus, and there are all kinds of charts and pilot books. It's all complete, and the engine works, and," his voice rose to a shout, "we're going to take her round to Flatfish Bay and live on her, and —" He could get no further.

With a wild shriek Sandy leapt to his feet, rolled James over, and followed him down the hill. They chased each other, yelling with joy, until at last they joined the others, panting and grinning.

"Was there ever such a blissful plan?" crowed Jean.

"When do we start? Why are we waiting? What's she called? Is there room for us all?" shouted Sandy and Hugh in turn.

"We'll have to do it properly or there won't be room," Fiona broke in on the chorus. "Watch and watch about, two at a time." Gosh, it's going to be fun!"

"When do we start?" It was Sandy again.

"We thought to-morrow or the next day," said Ninian. "You see, there are all the stores and blankets and saucepans to get on board, but we thought we'd leave it all until you got here."

"What's she called?" asked Hugh.

"*Fauna*," said Jean briefly.

"*Fauna*," repeated Hugh slowly. "You know, it's rather a good name."

"Lucky," said Jamie, "because it's bad luck to change the name of a ship."

"I can't wait to see her," said Sandy longingly. "Oh, Ninian, I never guessed it could be anything as good as this."

"If only the weather holds," put in Fiona.

"Well, it'll be fun whatever happens," said Jean. "Goodness, Hugh, I envy you not having seen her yet, she's simply perfect."

"When can we see her, Ninian?" asked Hugh.

"It's too late to-night," said Ninian, looking out at the setting sun. "We'll go to-morrow and spend the whole day there, getting her ready. There's lots to be done, because she was left in an awful mess."

"How long have you got her for?" Sandy lay back and tweaked Jean's hair, as she lay flat on the warm grass.

"We've got her till the end of August," said Fiona. "That's nearly a fortnight, isn't it, or is it more?"

No one could remember how the rhyme went, but still it did not matter very much. The main thing was that they had a golden prospect before them; a thrilling prospect of meals cooked on a Primus and of unlimited bathing and basking.

Ninian, too enchanted to speak, bit on his pipe stem, and frowned at the cloudless sky. Fiona and Jamie were feeling a little disloyal to *Black Swan,* but rapturously happy all the same. No such thoughts marred the minds of Jean, Sandy and Hugh. They were all six perfectly happy until Ninian broke the silence by saying in his maddeningly logical way:

"You know, if it does rain like mad it really would be rather hell, stuck down in that tiny cabin."

Immediately there were shrieks of "Ninian!"

"You do think of the most odious things!"

"Don't be so stupid."

"No, but it would," repeated Ninian, unperturbed.

"Nonsense," cried Fiona, jumping up. "Nothing's going to happen like that. It's going to be the most perfect summer that ever happened. Come on, now, if we run we'll get up to the rock and see *Fauna* before dinner!"

The others followed her flying figure up the track, and a few moments later they had crossed the burn and were charging up the hill to the rock, where so many of their adventures last year had been planned.

They stood for a minute on the summit, getting back their breath. The wind came blowing up to meet them from the sea.

"There," cried Fiona, pointing.

They followed her outstretched arm.

"*Fauna's* nearest us," said Jamie. "The other's *Black Swan.*"

"YES, IT'S TRUE," SHE SAID.

Hugh looked down on the tiny dot that was to be his home for the next week or two. He found it difficult to imagine that it was really a life-size boat with a cabin and bunks and an engine. It did not seem possible that, with a squash, all six of them would fit in comfortably enough to live there.

The sea was gold, the land was black, and the sky green and pink. The blue peat smoke from the crofters' fires hung in a haze over the village. Out on the golden sea a tiny black boat, the herring boat, chugged off towards Beanault.

Hugh turned. They had all gone back down the hill, all except Fiona.

"Yes, it's true," she said, reading his thoughts, "every bit of it." She looked down at the others.

"Come on," she said, "or we'll be late." And they ran down the hill together.

(The man stood still on the cliffs above Flatfish, staring west over the sea towards the Hebrides. It was dusk, and their far-away hilly outline was hidden by the night. In his mind the man could see them, and one in particular, his home which he loved, the place where he could not live. As he stood motionless it grew darker and darker till the sea was an iron-grey shield, barred with black, as the waves rolled in from the Atlantic. Slowly the beach faded and grew dim, the gulls dropped their clamour and were silent, and a small night-wind whistled through the grasses on the cliff. Gradually the stars came out one by one above the still figure on the cliff's edge.

He stood there until it was quite dark, his face inscrutable, expressionless, his eyes half closed. He stood so still that he seemed to have become part of the cliff, and yet his mind was more distant and more far away then the hidden rim of the sea.)

CHAPTER II

VICTUALLING SHIP
Friday, 6th August

THERE was so much to be done next morning that it was difficult to know where to start. At last it was decided that Hugh and the twins would get the stores, while the other three scrubbed and polished and overhauled the engine.

"We must all go down together," said Jean. "We can't possibly let Sandy see her without all being there, too."

"You could row across to the village," suggested Ninian. "There won't be such an awful lot to get," he added, seeing Jamie's face at the thought of rowing a heavy boat back.

"Well, let's make a list," said Fiona. "We're sure to forget otherwise."

Hugh produced a letter from his pocket and tore off a blank sheet. "This do?" he asked.

Fiona nodded, and took a pencil from Ninian. They were sitting outside on the grass, and there was no very convenient place to prop the paper. Fiona managed as well as she could.

It was sunny and windy and warm. The sea sparkled entrancingly beyond Hernsary and the sloping hill. Out by the mouth of the bay white horses galloped inland, and a motor boat crawled slowly towards Cove.

"What'll we start with?" asked Sandy.

"Cleaning things seem to be the most important," said Ninian. "*Fauna's* simply filthy."

Fiona was writing hard.

> "Vim.
> Rinso, plenty.
> Soap.

Scrubbing brush.
Dishcloths.
Brasso.
Rags and things.
Abraizo.
Soda.
Saucepan.
Frying pan.
Kettle.
Teapot.
6 cups.
6 plates.
6 knives, forks and spoons.
Bread knife.
Palette knife.
Dustpan and brush."

"We can get all these in the house," objected Jamie. "Hurry up with the food."

"I must put them down," said Fiona. "We'll never remember otherwise."

"Cocoa.
Tea.
Sugar.
Butter.
Bacon.
Bread.
Jam and things.
Cake.
Eggs.
Sausages or kippers, or and kippers.
Tinned fruit.
      "   meat.
      "   milk.
Dripping.

Matches, lots."

"Chocolate," said Jamie and Sandy loudly.

"Potatoes," wrote Fiona, frowning as the space on the paper got smaller and more and more things came crowding into her head.

"Don't forget water," said Ninian. "Put it down large. We mustn't forget to fill the tanks. And paraffin and petrol and oil."

"A bucket and brush for the decks," said Jamie.

"And blankets and pillows and clothes," added Jean.

"Don't forget sardines," said Hugh, "and salt and mustard and pepper."

"What an awful lot of things there are," sighed Fiona, rubbing her forehead.

"And there's sure to be masses more when we get there."

"Lots of oilies and jerseys," said Sandy, "if we're going to keep watch by night."

"Bathing things," said Jean, "and what about tooth brushes and sponges, or do they come in with clothes?"

"Yes, definitely," said Fiona. "Can anybody think of anything else essential, because there's only about half an inch left to write on."

"Torches might be useful," said Hugh. "And what about some cards — we must have something to do when it rains."

They were squeezed in at the bottom of the list.

"Rifle," said Ninian suddenly.

"Why on earth?" asked Jamie.

"Might be useful, we'd better take it," said Ninian. "And fishing lines, too, and the spear."

"We can't do any elaborate cooking," said Fiona, sitting up and stretching. "Not on a Primus anyway. We must take masses of bread and bacon and stuff — and cheese, of course."

"She may need some new ropes and things," said Ninian. "We'll have to see that when we get there."

"Do let's go," begged Jean. "I'm aching to start."

"Put a cross beside the things we can get in the house," suggested Sandy. "Then we won't get in a muddle."

"We will," said Fiona, staring at the illegible mess on the paper. "Oh, well, can you read it, Hugh?" She handed it to him.

"Good enough," said Hugh. "I can guess half."

Sandy jumped up. "Let's be off, then," he cried. "Bags I get the car!" He and Jamie raced towards the shed.

Ninian stood up and felt in his pockets. "Jean," he said, "here's a pound for all those stores. Well, perhaps you'd better have two, in case."

Jean took the money.

"I'm paying half," said Hugh.

"Rot," said Fiona. "Father sent us some on purpose. Now, shut up, and don't say another word," she added, as Hugh opened his mouth to protest.

With a roar and a grind, the Ford emerged backwards from the shed. Sandy had won, and was sitting triumphantly in the driver's seat.

"Beast," Jamie said, as he followed. "You've learnt some horrible new tricks, Sandy."

"Oh, hurry up," said Ninian, his eyes on the sea. He was impatient to be down there; to feel *Fauna's* deck beneath his feet again.

Fiona came running from the house with a scrubbing brush, Vim, and various cloths in her hands.

"Buck up," urged Ninian, his foot on the clutch.

Fiona squeezed in at the back, the car jerked, and they were off. The twins had opened the hood and the air came rushing at them, cool and sweet. They had to shout at each other above the rattle of stones on the track and the clatter of the Ford, which sounded, as usual, as if it was about to drop to pieces.

Jean opened the gates, one two hundred yards or so from the house, one over the burn, and the other in the birch wood. The other Stewarts were too firmly wedged in the back to be able to move.

The river was low in its bed as they passed. Dry grey rocks by the score lay scattered where there should have been racing water.

"I don't wonder you caught nothing yesterday, James," said Hugh.

The last gate, by the river's mouth, was opened, and they were out on the smooth tarmac.

"There she is," cried Fiona, as they came within view of the bay.

Over by the slip, anchored where the chart said "Good anchorage, three fathoms." Hugh saw the brown shape of a boat. *Black Swan* was there, of course; he could see her dark against the grey rocks. But beyond her was another boat, paler brown and higher, with a row of portholes along the small raised cabin.

They sat with their eyes fixed on her, all except Ninian, and even he did no more than glance at the road.

Presently they were crunching down the cinders under the tall pine trees, brushing through the heaps of needles that had drifted along the path. It was dark in the wood, dark and cool, and they hurried out into the sunshine of the pier.

"There she is," breathed Jean.

Fauna was no longer something remote and undistinguishable; she was a real live boat, almost within reach.

"Come on," said Ninian, dropping the knapsack he was carrying. He untied the long rope that moored the dinghy and started to haul her ashore. Directly she came alongside they leapt down, almost upsetting her in their hurry.

"Got everything?" asked Ninian, with one hand grasping a bunch of seaweed to keep the boat steady.

"One, two, three," counted Fiona. "Yes, that's all. Do let's hurry."

Sandy pushed off. Ninian took the oars. The dinghy had sunk deep in the water. There was only just enough room for the six.

Quickly Ninian rowed out to *Fauna*. Sandy and James in the bows were ready to grab the gunwale directly they were along-side. The tide was strong here, sweeping them inland. Ninian rowed as hard as he could.

"Ship your starboard oar!" cried Sandy. A minute later there was the faintest of bumps, and Ninian looked up to see *Fauna* beside him.

Sandy heaved himself on board and tied the painter between two scuppers in the low bulwarks that were only three or four inches high. One by one the others followed him while James handed up the knapsacks.

Fauna had no deckhouse, but the roof of the cabin was raised about a foot and had three small portholes each side. Aft there was a canvas screen to protect the steersman from the worst of the weather. She was steered by a large wheel, and beyond that there was a glass skylight in the cabin roof that could be opened and instructions shouted up and down. Behind the wheel was a hatch into the engine-room, which was not so much an engine-room as an engine with hardly any room round it at all. Beside the hatch was the pump and several untidy coils of rope, and forward was more rope, a bucket, a squeegee and mop, and a small wooden bollard like a cross. Also, of course, the anchor and chain, as *Fauna* was tied to a buoy at the moment.

Jean was struggling with the forehatch into the cabin.

"It's awfully stiff," she said. "Come and help heave, Ninian."

Ninian gave it two or three kicks with his heel, and it flew back. Jean and Sandy were the first down, and the others followed or stood on the companion, as there was not overmuch room in the cabin.

Opposite the foot of the ladder was a sink and shelf for the Primus, as well as cups hanging on hooks, a few kitchen utensils, and odd spoons and knives in the drawer. A little water tank hung above the sink over a grimy porthole. On the right was a door leading to the fo'c'sle, in which there was just enough room for two bunks to be squeezed in with the feet up in the bows. Opposite the sink was a tiny lavatory and between the two was the doorway to the main cabin.

Hugh's first impression of this was that it was very small, and his next that it needed cleaning badly. However, he was sure Fiona could cope with that, and had seen her stowing into one of the knapsacks a tin of Vim, a scrubbing brush and cloth.

There were two bunks built in each side under the decks, and over the water tanks. Aft, a piece of the bulkhead could be taken down, making room for someone to crawl over a cushioned seat through to the engine. A long table stood in the middle of the cabin, and two flaps attached to each bunk could be put up for seats. On the right inside the doorway was a cupboard with a few pilot books and charts on top.

Jean was delightedly showing him and Sandy everything.

"There's even electric light," she said, "although we can't use it until the engine's been run a bit more."

"Luckily there are plenty of lanterns," put in Jamie.

"The portholes open, too," said Jean, unscrewing one.

"Let's open them all," said Fiona. "That'll air it a bit."

Ninian was grappling with the screw of one of the water tanks.

"They're rather inconvenient," he said, "because unless one pumps a lot one has to get all the water out with a cup."

"Oh well," said Fiona, climbing back up the companion, "you'd better get going with that engine, Ninian. I've an idea it'll be as stubborn as most engines are."

"You're probably right," said Ninian

Hugh joined them on deck. "Isn't it about time we were starting for the village?" he asked. "There seems to be a good deal to do there."

Ninian was already half-way down to the engine-room,

and Fiona had the bucket in her hand.

"These decks do need a scrub," she said. "I'll get Sandy on to them. Yes, perhaps you'd better go."

"Come on, you two," called Hugh, and with difficulty dragged the twins away from an intent study of the chart.

"They've got Flatfish Bay there, only they call it something quite different," said James.

"And look — there's the lighthouse, and there's rocks, and what are all those squiggles?" asked Jean.

"Currents," suggested Sandy. "And look — one fathom, two, then ten: it must be a drop."

"Come on!" shouted Hugh again.

"Look at Foura with the gully," cried Jean.

"And the Hebrides," said Jamie. "I say, Ninian," he called through to the engine-room, where his brother was crouching, "how far is it to Faraway?"

Ninian did not hear, and at this moment Hugh appeared and dragged them forcibly to the companion.

"I'll ask him later," thought Jamie, and forgot about it.

Jean seated herself in the stern and the others each took an oar.

"We can go up the river nearly to the bridge," explained James. "There's a place to tie up there."

Fiona watched them go, the bucket still dangling from the rope.

"Here, Sandy," she said, "you start on these decks, only don't go pouring water down the ports."

"What are you going to do?" asked Sandy suspiciously.

Fiona grinned. "Don't think you're having the worst of it," she said. "There's more to be done below than up here." She slid down the companion and reappeared with a bucket that she filled, and narrowly missed having her feet soaked by a stream of water sent along the deck by Sandy.

Ninian, meanwhile, was getting oily and hot in the cramped space round the engine. There was nowhere to stand, except on the ribs of the boat and her sides. Under the engine a revolting mass of oily water slid up and down. Seeing Fiona taking up the strips of matting from the cabin, he called through: "I'm going to pump out the bilges; it's simply beastly in here."

"You certainly do look hot," said his sister.

She took the mats up on deck, to brush and beat, and left them while she scrubbed the lino and woodwork. Indeed, everything had to be scrubbed most thoroughly, but it was not unpleasant, as she kept finding new exciting things and calling them through to the boys.

Softly a few ripples flew across the water. Sandy, peering over the gunwale, could see faint green fronds of seaweed and some shells below the boat. It was low tide, and a long stretch of muddy sand lay all along the shore between the pine wood and the village. A curlew gave its bubbling call as it flew low over the mud. Sandy remembered how they had used its call for their danger signal last year, and remembering it, wished that they could have the same sort of holiday this year, too. Although going round to Flatfish was going to be heavenly, it would lack that tremendous excitement that the poaching had had.

"Sandy," called Fiona, "you might empty this bucket."

By the time the tide was half-way up the shore again, *Fauna* was looking very much better than she had some two hours earlier. In the sea all round her floated scraps of cotton waste, chips, dust, rags, and bits of paper, and a patch of oily water showed that the bilges had indeed been pumped out.

"I wish the others would come back," said Sandy. "I'm getting hungry."

"There are the water tanks to fill, too," said Fiona.

She and Ninian had decided the best place to keep the paraffin was in the fo'c'sle. There was room for a big tin at the foot of the bunks. They would fill up to capacity with petrol and the extra tins could be wedged in somewhere with the engine.

In her mind she was running over the cupboards and drawers in the cabin as she sat with Sandy on deck. There was not much room for stores or clothes; anyway they would not be taking many of the latter. There was the cupboard under the sink and the one in the cabin, and the shelves where the cups and plates were, and also two big drawers under the fo'c'sle bunks and a place for things under the cushioned seat.

"She certainly does look lovely now," said Sandy, who had been below inspecting the results of Fiona's hard work.

"She's a blissful boat," said Fiona. "Absolutely perfect. I don't think she could be better in any way."

"We don't know how she behaves yet," said Sandy. "I say, Ninian, how's that engine?"

Ninian's voice came muffled up through the hatch: "Filthy, but she should start any minute now."

And just as Fiona sighted the laden dinghy creeping towards them, the calm peace of the morning was shattered by a fearful roar. A hot dirty face was poked up through the engine hatch.

"Pretty good," said Fiona. "Oh!" as the noise stuttered and died.

"That's all right," said Ninian, diving back, and in a minute the roar steadied to a rhythmic beat.

"Do her good to run for a little," said Ninian.

At last the store ship arrived, and large and enticing looking parcels were handed up by Jean.

"You couldn't imagine how long it took to get these things," said Hugh. "To begin with, there were about a hundred people there first, and then the man couldn't find a thing. But we got them all eventually."

"Even some chocolate," interrupted Jamie.

"Gosh, it looks bliss down there," cried Jean. She was peering down the hatch. "You have worked hard. What's that on the stove?"

"Help!" cried Fiona. "I'd forgotten it. Any one hungry

except me?"

"Hungry?" said Ninian. "Don't let's store the things till after lunch."

It was too fine to eat in the cabin, so the sandwiches were spread on the roof, and Fiona produced mugs of cocoa, that had been boiling on the Primus.

"The first meal we've had in *Fauna*," said Jean, taking a bite of ham sandwich.

"The first thing we've cooked here," said Fiona, trying to sip her drink.

Hugh lay on his back and watched the gulls wheeling and crying overhead. It was hot, and a warm wind blew from the pine wood, so soft that at first he could not think why he could smell the resin. Oh, but it was good to be back at Carrick.

Ninian was speaking.

"Did you get the petrol and stuff?" he asked.

"Not all," said Hugh. "There wasn't room. We'll have to get the rest when we've emptied out these tins."

"It'll take some time putting all the stores away," remarked Jean.

"And there's the water to get in," added Sandy.

"We don't need to bring cups and things, and a kettle and saucepans, because they're here already," said Fiona, "and a few knives and spoons."

"There won't be time to go for a trial trip to-day," said Ninian, "and we simply must do that before we go right out. The engine seems all right so far, but we don't want her to die on us."

"Then we can't start till the day after to-morrow — Wednesday," said Jean, and sighed. "It seems such a long time."

"Plenty to do," Sandy reminded her.

"It's wasting a day," objected James. "After all, Ninian's not up here for long."

"What sort of time shall we start on Wednesday?" asked

Jean.

Ninian rolled over and looked at her. She was trying not to look disappointed that they were not starting at once.

"Don't smile like that," she said. "What is it?"

Ninian turned back and looked out to the headland. He was smiling at a thought he had, of a way of making her not disappointed after all.

"I don't know what there is against starting to-morrow evening," he said at last.

"Ninian!" shrieked Jean, leaping up and running round the deck in her excitement. "Really to-morrow?"

"Well, why not? Not that twelve hours could make much difference, but still —"

"Oh, don't be so patronising," said Fiona. "You talk as if all this was your idea, and you were kindly letting us help, in an amateurish way."

"D'you consider yourself a professional, then?"

"You wouldn't be doing this if it wasn't for us," said Fiona, ignoring his question.

"Why not? There are plenty of chaps I know who would have come up, and probably been more efficient than you, too."

"And run you on the rocks in the dark," said Fiona scathingly.

"And not have quarrelled like a schoolgirl."

"If you're so mad about them, I wonder you didn't ask them up here."

"They wouldn't have come."

"Just like old times," said Hugh, "hearing you two quarrel again!" At which they both laughed, and Jamie said:

"Twelve hours will make a difference, Ninian, because instead of waking up at Carrick, we shall wake up at Flatfish."

"Really, he's longing to just as much as us," said Fiona, "only he thinks that as an embryo subaltern, he mustn't show enthusiasm. Goodness knows why," she added.

"You really do talk nonsense," said Ninian, laughing in spite of himself. "Let's get going with the petrol."

Eventually they decided that Ninian should take the tins to be filled in the Ford while the others filled the water tanks. This proved a very messy job, but at last it was done.

"Well," said Fiona at last, as she screwed the top on the second tank and looked proudly round the gleaming cabin, "no one could say she was dirty now."

Jean ran her hand affectionately down the bulkhead.

"I wonder how she will go to-morrow," she said. "And I still can't believe that we will be living in her soon."

"It does seem too good to be true," agreed Hugh, climbing up the companion.

On the deck, Ninian was tying down the last petrol tin.

"All finished," he said, wiping his hands on a piece of cotton waste. "There's nothing more we can do to-day. Let's have a bathe before tea."

They dived off *Fauna* and swam in circles round her. Sandy tried to reach the bottom, but came up puffing and scarlet before he had got half-way.

"Silly," said Jean, "the tide's gone in."

They boiled the kettle for tea on the Primus, which refused to light for some time, and Ninian had to go and pump and poke about with a little prong.

"You'll be an expert this time next week," he said, grinning.

"Hope so," said Fiona dubiously. "I'm always afraid of it bursting or something."

"What'll we do besides go to Flatfish?" asked Jamie, during tea.

"Well, we can go to Melvaig; perhaps round to Fairloch," said Fiona.

"We could go farther," said Ninian. "We could pay a call on Hugh's Uncle Frank at Corriedon."

"We could sail all night," said Jean, her eyes sparkling, "On and on, steering by the stars."

"Can you find the Pole Star?" asked Ninian derisively.

"Pole Star," said Jean. "You showed it me yourself."

Fiona lay back against the canvas screen. Pictures floated through her mind; early morning at Flatfish with the dawn coming up beyond the cliffs; long days on the hot beach; stalking seals and finding gulls' nests; climbing everywhere that a foot could be wedged on a rock; sailing through a golden day; sailing with the summer rain warm on your face; sailing at dusk and under the moon; evenings in the cabin by lantern light; nights tucked up in a bunk with the water racing past and gurgling close to your ear.

Jamie flung his crust at a swooping gull and looked affectionately across at *Black Swan*. She looked pathetic and neglected with her brown sail furled, all ready for a voyage.

"I say, Ninian," he said. "Let's take *Black Swan* out this evening. After all there is some wind and we shan't get many chances of sailing her this summer."

"Yes, that's the one thing I could wish for *Fauna*," said Sandy, looking at the stump on the deck, that looked somehow as if it should have been a mast.

"There's no way of rigging one up, either," said Ninian. "Come on, we'll have time to go to Isle Carrick and back before dinner."

They rowed across to the fishing boat and climbed aboard. They knew her so well that it only took a few minutes to haul up the sail and cast off. As they tacked up the loch towards the headland Jean dipped a rag into the sea and cleaned the thwarts and engine case, while Jamie collected pieces of dried seaweed that had been flung on board by the high spring tides and storms.

"We had better take the fishing lines to Flatfish with us," said Sandy. "Haddy will help out the menu."

"And the spear," said Ninian. "Don't let me forget." He pulled out his pipe and started to fill it, cutting off flakes of tobacco and rubbing them together between the palms of his hands. Slowly he pressed it into the bowl of the pipe and lit it.

The strong tang blew past Hugh. "Oh, black twist," he said. "D'you still smoke it, Ninian?"

"Of course," and Ninian laughed, remembering their arguments about it last year.

Hugh pulled his moustache.

"And that reminds me," added Ninian. "I shall grow a beard. It'll be an awful fag, shaving on *Fauna.*"

"Oh, gosh," said Fiona. "I say, Hugh, I wish you hadn't given Ninian these ideas about beards. You look bad enough yourself."

"Let's have a race," said Ninian, ignoring her. "I bet I grow a longer one than you in a fortnight."

"All right," said Hugh. "Only don't forget fair beards don't show as much as dark."

"Must you, really?" said Jean.

"Probably," said Hugh.

Suddenly Fiona said, "Look. There's the sea."

They watched it rolling in between the headlands.

"And to-morrow," said Jean, "we'll go out there, and won't have to come back."

(In the cool gloom of the cave the men leant over the table: their eyes fixed on the chief.

"Ready for another summer?" he asked, his eyebrows raised.

"Aye!" He knew that would be the answer, and smiled.

"Here's to it, then." The table was covered with an assortment of glasses and mugs: both dirty and clean, chipped and whole. He tilted the whisky bottle that was beside him and half filled each glass with the raw spirit. The men watched him intently, the candle-light shifting on their faces. Whether young or old, their expressions were the same: strong and purposeful, backed by a strange secrecy. It would be impossible to find out what any of these men were thinking, impossible to persuade them to change their minds.

The Chief filled his own glass to the brim.

"Slainte!" he said, and raised it.

"Slainte!" The heads went back and the throats gulped under the blue jerseys. The Chief's glass was the first on the table.

"Back to work," he said, and slid his fingers through the dust on the table. The men filed out and he was left alone amidst the cobwebs and the silence, and the creeping shadows of the cave.)

CHAPTER III

"REMEMBER THE LAST TIME WE WERE HERE?"
Saturday, 7th August

IT WAS a perfect morning, so still that they could hear the river from the lodge.

Luckily they had wakened up early, as Maggie had told Ninian there was the hay to be cut, and if they were going away for a week or more it would spoil. This was not such a long task as it sounded because the field was only three or four acres, a rough square walled off from the hill by stones and bracken. Lumps of rock stuck up every now and then, and there were plenty of thistles and ragwort among the grass.

Ninian, Fiona and Sandy were fairly proficient with a scythe and they started off first, cutting as fast as they could, although they knew they could not keep it up for long.

The twins and Hugh were sent to weed the garden, and spent most of the time eating green peas and lettuce.

Fiona's scythe swept through the grass, leaving a patch of stubble behind it. On and on, one foot at a time: it was going to take ages to mow the field even with two of them. And how heavy the scythe was getting. Her shoulders and arms began to ache. Looking round, she saw Ninian, with a scarlet face, stop to wipe his forehead. Behind them the grass lay in even swathes, with here and there a golden head of ragwort or a purple crowned thistle amongst it. There were a few fronds of bracken too, and Sandy was picking the worst out and flinging them on to the moor. Presently he changed with Fiona, and Ninian produced a whetstone and ran it over his blade with a steady "weet weet" until he had it sharp again.

The others in the kitchen garden had just found that the

raspberries were ripe, and were having a feed off them. They were over-ripe and presently Jean said:

"You know, we ought to do some weeding."

"All right." Jamie seized a huge dock and tugged as hard as he could. Of course it broke before the root came out, and he had to dig miles down for that. Meanwhile Hugh and Jean were attacking a large clump of nettles and trying vainly not to sting their hands.

"Beastly things," said Jean, rubbing where one smarted on her leg. "They're as tough as anything."

Jamie had finished with his dock and was walking up a row of cabbages, hauling out handfuls of groundsel and shepherd's purse. At the end of an hour parts of the garden looked almost respectable.

It was half-past ten by the time there was an exhausted shout from the hayfield, and the mowers returned triumphantly, although with aching backs and blistered hands. "Has any one got any Elastoplast?" asked Fiona, tentatively inspecting her palm.

"I think so," said Ninian. They had reached the deer fence round the kitchen garden. "Hoy!" he called. "How much weeding have you done?"

"Lots!" shouted Jean. "We nearly caught a rabbit, too."

"Well, I don't know how much longer you want to go on, but we're ready to start."

There was a clatter of garden implements and the twins rushed across several beds and out of the gate.

"Mind the carrots," shouted Fiona, who had planted them in the spring.

"Bother carrots," said Jamie.

They loaded up the car with clothes, toothbrushes and sponges.

"It doesn't matter if we do forget some things," said Fiona, "because we're coming back here before we start properly."

"Lucky," said Sandy, "because once we get to Flatfish it

won't be much good remembering the soap."

"Do let's start," begged Jean. "We shall never have time for a proper trial trip and get to Flatfish before dark."

Fauna was still there and looking as inviting as ever. Even more so really, because she was clean and full of stores. Every kind of tinned food was piled in all the cupboards.

"We'll never eat it all," said Jean, looking at it as she squeezed her pyjamas in on top of some tinned soup.

"Doesn't matter," said Ninian, who liked to feel that if he wanted he could stay away a month.

"We can eat as much as we like," said Sandy appreciatively reading the labels on the jam pots.

Ninian had already climbed through into the engine-room and was wielding a long-spouted oilcan.

"Who wants to steer?" he said.

There was a tense silence. Every one longed to but did not want to be the first to be responsible for *Fauna* while her antics were yet unknown.

"Fiona had better," said Hugh at last. "She knows the loch best."

"Torture," said Fiona, feeling thrilled all the same. "She's sure to get out of control."

Hugh scrambled aft to help Ninian with the engine and the others went on deck.

"We don't want the dinghy, do we?" asked Sandy. "Shall I tie it to the buoy?"

"Do we want the dinghy?" called Fiona down the hatch to Ninian.

"Yes, we may break down," was the comforting answer.

Sandy tied the painter to a ring bolt in the stern and Jamie went forward to cast off. Fiona turned the wheel experimentally. It seemed all right.

The glass-calm loch glittered under the sun. It was so smooth that the hill by Naast, opposite, looked one with the water. A heron, like a grey ghost, stood motionless amongst the seaweed below the pine wood. Everywhere there were gulls calling and crying.

At last Ninian and Hugh's efforts were rewarded and the engine came to life. The water round *Fauna* was shattered with ripples, a handful of greasy cotton waste was flung overboard. Jamie cast off, and *Fauna*, no longer merely a store ship and houseboat, became a living vibrating thing with a will of her own, as Fiona, clutching the wheel, soon found out. Ninian adjusted the throttle and the engine settled down to a steady chugging.

"Oh, *Fauna*," breathed Jean, as Fiona steered the little ship out beyond the point. A gentle wave rippled back from her bows — it was too calm for anything else. Jamie was already longing for it to be rough to see how she would ride big waves.

Fiona, her eyes fixed ahead, could feel the warm air rushing past her face and blowing back her hair. Below her the engine throbbed and she could feel it vibrating up the wheel. She tried turning it a fraction either way. *Fauna* answered the helm beautifully, although she was inclined to pull away to starboard. Fiona decided she was perfect, almost better than *Black Swan*. She was not really much bigger, but the fact of her having a cabin made her more exciting. If only she had had sails.

Although the engine was running all right, Ninian decided to stay below for a bit longer to see how it ran. Hugh stood up and poked his head out of the hatch. It was horribly hot and smelly down there and there was hardly room for one, let alone two.

"Where shall we go?" asked Fiona.

"Let's go round the island," said Sandy, who was sluicing down the decks.

"Don't let's go too far," said Jean, coming aft down the cabin roof. "There won't be much time if we've got to come back again."

"Let's go and anchor in Mellon Charles," said Hugh. "We could bathe then."

"OH, FAUNA," BREATHED JEAN.

"Yes, we must try out the anchor," said Ninian, poking his head up out of the hatch.

"What happens if it doesn't hold in a storm?" asked James.

"Wait and see," said his brother. He hoisted himself up and sat with his legs dangling into the engine-room. "Take

a turn with the pumps, Sandy, and see if there's any bilge
come in since yesterday."

"How fast can she go?" asked Jean.

"About five or six knots, I should think," said Ninian.
"We'll have to find out."

They had passed the second point and could see ahead
of them out to sea.

"She's going awfully well," said Fiona. "Someone else
come and steer."

Jamie took the wheel on the condition that he was not
responsible for coming alongside anywhere or anchoring in
any exact place.

"I'm going below to see what it feels like," said Fiona.
She pushed open the forehatch and disappeared down the
companion.

The throbbing of the engine was much louder down
here, and the saucepan and kettle were clattering, so Fiona
wedged them up against the tins of Vim. A good many of
the stores were rattling too, and she silenced as many as she
could by wrapping various pyjamas and jerseys round them.
She put back the panel between the engine-room and cabin
and decided there should be a lantern swinging from the
beam. There were two or three hurricane lanterns in the
fo'c'sle and she got one out, filled it and hung it from a
hook. It did swing slightly. She tried lying on one of the
bunks. The hay mattress was comfortable, and she could
hear the rush of the sea against the planking.

"What are you doing?" said Sandy, coming down the
companion.

"Seeing what bliss it is in one of the bunks," said Fiona.
"You try it."

So for a little they lay opposite each other until Sandy
said: "Let's open the ports."

The brass framework and screws were gleaming after the
hard work of yesterday.

"I'm longing for a meal down here," said Fiona, "and to

start cooking on the Primus."

"Won't you get tired of it, too?" grinned Sandy.

"You can do the washing up," said Fiona.

They went on deck to find they were already passing between Carrick and Inverasdale. Two boats were out fishing and they could see the men hauling in the haddy.

Fiona took over the wheel and steered them into Mellon Charles. Ninian dropped back to the engine; Hugh and Jamie went forward. Gradually they slowed down and stopped. The anchor was flung overboard.

"Give her two fathoms," called Ninian.

The chain rattled out into the green sea and Hugh made it fast.

They had brought a sandwich lunch and ate it on deck.

"She went well," said Jamie. "Are you satisfied, Ninian?"

His brother had too much in his mouth to answer, but nodded.

"She'll do," he said eventually, "although she seems almost too good to be true."

"Now don't be a wet blanket," said Jean. "You are maddening this summer, Ninian."

"I can see a flatfish," called James from the bows. "Only a little one."

"We must remember the spear," said Hugh, looking up into the sky and watching the gulls hovering expectantly.

Small waves were breaking on the beach of Mellon Charles and oyster catchers whistled from the rocks. The tide sucked back from the seaweed and left the limpet-covered rocks to dry in the sun. On the way home after lunch they stopped at Beanault to get a store of fruit and chocolate.

"We couldn't do without chocolate," said Sandy.

In the end they did not start until after tea. They spent longer than they had meant up at the lodge collecting last-minute things, including four lobster pots. Then the engine had refused to start, and, when Jean had reluctantly decided that they would have to wait till the next day, it roared to life, spluttered for a minute, then steadied. The propeller churned up the water astern and, as they moved off, left an ever widening wash.

Sandy was steering this time; the twins were admiring him; Ninian and Hugh were grunting over the engine, and Fiona was choosing what they should have for supper. She lit the Primus and put the kettle on. Whatever they decided on, hot water was sure to come in useful. Really it was much too soon to start thinking about eating, so she called Jamie and Jean down to help her make up the bunks. At the moment the blankets and pillows were lying in an untidy heap in the fo'c'sle, together with the oilskins and a few last-minute stores.

"Luckily it's hot, so we won't need much on in bed," said Fiona, picking up a flea-bag, and shaking it out. They spread one on each of the four bunks, and rolled the other two up, so that whoever was taking first watch would have to change them over when he came below. Then there was another large blanket that could be tucked in or folded.

"Don't they look comfortable?" said Jean, turning down the corner of a blanket in a professional way. "I'm longing to try one."

"Who'll sleep where?" asked James.

"Well, whoever is on watch together had better share a cabin," said Fiona. "Let's go and ask the others."

Jean hung the oilies from hooks behind the companion and followed Fiona on deck.

Apparently the engine was going all right, as Ninian and Hugh were sitting on the cabin roof smoking.

"What have you been doing?" asked Hugh.

"Making up the bunks and things," said Jean. "I say, Ninian, who shall be on watch together?"

Ninian leant back and crossed his hands behind his head.

"The twins had better be on with Hugh and me," he said,

"and Sandy and Fiona together. That all right?"

"Can I be with you, Ninian?" asked Jean.

"I don't seem very popular," said Hugh.

"You'll have to put up with me," said Jamie, smiling.

"I suppose that is the best way," said Sandy, "and if we quarrel too much we can change over after a bit."

"How long shall the watches be?" asked Sandy, his eyes on the white waves that were breaking on the rocks by Cove.

"Wait a minute," said Hugh, "that'll take a bit of working out. We'll have to divide the night into three. How early need we begin?"

"We'll have to start early, otherwise we shall get so tired," said Jean.

"I think it will make you twins too tired," said Ninian, suddenly becoming the elder brother.

"Hoy!" protested the twins.

"You mean only have two watches," said Fiona. "Yes, perhaps that is a good idea."

"Oh!" said Jean. "I say, you might let us. We shan't get any more tired than you will. You'll get completely done in if you stay up almost the whole night."

"Let's do it in threes for the first time," suggested Hugh, "and the twins can be on every other night."

"Yes," said James firmly, "let's do it like that."

"Then the first two go from ten till one," said Fiona, who had been doing frantic mental calculations, "the next from one till four, and the last till seven, or won't we be awake by then?"

"I should hope so," said Ninian.

They arranged that he and Jean should take the first watch; Hugh and James the second.

"We shall have much the longest-seeming one," grumbled Sandy.

"We shall see the dawn," Fiona reminded him, "and if we're very tired we can sleep after breakfast. I shall be up already to cook it."

35

"You'd better take over here," said Ninian, rolling over so that he could see out beyond Foura Island.

Fiona changed with Sandy and turned *Fauna* south. She did not attempt the channel between the island and the mainland, although there would really be enough room.

As she gave the rocks a wider berth than they needed, Jamie caught her eye and grinned. They had both seen the swell that came rolling in across the Minch. As they reached it, *Fauna* started to roll gently and Fiona suddenly remembered the kettle.

"Jean," she called, "have a look at the stove. We don't want to set anything on fire."

Jean peered down the hatch and reported that everything was all right.

"The Primus doesn't seem to mind a bit," she said. "A little water has sloshed out, but not much."

Gradually it was growing darker, so slowly that it seemed only imagination. Ninian, noticing it, got up and tried to coax a little more out of the engine. *Fauna* hurried on through the evening. The gulls were black against the sun. The cliffs ahead were black against the coming night. Fiona had steered so far out that already she could see the long curve that was Flatfish Bay.

The twins and Sandy stood in the bows balancing precariously on the gently heaving deck. Hugh came and leant against the canvas screen by Fiona. She smelt the whiff of tobacco from his pipe and turned her head.

"Remember the last time we were here?" she said. "How we climbed the Stack and said we would come back and spend the night at Flatfish some day? I never thought we should."

"I did, somehow," said Hugh, "although generally the things one wants most don't happen, or at any rate not until one's forgotten one wanted them."

"It doesn't seem so very long ago, last summer." Fiona turned the wheel slowly and they swung round into the bay.

The two long beaches with their barrier of rock were still the same and as deserted as ever.

"I wonder if those dead sheep are still there," said Hugh, smiling.

"And the trolls," added Fiona. "We will have to see if they come out at midnight this time."

Ninian's head appeared out of the hatch. "I say, Hugh," he said, "can you manage the engine? I'd better be forward."

"Heavens," said Hugh. "All right, I'll try." He changed places with Ninian, who went into the bows. The tide was low.

"Don't go too far in," he called to Fiona.

"Go slow."

Fauna gradually lost way, the engine slowed.

"Starboard a bit," called Ninian. "As you are. Stop!"

As he spoke, Sandy threw out the anchor and five fathoms of chain. Hugh stopped the engine. Ninian peered anxiously over the side and watched the anchor chain straighten.

"Hope she'll be all right," he murmured.

"Fiona, what about some supper?" said Jamie.

"How hungry is every one?" asked Fiona.

"Frightfully!"

"Incredibly!"

"I've never been so hungry in my life!"

"I don't mind what it is as long as there's plenty of it!"

"Don't bother about anything elaborate, let's have it quick!"

"All right," laughed Fiona. "You might tidy up on deck," and she slid down the companion.

"Go and help, Jean," said Ninian, who was hungry.

"Lazy bones." But Jean followed her sister below.

"Let's have it on shore," called Sandy. "Just to feel we're really in Flatfish."

"Oh — all right." Fiona changed her ideas about supper

and stuffed some tins and bottled beer into the knapsacks. Bread and cheese and chocolate followed.

"And don't forget the tin-opener," added Jean.

"Nor the beer-opener," said Fiona.

They heard a bump as the dinghy was hauled alongside and thuds as the boys dropped into it.

"Come on," came Ninian's voice down the hatch. They charged up the companion and on to the deck.

"We can tie the dinghy where we used to last year," said Fiona.

"We shan't need a flare this time," said Sandy.

He was the first ashore and the others followed him over the rocks and then at full speed across the smooth beach.

They had landed in the second bay and chose a place to sit on the dry sand among the rocks.

"I am hungry," said Jean, her eyes larger than ever.

"Give us a chance," said Fiona, winding madly at the sardine tin.

(Slowly, carefully, the man shifted his cramped position. He had been lying still for over an hour and he was almost numb. He knew that if he did not move no one on the beach below or anywhere on the surrounding cliffs could see him. He knew too, that he must remain invisible at all costs. He had orders from the Chief. He rested his chin on his arms and gazed down through the grass at the unconscious figures below him. He wished they would go away.

Suddenly, from some way behind him came the cry of a tern, repeated three times. To most people, the Stewarts included, that would mean nothing: at the most a tern disturbed off its nest, scolding the intruder. To the man lying so still in the crevice between boulders, it meant "Have they gone yet?" After a moment he answered with the deep bark of a black-backed gull.)

"Can you see him?" asked Jamie, looking up at the cliff.

"Who?" said Jean.

"That black-back, he's making an awful row." James sat

up scanning the rock-strewn cliff.

(The man sank his head lower into the heather and lay very still.)

"He's probably round the corner," said Hugh.

"No, he was quite close, perhaps he's got a nest." Jamie got up. "I'm going to see."

"I shall eat your chocolate if you do," said Sandy.

"Oh! all right." James subsided. "Only we must look after supper."

(But he forgot, and the man stayed on in the shelter of the heather until the shadows lengthened, and "Fauna" was a dark shape on the grey water.)

"Come on," said Ninian.

He rowed them back on board. Presently lights were twinkling from the portholes. The open hatch was a golden square. Laughter and voices floated up into the night. Gulls returning late to the ledges from a day's fishing were surprised at it, and for a long time their voices cried out into the dusk, and even when the night came they were not silent.

CHAPTER IV

NIGHT AT FLATFISH BAY
Saturday, 7th August

THERE was not much room below decks with four people undressing and two getting in the way. The thrill of it being the first night in *Fauna* made even more confusion.

Sandy and James were flinging clothes and pillows between the cabin and the fo'c'sle. Fiona was trying to clean her teeth and Hugh was making desperate efforts to stop the hurricane lantern from smoking. Ninian and Jean were pulling on extra jerseys and fishing their oilies out from among the pile behind the companion way.

"Let's set our watches the same," said Hugh, who had mastered the lantern and hung it up again. Jean switched off the light as the battery was not too good.

"We'll need a lantern on deck," said Ninian. "At least we ought to have a riding light, but it's most unlikely that anything will come along."

"It's starry anyway," said Fiona, "but I suppose a storm might get up."

"Not very likely, but still —" Jean pulled on a fisherman's jersey.

"What about some chocolate?" asked Ninian, wondering whether it would be light enough to read but deciding regretfully that it would not. "What on earth we shall do all that time, I can't think," he said.

"Ruminate," suggested Sandy.

"Only cows ruminate," said Jean.

"You'll have plenty to do trying not to go to sleep," remarked James. "Gosh, these bunks look comfortable. Where'll we sleep?"

"The watches will have to share cabins," said Ninian.

"Otherwise we shall get in a muddle."

"Let you and I have the big bunks," added Hugh. "At least, I imagine these are the largest," and he looked at the ones in the cabin.

Sandy paused in brushing his hair and said, "Cheek — I shall get cramp.

"Well, why not?" asked Ninian, half-way up the companion.

"We'd better turn in," said Hugh, catching a sandshoe on its way to Ninian. He looked at his watch. "Quarter-past ten already."

Jean followed her brother up into the dark. "D'you want the hatch open?" she called down it.

"Yes, definitely," said Fiona.

She and Sandy went through into the fo'c'sle. It looked very small and dark with only the light from the lantern glowing through the doorway.

"They look a bit curved, these bunks," said Sandy, standing dubiously between them.

"Hurry up and get in: they'll be comfortable enough," urged Fiona, climbing into the port one. She wriggled down into her flea-bag, made of army blanket.

"Umn, a bit scratchy." She slid farther in and lay back. The bunk seemed narrow: she could feel the planking on one side and the board on the other. The hay mattress was none too soft either.

"Ouch," said Sandy, who had sat up and bumped his head hard on the deck above him. "I say, one can't even sit up!"

"Don't grumble," called Hugh. "Are you ready for lights out?"

"Yes," said Fiona. "What's it like through there?"

"Lovely," said Jamie. "These bunks are bliss."

"These curve a bit towards the feet," said Fiona, "but they're nice all the same."

The glow in the doorway died as Hugh turned down the

lantern.

"How are we going to wake up at one?" asked Jamie suddenly.

"They'll have to come and wake us up," said Hugh, and he called up the skylight to Ninian.

"We'll wake you all right," said Jean, laughing. "Good-night, all."

"Good-night," called four voices from below.

For some time Fiona lay still in the darkness. She could hear James and Hugh talking softly in the cabin, then they too were still. Sandy grunted and turned on his hay-bag; she wondered if he was feeling as cramped as she was.

Overhead she heard Ninian walking up and down and the murmur of his voice to Jean. A faint light was still coming in at the ports although she could not see through them from her bunk.

The water splashed and rippled on the planking near her head. She could hear the waves breaking away on the beaches. From the noise they made she guessed tide must be high. She could imagine them rolling in over the sand and shells, beating up on the Stack, and gurgling and sucking in the gully. The gulls would be asleep, cuddled together on their ledges, hearing the sea far more loudly than she could.

Every now and then, *Fauna* rolled slightly as the seventh waves came in from the Hebrides. She wondered sleepily if the watch on deck could see the lights from the Outer Isles.

Certainly the beam from the lighthouse must be sweeping the sky; like the Starer's searchlight last year; the northern lights too. And the moon and stars... and stars... and stars...

To the chuckling of the waves by her ear, she fell asleep.

In the darkness of night on deck all things were hushed and muted. Ninian and Jean talked softly, but were, for the most part, silent. The shshsh, shshsh, shshsh of the sea was pleasant to listen to, and occasionally a gull called from the

Stack, and a sheep from the moor. But mostly it was silent.

On down the coast the beam from the lighthouse swept out in regular intervals, a thin point of light over the dark sea. That was the only human light that could be seen at present — the Hebrides were too far away.

The night wind was cool. They were glad of their jerseys. They sat in the stern on their oilskins, leaning against the canvas screen and staring out across the slowly moving sea. Behind them the waves broke with steady rhythm, sleepily, and *Fauna* rocked them like a cradle.

Presently Ninian took his pipe and started to fill it.

"It's lovely to think, isn't it," said Jean, "that there's nothing between us and the Hebrides?"

"Maybe a few steamers." Ninian struck a match that flared like a torch in the night and lit up his dark face. Jean watched as he put the flame against the tobacco and sucked it alight. She hoped he wouldn't grow a moustache: she liked him as he was.

"You can't count ships, silly," she said, continuing their conversation. "They're the same as us. I say, Ninian, I can't believe we're really going to stay here in *Fauna:* no house or anything."

"You can go home if you want," he reminded her.

"As if I did." She sniffed luxuriantly at the salt air. "What shall we do to-morrow, and the next day, and the next?"

"Don't ask me," shrugged Ninian. "Fiona's sure to change it."

"Why should she? Anyway, think of something."

"Well" — Ninian leant back and closed his eyes — "there are the pots to set, which reminds me, we must get some bait. We can go and see Hugh's uncle one day, might stay the night. Then there's all the bay to be explored again. You know, we've never really been right up to the Stack by land."

"Well, one can't go right up, there's sea all round it," said Jean.

"Idiot." Ninian puffed smoke at her. "I mean along the cliff. We might take the dinghy along the gully between the Stack and the cliff too."

"We could go to the lighthouse," said Jean. "And to Melvaig. I've never been there. Don't they make illicit whisky or something?"

"Used to," said Ninian. "Years ago. I'm afraid there's nothing so romantic as that now."

"Well, let's go and see— and how do you know anyway?" asked Jean.

Ninian looked knowing. "Ah," he said, "there's not much I don't know."

"I should say there was a good deal," said Jean. "Perhaps not about whisky, though."

Her brother laughed. There was the difference between his two sisters. Fiona would have said, "Even about whisky."

"What are you grinning at?" asked Jean. "You're not as clever as all that!"

"You should know," said Ninian kindly.

"You must be a success with the smart young ladies in London," said Jean.

"Oh, I am. They fall for me in hundreds."

Jean, looking at her brother, was sure they did, but for his good she raised her eyebrows sceptically.

"They do, really," Ninian assured her gravely. "Just ask Fiona."

"I have," said Jean, laughing. "One of you must be exaggerating! But, I say, have you got a special one? You must have, surely, Ninian."

"Oh, masses."

"No, but do tell me. I won't tell Fiona, I promise."

"Isn't it about time you went and had a look round? A pirate ship may be creeping up at this minute." Ninian felt his young sister's questions might get rather embarrassing.

"You don't really think there might be anything?" asked Jean anxiously. "You haven't heard anything?"

"Not a thing. Shout if you see anything. And don't walk over the cabin roof," as Jean prepared to run across it.

She walked up to the bows, and he saw her, a black figure against the grey sea. She went right round and came back the other side of the screen.

"All clear," she reported, and sat down by Ninian.

The moon had not yet risen, but the stars were very bright. Several of them were reflected in the sea. Jean wondered whether the flatfish could see them. She imagined the light glowing like a green shaft down into the dark water. Where it was not too deep it would reach the sand and throw black shadows from the weed and stones. The fish would flap along from one pool of light to the other, stirring up the sand as they went, and a shoal of sand eels would flick like sea bats between the stars. She leant over and looked down. It was inky black; she could hardly see where the boat ended and the water began.

As the hours crept past Jean began to long to try her bunk and the hay mattress. She stifled two or three yawns and at last Ninian turned round. "Sleepy?" he asked.

"Umn," Jean yawned openly. "Not very, really. I wish we could read or something."

Ninian heaved himself to his feet. "I must go and look at the anchor," he said. "I hope it's holding all right."

"What happens if it isn't?"

"We go on the rocks."

When he got back, Jean said: "Let's play the guessing game."

"All right; you start, then."

"Well, I've thought of someone."

"Is it a he or a she?"

"You can only ask one."

"Well, a he?"

"Yes."

"Is he nice?"

"Yes."

45

"Does he live up here?"

"No."

"Do we know him well?"

"Yes."

"Hugh?"

"Yes. I say, Ninian, that was an awfully short one. Try and think of someone more difficult."

"Wait a minute. Yes, I've got one."

"He?"

"Yes."

"Is he nice?"

"No."

"Mr. Drake?"

"Yes, blast you. This doesn't seem a very good game."

"What shall we do, then?"

"It's too dark to play consequences. Tell me a story, Ninian."

"What about?"

"Oh, life in the army or something. Or one of your many successes in London."

Gradually as they talked the night passed. It was nearly one o'clock. The moon was rising behind the cliff. They could see it glow in the sky. Presently Ninian got up.

"Time to rouse up those others," he said.

"Shall I go?" asked Jean, starting towards the hatch.

"Yes, go on. Don't wake Fiona and Sandy. You needn't bother to come up again but get in Jamie's bunk. You know where your sleeping bag is?"

"In the fo'c'sle, I think." Jean pushed back the hatch as softly as she could and tiptoed down the companion. She could hear steady breathing coming from the four sleepers and a grunt and rustle as one of them turned over. Gosh, but she was sleepy too.

She shook her twin by the shoulder. He only turned and burrowed farther under the blankets. "Come on, wake up," she hissed into his ear. Jamie opened his eyes.

"Is it our watch? Sorry. Ugh, but I'm sleepy."

"Well, so am I," said Jean. She went across to Hugh, who was easier to wake. It did not take them long to dress, even though they stubbed their toes in the dark and kept dropping their clothes. Jean found her flea-bag and spread it out on the bunk. Directly she was in it she was asleep.

Ninian showed Hugh what to do in case the anchor dragged, and then went below, where he fell asleep almost as quickly as Jean had.

"Umn, it's cold," said James, yawning. As the night wore on a wind had sprung up and splashed little waves up against *Fauna*.

"How bright the stars are," said Hugh, looking up. "It's almost light enough to read."

"Anything in sight?" Jamie strained his eyes towards the invisible Hebrides.

"Yes, look," said Hugh. "Those lights are moving."

Far out to sea, very slowly, a bright speck that might have been a star crept along the horizon.

"A trawler," said Jamie. "Or perhaps a cargo boat."

"It must be something fairly big or its lights wouldn't show," pointed out Hugh. "I say, does anything ever come in here?"

"What, to Flatfish? Only trawlers sometimes. There's nothing to come for."

The tide was creeping in again. *Fauna* swung round and the boys moved to the other side of the screen. Up to the north, very faint, was the beam of far distant lights. As they watched another and yet another crossed the sky.

"The Northern Lights," said James. "How faint they are."

"I remember seeing them from the Carna Loch last year," said Hugh.

"They're better in the winter," Jamie told him. "Sometimes they're quite bright. I'd love to go somewhere

where one could see them properly."

"We ought to make an expedition to the North Pole," said Hugh. "At least, I don't think *Fauna's* quite big enough for that, but we might go to Iceland or somewhere."

"Wouldn't it be fun? Are there icebergs there? We might almost explore some unknown territory."

"Perhaps we'd find a new country. There easily might be one."

"I wonder if Ninian ever would?"

"Why not?"

"He'd say we weren't good enough. Probably right too."

"I think we'd be good enough, but *Fauna's* rather small for coping with icebergs."

"Perhaps one year we'll get something bigger. I think a converted fishing boat would be about right. But we ought to get something with sails."

"Are you going into the Navy, James?"

"Didn't you know? I'm going to Dartmouth next term."

"What's Sandy going to do?"

"I don't know. I don't think he knows himself. Not the Army or Navy anyway. Perhaps the Air Force."

Hugh got up and went forward. He looked at the anchor and wondered whether it was all right. He was not sure he remembered how to tell if it was dragging or not. If they were going to stay permanently in the bay it might be a good thing to lay a buoy. He was fairly certain the Stewarts would know how: anyway it would not be difficult.

"I say," came Jamie's voice from the stern. "D'you know what? I've just found that there's no compass in the binnacle!"

"Don't be funny," said Hugh, hurrying aft. "Oh, blast. D'you suppose there's one on board at all?"

"I don't believe we ever brought that one from *Black Swan*. That is rather hell, because unless we go back and fetch it we'll never be able to do any sailing at night, unless we steer by the stars, and I'm sure we don't know them well enough."

Hugh looked up at the sky. "They're certainly bright enough to-night," he said. "But what happens if it's cloudy?"

"We stay at home," said James. "Why?"

"Well, I know the stars pretty well," said Hugh modestly. "We could make a chart of them and steer by that; at least I suppose we could."

"Why not?" said James. "It's a marvellous idea. D'you think it would really work?"

"I suppose so. You always hear of people steering by stars, or perhaps that's only in mid-Atlantic or somewhere."

"We could try." To Jamie it sounded wonderful. He vaguely remembered hearing that the stars moved in the night, but he did not think that would matter. Anyway, they could make some sort of landmark to show the four points of the compass and choose the stars from them every night. And of course the Pole Star always pointed north. He looked up at the sky.

"D'you know any of them?" asked Hugh.

"Only the Great Bear and the Pole Star, and the Pleiades and Orion's Belt, when they're showing," said Jamie, looking round for them.

"Unfortunately they're not at this time of the year," grinned Hugh. "But the others don't take long to learn." He leant back and stared up at the speckled sky. It was such a fine night that the whole heavens were powdered with stars, some so faint and far that they seemed to be there one moment and gone the next. Hugh pointed out some of the clearest constellations: Cassiopeia and Aquila, Pleiades, Pegasus, and Ursa Minor.

"It doesn't take long to learn them," he said. "But I do wish I knew how much they moved in a night."

Jamie felt in his oily pocket and produced a bar of chocolate. There was a rustling of silver paper and then crunching as the two boys staved off pangs of hunger.

They watched the moon, silver on the tossing sea. It shone on the cliffs and the heaps of tumbled rocks and on the wet sand. The tide was nearly out and the seaweed glistened on the beach. It was so light that they could see the dark jagged openings of the caves in the cliff's face and could even make out the sheep paths in the grass.

As *Fauna* swung round with the tide Jamie looked towards the north. The lights were still patterned in the sky like the sticks of a fan; black against the stars was the ridge of the headland, and over it, very faint, the tall sides of Ben More. They were too near in under the cliff to see up to Carrick, and the coast curved out beyond the mouth of the bay. Only the lighthouse along by Melvaig still swung in a steady rhythm out across the sea. Hugh, watching it, felt almost mesmerised.

"I shall be asleep soon," he thought, getting to his feet and stretching. He walked softly along the deck and peered over into the inky water. As far as he could see, the anchor looked all right. He buttoned up the neck of his oily and shoved his hands into the pockets. He began to wish that *Fauna* had got six bunks. Surely this keeping watch in a deserted bay was a bit far-fetched. What could happen among these lonely rocks which had only known gulls for hundreds of years?

The night wind was salt and cold and blew Hugh's hair over his face. He imagined himself the night before last. At this time he would have been in his sleeper on the way to Inverness. Of all the things he had then imagined he might be doing, this was not one of them.

He returned to Jamie, hunched and cold by the wheel. He sat down too and, unbuttoning at least five buttons, at last reached his pipe and tobacco. The red glare of the match blinded them both for a moment, then Hugh tossed it overboard and they heard it hiss into the sea. Slowly the time passed until four o'clock.

Fiona woke reluctantly. Her warm flea-bag had never seemed more inviting; even her straw mattress was bliss.

"Get up," hissed Jamie, shaking her. "It's almost light out."

Fiona yawned loudly and sat up, shivering. Then, while James was tussling with Sandy, she leapt out and pulled on her thickest jersey and trousers. She pushed open the door into the cabin. The regular even breathing of Jean and Ninian filled it, and she could hear Hugh walking on the deck. Through the hatch was a square of dark grey sky in which a few stars were palely shining. It looked horribly bleak and cold. Fiona seized a handful of ginger biscuits from a tin and went up the companion.

"Hallo," said Hugh. "Good-morning." He looked grey and tired.

"It isn't a good morning, it's beastly," said Fiona, rubbing her eyes. She gave him a biscuit. "You must be tired. Any excitements?"

"No, nothing," said Hugh. "Oh, we found we had brought no compass, which is a bore."

"Gosh!" Fiona was still too sleepy to take much in. She stifled a yawn and looked about her. The sea was grey and chill in the half light. She thought longingly of her bunk and warm blankets.

Sandy came shivering up the companion. His eyes were still half-closed with sleep and his hair was on end.

"Well, good-bye," said Hugh. "Mind you cook us some nice breakfast. And," he added, as he disappeared into the cabin, "don't make too much noise about it!"

Sandy and Fiona looked at each other gloomily as they munched their biscuits. It was not yet light enough to see much, except the black shape of Foura and the headland against the grey water. The stars were growing dim in the sky and the ever-moving sea beneath looked sullen and cold. Imperceptibly it grew lighter; the rocks stood out on the shore; the sand became paler than the sea.

"I wish the dawn'd hurry up," grumbled Sandy. "How much longer will it be, d'you suppose?"

Fiona sniffed the keen air. "Not much longer," she said. "Half an hour — an hour — I don't know what time it gets light."

There was dew on the deck and on the cabin roof. Gradually, their hair and oilies grew damp too. They walked round the deck to keep warm.

"The others'll be sleeping much too soundly for this to wake them," said Sandy. "How long, exactly, have we got here, Fiona?"

"Wait a minute, I must think." Fiona frowned with the effort of concentrating. "It's Ninian who has to get back first. On the twenty-first, I think. That means he'll have to start on the twentieth."

"What's the date to-day?" asked Sandy.

"The seventh, or the eighth now. That gives us twelve days here. Of course, if it's boring we needn't stay so long, but as those people have got Carrick there wouldn't be much to do."

"I suppose we *could* poach."

"No, we couldn't," said Fiona firmly. "They're friends of father's and there'd be an awful row if we were caught."

"We weren't caught last year," Sandy reminded her. He was longing to feel a rod between his hands once more or to look at a stag over the sights of a rifle.

"What we could do," said Fiona slowly, "is to ask at Fairloch when we go there if we can fish the lochs over the top of this cliff. There are a few there and I'm sure no one ever goes there, they're so far away."

"Are they any good?"

"I don't imagine they're quite up to Carna standards, but I expect there are masses of little trout in them."

"Rather fun."

"Great fun."

"Have we got a rod?"

"Jean's brought hers. I think Ninian has, too. Perhaps we could get some fishing at Corriedon. Might almost get a day's stalking."

"D'you know Hugh's Uncle Frank?"

"Yes, I've met him. He's a funny old man, but kind, I should think."

Gradually the sky grew lighter. They could see the gulls still huddled on their ledges, round white blobs against the cliff. Already one or two of them were flying round in circles, lazily, as if they too were hardly awake.

"It'll soon be light," said Fiona. It seemed impossible that the night had already gone and that soon they would all be up; might even be bathing.

"Oh, look," said Sandy. "The sunrise."

They turned from watching the far horizon and looked towards the cliff on the left.

Above it the sky was faintly pink. A narrow bar of cloud was black with a lighter rim. As they watched it grew lighter. From palest shell pink the sky turned to rose. More and more of it lightened above the cliff's rim. The dull chill grey was shot with gold; the clouds were gold too. Even the sea started to sparkle, each incoming wave tipped with fire.

"It's lovely," breathed Fiona.

Against the dawn gulls were flying, black shapes like leaves, calling to waken each other.

"It's ages since I've seen the dawn," said Sandy.

"Wish we were on the top of the cliff," said Fiona. "We could see over to Ben Carrick."

"Oh, well," Sandy stretched. "It's morning now. We've hours before breakfast, too."

"Let's row ashore. It's too cold to bathe, but we could collect driftwood in case we want a fire."

Sandy hauled the dingy alongside and they dropped down into it.

"The sun's nearly up," said Fiona, as they reached the rocks.

"I think it's going to be another blissful day," Sandy said.

The tide was half-way in and the waves creamed up on the firm sand. They walked along slowly, watching *Fauna* bobbing in the bay.

"A very uneventful night," said Sandy.

"What did you expect to happen?"

"Oh, I don't know. A ship might have passed close or a trawler come in."

"I'm glad one didn't," said Fiona, kicking a heap of seaweed. "They'd have probably run into us."

The sun reached the top of the cliff and shone down on to the Stewarts walking on the beach.

The gulls were screaming from the Stack. More and more came wheeling out from the ledges and setting off down the bay.

Sandy and Fiona suddenly felt awake and very hungry.

"Hours till breakfast," said Sandy gloomily.

"We might almost go back and make some tea," suggested Fiona. "I don't think that could wake them, although that Primus does make rather a noise."

"Let's risk it," said Sandy, hauling a plank out from under the seaweed and balancing it across his shoulder. The end that had been buried was covered with horrible brown slimy stuff, and smelt. Fiona had an armful of scraps of wood. They dumped their gleanings by a rock beyond high-water mark and went back to the dinghy.

Fiona took off her oilskin and spread it on the wet thwart. Sandy rowed back to *Fauna* and they hauled themselves on board as silently as they could.

They tiptoed along the deck and leant down the hatch. Someone was snoring slightly.

"They seem to be asleep," whispered Fiona. "You stay here and I'll go and light the Primus."

"It's pitch dark down there, though."

"All right, I think I can see enough." Fiona slid down the ladder and presently Sandy heard noises of the kettle being

THE SUN REACHED THE TOP OF THE CLIFF.

filled and cups being clattered. Then there was the roar of the Primus, and he heard Fiona saying, "Gosh!"

"Probably nearly blew it up," he thought.

"I didn't put much water in the kettle," said Fiona, reappearing. "So it shouldn't be long."

They sat for a bit on the cabin roof, watching the gulls and a trawler coming down from Ullapool.

"There goes the herring boat," said Sandy, pointing to it

as it emerged from Loch Carrick."

"I wonder where it's going?" Fiona watched it as it breasted the first of the rollers.

"Faraway, I expect," said Sandy.

There was a hissing, bubbling noise from the cabin.

"Kettle's boiling." Fiona darted down the companion. Sandy heard her making the tea.

"I like sugar," he hissed down at her.

"Here, take this," and her hand appeared with a steaming cup in it. She followed it with her own tea and two large paste sandwiches.

"Umn! Bliss!" said Sandy.

"We might almost bathe," said Fiona, stirring her tea and handing the spoon to Sandy.

"Yes, later, when the others are up," said Sandy, munching.

CHAPTER V

LIGHTHOUSE AND STACK
Sunday, 8th August

THE SUN was high when Fiona woke the others. It was a fine, windy day, much too fine to be spent below. The twins and Ninian were first on deck, in bathing things, and they joined Sandy, who was swimming in circles and telling them how lovely it was.

Hugh came more slowly. He had remained a little longer in his bunk to savour fully the delight of being in *Fauna* at this early hour, and to watch the sea's reflection dancing in a dappled shadow on the ceiling, and to see the early sun glinting on the brass round the scuttles. He stretched warily, because he knew the bunk was only just long enough for him. He could hear the others pounding on deck and splashing in the sea and shouting. For a minute he felt it was too good to be true, that he must be still dreaming; then he saw the Primus burning under a saucepan, felt the roughness of the blankets against his chin, saw the row of pilot books and charts on the cupboard, and knew, delightedly, that it was not a dream.

He hurried up the companion and out into the sunlight. Fiona was standing there, tall and slim, with her black hair blown away from her face.

"Good-morning again," she said, laughing. "It is a good morning this time, too."

"It is indeed," said Hugh. "It's the best there ever has been."

"Yes." Fiona looked at him. "And the best there ever will be."

"It couldn't be anything else," said Hugh.

"Why not?"

"Race you to the others and back," Hugh said.

As they came up after their dive, Fiona asked again:

"But why couldn't it?"

"If you don't know, I shan't tell you."

"How could I know?"

"It's easy." Hugh watched a bead of water trickle down her forehead into her eye.

She was silent for a minute, and then said: "Is it because this minute is the only one that really matters?"

"No, not really. It's because there's going to be a week of this, and —" But somehow Hugh could not finish.

As they swam back to *Fauna* he said again: "D'you know now?"

"No," said Fiona, and laughed at him.

There was porridge for breakfast, and bacon and fried bread. They were so hungry that they finished every scrap as well as masses of bread and marmalade.

"The first thing to do to-day," said Ninian, brushing a wet strand of hair off his forehead, "is to set the lobster pots."

"What about bait?" asked Sandy.

"Couldn't we spear some flatfish?" suggested Jean.

"Where'll we set them?" asked Hugh.

Ninian looked over his shoulder to where the Stack rose out of the sea. Waves were beating up on the rocks round it.

"That looks the best place," he said. "We should get a good many out here, as I don't imagine people set pots as far along as this."

"How many did we bring?" asked James.

"Four," said Fiona, getting up and going down into the cabin for some more bread.

"Any one else want any?" she called.

"Yes," said every one, so she brought the whole loaf.

Up on deck, Sandy and the twins were already peering hopefully over the side in case they could see a flatfish. Hugh and Ninian were sitting on the cabin roof, drinking coffee from enormous mugs, and wondering how soon Jean would fall in.

"Has Hugh told you that we've got no compass?" asked Fiona.

"No. What do you mean?" Ninian frowned.

"It's true," Hugh said. "There should be one in the binnacle, but it's empty."

"Oh, hell!" said Ninian furiously. "That means we can't do any night sailing unless we go back for *Black Swan's* compass."

"That would be too ignominious," said Fiona. "Couldn't we get one in Fairloch?"

"Not very likely — you know how small the shops are. Perhaps Hugh's uncle has one."

"Jamie and I were thinking we might steer by the stars," Hugh said. The others looked at him.

"One hears of people doing it," said Fiona at last.

"The only drawback is that the stars move a bit in the night." said Hugh.

"Enough to matter?" asked Ninian.

"I don't know, we must find out somehow. Perhaps the pilot books say how much." The twins and Sandy had given up looking for flounders and were listening.

"I've got a blissful idea," cried Jean, suddenly. "Let's go and ask the lighthouse man, he's sure to know."

"Yes, do let's," said Fiona. "Even if he doesn't know, it'd be fun."

Sandy had gone down to the cabin, and now reappeared with something in his hand.

"This is minute, but it might be some good," he said. He put what he was holding on the cabin roof. It was a tiny compass in a blue box about the size of half a crown.

"It's very small," said Ninian disparagingly, "but it'd be better than nothing in an emergency."

Fiona and James felt sorry that they were not going to be completely at the mercy of the stars, and Fiona said: "Don't let's use it if we can help it. We could make a star map and try and steer by it as much as possible."

Even Ninian agreed that that would be more fun.

"But I don't know how dependable they are," he said.

"Surely if the Pole Star always points north, we can tell which way we're going?" argued Sandy.

"What if it's cloudy?"

"If it's cloudy we can't use them at all. We'll have to go by my compass."

"Better stay at home altogether."

"You would say that," said Fiona. "Come on. Let's wash up, then we can set the pots."

The cabins had to be tidied and the flea-bags brought up on deck and left to air. Then the dinghy was pulled alongside and they took the spear and set off.

The wind was in the west and strong enough to cause a ripple.

"Lucky we brought the water glass," said Sandy, who had "bagged" the best place in the stern. The glass was a deep strong wooden box, about a foot square, with a glass bottom. If it was pushed into the water, one had a clear view through the waves. The only difficulty was that one could not see very much at a time, and also one had to direct the person with the spear.

They rowed on for some time; Ninian looking over his shoulder, and pulling into the shore. The tide was going out, but was not low yet.

"I don't expect we'll get much," said James, as he saw how high it still was.

"On the contrary," said Sandy, "I can see one now. A big one, too."

Fiona, who was holding the spear, rushed to the stern and stood with it poised above Sandy's head. She craned over his shoulder, trying to see into the box.

"Keep it still, Sandy," she cried. "I can't see a thing!"

"We're moving," objected Sandy. "Ninian, backwater, for

goodness sake. Now, steady."

"I see it," shrieked Jean, with her head nearly under water.

Hugh could see nothing but the blurred outlines of rocks and seaweed below the ripples. Fiona and Sandy were having a violent argument, and of course lost the fish altogether.

"You are mutts," said Ninian. "For goodness sake stop quarrelling and look properly."

"Well, you come and take the spear," said Fiona, who would not have given it up for anything. They went on.

"Now, there's one," said Sandy. "You must be able to see him, he's vast. I can see even his spots."

Fiona knelt on the thwart beside her cousin and leant over his shoulder.

"Yes, I do see him," she said. "Hold the box like that, Sandy, and port a bit, Ninian."

With her eyes still on the fish, she slowly stood up and lifted the long spear. Swiftly she slid it into the water, frantically trying to keep her balance. Jamie held her by her belt; she leaned even farther over. A plunge, and the fish was firmly skewered.

The twins took the box and spear next, and succeeded in missing three, and catching one.

"You must try," Fiona told Hugh.

"What? Spearing or looking?"

"Either."

Hugh chose the box, and eventually saw a big skate which Sandy speared. Then he and Ninian had a go and got one lemon sole.

"We really have enough," said Jean.

"Too much," said James.

"Couldn't we give some to the lighthouse keeper?" suggested Jean. "He might be glad of some fish."

"Yes, let's," said Fiona. "Anyway, we can eat anything that's left over."

They rowed back to *Fauna* and Sandy and Ninian started cutting up the fish and baiting the pots. Any scraps that were left over they put in a bucket with some kitchen salt so that it would keep.

"It's sure to go bad," Jamie said.

"I should think these blankets have been aired enough by now," said Fiona, picking up her sleeping bag and carrying it below. Hugh gathered up an armful and followed her down. Between them they did not take long to make up the four bunks and tidy the cabins. They left the scuttles open but shut the hatch after them as they came on deck.

"Thanks for doing my bunk," said Ninian. "But I would have made it a bit fishy in this state."

"Well, yours and Jean's were the ones we didn't do," said Fiona. "You have first watch. Have you finished those pots?"

"Yes, and here's a nice flounder left for the lighthouse man," said Sandy, wiping his knife on his trousers and scraping a cluster of scales off his arm.

James and Jean were in the dinghy, piling the pots up between the thwarts. In each was a repulsive looking piece of fish wedged through two pieces of string and secured there. They were the lung kind of lobster pot, netting over a wooden framework with a hole in the side, and a big flat stone at the bottom. The Stewarts had made them several years ago and consequently they were getting a bit dilapidated. However, Ninian had been patching up the largest holes and there were none left big enough for a lobster to creep through.

Sandy and Ninian each took an oar. The twins went forward and Hugh and Fiona sat in the stern. The dinghy was low in the water as they pulled slowly off towards the Stack.

No one spoke for some time, Sandy and Ninian chiefly because the boat was heavy, the others because they were too busy thinking.

The warm sun and the wind were very pleasant. "How my face will burn this evening," thought Fiona. As they neared the Stack the gulls' cries became louder and yet more piercing. The sea was black with the bobbing heads of shag and cormorants and countless small guillemots and razorbills. Jean looked longingly for a puffin, but could see none. All around them the birds were diving, and occasionally a cormorant would flap along the water, trailing his legs and sounding like a small motor-boat. Hugh looked up at the Stack's sheer sides and remembered climbing it last year when he had thought he must fall into the sea. Sandy and Ninian altered course a little as they pulled round the seaward side of the Stack. There was enough swell rolling in for there to be a chance of being washed against the rocks.

"Listen!" said James suddenly.

"What to?" Ninian rested on his oars and the drips ran down them into the water forming ever-widening circles.

They strained their ears.

"I can't hear a thing," said Hugh.

"Oh, shut up a minute." Jamie leant forward, frowning. "There it is again — someone whistling.

"I can hear it too," cried Sandy.

It was distinct but very faint, a tune none of them knew.

"Oh, it's gone," said Fiona.

"I never heard it," said Hugh.

"Probably a shepherd," said Ninian.

"You would," said James.

Fiona stood up and lifted one of the pots clear of the others. She balanced it on the side of the boat, waiting until they would be near enough in to drop it over.

"Let's go the other side of the channel and along towards the shore," said Ninian.

"All right, but mind the swell in the gully," said Fiona.

"Why not row out a bit and set the last pot along there?" asked Hugh, pointing towards the lighthouse.

"Yes, how deep is it?" asked Ninian, looking over his shoulder.

"It's all right here," said James.

Fiona moved the pot across and as they passed a likely looking rock, flung it into the sea. It sank in a great foam of white bubbles and she paid out the rope until she felt it touch the bottom. Then she flung the rest of the rope, with its string of corks, out into the sea.

"Let me set the next," begged Jean, starting to scramble over Ninian and nearly putting her foot right through one of the pots. The boat rocked.

"Do have a care," said Ninian, steadying her.

"Sorry," said Jean. She joined the others in the stern and got ready the next pot. Presently all four lines of corks were bobbing in a row, about one hundred yards apart.

The lightened dinghy flew back to *Fauna*.

"Let's start fairly soon," said Fiona. "What's the time, anyway?"

"Surprisingly it's twelve already," said Hugh. "Or quarter-to, really."

"It's rather frightening how quickly time goes," said Fiona, as they crossed the cabin roof.

"Only when it's being fun," Hugh reminded her.

"That's the only time that matters," said Fiona.

"That rather depends," said Ninian, joining them. "It's often those times which matter least in the end."

"Well, which would you rather, being happy at the moment which will be the past, remember, very soon, or have the advantage of having learnt or read something that was dull at the time, but helps you afterwards?" asked Hugh.

"Happy at the time, I'm afraid," said Fiona. "After all, the chance for using the dull knowledge may never come, and if it did, you would probably get on all right, although you only had a happy memory to sustain you."

"I agree," said Hugh. "Anyway, this moment couldn't be more perfect, and nothing one could ever learn could make up for having lost it."

"Who wants to talk of time?" asked Fiona, feeling the west wind in her hair and the sun on her face. "No one has ever been able to find out anything about it, and already we've wasted about ten minutes of it talking instead of getting lunch ready. And starting the engine," she added.

"Yes, let's get going with that engine," said James, who was feeling cross because *Fauna* had no sail and the breeze was being wasted. In a way he half hoped the engine would not start; he had no faith in engines. However, the engine did start after a good deal of tinkering from Ninian and Hugh, and after the plugs had been removed and cleaned as well as various other things.

Fiona was in the cabin making a stew for lunch. They had brought some meat with them and she thought that it had better be used fairly soon, as otherwise it would be sure to go bad.

She scraped and chopped carrots, onions and turnips; made gravy from Bovril; poured it all into a saucepan with the meat; added salt and pepper; decided that it already smelt good, and put it on the Primus. She also peeled and chopped up some potatoes and left them in a bowl of cold water to be added to the stew at the end. Their lunch was almost ready.

Ninian had removed the partition between the cabins and was looking at her from the engine.

"Are you nearly ready?" he asked. "Because if so, you might go on deck and steer, the engine's about to start."

"One minute," said Fiona, shovelling a few last scraps of carrot into the stew and drinking the end of the Bovril from the jug. She licked her fingers, wiped them on her trousers, and climbed up on deck.

Hugh and Sandy were standing forward by the anchor, the chain already in their hands. The hatch above Ninian was open and Fiona called down it that they were ready. The engine sprang to life; James ran to help haul on the anchor chain; as they moved off, Fiona turned the wheel, and *Fauna* swung round.

"Give the Stack a good margin," called Ninian, "there may be some rocks off the point."

Fiona steered farther out, waves broke up against *Fauna's* bows, splashing on to the deck. Sandy stooped and pulled some weed out of the anchor chain and threw it back into the sea. Runnels of water trickled down the deck and out of the scuppers. A passing gull swooped at the weed Sandy had thrown, and soared disappointedly up again.

"Jean, there's some potato peelings and scraps below," said Fiona, watching the gull. "Throw them out and see if he likes them."

Jean obediently went below and returned with a colander full of parings and a crust of bread. She broke it up and tossed it overboard. Annoyingly, the gull would not take any notice of it until it had sunk, then he suddenly realised something was going on. He swooped, missed the bread, and cried plaintively. Jean emptied the colander and threw out the rest of the crust. Immediately there were masses of gulls fighting in the water, diving and swooping.

"You'd never think they would catch enough fish to keep alive," said Jean, watching them.

"I suppose lots of crabs and star fish and things get washed up," said Fiona, looking back over her shoulder. Their wake was cutting a white path through the sea and already the beaches seemed distant.

Ninian, who had heard the clamour of the gulls and poked his head through the hatch, swung himself up and sat with his legs dangling. He wiped his oily hands on a piece of cotton waste, then tossed it into the sea where it was instantly sucked under by the waves.

Looking back at Flatfish Bay he thought, not for the first time, what a strange and lovely place it was. He wondered if it liked having them there, breaking its silence with their shouts and laughter, disturbing its sand and spearing its fish.

It probably preferred hearing only the gulls' cries and the whistling of oyster-catchers along the shore. Perhaps the gruff bark of a seal or the honking of wild geese in the winter broke that calm, a silence more intense because there was always the whisper of the sea. Ninian felt that there was something strange about the bay, something secret. He loved it, as he loved all the country round, but it could not compare with Carrick. Although he pretended to laugh at the others when they spoke of their love for Carrick and the places round he was as fond of it as they were, but Fiona was the only person he would ever talk to about it.

Jamie had gone below to fetch the pilot books which he brought back on deck. On the way he stopped and looked into the saucepan. Already steam was rising from it and it smelt extraordinarily good.

"Your stew's doing beautifully," he told Fiona. "It's quite hot already."

The others crowded round as he spread the chart and books on the cabin roof.

"How far is this lighthouse?" asked Hugh, bringing out his pipe. Sandy leant over Jean's shoulder and stared at the coastline drawn on the chart in minute detail.

"It looks about four miles," he said, putting out his hand to pin down a corner of the paper that was fluttering in the wind. "More than that," said James. "I should think it's about five."

"How long'll that take us to get there?" asked Hugh.

"Oh, about an hour." James was vague.

Out to sea a school of porpoises were tumbling through the waves. Their black shiny bodies gleamed under the sun, as they rolled slowly along. Beyond on the horizon were the Hebrides, faint and dim; fairy islands; blue clouds; mirages; imagination; anything but real islands. A trawler's black spiral of smoke smudged across their beauty, bringing the mind back to the ordinary.

James was measuring out the distance to Fairloch.

"It's quite a long way," he said. "Farther than I thought."

"About ten miles?" guessed Jean.

"Oh, more," said James. "It'd be fifteen to the point and beyond that is the bay. From Flatfish, I should think it's about twenty miles."

"Rather fun being so far," said Jean. "It'll take us ages to get there, when we do go. But how far is the lighthouse?"

"Umn!" Ninian frowned. "About five miles, that should take us an hour or more. By the way, we can't all land because I don't think there's an anchorage."

"Oh, bags land," said Jean.

"Bags," said James and Sandy together.

"You'd better go with them, Ninian," called Fiona. "And stop them falling in or off or anything."

Hugh lay at full length along the cabin roof, his chin propped on his hands. *Fauna* was tossing gently, it was warm: the day was going to be fun.

Ninian sent James and Sandy to swab down the decks and tidy up generally. Jean went below to look at the stew. She was fascinated by the inside of the cabin, by the noise of water slapping against the planking, by the lantern swinging from the cross beam. She decided that it looked a bit dirty and unhooked. With a rag she rubbed the black from the glass and the dust that had collected round the bottom. Then she filled it and hung it up.

The stew was bubbling away on the Primus, smelling more and more good every moment. Jean tentatively prodded a carrot with a fork. It was still hard, and so were the turnips. However, she turned the stove down a bit, in case it was too hot.

Through the square of the hatch there was a patch of blue sky, flecked with small mackerel clouds. Occasionally a gull or a gannet flashed across and she could hear the others talking and discussing what they would do next day. A pity to miss anything, so she climbed up the companion and leant out.

THE STEW WAS BUBBLING AWAY ON THE PRIMUS.

"Let's go to Fairloch to-morrow," Jamie was saying. "It will take so long that we can stay the night. That'd be almost as good as a real voyage."

"We can get stores there too," said Fiona.

"Greedy," said Sandy, thinking of the cupboards full of

tins below.

"I mean milk and bread and things, silly," said Fiona scathingly. "We've got enough otherwise to last for months."

"Let's ask about the loch over by Inverasdale," said Jean; her mind as ever on fishing. "We might be able to get a day on that."

"We can go and see it, anyway," said Ninian, who was the only one who had ever been there. "It's a blissful place, if I can remember."

"What sort of place?" asked Hugh.

"Oh, woods," said Ninian. "There are two lochs, at least I think so. It's years since I was there, and anyway I came from the Inverasdale side."

They rounded the first point and turned slightly left to follow the coast line.

"I believe there's an enormous sandy bay coming," said James. "At least, I seem to remember one."

"I can see it," said Fiona, screwing up her eyes and peering into the distance. "By the way, would any one like to steer?"

"Oh, may I?" asked Jean.

Fiona handed over the wheel.

"Steer for the farthest point," she said.

She went over and sat on the cabin roof beside Sandy. The charts were beside her.

"Let's see," she said, looking at them. "There are some things we simply must do, what are they?"

"Go to Corriedon," said Hugh.

"The loch," said Jean.

"Melvaig," said Sandy.

"Let's sleep on the Stack one night," suggested Ninian suddenly.

"Oh, bliss! Oh, do let's," said Fiona. "All among the sea birds. We'd hear them crying at night and in the early morning. And we could make a fire, too."

"Wouldn't that frighten them?" asked James.

"There are so many, they couldn't be really frightened," said Fiona. "Anyway, they'd all come back next day."

"Some of us'd have to stay in *Fauna*," Hugh reminded her.

"Oh, bother!"

"Well, we needn't have such a conscientious watch that night," said Ninian. "Anyway, some of us'll be awake on the Stack till quite late."

"It'll be rather tricky hauling blankets and things up there," said Hugh, thinking of the precipitous climb he had had last year.

"We could use a rope," said Sandy. "Or take them on our backs."

"Thank you so much," said Hugh. "I think I'll volunteer to remain in *Fauna* that night."

"Oh, but think of the view by moonlight," said Fiona.

"Think of the journey back to Carrick with a broken back," retorted Hugh. "No, thank you very much. As a great favour, I might climb that Stack very slowly and unencumbered. But if you suggest heaping piles of blankets on my back I shall strongly object."

The others laughed.

"I say, I can see the lighthouse quite clearly," said Jean, who was the only one looking out.

Ninian stood up. He could see the top of it like a black finger over the point.

"Mind the rocks here," he said. "I seem to remember some pretty nasty ones.

"They were miles in," said Fiona.

"Don't be too sure," said Ninian. "I don't want to crack up *Fauna* as (a) she isn't ours, and (b) it would wreck the holidays, and (c) there's quite a swell on."

"Perhaps I'd better steer," suggested Fiona, getting up.

"All right," said Jean. "I'll go forward and keep a look-out."

Sandy joined her in the bows and Fiona turned the boat

"I SAY, I CAN SEE THE LIGHTHOUSE QUITE CLEARLY."

out to sea.

"We're pretty safe really," Ninian said. "*Fauna* doesn't draw much."

Fiona suddenly remembered the stew and sent Jean down to see it.

"The gravy's getting a bit low," she called up.

"Add some water,' shouted Fiona, her eyes on the lighthouse.

"I say, it's half-past one," Hugh reminded her. "Let's have lunch soon."

Sandy pricked up his ears.

"Let's have it before landing," he suggested.

Ninian looked at the coast. The tide was coming in,

there was nowhere to anchor off the lighthouse. The wind was west, blowing in shore.

"Steer some way out," he told Fiona, the wind blowing his hair on end. "We'll let the tide take us in and have lunch on deck."

Fiona swung the wheel and turned *Fauna* even farther out to sea.

Below, Jean was getting out plates and knives and various other implements.

"What shall we have for sweet?" she called.

"Tinned peaches," shouted Sandy quickly.

"All right," Fiona grinned. "Can you open them?"

"Yes, if I can find the tin opener," retorted Jean. Jamie, by the hatch, heard her rummaging in the drawer and then a noise of struggling as she tried to force the point into the tin.

"You don't seem to be having much success," he remarked. "Like me to try?"

"Ouch! Yes, perhaps you'd better," said Jean, sucking her finger where she had hit it on the tin. James swung himself down, and between them they managed to cope with the peaches and pour them out.

Meanwhile Ninian had decided that they were far enough out. The engine was stopped and they were left in silence.

They had lunch on deck, watching the coast line grow nearer as wind and tide carried them in shore. Every now and then a wave would break beside them and they could hear them beating upon the rocks. The dinghy kept on catching them up and bumping the stern.

"Bother," said Sandy, as he was sent aft to fend her off for the fourth time. "She can't do much harm, surely."

"Well, eat up," said Fiona. "Then you can go ashore."

"Gosh, it's a blissful day," said James, leaning back and watching the clouds.

Indeed it was one of the best kind of days; warm and

windy. The sea was bright blue and flecked with white; lumps of saffron seaweed kept bobbing past, and the wavy forms of jelly fish.

Gradually they were swept inland, and by the time lunch was finished they had almost reached the coast.

They arranged that Sandy, the twins and Ninian should go ashore.

"Can you cope with the engine?" Ninian asked Hugh.

"Yes, I think so," Hugh grinned. "I think we'd better take her out again and drift back."

"All right." Ninian was obviously longing to go to the lighthouse. "Hurry up, you." This to Sandy, who was looking for chocolate in the cabin. He was hustled overboard into the dinghy and Hugh threw the painter in after him.

Fauna swung round and headed out to sea once more.

"I say," said Jean suddenly. "D'you think the man'll let us land?"

"Oh, of course," said Ninian. "We can give him the fish to appease him if he seems fierce. By the way, we never told Fiona when to come back for us."

"I don't expect she'll be too long," said James. He looked up at the lighthouse ahead of them.

A jetty was built against a small cliff with a dinghy tied up to it. There were a few rough steps cut in the rock up to the lighthouse. They could see the figure of a man standing at the top.

"There he is," said Jean, hoping he would be nice.

Ninian looked over his shoulder. He had never landed here before and did not know the keeper, but he had always had a longing to see over the lighthouse, perched on its jut of rock.

They bumped against the jetty and Sandy scrambled up the iron ladder. They tied the dinghy up and climbed the steep steps.

It was very bare on this headland; bare rock with only a few clumps of thrift and sea campion growing in the crevices. There were gulls too, but not so many as at Flatfish. The steps were worn and in some places were so far apart that Jean could hardly stretch from one to the other.

The lighthouse keeper greeted them at the top. He was a short sturdy man of about fifty with a weather-beaten face. He seemed genuinely glad to see them.

"Aye, you're verra welcome," he said, shaking them by the hand. "It gets gey lonely on this bittie rock. I watched yon wee boat coming round the head and never thought ye'd pay me a visit."

"We've brought you some fish, too," said Ninian, handing him the lemon sole and a flounder on a piece of string.

"Thank you," said the keeper. "If ye can spare them?"

"Oh, yes," said Jean. "We've got masses."

"Ye'd like to see over ma hoose?" asked the man, noticing how longingly James and Sandy were staring up at it.

"Oh, yes, please." Jamie had always wanted to find out the workings of a lighthouse, this one especially, as they had seen it so often flashing at night.

The man led them the rest of the way up the path. He told them he was an East Coaster, that his name was MacDonald, that his mate was away on holiday, leaving him alone.

The main room of the lighthouse was small and snug. It had two bunks in the walls, like those in *Fauna*. There was a stove on which a kettle was boiling, two dilapidated armchairs, a table, and a cupboard against the wall. Rather surprisingly a canary was hanging in a cage by one of the narrow windows. Directly it heard voices it burst into loud shrill song. MacDonald did not seem to notice it.

"Och, there's no much to see in here," he shouted above the canary, and led them up a spiral stairway to the top.

The full force of the wind hit them as they came out on to

the narrow platform. There was a grand view of all the coast; they could see the Summer Isles up by Ullapool and all the hills to the north.

"I say," said Jean, pushing her hair out of her eyes. "I'm sure I saw a boat going into Flatfish."

"Nonsense," said Ninian. "No one ever goes there. There's nothing for any one to do."

"All the same, I'll bet anything I saw a boat," insisted Jean. "Bother that hill, we can't quite see into the bay."

None of the others would take any notice of her; they were all too busy inspecting the lamp and asking the keeper about storms in the winter.

"Aye, they're verra fierce," said MacDonald, screwing up his eyes and peering out to sea, as if he anticipated a gale at that moment. "Sometimes ye'd think the hoose'd be blown awa', an' we get a few boats up on the rocks yonder," and he pointed down towards Fairloch.

"We're going there to-morrow," said Jamie. "Are there any specially dangerous ones?"

"Och, no, not in your wee boat. It's at night when there's a big sea running that ye have tae be carefu'."

"It must be fun, living here," said Jean, looking out over the sea and hearing the gulls screaming all round her. "How do you get food though?"

"Och, a boat comes oot frae Fairloch once a week, if it's calm," MacDonald told her.

"And if it's not?" asked Sandy.

"There's no boat," said MacDonald.

They went slowly down the steps, out of the sun into the cool gloom of the lighthouse. *Fauna* had nearly reached the rocks and they had seen almost all there was to see.

"Ye'll have a cup o' tea," the keeper insisted, "and a bit of the scone I baked."

"Can you bake?" asked Jean, in surprise. MacDonald did not look as if he could.

"Taste a bit o' ma scone and tell me then," he said,

smiling. He gave them each a piece, spread with apple jelly. They all agreed that even Maggie could hardly bake them better.

"We must be going," said Ninian at last. Out of the slit of the window he could see *Fauna* tossing on the swell.

"Come and pay me another visit some day," said the keeper. "And thank you for the fish."

"He must be lonely living there," said Jean, as they rowed back to *Fauna*. "Rather fun in a storm though."

"I wonder if he's rescued lots of people," said Sandy. "How silly of us not to have asked him."

"I hope he doesn't have to rescue us," said Ninian over his shoulder. "If we start careering about at night without a compass he probably will."

"We have got a compass," said Sandy. "And anyway, we won't be careering."

"You missed some lovely scones," Jean told Hugh, as she caught hold of *Fauna.*

"We could see you standing at the top," said Fiona. "Was he nice, the man?"

"Yes, he had a lovely little room and a deafening canary," said James. "He was all alone there, so I expect we cheered him up a bit."

"He had a wireless," Ninian put in.

"I say," said Jean. "Did you see a boat going into Flatfish?"

Fiona and Hugh looked at each other.

"No," said Hugh at last. "Not a sign. Not that I looked, but still —"

"I'm sure I saw one," Jean insisted. "Do let's hurry back and see."

"We might as well go back really," said Ninian, looking at the sun. "It must be about three or something."

"Let's bathe when we get back," said Sandy.

"And see if that boat's there," put in Jean.

"Oh, you and your boat," said Fiona. "What would a boat

be doing in Flatfish anyway?"

"Just what I said." Ninian started to fill his pipe.

"If there is one it's probably getting wood or seeing the sheep or something," said Sandy.

"I think it's smugglers," said Jean.

"Oh yes, of course, in broad daylight. Honestly, you are an idiot, Jean." Fiona was scathing.

"It *might* be smugglers," said Sandy. "Flatfish is so deserted that it would be a perfect place."

"You've got smugglers on the brain," said Ninian. "Smugglers or secret societies."

Hugh had started the engine; Fiona turned the wheel, and already the lighthouse was behind them. They could see MacDonald standing by the door and waved to him. He waved something white in reply.

"It must be the flounder," said Jamie, laughing.

The wind had veered to the north slightly, so it took them longer to get back. The coast was a mass of cliffs and caves, and small bays, every one of which Jean and Sandy were convinced, was a smuggler's den.

"Hardly likely with the lighthouse man peering in at them at every minute," said Fiona.

"And with trawlers steaming up and down all day," added James, his eyes on a far spiral of smoke, the only one they had seen that day.

As they were rounding the point before Flatfish Jean gave a shriek of excitement.

"A boat, look, there is a boat."

They all turned. Indeed there was a boat, some way out to sea, heading for the Hebrides.

"Probably just been in to Carrick or Beanault," said Ninian.

"I'm sure it's the one I saw before," said Jean.

"All these fishing boats look exactly alike," said Hugh. "At least I can never tell them apart."

"You wouldn't." Jean was cross. She had been so sure

they would find a boat anchored in Flatfish and now there was nothing to prove she had been right. But however much the others teased her she still insisted that she was.

That evening after they had bathed and had supper, Ninian rowed Fiona, Hugh, Sandy and James ashore.

"There's something funny about this place," said James.

"I know." Fiona looked over her shoulder. "I felt it too."

"As if someone was watching us," put in Hugh.

"Nonsense," said Ninian, but he too had had that strange feeling and a glance round at the empty cliffs did nothing to reassure him.

"Trolls, I expect," said Sandy. He laughed, but Fiona could hear the same tone in his voice that she had heard in Ninian's.

"It's probably because this place has been deserted for so long," she said. "Perhaps it doesn't like having us here, but it'll get used to us." She looked round at the smooth stretch of sand and the darkening sea. After all it was Flatfish, their own especial bay. There was nothing here to hurt them.

"Well, good-night," said Ninian. "I'm not sure I envy you."

"We're not afraid." Fiona looked up at the Stack. "Anyway, we shall be safe there."

They pushed off the dinghy and Ninian rowed back to *Fauna*. Then they turned and climbed the Stack.

They hauled bundles of bedding and extra clothes and a few provisions up on all the rope they could find tied together. Sandy and James were sent to gather driftwood for a fire, while Fiona and Hugh built a fireplace and laid out the beds as near to the middle as they could. Privately, Fiona had resolved to drag hers to the edge when it got dark, so that she could lean over and see the water beneath. Almost as good as being a gull on a ledge then. These, of course, were setting up a deafening clamour at finding their nesting place inhabited. However, as night drew on they grew more peaceful, although hundreds of them were circling round afraid to roost in their accustomed places.

As it grew dark Fiona called the others. It was a dangerous place to climb in the night and she hoped that they had left nothing behind. However, they left the rope hanging down so that Ninian could always row across with anything if they shouted.

The sun had set behind the Hebrides in a blaze of gold and scarlet. Everything was a dim misty blue and the clouds that had been so brilliant were like black bars in the sky. Already the lighthouse had started to flash and a pin-point gleam betrayed a steamer on the horizon. The rim of the cliff above the Stack was inky black, the wind had dropped and the cries of sheep and gulls came very clearly. The waves beat monotonously against the rocks, and now and again a tremendous clamour would break out among the gulls and then die away as they shuffled each on to his own ledge. *Fauna* was a small black ark in the bay, each porthole blazing and a square of light for the hatch. If Ninian and Jean shouted the others could just hear what they said.

The waves broke again and again on the sand and gurgled up the gully between the Stack and the cliff.

"What a horrible noise it is," said Fiona, who had been listening to it in the silence. There was a moaning roar every now and then as the waves broke in some underground cavern. They were all glad when Hugh said at last: "Come on, let's light the fire."

The dry driftwood caught easily, and soon a pan of bacon was sizzling on the first fire that had ever been lit on the Stack.

It disturbed the gulls, however, who flew round screaming in terror until the flames died down and all that remained was a glow.

The Stewarts and Hugh were already in their flea-bags, crowding round the embers and talking loudly. It was one of the blackest nights they had ever known and the Stack was a ghostly place.

Fiona was glad Jean was not with them, and looked rather enviously at the bright lights of *Fauna,* swinging out in the bay. Ninian was going to watch there alone to-night until the early morning when it grew light and Jean could come up. He had left instructions that on no account was he to be disturbed until at least eight or nine.

The fire had died down to a heap of red ashes. It was still pitch dark and there was an hour or two before moonrise. Sandy and James were already asleep. Hugh put down his empty cup and lay back. The wind was still strong enough to blow his hair about, so he pulled the blankets right over his head, only leaving out his face. The gulls were quarrelling on their ledges and the waves seemed to beat even louder on the rocks. He heard Fiona get up.

"What *are* you doing?" he said. It was as black as pitch. "Do be careful."

"I must look over into the sea," said Fiona, moving cautiously across the top. Her bare feet sank into clumps of thrift and occasionally crunched on an empty eggshell.

"For Heaven's sake, look out." Hugh expected to hear her splash into the sea at any minute.

She reached the edge of the Stack and, on hands and knees, crept as far as she could. Her eyes by now were fairly accustomed to the darkness after the bright light of the fire, and she could make out the white dashes of foam as the waves broke on the rocks beneath. It was cold out on the edge, with the wind sucking up the gully. An extra large wave broke and sent a bead of spray up on to her cheek.

"Are you still there?" called Hugh. She turned and saw the red glow of embers where their blankets were.

"Coming," she said.

She snuggled deep into her flea-bag, pulling it right over her head. She was glad they were not sleeping here every night.

For some time she and Hugh lay looking up at the stars and talking in undertones. Sandy and James slept like logs, unperturbed by the noise of the waves. Fiona stretched out her hand and picked off a head of thrift. She rolled it between her fingers until the dry petals fell off.

After Hugh had been silent for a minute or two she called his name softly. There was no answer. She alone was awake. Dimly she hoped a gale would not blow up. Dimly she wondered if the ashes were blowing on to Jamie, who was lying that side of the fire. Suddenly she realised her eyes were shut and opened them again. Above was a blaze of stars and, half asleep, she imagined the Stack was rocking beneath them. There was a sudden chattering from the ledges, and then silence. After that Fiona was asleep.

Hugh woke once in the night. A bright lop-sided moon was up in the sky. The wind had stopped. The other three were sleeping. With a great effort he raised himself on his elbow and looked across at *Fauna*. There were no lights there now, only a small glow.

"Poor Ninian," thought Hugh, "he must have smoked pounds of tobacco!"

CHAPTER VI

VOYAGE TO FAIRLOCH AND CORRIEDON
Monday, 9th August and Tuesday, 10th August

JEAN had decided last night before she went to sleep that she would relieve Ninian as early as possible. She set the alarm for half-past four. It was grey and cold when she got on deck. It had taken a bit of doing, leaving her warm bunk for the bleakness of early morning, and only the thought of Ninian, tired and probably cross, watching the sky grow slowly lighter, spurred her on. She lit the Primus before going on deck. Tea would cheer them both up.

She climbed up the companion and shivered as the cold morning met her. The deck was wet with dew and in the half-light she very nearly tripped over the canvas bucket someone had left lying about.

Ninian was sitting by the steering wheel, propped against the screen and fast asleep. His pipe, full of cold grey ash, lay beside him. His oilskins shone with dew and his hair was wet. He looked extremely uncomfortable.

Jean laughed as she looked at him. Here was Ninian, always so firm about them staying awake on watch and so good at doing it himself, now caught beautifully. She would leave him there till the kettle was boiling and wake him with some tea. On second thoughts she decided not to tell the others. After all, Ninian was her favourite brother and how Fiona would crow.

Thinking of Fiona reminded her of the others across on the Stack. She looked that way but it was still too dark to distinguish it from the rest of the cliff.

"I bet they're all asleep up there anyhow," she said. "Lucky nothing came in here in the night." She peered round, half hoping she would see the mysterious fishing boat, but there was nothing there.

Meanwhile the kettle had boiled so she made tea and carried a cup of it forward.

It seemed a pity to disturb Ninian who was sleeping so soundly. However, she shook him by the shoulder.

"Come on, wake up, watchman," she said.

Ninian blinked, gaped, rubbed his eyes.

"Had a nice sleep?" laughed Jean, handing him his tea.

"I — Gosh! — I *have* been to sleep." He looked at her in dismay, half asleep, and then grinned.

"All right," said Jean, who knew what he was thinking. "I, won't tell the others."

"Thanks." He took a sip of tea. "I say, I wonder how long I've been asleep?"

"All night, I expect," said Jean. "You really are helpful. There's a trawler in too; anchored quite close, I should have thought that would have woken you."

"Where! What!" Ninian leapt up, spilling his scalding tea over his hand. He swore loudly and then saw Jean laughing.

"Beast," he said. "It's too early for that sort of thing. Well, can you carry on from here?"

"I should hope so," said Jean. "I wonder who's the most helpful, you asleep, or me awake?"

Ninian disappeared down the companion.

"Don't wake me too early," he called.

"You won't sleep long when Fiona and Sandy get back," Jean retorted.

The wind had dropped completely; it was cold and still and grey. Gradually the sky lightened and in the east it turned pale yellow.

Hugh was wakened by the gulls, who started the day much too early for his liking. They did not seem to mind the four log-like figures under their humps of blanket, and Hugh lay still so as not to frighten them. He tried to go to sleep again but without much success. He could hear the sea sighing in the gully and the incessant squawking of a black-back down on the rocks. He pulled the blankets over his head and shut his eyes. When he next opened them the sky to the east was lemon coloured, with a few curly black bars of cloud straggling across it.

Hugh rolled over and looked out across the oily sea. He could distinguish *Fauna*, and was glad that he was not sitting on the hard deck keeping watch. At that thought the extreme sharpness of the rock he had been lying on came home to him, and he tried to hump up a bit of sleeping bag and lie on that.

The other three lay like the dead, curled up in their blankets. The fire was a sodden heap of ashes among blackened stones: the greasy frying pan and heap of plates looked horrid. Hugh felt extremely depressed and wished he was in a proper bed. He turned over on his side and pulled the blankets up.

Sandy prodding him was the next thing he knew. He sat up. It was broad daylight, and windless, and the sea was flat calm. James was in his pyjamas peering over the edge of the Stack. His fair hair was sticking up and he looked very sleepy.

Sandy was whispering.

"Fiona's still asleep," he said. "Let's go down and bathe — it looks lovely!"

Hugh felt sure it did not. However, he felt more cheerful than he had an hour or two earlier, so he regretfully left his flea-bag and followed the others over the cliff.

The Stack was deserted except for the still figure of Fiona. One by one the gulls swooped lower and lower, until, at last, one or two dared to land. They shuffled about among the thrift and squabbled greedily over some crusts they found in a puffin's nest. A bold herring gull perched on the foot of Fiona's bed and started quarrelling loudly with a kittiwake.

Fiona slowly opened her eyes.

Three feet away a gull was busily trying to swallow an enormous crust, while several more birds were swooping over his head, shrieking with envy.

At first she could not imagine where she was; then suddenly it dawned on her and she rolled over to see if the others could possibly be sleeping through all this din.

Their beds were flat.

Fiona sat up. From every corner of the Stack gulls rose up screaming. Half deafened, she got up and looked over the cliff just in time to see Hugh dive into the sea.

"Hoy, don't come down — we haven't got anything on," shrieked Jamie, who had seen her.

"You're telling me," said Fiona.

She returned to the fireplace and collected the wood they had not burnt the night before. There was still some water in the kettle; not much but enough for a cup of tea each.

It did not take long to boil on the flaming sticks, and by the time the boys had swum across to *Fauna*, got the dinghy and rowed back to the stack, tea was ready and very much appreciated.

Ninian shut his ears to the stamping of footsteps on deck and half-stifled laughter that came down the hatch, but at last he could bear it no longer and came thundering up in a black rage.

"For Heaven's sake," he said, scowling. "I was awake till about six this morning."

Jean caught his eye.

At the sight of his wild black hair and unshaven face the others gave a shout of laughter.

Ninian, pleased at seeing the sun and feeling it warm on his back, came farther up the companion.

Hugh whispered something to Sandy and James, and they sat looking very solemn while Fiona stirred a saucepan full of porridge.

"Have some tea," said Sandy, holding up the pot and shaking it. "We brought some across for Jean, and I think there's enough left."

Ninian came right up on deck, still looking furious and sleepy.

"Inconsiderate brutes," he grumbled. "Now you've wrecked what probably would have been a jolly nice day." He looked at Sandy's sleek hair and a trickle of water that was running down his neck.

"Gosh, have you been bathing already?" he said. "You must be insane."

Before he knew what was happening, Hugh and James had rushed at him. For a moment he struggled with them on the edge and then shot into the sea.

"You wait till I get back on board," he gasped, spitting. "I've swallowed mouthfuls, blast you. Just wait till I get back on board."

"We won't let you if you talk like that," cried James. "But you must admit, Ninian, that it's blissful?"

Ninian had to agree that it was, and after being fended off by the mop handle once or twice, decided it was better to postpone his revenge until later.

The porridge was more delicious than anything that could have been imagined and every last lump was eaten.

"We must get the pots up after breakfast," said Jean, taking a mouthful of bread and marmalade. They could not cope with toast on a Primus.

"I'm longing to see what we've got," said Fiona. "I haven't the least idea if this is a good place or not. Probably we'll get nothing."

"Probably we'll get millions," said Sandy. "We can give them away in Fairloch."

"Yes, of course — we are going there for the night," said Ninian, wriggling as a drip went down his back. His bad humour had worn off after the porridge. From the look of the sky it was going to be the most glorious hot day.

"Well, let's get a move on with the washing up," said Fiona, heaping plates on top of each other.

Eventually the last spoon was dried and the saucepan stood soaking by the sink.

Fiona filled her pockets with thin string and a knife, and they set off in the dinghy for the row of pots.

"We must make that buoy sometime," said Ninian, as he pulled towards the shore.

"Well, why not now?" asked Hugh.

"All right, but two of you had better go: the stones will be a bit heavy for one," said Fiona.

No one wanted to go much, so they drew lots and it fell to Jean and Hugh.

"We probably won't get anything," said Sandy reassuringly.

"You might," said Jean.

Ninian landed them on the second beach and they wandered up to the tide-mark to look for an airtight tin of some sort. The others rowed on towards the pots.

The sun, not yet high in the sky, was warm; there was not a ripple on the sea. You could see lumps of weed showing above the surface as they floated by, and drips fell in clear rings from the oars on to the water. A white gull's feather seemed hardly to move as it floated by like a petal, it was not even wet. The sand, reflected through the water, made the sea startlingly green. It would be a perfect day for spearing. Every detail below was revealed, every frond of weed, every shell and pebble, every sand eel.

As they neared the first row of corks the excitement grew intense. Jamie was up in the bows, ready to grab the first one as it came near. Sandy had the gaff in his hand, hoping his cousin would miss.

There was a slight swell by the rocks and Ninian rowed more slowly.

Jamie stood up and leant over. He snatched, and the corks were in his hand.

Slowly he began to haul, easily at first as the slack came in, then heaving at it.

"It's coming," squeaked James, nearly out of the boat.

"I can see something." Sandy's face was almost under water. "It's the stone, silly," said Fiona, no less excited. Surely there was something shimmering white down there.

The sodden top of the pot appeared and Jamie seized it with both hands. He heaved and got it aboard. It was quite empty.

"Blast!" he said.

"Typical," said Fiona.

Ninian looked up. As he did so something moved on the cliff and caught his eye. He screwed his head round, and Fiona, seeing him, followed his gaze. A man was hurrying along the cliff and as they watched, disappeared behind the Stack.

"Who on earth?" said Fiona.

"Goodness knows — must be a fisherman: he was in blue," said Ninian.

"Who?" asked the others.

"The man, didn't you see him?"

"No."

"Well, you will when we get a bit farther along," said Fiona.

But when they could see along the gully behind the Stack there was no sign of any one.

"Where could he have gone?" asked Jean.

"Just disappeared," said James.

"I told you so." Sandy sounded triumphant.

"What?"

"A smuggler, gone into his cave."

"Idiot," said Ninian. "He's probably hared along the rocks and is on the beach by now."

"He couldn't have," began Sandy, but the next lot of corks were bobbing alongside and everything was forgotten in the excitement.

"This one seems heavier," James said hopefully. But it was as empty as the other.

"Something's taken the bait, though," said Sandy.

"Probably little crabs," Fiona told him. "They have a habit of sucking it off."

"Perhaps we'll be luckier with the next," said James. "It does look such a lovely lobstery place, too."

"Shall we set them again?" asked Sandy. "We've got some bait left."

"Might as well, just to use it up. A pity this is no good, though," said Ninian,

James had caught the third string of corks and was hauling in the rope. No one spoke: they were all afraid that the black object in the pot was only their imagination.

"It is one," shrieked James at last. "An absolute whopper!"

Sandy helped him lift the pot on to a thwart. He undid the sodden string at the back and gingerly put his hand in. There was a good-sized lobster inside, snapping its claws wildly. Jamie seized it behind the head and dragged it out.

"What a beauty," he said. "Look at its huge claw."

"Poor thing, he's only got half a whisker one side," said James. He put the lobster down and it made a rush for Sandy's sand-shoed feet. He gave a shriek and lifted them up, balancing them either side of him on the thwart.

"Do tie him up, Fiona," he said. "He looks frightfully savage.

"He'll be all right," said Fiona, her eyes on the last pot.

Jamie hauled it on board.

"Another one," he cried. "Not such a big one, but still."

"Do look, it's only got one claw," said Fiona. "And there's a funny little pink one growing."

They all craned over to see.

"It must have lost it fighting." said Ninian.

In place of the claw there was a small soft one.

"How convenient for it, being able to grow spare claws."

Sandy touched it carefully. "I wonder how long it takes."

"Ages, I expect." Fiona lifted the last pot into place on

the top of the others.

"Where shall we set them, Ninian?"

"What about round the Stack?"

"All right."

Sandy took the old and chewed-looking bait out and put in some fresh. Fiona quickly mended yet another hole in the netting. James picked bits of seaweed and a few starfish off the bottom boards and flung them back into the sea. Two whelks had come up in the pots and fallen out.

"Are they worth keeping?" he asked.

"No, not only two," said Fiona. "They're awful to cook, and a bit rubbery at the end of it."

"Here's a hermit crab." Jamie picked a whelk shell off the bottom.

Out of the shell waved two orange claws like those of a tiny lobster.

"Funny thing," said James. "Oh, do look at this!" He bent down and picked up the tiniest flatfish imaginable.

"How sweet," said Fiona. "It's as thin as paper, almost."

"Like cellophane," said Sandy. It certainly was almost transparent.

Ninian turned the dinghy and pulled slowly towards the beach. Hugh and Jean had got two rocks and a large tin, perfect for a buoy.

"I suppose the pots will be all right for two days?" asked Jean.

"Oh, yes." Sandy grabbed the gunwale and swung himself on board.

"We shall have to use rope, there's not enough chain," said Ninian, diving into the cabin.

He pulled the rope out from under one bunk, where it was stowed.

"Bung the tin well up," said James. "We don't want it to go and sink."

Sandy held it up against the sun. There was not one pinprick of light.

"It has got a sort of cap screwed on," he said. "Looks as if it's rusted together, too. What d'you suppose it was — an oil drum?"

"Yes," said Hugh. "It makes a perfect buoy, if a little big. It's even got a handle at the top."

Ninian tied the rope to the two stones. He cut a bit off and made a loop with it in the handle of the drum.

"Very professional," said Fiona.

With great difficulty the rocks were hauled to the edge and dropped over. They thundered into the sea, and went roaring down, a cascade of bubbles all round them. After a minute or two the water calmed enough for them to be able to make out a whirl of sand at the bottom, and the rope stretching on and up like a snake.

"It would take a frightful gale to move those," said Sandy at last.

"Yes, but we must watch out for the rope fraying," said Ninian.

"I'm longing to use it," said Jean. "I wish we didn't have to wait till we got back."

"The tide *would* be low," said Fiona. "We won't know how much slack to leave until high water.

"We shall have to guess at it," said Ninian. "But whoever is on watch at four can see, because it'll be high then."

"James and I are," said Hugh. "At least we're relieved then. Between four of us we should get it right."

The dinghy was tied up; the engine started; Hugh and Sandy pulled up the anchor. With Fiona at the wheel they moved out of the bay.

It was flat calm and very still and quiet. There was no sound but that of the engine and the crying gulls from the Stack. Smooth ripples broke at the bow and *Fauna* heaved gently on the swell. Patches of scum floated on the water and out to sea a flock of sea birds were diving and screaming over a shoal of young herring. The sky was cloudless and it was scorching hot. The sea glittered and flashed like gold.

The line of the cliff was hard against the sky.

They were too near in to see any of the hills and the islands were lost in a heat haze.

"I bet all those caves aren't wasted by being empty," said Sandy. The cliff was studded with black holes of varying shapes and sizes.

"Most of these are impossible to get to." Ninian pointed out. "The cliff is completely sheer and one couldn't possibly land on those rocks."

"There may be some secret bay or something," said Jean, upholding her cousin.

They sailed on down the coast in the heat of the morning, past the lighthouse, past Melvaig's scattered houses, past the long bare beach of sand into Fairloch.

Across the bay was a hill of grass and heather and beyond that the Corriedon mountains. West was Skye, rising steeply out of the sea, misty in the heat haze. A fishing boat was coming in round the end of the island, nets piled on the deck, and the red sail swinging in the light wind.

On their left were crofts scattered on the hillside, gradually growing more plentiful as they neared the end of the bay. Slowly they rounded the last point and as they did so the curve of Fairloch's sandy beach came into view. In this hot August weather it was plentifully sprinkled with trippers, and there were even more outside the huge hotel, built just across the road above the bay. There was a high grassy hummock on the right, stretching into the sea, and left was the village, a few stores and cobblers and the inevitable petrol pumps. The hotel was in the middle, a huge grey pile with turrets and a gravel sweep in front that was covered with deck chairs.

Fiona turned the wheel slightly and they edged in towards a pier on the left by the huddle of houses. There were several fishing boats there already, but Fiona, her bottom lip caught between her teeth, was gauging the distance to a nicety. Ninian slowed the engine; James and

Sandy were in the bows; gently, softly *Fauna* came alongside. Not a chip was scraped off the boat ahead nor was a splinter knocked from the pier.

"Well done," said Hugh, but Fiona was not listening. She threw a rope to Jean, already up on the jetty. *Fauna* crunched gently against the limpets and sent waves washing amongst the wooden piles.

"Well, what'll we do?" Ninian slid back the engine-room hatch.

"*Fauna'll* be all right here, won't she?" asked Jean.

"Yes, why?"

"I say," Jean looked rather tentative. "Let's go and have dinner at the hotel. Just for fun," she added quickly, seeing Fiona and Ninian look at each other.

"Have we got enough money?" asked James practically.

"Umn, yes." Ninian looked at the others, his eyebrows raised. "Well, shall we?"

"Yes, let's give all those old trippers a shock by arriving looking like this." Sandy grinned as he looked at their old and stained clothes.

"Who cares?" Fiona wriggled her bare brown toe through a hole in her sandshoe and stuck her hands in her pockets. "Let's present Sanderson with some fish in case he doesn't like the look of us."

They wandered on down the street, remembering various stores they wanted as they passed the shops.

There were a good many hikers on the road, all pressing forward with eager hot faces, huge packs on their backs and red arms and legs.

"Funny how fat hikers always seem to be," said Jamie.

"And why do they wear such unattractive clothes?" asked Fiona, hunching her shoulders and knowing that, with her long legs, she looked like a boy in trousers.

"There's a hiker's hostel up by Sand," said Ninian. "But the road ends at Melvaig. I wonder where they're going?"

"Just curiosity," said Sandy. "They'll have to come back

this way."

"Why so scathing about the hikers?" asked Hugh. "Poor things, it's probably all the holiday they get and if they're enjoying themselves —"

"Well, I wish they'd enjoy themselves somewhere else," growled Ninian, who viewed the ever-growing hordes of trippers at Carrick each year with horror.

They walked on along the dusty road in silence. Worn lumps of rock stuck up every now and then and a few tufts of grass were growing along the middle. It was hardly more than a track and had never been tarred. An orange van swept past in a swirl of dust. Joan waved to the driver; it was the butcher. No clouds moved in the sky; the sun burnt down, bright and brassy; by the rocks the waves sucked and sighed, washing among heaps of shiny weed, cool and inviting.

"Do let's bathe when we get to the beach," said Jean.

"I wish there were Stop Me and Buy Ones in this part of the world," said Hugh.

They were so hot when they did eventually reach the hotel that there could be no thought of anything but bathing. As they walked along the road, less dusty here where the traffic passed, the hotel was on their left and the beach on their right, below a small cliff. They plunged down the path, steps cut between gorse bushes and out on to sand. There was a stretch of hot dry sand to be crossed first, covered with orange peel, half buried bits of rag and dirty dried seaweed. The Stewarts hurried across this, picking their way between trippers.

"How they can sit there," whispered Fiona, wrinkling her nose.

The sight of these fat unappreciative bodies was too much for Ninian. He started to run, and, followed by the others, charged along the wet sand, dodging groups of brown and oily young men, until he reached the rocks on the left of the bay. He climbed along these at a tremendous speed until he was out of sight and sound of the trippers.

"Gosh," he said, taking a deep breath of the cool salty air, "this is better. Let's bathe quickly."

"And we can see *Fauna* from here, too," said James, looking across the calm blue bay. There were several small figures moving on the pier and one of the fishing boats was getting ready to go to sea.

"She's all right," said Ninian, pulling off his shirt.

As Fiona emerged from behind a rock, pushing her hair out of her eyes, she was just in time to see his brown body dive into the sea.

"Mind the current," he called, as he came to the surface, and Fiona remembered how the tide raced past this point.

As she came up after her dive she felt the water pull at her body and saw Ninian already some yards down on her left, swimming back to the shore. For a minute or two she relaxed and let herself get swept on past the point and out to sea, then she rolled over and struck out against the current.

"Don't go too far out, Jean," called Ninian, who had reached the rocks and was hanging there, resting.

They did not stay in long: it was too hard swimming against the race all the time.

"Blast those trippers." Ninian scowled and ran his fingers through his hair, while the water trickled down his back, sparkling in the sun.

"Won't take us long to dry." Fiona hunted about for a fairly smooth rock and found one where a clump of heather made a soft seat.

"You look like a colony of gulls," grinned Sandy, who had climbed to the top of the cliff and was lying on his face looking over at them. He picked off a head of thrift and dropped it on Jean. She looked up and smiled at him and at the whole hot day; at the warm sun that was drying her; at the gulls, white like blown paper; at the slow beat of the sea below.

Lazily they watched the fishing boat leave the pier

SANDY HAD CLIMBED TO THE TOP OF THE CLIFF.

opposite, the throb of the engine came to them clearly and they could see the white V of the wash. The shouts and laughter from the trippers on the beach were the only blot. Hugh, more tolerant than the Stewarts, was the only one who felt a slight sympathy for them. After all, as he had said before, it was probably the one holiday they had that year. The others would have joyfully killed them all.

"Tea, I think," said Ninian at last.

Drowsily Sandy rolled over and pulled the knapsack nearer to him. The others listened expectantly while he rustled among the paper bags. "Hoy, catch!" he called, and sandwiches came scattering down amongst them.

"Do look out," said Fiona, rescuing one off a clump of heather. Tea finished, they lay back digesting for a while, then Ninian, looking up at the sky and stretching, said, "Come on, let's go across to Flowerdale."

"All right." The others got up too.

"Let's leave these here," said Fiona, pointing to their clothes and towels.

"All right, stuff them well into a crevice, though, or those trippers will probably snaffle them," said Ninian.

They went back over the hump of grass to where a narrow gully in the rocks joined the bay of Flowerdale to Fairloch. It was only at spring tides that the sea came through this gully, and now the sand was hot and dry.

On the left, through the gully, was a tiny village where a wooden pier, inaccessible at low water, was built under a row of shady sycamores.

"This is where we got *Black Swan*," Jean told Hugh, as they approached a cluster of grey cottages built against the hill. Several boats were pulled up on the stones, a heap of lobster pots lay there, nets were stretched between poles and a couple of collies lay asleep in the sun outside the crofts. These leapt up, barking wildly, and Hugh was reminded of a certain dark night when they had landed at a farm on Loch Marba.

"Shut up, Doolay; quiet, Taraf!" shouted Jamie. On hearing all this noise a woman came out of the nearest cottage and said something in Gaelic to the dogs, who subsided and slunk away, their tails between their legs.

While Fiona and Ninian talked to her the others wandered down to the sea and played ducks and drakes with broken slates they found among the rocks.

At last Ninian called them and they climbed back up the hill to their clothes, still there in spite of their doubts about the trippers.

"We shall look smart in the hotel," said Fiona, grinning. Vainly she tried to comb out her hair with her fingers. The salt water had made it into a curly sticky mat. "Oh, hell," she said. "Has any one got a comb?"

No one had, and Ninian's hair was as bad as her own.

"Perhaps they'll have one in the hotel," suggested Sandy.

"Ugh, it'll be all trippery," Fiona shuddered.

"Come on, I'm getting cold," said James, and started to run. The others followed him across the sand and up through the marram grass and gorse bushes. Their feet slid on the gravel in front of the hotel and they arrived breathless on the steps.

Fiona made one last desperate effort to smooth her hair and then pushed round the revolving door.

The hall was full of people, people who had just changed for dinner and were sitting drinking sherry and dry martinis. Every one looked round as the Stewarts came in, for the noise the younger members of the party made was unusual.

Most of the people quickly looked away again, but to Fiona's fury she heard some of them sniggering, and turned round to give them one of her blackest looks. That quelled them, and she followed Ninian across the hall to the manager's office. Mr. Sanderson was a friend of theirs, one of the people to whom they had sold venison last summer. He was delighted to see them again and promised them a table for dinner. "Although we're terribly full," he said. "And booked right up to the end of the summer, too."

"I say," said Ninian, balancing on the edge of the desk. "Do you own the fishing rights on the lochs beyond Inverasdale? Loch an Draing and the other little one?"

"Yes," said Mr. Sanderson. "Why? You're surely not tired of your own lochs?"

"No," said Fiona. "But you see we're — well — sort of camping in the bay by the lighthouse and we wondered if we could go and fish those lochs sometime when there's no one there?"

"Oh, there's very seldom any one there," said the proprietor. "You have to walk a mile or so, whichever way you go, and it's not many nowadays that'll do that."

"We will," said Jean. "The farther from civilisation the

better."

"Well, mind you're not stolen by the Green Laddie," said Mr. Sanderson, as they went back in the hall and they all laughed.

"Who is the Green Laddie?" whispered Hugh to Jean.

"The last fairy to be seen in Scotland," she told him. "But he was a nice one, really."

The other guests were already filing into the dining-room.

"We might as well, too," said Ninian, looking at the clock. "It's early, but I'm ravenous."

They found they were at a table looking out of the window over the bay. More boats were putting out with herring nets, and they could see the brown hulk of *Fauna* against the pier.

The dining-room was nearly full. Waiters and waitresses were hurrying about with menu cards, and one of these was placed in front of each of the Stewarts. To James and Sandy and Jean they meant less than nothing as they were in French, but the other three started to argue violently, with, as Sandy had to admit afterwards, marvellous results. They had smoked salmon, clear soup, whitebait, roast duck with most excellent garnishings, and ices. There were more discussions about the wine.

"We might as well do it in style," Ninian said. "And have wine while we're about it."

Fiona backed out of this argument and left it to him and Hugh. The great difficulty was: red or white?

"Red, with duck," said Hugh, but eventually they decided on Liebsfraumilch.

When they had chosen the menu they had time to look round. Every one seemed to be staring at them.

"Apes," growled Ninian.

Fiona grinned. She could see that all the girls were staring at him and Hugh. And she agreed really. Wild looking though they might be, they were certainly more attractive than the other young men in the room.

To begin with, they talked and laughed, principally about the other diners. Fiona had difficulty in making James and Sandy lower their voices sufficiently so that they would not be heard across the whole room. As the evening wore on the heat began to make them sleepy. One by one they grew silent until in the end it was a kind of race to see who could be finished first.

Fiona was, and beckoned to the waiter.

A band had struck up and couples were dancing in a small space between the tables.

It was growing dark outside.

Sandy scooped up the last of his ice and opened his eyes very wide. It was insufferably hot and the chatter of the other people sounded like a monkey-house.

Ninian and Hugh between them settled the bill. Fiona swallowed the last of her coffee and pushed back her chair. The others followed her from the room; they almost ran.

Out through the swinging door and into a rush of cool air. Across the gravel and down the small cliff between gorse bushes. And along the deserted beach. Her feet did not make a sound on the sand. The tide was going out and waves broke crisply and evenly out of the calm sea, dragging back with them limpet shells and bunches of weed.

"Oh, night, night!" whispered Fiona, as she stared up at a pale and twinkling star. The wind was cool in her hair and an impatient wave broke over her feet. The others were still slithering down the cliff. For the moment she was alone on the beach. She lifted her head again and looked at the stars.

"I say, Ninian, the rope's swollen in the dew."

"Hurry up with that warp aft, Sandy."

"I can't see, it's pitch dark. Ouch!"

"Don't make such a row, you'll wake the whole village."

The sudden roar of the engine shattered the stillness of early morning. To the Stewarts it seemed ear-splitting.

Ninian's black head poked up through the hatch; Sandy and James threw the wet ropes down from the pier and jumped after them; Fiona turned the wheel and slowly *Fauna* moved out into the still bay.

It was dark with the greyness of half an hour or so before dawn.

Half-past four, to be exact.

It was cold, before sunrise. The Stewarts rubbed their fingers as they coiled the ropes, and Fiona wished she had brought gloves with her. It had been Ninian's idea to start so early.

"Let's be at sea when the sun comes up," he said. "Besides, it'll take us some time to get down to Corriedon."

The sky was still speckled with a few faint stars. Out in the bay the water was ruffled by a breeze.

"And half an hour ago," thought Fiona, "I was still asleep."

She rubbed her eyes for the tenth time. She was really awake now.

The fore-hatch was pushed back and Jean appeared, holding two cups in each hand. She slopped some out on to the deck as she came down.

"Here, Fiona," she said.

Her sister took one and sipped it. It was scalding hot and rather strong.

"Who made it?" asked Fiona. "You or Hugh?"

"Why? Is it nasty?" Jean was cautious.

"It's not bad."

"You ought to be grateful for any," said Hugh's voice behind her.

"Oh, so you made it!" Fiona turned the wheel slightly. She hunched her shoulders into her oily. "Hurry up, dawn," she said.

Behind her, Ninian pulled to the engine-room hatch. Through the skylight she watched him crawl into the cabin and spread out a chart on the table. Sandy, James and Jean joined him down there, the hurricane lamp swinging slightly over their heads. There was a bit of a swell out here in the bay, just enough to slop the tea out of Jean's cup on to the corner of the chart. Fiona could see Ninian swearing at her and telling her to get a cloth to mop it up. On either side of the cabin the bunks were still heaped with rumpled blankets and pillows. Fiona resolutely turned her eyes away. Up here on deck the wind was stronger, and already an occasional bead of spray pattered on the cabin roof.

Hugh came and stood beside her, his hands in his pockets.

"How long'll it take us to get there?" he asked, rocking from toe to heel as *Fauna* pitched.

"Oh, umn, we ought to get there by about nine," said Fiona. "Unless we run on a rock — or I get frozen to the wheel," she added.

"Let me steer for a bit, then."

"No, we might as well freeze one at a time. Anyway, it'll soon be light."

The sky was pink behind Fairloch. There were woods cloaking the side of a low hill above the Asheenach road. Along the summit several giant and sturdy pines were cut in sharp silhouette and the tops of firs in the plantation by the Kerry were just visible.

Ninian had given no instructions about rocks near here, and Fiona did not believe there were any, so she picked her own land-marks and steered for them.

On her right Skye was emerging from the dark. Its huge bulk of mountains were clear against the paling sky, and becoming every moment more distinct.

Fauna, her decks wet with dew, slipped on into the morning. The beat of her engine shattered the silence and drowned even the slap of waves against her sides. By the time it was really light they had left Fairloch behind them.

Half-past seven.

For some time now, through the hatch, Fiona and Hugh had watched signs that could only mean the preparation of breakfast.

First Jean had got up and pushed back the charts while Sandy rescued two cups that nearly overbalanced. Then she disappeared forward.

Ninian pulled down the pilot book and started to flick over the pages. Sandy leant over his shoulder and kept on trying to stop him from passing all the exciting-looking maps and tide tables.

Then Ninian looked up, appeared to be explaining something, and eventually slammed down the book and got up, scowling.

"Jean can't light the Primus," guessed Hugh.

"Or the plug's stuck again."

It was rather like watching a game of Dumb Crambo or a silent movie. Presently a string of sausages and two forks were thrown on the table. James and Sandy each seized one and started to prick the sausages.

Then the hatch was pushed back and Ninian came on deck.

"Gosh, it's light," he said, as he looked round. "And we have come far."

"How's the breakfast?" asked Hugh longingly.

"Oh, Fiona, I think you'd better go and cope, just in case Jean's bungling it."

"All right. By the way, I suppose there are no dangerous rocks anywhere here, because you haven't told us of any?"

"No, not yet." Ninian took over the wheel.

Fiona went down the companion into a reek of sausages and paraffin. "What have you been doing?" she asked resignedly, as she hung her oily on a hook.

"Well, Ninian was filling the Primus and it overflowed," said Jean, scooping up a sausage on the palette knife and flicking it over in a shower of fat.

"Here, don't you burn them." Fiona sprang at the frying

pan.

"Stop it, Fiona, they're all right. Let it go, I can do it." Jean's temper was obviously not improved by the early hour.

Neither was Fiona's.

"Jean, you're burning them all. Do scrape underneath, you gump! There now, look, it's burst!"

"Well, they always burst when you do them, anyway."

Fiona turned her back on this scene. At home she would have stalked out of the house and up the glen, and probably slammed the door, but there was no point here in slamming the hatch, and you could not stalk far on *Fauna's* deck.

"You two can lay the table," she announced to Sandy and James. She swept the chart and pilot book on to the bunks.

"Come on, breakfast's nearly ready." She pulled open the drawer and scattered a handful of cutlery over the table.

"Don't do that with the cups," warned Sandy, and nearly had them thrown at him.

The sausages were done. Jean put a lid over them and replaced the kettle that had only just boiled.

Jamie shouted to Hugh, who came clattering down the companion.

They had grapenuts first, with bananas sliced on them. Food had a marvellous effect on every one's temper, and even Fiona forgot to be angry and scooped up her last crumb of sausage.

Ninian let them stop for an hour or so later and bathe off a long shelving rock that ran into the sea like a pier. They brought *Fauna* alongside in grand style and made her fast, keeping one eye on the tide.

They had lunch on deck and threw scraps to the gulls. There was a cloud of these following the boat, principally because Ninian had found the very old remains of bait in a bucket and had hurled it overboard.

"We might almost be a liner," said Jean, watching them.

"Ploughing our way across the Atlantic," said Fiona.

"Throwing out bucketfuls of stuff, rolls that had been

hardly eaten, and cake," said Sandy.

"There might be an albatross or two, or is that the Pacific?"

"Probably." Ninian half-shut his eyes and stared back the way they had come where, beyond the gulls, there was nothing but open sea, that is, if you shut your right eye. He tried to imagine them crossing the Atlantic in *Fauna*.

"We'd need something bigger," he said.

"What?" Hugh, who was steering, thought he must have gone mad. Fiona, whose thoughts had followed her brother's pretty closely, explained.

As they grew nearer to Corriedon it was Hugh's turn to show off and tell them the names of the different hills, where he had shot the biggest stags, where an eagle nested, where there was a loch high up between two peaks.

Soon the grassy foothills gave place to the mountains themselves, that dropped more and more steeply into the sea. Corriedon was a loch almost overshadowed by hills, more like Loch Marba than Carrick.

"What'll we do this afternoon?" asked Jamie, looking at Hugh.

"Some of us might fish," he said. "It's too early for stalking, which is a pity."

Jean, who had pricked up her ears at the mention of fishing, said: "Fishing the river?" She had heard of the excellence of the Corriedon river.

"Why not? The rest of us might try and get a rabbit or something."

"We've only brought one rod," said Jean.

"There are plenty at the lodge," said Hugh.

The hills grew higher and higher. Ninian reached down the hatch and unhooked his glass from under the companion. He pulled it out, leant back against the screen, and started spying for deer.

The engine beat with a steady throb-throb.

"Bother the vibration," said Ninian, resting his elbow on

his knee.

"I can see some," cried Sandy triumphantly. "By that black gash on the right." Fiona looked where he pointed. She too could make out the tiny brown specks in the heather.

"Stags," said Ninian at last. "Still in velvet, though."

Ahead they could see the coast curve in to Loch Corriedon and then continue on in a line of equally steep and rocky hills.

The loch narrowed half-way down and broadened out again, although not much. The hills round the inner loch seemed steeper than ever, and it was at the end of this strip of water that Hugh's Uncle Frank had his house. It was there, too, that the famous Corriedon River ran into the sea. The outer loch was about the same length as Loch Carrick, and the inner loch about half. It would take them two hours at least to reach their destination.

"To-morrow what'll we do?" asked Sandy.

"Non-stop journey to Flatfish," suggested Ninian.

"What happens farther down the coast?" Jean was a bit vague on geography.

"Another loch like this. We could, of course, go on and on down."

"No, let's go back," said Fiona. "We must try and find the Green Laddie."

"And there are all those caves to be explored," added James.

"Perhaps the boat'll come in again," said Jean.

"Still harping on that?" said Ninian, lying back on the cabin roof, his head on his arms. He watched a heap of stately clouds sail on eastwards and a couple of terns, the most graceful of all sea-birds, dart and hover above him, crying shrilly as they swooped. He remembered coming into this loch years ago with his father and finding masses of terns' nests on a little shingly island. There had been eggs there as well as babies, spotted like the rocks, and you had to tread carefully because they were thick on the ground. The noise the parents had made, circling and shrieking overhead, was even more piercing than the Stack at nesting time. August was late for nests, but there might be a few babies left.

They were going east now, straight into the heart of the hills. The slopes were strewn with huge rocks, and brown-green grass and heather seemed the only form of food for deer. Ninian would have loved to have stopped just where they were and climbed these hills; here where there was no habitation whatever. Every hundred yards or so a small burn came racing down the rocks, hurling itself from fall to pool, roaring even above the noise of the engine. Sometimes where they ran down a gully cut deep in the hillside, clumps of hazel and rowan trees grew between the rocks, trailing their leaves in the hurrying water. Sometimes the burns would run underground for a few yards, gurgling deep in the peat where they had worn themselves a channel. Beside one of the largest of these, where it ran out over the short rocky beach, was the ruin of a cottage, nothing left standing but one old wall and chimney, the other stones lying heaped in a rough oblong. Nettles were growing in the corner of one room and out of the chimney waved a tiny rowan tree. The ground beside the cottage must once have been cleared for a garden, but now there was only the brilliant turf, shorn close as velvet by rabbits and sheep.

"What a blissful place to have a house," said Fiona, looking at it. "Think how quiet; no sound but the burn."

"And a few waves on the rocks," added James.

"An occasional eagle or buzzard, and sheep," said Sandy.

"And stags roaring in the autumn," said Ninian. "Right in the garden, I should think."

"I wonder why it's a ruin?" asked Jean.

"Perhaps Cumberland sacked it," suggested Fiona. "Although I don't think he came just here. Probably all the inhabitants died of consumption; that does happen sometimes."

"Or they may have found it too lonely," said Hugh. "Imagine living in that place, for years and years, never seeing other people."

"There may have been some other crofts there," interrupted Sandy.

"Snowed up in the winter," continued Hugh, ignoring him. "And the nearest village Corriedon, which consists of at least two houses."

"Derbaig's nearer," reminded Ninian.

'There isn't even a shop at Derbaig," said Hugh. "At least I don't think so."

"Is that Derbaig?" asked Sandy, pointing. A curl of smoke seemed to be rising from the middle of the hills on the left of the Narrows.

"Yes, and Sheildaig's opposite," said Hugh. "That's a very grand place and boasts a pub, and they say the men row across there from Derbaig every night."

"It must be nearly two miles," said Ninian. "You'd think they'd build one of their own."

As they got opposite they could see that Derbaig was a tiny horseshoe harbour cut in the side of the steepest hills. The most inland slope had houses perched on it and a track running diagonally across it. Several fishing boats were moored in the tranquil water of the harbour, which looked as if it could never be disturbed by wind or wave. The road ran up the hill behind the village in hairpin curves and disappeared over the neck of land that formed one side of the Narrows.

"Steer for the middle," Ninian told Hugh, "because there are rocks underwater on either side."

"Strange though it may seem, I did know," said Hugh sarcastically.

"Sorry," Ninian laughed. "I was forgetting you came from here."

They passed the Narrows, their wash breaking over the

rocks either side, and were on the last lap of their voyage. Uncle Frank's house was round a corner and out of sight as yet, and the hills grew ever steeper. On their left the road ran like a ribbon, slanting down the side of the hill, until it was almost on a level with the sea.

A little figure on a bicycle toiled upwards.

"Poor thing, he must be hot," said Jean.

"It must be fun coming down, though," said Sandy. "Think of those hairpin bends the other side."

At last they were round the corner and in front of them were the scattered houses of Anat, Facaig, Corriedon and Alligin. These places together would number about one hundred houses, but they were called separate villages.

Uncle Frank's house was on the hill opposite, grey against its thick background of firs. Fiona remembered the lovely half-tropical garden hidden there.

"Where shall we anchor?" Ninian asked Hugh.

"There's a spare buoy near that white motor boat," Hugh told him. "We might as well grab that as nobody else wants it; at least, I hope not."

"I suppose the mooring's all right?"

"Well, it was last year. I don't think chains rot very soon, but we can ask Uncle Frank if you like."

"Perhaps we'd better," said Fiona. "It'd be an awful bore to get back and find *Fauna* on the rocks."

"Where's the river?" Jean had not been thinking of much else since Hugh had first suggested fishing.

"In the corner, on the right, past that little island," said Hugh. "You can't really see it well because there are trees in the way. There's a bridge over it just before you get to Alligin," and he pointed to the village to the right.

Ninian dropped down into the engine-room. Hugh, still at the wheel, was determined to bring the boat alongside the buoy as neatly as Fiona did.

The engine slowed and stopped. Maddeningly, the buoy danced up and down, and it was impossible to gauge the distance. *Fauna* seemed to have no way on at all and she would not answer to the helm. Hugh spun the wheel, found that she had turned much more than he had thought, realised that she was practically stationary now, turned the wheel again, although he was convinced it was too late, and Sandy, who had been expecting to pick the buoy up on the starboard side, rushed to the port and just hooked it in time. Hugh breathed again and at last dared look at Fiona, who laughed.

"Only just," she said.

The mooring chain rattled on board, slimy with weed. Ninian hoisted himself up and slammed the hatch back behind him.

"No need to lock it," said Ninian. "I'll leave the key in the first cup, as I'll probably lose it ashore." There was a hasp and small padlock on both the hatches and they had used these at Fairloch, but there was no one likely to come aboard here.

They rowed off to the pier on the left of the loch. The tide was nearly out and they had to climb up a flight of green and slimy steps which were extremely slippery.

"Can we leave the dinghy tied up, d'you suppose, or will it bump too much?" said James. "Because it's miles to pull it up on the stones."

"It'll be all right tied up," said Ninian, slipping the painter through a ring. "It's so calm nothing can happen."

They walked up the pier and on to the road.

There was only a path up to the lodge: the drive came in at the back of the house and did not join the road for another half-mile. Hugh pushed open the gate in the stone wall and the others followed him along the track which zigzagged up the hill between clumps of rough brown grass and boulders. The path was gravel except where it crossed a burn, and then there were stepping-stones.

The lodge was about two hundred yards up the hill, which was a steep one. Hugh led firmly, knowing that if either Ninian or Fiona were in front they would go at a tremendous pace and it was much too hot for that.

There was another gate at the bottom of the garden, the same one they had gone through last summer when they first met Hugh. Sandy and Fiona winked at each other again as they walked up to the house between the laurel bushes. On the gravel, in between the lawn and the house, a man was standing. He was dressed in check plus-fours and a deer-stalker. He had a large, white moustache, a pipe was in his mouth, and he was staring straight at the house.

"Hallo, Uncle Frank," said Hugh, as he pushed through the last of the laurels.

The old man turned.

"Hallo, Hugh, my boy," he said. "This is a surprise. I thought you were up at Carrick?"

"Well, I was," said Hugh. "But we came down in a yacht. These are the Stewarts, by the way," and he introduced them.

"Well, well," said the Colonel, twirling his moustache. "Have you had lunch?"

"Yes, thank you," said Fiona. "I hope you don't mind us all bursting in like this, but Hugh seemed to think you wouldn't."

"No, not at all. In fact I'm alone here at the moment and I hope you can stay for some time. Did you say you came in a yacht?"

"Yes, she's moored down there by the *Aloma*," said Hugh. "We came in for the night."

"How jolly," said the Colonel. "And now I suppose you want to fish," he added, having seen the rod in Jean's hand.

"Could we?" she asked.

"Yes, of course, delighted. You a keen fisherman?"

"Oh, very, but it's been too dry up at Carrick lately."

"Can we borrow another rod, Uncle Frank?" asked Hugh. "And I thought the rest of us might try and get a rabbit or something."

"Good idea," said his uncle. "Come on inside. By the way, I was wondering whether it would be an improvement to have some of the creeper off the front of this house. Shuts out the light, y'know, makes it a bit damp. I've bin gettin' rheumatism lately, not so young as I was, might be the creeper."

Hugh, who could hardly believe his cars when he heard his uncle suggesting an improvement to the house, was silent. However, Fiona said:

"Yes, I'm sure it would be a help. I always think too much foliage round a house does make it damp, but this has such a lovely view and is so near the sea that it shouldn't be."

Uncle Frank seemed pleased at this, and led the way in, through a porch festooned with mackintoshes that smelt awful, into a small room entirely surrounded by rods, rifles and guns. Leaning in one corner was a rod already up and this the Colonel gave to Hugh, saying:

"Might as well take this one, it's all ready. Now which of you wants to fish?"

Jean did, obviously, and it was decided that Sandy and Ninian should go too, and between them share the rods. The Colonel said he would come and show them the way. At this Ninian caught Hugh's eye and looked rather dubious, but Hugh managed to hiss at him that his uncle knew all the best places and was a patient ghillie too.

Slinging a fishing bag over his shoulder and handing Sandy a gaff, the Colonel walked across the hall and out of the front door. The others heard him telling Jean she might catch a salmon but was more likely to get sea trout.

Back in the gunroom, Hugh helped himself to cartridges and to two of his uncle's guns.

"You and Jamie shoot," said Fiona. "I'll carry the spoils."

"No, you must shoot," said Hugh, peering down the barrels of the gun. "I have often here."

"Honestly, I'd rather not. But we can change if we want to. Where do we go?" Fiona looked out of the window.

"YOU AND JAMIE SHOOT," SAID FIONA.

There was no very rabbity-looking place in sight.

"The side of the hill we came up is a goodish place."
Hugh handed Fiona the cartridge bag. It was heavy.

"You've got enough, anyway," she said, thinking of the others he had put in his pocket.

"Might as well be prepared," said Hugh. "And you can carry this game bag as well."

Fully laden, they went through the stuffy porch, and out into the garden. *Fauna* was rocking peacefully below them.

"She looks more like an ark than ever," said Jamie.

A seagull had settled on her deck and was walking slowly round on the look-out for any scrap of food. The tide was low and in the shallows a heron was standing as still as the rocks around him. He never moved until suddenly he spread his wings and flapped awkwardly across the loch. The tide was slowly creeping in over the mud, swirling round the bunches of seaweed that clung to the stones. There were plenty of mussels here, too, and winkles, but Jamie, who suggested collecting some, was squashed by Fiona, who said it was much too drainy.

They spread out in line along the slope of the hill, Fiona in the middle, and walked in the direction of the pier. There was not much cover here for rabbits, and any they did see were too far away. Fiona beat through a likely looking patch of bracken and two ran out. She could not see what happened as the fronds reached right over her head, but she heard a shot, and on reappearing, found that James had got one.

"Well done," said Fiona, pulling bracken out of her hair. She picked up the rabbit, a fat young one, and stuffed it in the game-bag.

They went on, more uphill now, so as to avoid the crofts along the road. They skirted round a hayfield full of stooks, through a wire fence, and into a cornfield that was just being cut. Women were following the cutter, gathering up armfuls of corn and twisting several stalks round to keep them together. The Stewarts often did this at home, and felt rather guilty at not stopping and helping. However, the farmer called them out into the field, where they were just coming to the end of a patch, and Hugh shot a rabbit as it ran out.

"One each," he said, as he gave it to the farmer. "Come on."

They walked along the hedges of two more grass fields without any success. Hugh just managed not to shoot a red squirrel as it leapt into an ash tree, and Jamie missed a rabbit, but apart from that they saw nothing.

"Well, perhaps these woods'll be better," suggested Hugh. They were above the pier now, and a thick plantation of firs grew in a square on the hill. Fiona and James stayed where they were and Hugh went round the other side. Then, when he whistled they walked up, until the plantation ended. Jamie missed a pigeon that came hurtling out overhead, smashing its way through the twigs and sending showers of fir needles to the ground. He also hit a rabbit, and they heard Hugh blazing away on the other side.

"So many shots must mean a miss," said Fiona, picking her way through a bog. As she stepped in a clump of rushes a snipe bounced up and went zigzagging away.

Of course Jamie missed.

Fiona said nothing, just looked at him.

"Sorry," said James, but he did not relinquish the gun.

They reached the top before Hugh, so they walked along to meet him. The hill slanted on and on upwards, scattered with rocks and occasionally a small rowan tree. Every now and then the wind whistled through the thin grass, or breathed rather than whistled — it was not cold enough for that. Clouds like wisps of cotton-wool sailed on past the tops of the hills. Fiona, watching them, saw that they moved much faster than the wind blew down on earth. High up on the hillside she could see a dozen or so hinds feeding, and longed for stalking to start.

Hugh met them at the corner, very pleased with himself, with a couple of rabbits dangling from his hand.

"Lovely shooting," he said.

"How many shots did you have?" asked Fiona suspiciously.

"Only one each for these."

"But we heard masses," said James.

"Oh, well, there were masses of rabbits," said Hugh.

They wandered on for a bit but the hillside seemed bare. So at last they found a comfortable patch of heather and lay back in the sun, watching the waves flicker across the loch, an occasional motor creep down the road opposite, and listened to gulls, the whistling of oyster catchers, and the steady roar of the river away on their left.

The fishing party walked along the road across the head of the loch until they came to the bridge. Here the Colonel stopped and looked speculatively into the water. The river was almost as low here as it was at Carrick, and hot grey stones stuck up every now and then and a long ridge of shingle showed by one bank.

"Humph, it's a bit too low," said the Colonel. "Still, we'll have a try."

Jean put up her rod and, frowning, tied on the cast. Ninian had taken the other rod, and Sandy was determined to stay with him. He was sure that the Colonel would be unable to resist fishing himself, and he did not feel up to arguing with him. Ninian caught Jean's eye and winked. Then he said:

"Is the sea pool any good, sir? It looks as if there might be a salmon there."

"Well, you can try," said the Colonel. "But it's not a very good place as a rule. Shall we try up stream, young lady? I know several nice little pools." They went on for a hundred yards or so.

"It's all too shallow," said the Colonel, shaking his head sadly. Undaunted, Jean jumped on to a steady rock and started to fish. The Colonel watched her, pleasantly surprised.

After catching her tail fly twice on a rock, she too had to admit there was not enough water.

"Never mind, there are plenty more pools to try," said Uncle Frank, leading on up the shore. However, he went on and on, passing every pool with a shake of his head, and Jean saw too, the ominous grey stones sticking out of them.

They had gone about half a mile without stopping once. The river now began to get much narrower, and they gradually found themselves climbing as they left the valley behind.

"We'd better cross here," said the Colonel, indicating a precarious looking chain of stepping stones. Jean followed him across and climbed up the opposite bank. There was a boggy field on their left, edged by a tumbledown wire fence. Across the river a hill rose steeply and the heather came right down to the bank, dripping its tough brown stems into the water.

The river gushed over a fall, splashing from rock to rock among a tangle of bare smooth branches that had been left there the previous winter.

"Goodness," thought Jean, "if it gets any rockier there won't be room for a fish."

However, the Colonel had one last hope, and that was round the corner. Here the river grew suddenly smooth and deep, as it slid between sheer rocks. There was a curve in the cliff opposite, which was higher than the one they stood on, and in this curve, sheltered by a rowan tree, was a still dark pool on whose surface cakes of foam circled slowly.

"There," said the Colonel triumphantly. "If you can get a fly in that, it's the best pool on the river."

Jean could not help agreeing.

"You have to be careful, though," he warned her. "Because if you get tangled on that tree, it's a long way round to reach it."

"Yes," said Jean, thinking whatever it was like it could not be much harder than fishing their own wooded Carrick at night.

She made one or two trial casts across the pool, having first offered the rod to her escort. Then, softly, she dropped a fly under the lowest branches of the rowan. And nothing happened.

Again and again she tried, still with no success. She heard the Colonel clicking his tongue in sympathy, which was maddening. She cast, not only on the chosen place, but all over the long pool, with no results.

"You have a try," she said at last.

The Colonel, who had obviously been longing to have a go ever since he got up here, took the rod and started pulling out handfuls of line.

Jean, watching him, saw that he was a good, if rather wild and impatient fisherman. She leant back against a boulder and prayed for a fish. She stared at the peaty water, trying to will one out of it. It was so dark and black just here, anything might be hidden in it. It was brown really, shading to gold round the edges. Bubbles winked past on its surface and leaves, upturned, and tufts of grass. Sometimes a feather or a draggled wisp of sheep's wool or a half-submerged twig was swept on down to the falls.

She heard the Colonel come scraping back over the rocks.

"No luck," he said despondently. "I really did think we should get something here. It's the first time I've ever known this pool to be blank."

"It's not really fair on the pool," said Jean. "It's too low and bright."

"All the same this is our prize pool," said the Colonel. "And this'll be the first blank day I've ever known on it."

"Well, we can't go home empty-handed after that," Jean smiled. "Let me have one last try." She took the rod and examined the flies.

"Shall I put on a Jock Scot?" she asked. "It's bright enough for one."

"If you like." The Colonel was convinced that no fly would coax a fish out of the Corriedon to-day.

Jean disentangled a Jock Scot from her fly book and tied it on. She looked up and down the river, choosing the best place, and decided on a spot just below the overhung pool.

Once, twice, her line dropped on the water. She was determined to get a fish. She did.

Directly she felt it she struck, and knew that it was on. Not a big one, probably a sea trout, but she was going to cling to it whatever happened.

The Colonel, who had been sitting on a stone, disconsolately filling his pipe, dropped it, jumped to his feet and ran forward to help. Jean needed no help as yet. She could manage this fish all right.

He played for about five minutes, although it seemed longer, and then Jean reeled him in. The Colonel slipped a net under him, and together they looked at him lying there.

"Not a bad little fish", said the Colonel at last. "Must weigh about two pounds. Well done, young lady."

Jean wondered whether he had forgotten her name, or whether he always called girls that. She thought he probably did.

"We must be getting home: it's tea time," said the Colonel, stuffing the fish into the bag. Jean looked longingly at the river, although she did not think it was likely that she would get another out of it on such a day. However, the Colonel was hungry and already disappearing over the rocks. Jean picked up the rod and followed him.

They found Sandy and Ninian sitting on the bridge, throwing sticks into the water, and watching them float out to sea. They looked rather bored.

"Any luck?" asked Jean.

"Not a fin," said Ninian, staring at the tail of the trout protruding from the bag. "I say, don't tell me you caught that legally?"

"Course we did," said Jean.

"Oh, well." Ninian lifted his rod out of the heather and they started back along the road."

"I heard a lot of shooting," said Sandy.

"I expect you did," said the Colonel, laughing.

They met the others at tea, as satisfactory a tea as they had last time, Sandy was pleased to find.

"You must stay to dinner," said the Colonel, and Fiona, with visions of one Primus between three saucepans, said:

"Thank you very much, we'd love to."

They walked up the glen after tea and watched deer and buzzards and a golden eagle. They did not feel homesick for *Fauna* until dinner, when Jamie, looking up suddenly, caught Fiona's eye across the shining table, laid with silver and flowers. He knew that she, too, was thinking of a smoky lantern swinging from the beam; a disorder of cups and plates, and a friendly reek of cooking; the slap of waves against the planking, and, through the hatch, the sudden coolness of night, the scented wind and the thousand stars beyond the hills.

CHAPTER VII

"IT'S THE TWELFTH!"
Thursday, 12th August

THEY had a hot and uneventful journey back from Corriedon. They started late and Ninian refused to stop and let them bathe, saying they would never get back in daylight if they did.

However, they arrived before dusk and tied up to their buoy for the first time.

"We shall have to guess at the amount of slack to leave," said Ninian. "Don't forget to keep an eye on it, Hugh and James."

"No, we won't," said Hugh, wondering what he would have to do. He yawned, tired after the long hot day.

Fiona and Sandy, coming on deck at four a.m., helped the sleepy watch they were relieving to test the buoy.

"Better leave a bit of slack, even now," said James, rubbing his eyes.

"Yes, in case it gets rough." Hugh had hauled in as much rope as he could. It was wet and cold, and he shivered.

"How much shall we leave?"

"Well, it's almost the end of the rope; let's shove it all over." This was Sandy.

"There's nearly a fathom." Fiona had uncoiled it. "Gosh, it's much colder."

"Well, good-night," said Hugh, hastening towards the hatch.

He slid it back. Since Ninian had greased it, it ran smoothly. A dim light filtered through from the fo'c'sle into the dark, and then it was shut out. The portholes threw small golden discs across the sea, then they too faded.

Up on deck it was grey and windy. The fading stars were

hidden by hurrying clouds; the moon was a pale glow, hastily obscured; it was difficult to see the land and the breakers on the beach. The wind was steadily rising, and waves came splashing up on deck. Sandy and Fiona huddled together. After the heat of the day they felt cold.

"Blast!" said Sandy, as a gust of rain pattered on his cheek.

"Don't say that's going to start." Fiona began to button herself more deeply into her oily. As the rain did not seem to be abating, she crammed a sou'wester on her head and firmly tied the strings. Sandy did the same.

Their watch seemed longer than it ever had before. For hours they walked up and down, swaying as *Fauna* swayed, their rubber boots slipping on the wet deck. They tried sitting in the lee of the canvas screen, but somehow the water found a way to trickle down their necks and on to their knees.

They had never welcomed any dawn as much as they did this one.

Ninian awoke pleasantly to the smell of bacon frying. For some time he lay, half asleep, listening to it sizzling in the pan, and to the muffled clatter of cups and plates as the table was laid. Presently he became aware of a new sound, one which made him open his eyes: the steady patter of rain on the deck above. It was drumming down hard now, especially on the thin covering of the cabin roof. He looked up and saw the skylight swimming with it. A trickle of water had crept through one corner, and was splashing on to the cushioned seat below. Bother, that was where he sat. He turned over, stretching luxuriously in the blankets.

"Hallo," said Sandy. "Charming sort of day outside. The rain's simply sheeting down."

"Did you get wet?" Ninian crossed his arms under his head. *Fauna* was rocking slightly, and he heard the water sloshing about in the tanks underneath him.

"Soaked," said Fiona, putting in more bacon. "Our oilies are dripping in the lavatory."

Steam was slowly forming on the skylight and scuttles.

"Let's open something," said Ninian. "It's like an oven in here!"

"Water simply pours down the hatch if you open that." Sandy balanced precariously on the end of the table.

"Try one of those portholes." Ninian reached out a long arm and unscrewed one of the scuttles. A gush of cool air swept in. He crawled from his blankets and looked out at the day. A wall of grey rain was sweeping across the bay, blotting out everything. The beach was hardly distinguishable; the cliff was a faint hump; the sea was pock-marked with rain drops. The wind had dropped a bit since early morning, but the rain had increased.

"Breakfast's practically ready," said Fiona. She opened the door in the fo'c'sle and woke Hugh and James. They and Ninian and Jean ate it in their pyjamas, and every one grumbled about the rain.

"It's so hard," complained Jean. "If only it was a drizzle."

"There's one thing we must do," said Ninian, scooping up some bacon fat on a piece of bread. Every one looked up.

"The water tanks must be filled."

There was silence. It would not have been a bad job on a fine day, but now, in the sousing rain!

"Couldn't we have a sort of gutter from the deck?" suggested Sandy hopefully.

"Rather repulsive," said Jean. "Imagine all those old bits of bait and things."

"That's quite enough," said Fiona. "But Ninian, how'll we fill them? I mean, what with?"

Ninian looked at her in dismay.

"There's nothing but petrol tins," he said at last.

"Worse than the decks," said Jean, unsubdued.

"If we wash them out thoroughly, they should be all

right," said Hugh. "I know I have seen petrol tins used for water. It evaporates like anything," he added, seeing Fiona's face.

"We've got a pipe to pour it down," said Ninian. "We'll stick that through the skylight and into the tanks."

"Everything'll get soaked," objected Fiona.

"Well, through a porthole, then."

"Don't let's all go. Six wet oilies in that lavatory would be beyond a joke."

"Couldn't we wear bathing things?" This was Sandy.

"Well, you can. Personally, I should hate it." Hugh had visions of himself, cold, wet and covered with sand.

"It might be an idea." Ninian edged away from the drip. "Let's see how warm it is."

Breakfast was eaten and washed up. It was terribly cramped in the cabin and rather dark.

"Still the battery must be beautifully charged, after that long voyage yesterday," said Fiona, switching the light on experimentally. It did not make much difference, and she decided to save it for the evening.

Ninian borrowed Sandy's wet oily, and went up on deck. It was raining harder than ever, and the wind buffeted him and blew his hair on end. He went forward to have a look at the buoy. The tide was swirling out: he could see it racing past the rope round which already were tangled fronds of seaweed. Waves were splashing up on the rocks on the left of the bay, the spray flung high. Out to sea there was nothing visible except white horses galloping inland under the mist.

Ninian ran back to the hatch and slithered down in a cloud of drips.

"What's it like?" asked Hugh.

"Foul."

"Let's wait until it clears a bit. It can't go on like this for long." Ninian forced the wet buttons undone, and peeled off his oilskin.

"Do hang it up," said Fiona. "You're soaking everything."

Bunks were re-made and scuttles opened. The Stewarts seemed larger than ever, cramped in the cabin. Everything they sat on seemed harder than the last; it was impossible to use the bunks unless you lay at full length; they roamed up and down.

Presently Ninian, feeling stifled, took down the partition and crawled into the engine-room. Hugh joined him, and together they overhauled the engine and cleaned the plugs.

Rain came pouring in through one row of scuttles. In fact it seemed to keep on coming in somewhere, and Fiona spent hours with a cloth, mopping up.

For the tenth time Jean peered through a scuttle and was rewarded by the sight of the rain sweeping across the bay, becoming even thicker. It hammered so loud on the deck that they had almost to shout at each other.

Fiona sat hunched on the dry corner of the seat. She did not mind in the least being out in the rain, none of them did, for no one who lived in Scotland ever really bothered about it, but the prospect of drying six lots of clothes in *Fauna*, and with nowhere to dry them, was awful. However, soon she would have to go out, if only to get a breath of air.

Her eyes wandered gloomily over the cabin; the shelf of books, she would read if only the others were not making such a noise; the lanterns; the companion ladder, still wet from Ninian's feet; the bunks; the screw-top of the tank, a horrible reminder; the drip on the end of the cushion. Nothing very inspiring. On her right, Ninian and Hugh were crouched over the engine, covered in grease, and making strange technical remarks. Better put on a kettle of water: they would need something hot to wash in.

Sandy and James were having one of those pointless arguments that could not end.

" 'Tis!"

" 'Tisn't!"

126

" 'Tis!"

" 'Tisn't!"

"Oh, shut up," said Fiona, springing up. She lit the Primus and filled the kettle. The water ran slower and slower. The tank must be empty.

"Try pumping, Jamie."

He sprang on to a bunk and started pumping violently. After about ten minutes Fiona tried the tap again. There was only a trickle.

"Ninian, there really isn't any water," she said, peering through into the recesses of the engine-room.

"Won't be long," grunted Ninian, up to the elbows in grease. He produced a complicated piece of mechanism and blew into it.

"He won't really mind if the water does taste petrolly," thought Fiona.

Sandy and Jean both had a turn pumping.

"There simply isn't any water left." Jean had unscrewed the cap of the tank and was squinting in.

"We shall have to get it soon,' said Fiona, and turning once more to the engine-room, she said:

"What about these tins? Can't I wash them out?"

"What? Do wait, I shan't be long. Chuck us some cotton waste, Hugh."

Fiona retreated. It was no use talking to Ninian when he was in that sort of mood.

The others were playing Snap on the table. They had a pack each and looked as if they would be there indefinitely. However, Jamie was usually a card or two behind the others, and whenever he said "Snap!" he was told it did not count. Soon he was out and he and Fiona watched while Sandy, and Jean, with bulging eyes, slammed down the cards as if their lives depended on it. Fiona thought that even if a gun was let off behind them they would not move, so great was their concentration.

"Snap!" they shrieked together.

"I was first."

"No, I was."

"You weren't."

"Fiona, who was?"

"Both the same."

"Bother, that makes it 'pool'."

They went on and on until Jean only had two left. She turned these over with lightning swiftness, her eyes fixed on Sandy. Gradually she won back half the cards. Fiona got up and wandered over to the Primus. This game might go on for ever.

The engineers crawled back into the cabin. They were filthy.

"I must say you are rather efficient, Fiona," said Ninian, gratefully, as he poured out a basin of water. Between them they used nearly a whole cake of soap and coated the basin with black. Ninian slooshed it round with the remains of the warm water. He was hot and sticky from working over the engine.

"I must go out," he said. Two steps up the companion-ladder and he pushed open the hatch. Cool rain fell on his face and the wind lifted his hair. He drew in great breaths of air. Fiona was behind him.

"What's it like?" she asked.

"Umn, lovely!" Ninian came farther out. "It's not raining hard now; let's go and get the water."

He ran up into the drizzle and collected some of the empty petrol tins. "Let's fill them with sea water and sloosh," he said, dipping the bucket and hauling it on board again. One by one the tins were shaken, like cocktail shakers, and the frothy water poured back into the sea. Ninian sniffed them critically and rinsed them out again.

"Put in some Rinso." Fiona handed up a packet. The rain was abating every minute, but still fell steadily.

"Who wants to come?" asked Ninian. Jamie came scrambling up, buttoning his oily. He gave his brother one.

"I'm pretty wet already," Ninian said, and slipped it over his shoulders.

Sandy and Jean were still deep in the cards, with glazed expressions and bitten lips.

"Come on, you two." Fiona seized a pile of cards in each hand.

"What? Oh, bother, Fiona, I was winning," said Sandy.

"No, you weren't."

"Go on and help Ninian get the water; and put on your oilies," she added, as they stampeded up the ladder.

She and Hugh were left on board. They wandered about picking up the cards, and then laying and cooking the lunch.

"We can't do much with so little water," grumbled Fiona.

Ninian rowed on through the rain, the petrol tins piled between the thwarts. The twins and Sandy, wet, black figures, were huddled in the boat, water streaming down their backs, and seeping through in places.

They rowed as near in as they could and tied up the dinghy.

"Someone'll have to stay and fend her off, it's too rough to leave her," said Ninian, wedging his top-boot on to a limpet and scrambling ashore.

"Jean'd better stay," said Sandy, "because the tins'll be pretty heavy."

"All right." Jean sat down again and picked up the short gaff to use as boathook. She handed up the tins and watched the boys set off across the rocks.

She got wetter and wetter. The wind seemed to be rising too: she wondered if they were in for what Ninian would call "a dirty night." The dinghy tossed up and down, bumping notwithstanding Jean's efforts. The rain pattered on her oily and sou'wester and ran down her face. A wet wisp of hair clung to her cheek and she brushed it off. Her fringe was soaking too, and the water ran down from it into her eyes. As she lifted her arm to rub them she felt a horrid trickle creep up to her elbow.

Ninian led the boys across the beach. The sand clung to their wet boots and the rain drove unceasingly into their faces. Heads down they forced themselves along.

"Where is this blessed burn?" asked Sandy, screwing up his eyes.

"Over there by the rocks." Ninian jerked his head towards the right-hand corner of the bay.

A gust of wind spattered the rain against their sou'westers.

"Gosh!" said Jamie. "I hope it's stopped by to-night. We can't keep watch, Ninian, in this."

"Not unless we rig up some kind of a shelter," said Ninian, swinging the petrol tins. "Ah, here's the burn."

It ran down over the sand, spreading wider and wider until it reached the sea.

"We'll have to go up to the cliff," said Sandy. "We couldn't possibly fill them here."

As they neared the cliff the roar of water grew louder. Already the burn was in spate, hurling itself over the rocks. It was really more of a trickle than a burn, and, where it dropped for about three feet from the cliff to the ground it was like the jet from a giant tap.

They stood the cans beneath this convenient place and they were filled in record time.

"What with petrol and peat it will taste nice," said Jamie, screwing the top of his tin. They staggered back to the sea, Ninian with one in each hand.

Jean, looking wet and dejected, welcomed them back.

"How many turns will we have to have?" she asked.

"Only one more, I should think." Ninian dipped the oars and started to row back.

By this time *Fauna* was tossing on the waves and Sandy and Jean got ready to grab the nearest thing that chanced to hand as the dinghy came alongside. They seized hold of the bulwarks and hung on as Ninian and James heaved the tins on board.

Fiona, draped in oilskins, appeared in the hatch. She and Hugh had rigged up the pipe through one of the scuttles and fixed a funnel in the top.

"Is the water too foul?" she asked.

"It's all right." Ninian was not in the mood for arguing. He was much too wet.

Dubiously Fiona unscrewed the top of the first-tin and emptied it down the tube. As far as she could see it looked all right, and if a frond or two of moss or a blade of grass whirled past, what matter?

Ninian and she looked at each other. They were both thinking of the same thing. Firstly, if it got much rougher the buoy might not hold, and secondly, there was no sort of shelter in Flatfish Bay and the waves would soon be flying in from the Hebrides. The nearest shelter would be Beanault. It was unthinkable that their trip should end in a port.

"It'll have to get a good bit rougher yet," said Ninian, speaking for them both.

The tins were emptied.

"One more load," said Fiona. "That'll last us ages."

"Well," thought Jean, sitting once more in the dinghy. "I can't get much wetter, anyway."

As they neared the rocks she saw a family of eider duck bobbing serenely on the waves. The parents were looking very much at home, but the ducklings were so small that every now and then they had to go through the waves instead of over.

Ninian, ploughing through the sand, looked back towards *Fauna*. Beyond her, to his enormous relief, the sky was clearing. Perhaps after all they would be able to stay at Flatfish.

By the time they had emptied the tins for the second time the wind had almost dropped, although the rain fell harder than ever.

One by one the Stewarts climbed down to the cabin, spattering everything plentifully. Their boots and oilies were put to drip in the lavatory.

"Do keep still," Fiona scowled at Sandy. "You're soaking everything."

"Sorry." Sandy tried to undo the buttons of his mac without shaking himself too much.

Suddenly Jamie caught sight of something.

"Oh, bliss, Fiona!" he said. "Cocoa!"

In a few moments they were sitting round the table blowing their cups and cautiously sipping.

Ninian's hair was wet and consequently stuck up on end even more than usual, and the careful smoothing out that went on each day might never have occurred. He was leaning his elbows on the table, staring at his cup and concentrating on keeping it steady. *Fauna* was rolling enough for the cocoa to slop out if not carefully watched, and overhead the lantern was swinging sickeningly. Something in one of the drawers was rolling up and down, thump, thump, methodically. After a minute or two, Fiona got up and pulled open the drawer. There was a tin rolling about, so she stood it up on end.

The afternoon was interminably long. Slowly the wind dropped and the sea grew calm, but the rain continued.

Lunch was eaten and washed up; the cabin seemed to grow smaller and smaller. Poker and Consequences and other paper games were tried.

"Oh, hell," said Ninian at last, scooping all the cards together. "Whatever time is it?"

"Half-past two." Hugh put his watch to his ear to make sure it was still going.

Fiona started to play a long and involved Patience; Jean and Sandy watched her; Jamie climbed on to one of the bunks and started to write up his diary.

"I say," he sat up, bumping his head on the deck. "Does anybody realise what the date is?"

Nobody did. Nobody had any idea; time was of no

account in Flatfish Bay.

"*It's the Twelfth,*" said Jamie.

Ninian, sitting on the end of the table, stopped swinging his leg. Hugh paused with a match half-way to his pipe. Fiona looked up, a card in her hand. Sandy, the keenest poacher of them all, looked quickly round the cabin. Jean did not realise what they were talking about.

Ninian rubbed the misty scuttle with his hand and peered out over the running deck.

"It's nearly stopped," said Sandy, craning over his shoulder. Indeed, it nearly had. A steady Scotch mist was still hiding the headlands, but the worst torrential rain had stopped.

"We've only got the rifle," said Ninian, opening the lavatory door and extricating his oily from the heap of others.

"If we could see one we could stalk it," said Sandy.

"I did see some the other morning." James had put his diary away and was pulling on his mac.

"Coming?" Hugh asked Fiona. She shook her head.

"You four will be plenty. Jean and I'll stay and wish."

Ninian filled his pockets with cartridges and looked down the barrel of the rifle.

"All right," he said, and slipped it into the battered canvas case.

The others were up on deck already. Sandy was in the dinghy, fitting the oars in the rowlocks.

"Good luck," said Fiona, as Ninian raced up the ladder. He slammed the hatch behind him and they heard his feet sliding on the wet deck.

"Yes, but," said Jean, as the splashing of the oars died away, "what *are* they talking about? Why the rifle?"

Fiona looked at her little sister and burst out laughing. "Oh, Jeannie, it's grouse shooting to-day!"

"Of course we're raving mad," said Hugh, as they walked

across the sand again. "What chance on earth have we of hitting a grouse with a rifle?"

"In the pouring rain, too," James reminded him.

"We shall have to stalk it," said Ninian, unabashed. He was already half-way up the cliff, climbing in zigzags along the small paths that ran crosswise round the bay.

The rain trickled warmly down their faces, for they wore no hats, and started to creep beneath their collars.

"We shall never see anything in this," said Sandy, screwing up his eyes and peering into the mist. A couple of wet sheep scampered away ahead of them, their coats like sponges.

"Steady now," said Ninian, as they reached the top, puffing after the sharp climb in their oilies. He shifted the rifle in its sodden case to the other shoulder.

Gratefully they obeyed him and slowed down. The rain was stopping, very gradually, but it was anything but clear.

"How on earth —" began Hugh, but was shushed by Ninian. "Well, how on earth," he whispered, "are we supposed to see a grouse? One generally hasn't the least idea of their whereabouts until they leap up."

"Wait and see," hissed Ninian, advancing step by step, scanning every inch of ground. There was plenty of long wiry heather to hide the birds.

"One thing anyway," said Sandy. "They won't fly much in all this wet."

"Has any one ever seen any up here?" Hugh felt that unless he knew this, he could not bear a long wet walk with no object.

"Yes, a covey flew over the top there," said Jamie, pointing to the place where the cliff jutted out between the two bays.

They forged on.

For a brief moment the rain increased, and then almost died away. Ninian pushed his dripping hair out of his eyes and looked across to the other bay.

"It's not much use going over there," he said. "It's too grassy. So let's go inland a little way and then back to the boat."

The others agreed and they struck off through the heather. In places it was so long that it reached almost to Jamie's waist. He struggled along, kicking at the tough stems and stopping every now and then to have an extra hard look for grouse.

Suddenly a covey flopped up from under Sandy's feet. They must have been lying extremely low as the first thing he saw of them was the sudden whirl of wings and an angry chorus of kuk-kuk-kuk-kuk.

"Gosh," said Sandy, who had nearly jumped out of his skin.

"Bother you!" Ninian lifted the rifle futilely. Since the rain had stopped he had taken the cover off and it was ready loaded.

They went on gloomily, until Ninian beckoned to them to turn and they squelched back towards the cliff.

Hugh felt wet and depressed. Of course it had been a mad thing to do, and even if they had seen a grouse and been able to get a shot the bullet would have probably ruined the bird. He thought, longingly, of their past week of sunshine, and hoped the weather had not changed for the rest of his leave. The sky certainly was no lighter, it did not look as if it was going to clear up yet.

"Oh, well," said Ninian. They had nearly reached the cliff and he stopped to unload.

Suddenly there was a soft urgent whistle from James. A few yards in front of him he could hear the soft clucking of a grouse. It must be right on the edge of the cliff.

Cautiously Ninian walked across, the rifle in front of him. He stopped by Jamie. He, too, could hear the birds, but there was no sign of them.

Hugh and Sandy came up and watched Ninian advance on all fours.

Sandy was the first to see the bright eye of a grouse among the countless raindrops.

"Ninian," he hissed. His cousin looked round, saw the grouse, and carefully raised the rifle. The click, as he cocked it, made the bird look up. Holding his breath, Ninian aimed.

There was a shattering roar and the rest of the covey flew off.

"You've got it," cried James, running to pick it up. Apart from being headless it was in good condition.

"Lucky I was so close, I could hardly fail to miss," said Ninian, slipping the rifle back into its case.

"Triumph," cried Sandy, and charged off down the cliff, his oily flapping behind him.

Fiona and Jean had taken advantage of the ceasing of the rain to bathe. After being cooped up in the cabin all day, Fiona felt that she must do something energetic or die. The boys joined them when they had tied up the dinghy and shouted out the story of the great stalk through mouthfuls of sea water.

"How shall we cook it?" asked Fiona, hanging by one hand from the dinghy. "We haven't got an oven."

"Couldn't we fry it?" asked Hugh, whose ideas of cooking were vague.

"What about roasting it in the saucepan with the lid on?" said Ninian, lying on his back and keeping still, so that his nose was the only thing visible above water.

"Umn!" Fiona swam quickly in a circle. "I'm going back, it's cold."

The still-warm grouse was plucked and trussed.

"It'll be tough as leather," prophesied Fiona, as she lowered it into the bubbling dripping. She dropped potatoes in round it so they would all be cooked together, and the smell that arose every time she lifted the lid made their mouths water.

"This is the grandest meal we've ever had in *Fauna*," said Sandy, approvingly, when at last they sat round the table and Ninian carved the precious bird into six. There was silence as they tasted their first mouthfuls.

"Gosh, it's good," said Jamie in amazement.

"A bit tough." Fiona was the most critical, having cooked it.

"It tastes beautifully grousey anyway," said Hugh, removing a feather from the leg he was dissecting.

When at last they leant back, full and happy, and regarded the shining bones, they could not but agree with Sandy that they had had the best meal in *Fauna* that evening.

Ninian and Hugh went up on the rain-sodden deck. It was cool and windless and the colours on the shore were vivid, although night was creeping gently on. Ninian sniffed appreciatively.

"It looks as if the rain's gone," he said, looking at the sky. Jamie poked his fair head through the hatch. He had remembered a question that he had been meaning to ask his brother since they first sailed in *Fauna*.

"I say, Ninian," he said, "how far is it to Faraway?"

There was silence. The cries of the gulls came clearly and the splash as a wave broke against *Fauna*.

"Thirty miles." Ninian spoke slowly, his mind already racing on.

"It would only take five or six hours," continued James. "Oh, Ninian, do let's. That would be a real voyage."

"Yes, we must." Ninian bent down the hatch. "Hoy, Fiona, come up."

"Half a sec."

"No, hurry, and bring the chart."

They heard the sound of drawers being slammed, and Fiona swearing at Sandy. Then she appeared, the chart under her arm.

"What's this brilliant idea?" she asked, as Ninian

snatched it from her and spread it on the cabin roof.

"Faraway," said James. "We're going there."

"What?" Sandy and Jean came pushing up behind Fiona.

"Thirty miles, five knots, it should take us about six hours." Ninian had been to Faraway before, but not for some time, and never in *Fauna*.

"There's no compass," Sandy pointed out.

"Well, we won't really need one. If it's fine we can see the coast from here, and just hope for the best."

Fiona looked up. A much better idea had occurred to her.

"Let's come back in the dark," she said, "and steer by the stars."

"Could we?" asked Jean.

"No," said Ninian, "I've been looking in the pilot books. They move much too much, as much as the sun does. The only thing to do would be to steer by the Pole Star. That always points north."

"Bother." Fiona did not think that sounded as much fun as a Star Map. She had pictured looking up at the sky rather as one looked down at a chart for rocks and landmarks. "Still, we could make a map and watch all the constellations," she said.

"We might almost see them moving round," said Sandy.

"Hardly," said Ninian, "but it would be interesting to see just how much they do move."

"What about the tides?" asked Jamie.

Ninian, who seemed to have made good use of the pilot books, informed him that they were not too strong as long as the wind kept down.

"However, we can't do it at all unless it's a fine clear night," he said, "and if it is we should be able to get a rough idea of where we are from the coastline."

To Hugh all this sounded vague, but he supposed they knew what they were talking about. They seemed highly delighted.

"Oh, it'll be bliss," said Fiona, gazing rapturously at the chart and trying to remember what the harbour at Faraway looked like.

"We can fill up there with petrol, too," added James.

"There's a cinema," said Sandy, looking at his cousin and wondering what he would say. "How long shall we stay?"

"A night, and come back the next night?" suggested Hugh.

Fiona looked out over the darkening sea. It was very still and cool too.

"Time we were in bed," she said, rolling up the chart slowly. "You ready for the first watch?"

Ninian and Jean nodded.

"Let's get some jerseys," said Jean, dropping down the hatch. She threw an armful up on deck, and followed it with the oilies.

Fiona, in her narrow bunk, lay still, listening to the lapping of the sea outside. Jamie and Hugh were whispering to each other and rustling on their straw mattresses. In the warm gloom of the fo'c'sle all she could hear was Sandy's even breathing. Through the scuttles shone a grey light, slowly darkening. Fiona watched it drowsily until she could not be bothered to keep her eyes open any longer. Up on the deck above her someone kicked the anchor chain as they passed, and she heard the mutter of voices. She turned over and buried her head in the pillow.

"Beastly hard," she thought, and fell asleep.

(There was silence on the deck of the fishing boat but for the low whispers of men's voices and the hushed scrape of their feet on the deck. Occasionally a rope or block tapped the mast and creaked under the light wind. Always there was the steady ripple of water beneath the forefoot and the splash of small waves against the topsides.

"We'll never do it," came a murmur from a man amongst the group by the mast.

"We will," said another.

"We've got to go right by them. There'll be two of them on deck."

"We will do it," said the second man again.

"How do you know?"

"The Chief said so. He's steering. Have you ever known him fail at anything he said he would do?"

Again there was silence while all eyes were fixed on the black shape of "Fauna" riding at her moorings in Flatfish Bay. It was pitch dark, but their eyes, long accustomed to difficult and dangerous work at night, could see her clearly and the two figures hunched on the cabin roof. The ship slid on like a ghost and seemed to hold her breath with the crew. She, too, trusted her master. He had sailed her past danger before, and would do so again.)

CHAPTER VIII

STORMY PASSAGE
Friday, 13th August

THE CHART was made. All the large constellations were marked in; the Big and Small Bears, Pegasus, Sagittarius and Perseus, Hercules, Lyra and Cassiopeia, Leo, Libra and Aquila, Virgo, Bootes and Capricornus. Hugh had joined up the groups so that it was easier to tell which was which.

"We shall steer beautifully by this," said Fiona, looking admiringly at it during breakfast.

"I'll copy it out on a large piece of paper," said Ninian, turning it so that the Pole Star was pointing north.

Fiona pushed her cup aside, leaving a smear of coffee on the corner of the chart.

"Clumsy," said Ninian, and rubbed it with his handkerchief. He picked up the map and put it away.

"Let's get washed up before this place is a shambles," he said.

"Yes, quick, we want to get started soon." Sandy scooped up a handful of plates and dumped them in the sink.

"Look out! Oh, you fool, there's one plate gone!" Fiona rushed at her cousin and removed him forcibly from the sink.

"Have we got enough petrol?" Hugh and Ninian edged towards the companion. Presently they disappeared up it and Fiona heard their voices coming in a vague mumble down the hatch. It was really easier washing up in such a small place without them. They took up too much room.

They were later than usual this morning. It was half-past nine already. Fiona, impatiently rubbing at plates and cups, wondered why things always took so long just when you wanted them not to. At last everything was finished and she climbed up on deck with a colander full of scraps.

It was a fine day, with a north-west wind ruffling the water of the bay. In here it was sheltered enough, but out at sea there were white horses, not large enough to worry about, but enough to give the crossing an extra spice.

The decks were swabbed and Ninian and Hugh went below to start up.

"What's the matter?" Fiona called down the hatch, after she had been standing ready at the wheel for some time.

"Blasted engine won't start," grunted Ninian. "It would be this morning, of course."

"Do you mean there's something broken or is it just being obstinate like Sandy?"

"Obstinate. There doesn't seem to be anything wrong," said Hugh, and he and Ninian lapsed into silence. Fiona knew better than to ask them any questions. Engines have a bad effect on most people's tempers.

At half-past eleven it started. By then they had quarrelled with every one who had ventured to suggest anything to them. Everything that could be done was done, the plugs were cleaned again and again, the engine was primed time after time, and at last it did go.

With eager hands Sandy cast off the buoy and let the dinghy go. They had decided it would only get in the way on the journey. Fiona swung the wheel and they moved out into the bay.

The voyage had begun at last.

While the engine was being tinkered with, the twins and Sandy had rowed ashore and fixed two large white stones on the cliff. When these were in line you were facing due east or west.

Ninian waited until they were a little way out, then he fetched the chart up on deck; Fiona manoeuvred until the stones were in position; Ninian turned the chart and then pointed.

"*Fauna's* wake looks very waggly," Jean said.

"Well, it'll be straight from now on; at least as straight as I can make it," said Fiona. "I can just see enough of the Hebrides now to steer for them."

As they drew farther from the shore the well-remembered shape of Ben Carrick became visible. The sky behind the hills was a clear bright blue, but towards the north of the Hebrides there were faint wisps of clouds, too far as yet to tell what kind, and anyway too small to be of any consequence.

As they left the shelter of the mainland the waves came dashing up to them, wetting the deck. Away on Foura Hugh saw a column of foam shoot up and then another. Still, it was always rough on that end of the island.

It was a most glorious day; hot sun and a wind that felt as if it blew right through you, and yet was not cold. Fiona steered on, glancing over her shoulder every now and then, until at last the two boulders were out of sight. The engine seemed to have recovered from its obstinacy; its chugging was almost drowned by the slap and splash of the waves. An extra large one bounced up on deck and trickled away down the scuppers.

Fiona and Ninian looked at each other and then out to where the clouds were slowly piling up, thin feathery clouds, mare's tails. Fiona looked at her brother and raised her eyebrows. He was still staring ahead, frowning slightly. Then he turned and met her eye.

"Well?"

"Well?" said Fiona, holding *Fauna* steady on her course. It was in neither of them to turn back, but they had not expected the wind out here to be so strong.

"Well?" said Fiona again.

"Carry on," said Ninian in a low voice. "We've crossed in worse weather than this." He did not want the others to hear, they would only begin to imagine things.

Sandy and the twins were having a fine time in the bows,

dodging each wave as it came splashing aboard. There were not really big ones yet, and *Fauna* was only pitching slightly. Hugh, leaning on the canvas screen by Fiona, thought that to-day promised to be one of the best they had had so far. It was too windy for a pipe, and his hair felt as if it was being tugged from his head. Fiona was humming gently beside him. He could not hear what it was but could see her lips moving as she added a few words now and then. Her eyes were half shut against the wind. Her green shirt was open at the neck and her throat was burned as brown as her face and arms. She looked down and caught his eye.

"Will you take over, Hugh?" she said. "I want to get a jersey — it's a bit cold."

He moved over beside her.

"Steer for that largest hill," she said, pointing to a mass of blue peaks on the horizon.

"Bring me up one too," said Hugh.

"All right, I'll start on the lunch if you can carry on: it's getting late."

She appeared for a minute to fling him a thick fisherman's jersey.

It became increasingly difficult to keep one's balance below. Everything slid away just as it had been put down, the water slopped over, the Primus needed filling just to make everything more difficult, and the lantern, hanging in the cabin, swung to and fro in an annoying way.

After a bigger lurch than usual Fiona put her head through the hatch. In the short time she had been below the sea had grown considerably rougher. White horses were fairly flying inland, and the deck was running with spray. Ninian had taken over the wheel, and his more expert hand steered *Fauna* into the calmest sea. All the same, Fiona was rather perturbed to find how the wind and sea had increased. She looked across at Ninian. He was frowning, and turned to look behind him. They had come farther than she thought, but Faraway still looked a long way ahead.

Those dangerous mare's tails were piling up too, with bigger clouds behind them. A seagull was tossed by on the wind; *Fauna* gave another big lurch and Fiona ducked just in time as a green sea came swishing down the deck.

"Well, whatever happens we must have lunch," she thought, and dropped into the cabin once more.

The sea was racing along against the planking and the scuttles were running with water. Fiona screwed them up as tightly as possible, and then tried to wedge something that was rolling about in the cupboards. There was something very snug about being in a cabin when the boat was leaping beneath and the wind roaring above.

She opened the skylight below the wheel and saw Ninian peering down at her. His eyes were bright with excitement: the fun and adventure of being in *Fauna* on a day when a sea was running had got the better of his fears.

"How is it?" called Fiona.

"Fine," he shouted back. "Come up on deck."

She collected their jerseys and climbed up.

A tremendous buffet of wind caught her and nearly blew her down again. She caught hold of either side of the hatch and leant back for a moment.

They were well out in the Minch now, but were making hardly any headway as the wind was dead against them. All she could see of Sandy and the twins were their heads peering over the screen, behind which they were kneeling, sheltering from the wind. Clouds of spray were beating upon Foura, and a great line of white edged all the cliff. It was as sunny as ever, the same glorious day. It made you want to shout, and you had to, to make yourself heard.

"Come on," called Hugh from the shelter of the screen, and Fiona half ran towards it. She too knelt down, laughing and gasping, and handed out the jerseys.

"Isn't it marvellous?" cried Sandy. "It's getting even rougher, too." Sandy was never sick, but Jean and Ninian, who were, did not look so enthusiastic about it.

As she knelt, Fiona was able to see that they were appreciably nearer the islands. The coastline north along the mainland was much larger, and behind them Flatfish was hardly distinguishable from the cliffs.

They stayed silent for some time, watching the waves roll past and scatter spray along the deck. Then Fiona got up and stood by Ninian for a minute or two. She did not have to ask him if he thought it was all right: she could tell he thought so from his face. Herself, she was not sure. Squalls got up so easily on this coast and they were entirely unprotected out here. However, she would never have dreamt of turning back any more than he would, and as long as the wind did not get much stronger it would be all right.

She returned to her cooking: as little as possible to-day, when all she wanted to do was to be on deck. Corned beef, a big dish of potatoes, bread and butter and fruit. She handed it up through the skylight and they sat in shelter of the canvas, eating. The wind had given them tremendous appetites and everything was finished.

After lunch Fiona took the wheel for an hour or so; thanks to the wind they were hardly moving; it had taken them a good four hours to come nearly half-way.

Lewis still looked as remote as ever, and, although the wind had lessened, the sea out here was much rougher, so rough in fact that Ninian went below for the oilskins.

Presently the wind dropped to only a shadow of itself, and they were able to talk in comfort once more. Their faces were tingling, their hair in uncombable tangles, but they felt like gods.

"Are we half-way yet?" asked James.

"Yes, about," said Ninian. "More than that. What's the time, Hugh?"

Hugh looked at his watch, frowned, listened to it, and then said:

"Nearly five."

"What!" Ninian swung round. "Don't be funny."

"I'm not, it is that time."

"The wind's dead against us," Sandy reminded him.

"Yes, I know, but if it's taken us all that time to come half-way we won't be in till dark," said Ninian, frowning.

"Oh, bliss," said Sandy and Fiona together.

Ninian did really look worried now. He glanced at the clouds over Lewis, but there was no break in them and they were blacker than ever underneath. Although there was so little wind, the sea had not gone down at all, and the clouds were still racing towards them. He looked back. The mainland and the Hebrides seemed equally distant.

"Hell," he thought. Perhaps after all it would be safer to turn and run home before the wind, yet there would be no shelter in Flatfish to-night, and to go back into Carrick or Fairloch was unthinkable. Anyway, it was light for so long now, and the wind had dropped, so probably the sea would go down and they would be in Faraway before dark.

Sandy took over the wheel.

"It's much easier to steer now," he said. "That big hill on Lewis is quite plain. I think I can see houses below it."

"It's still a good way off," James reminded him.

"Yes, but look how the wind's gone down," said Jean.

Indeed it was strangely still after the buffeting of the last hours.

"What about some tea?" asked Ninian, reappearing from the engine-room, where he had gone for a brief examination. He glanced again at the clouds. They were still there, and it looked dark behind the hills. Spray was splashing up on the deck and they were making heavy going out here in the middle of the Minch where the currents ran strong.

Tea was eaten on deck.

Ninian was by this time silent with worry. He had no idea whether *Fauna* was seaworthy or not, it was nearly six now, and they were still about twelve miles from the harbour.

"I wish we had had *Black Swan* in all that wind," said

Jamie longingly.

"We should have had to tack," said Jean.

"Still, think how we would have rushed along."

Ninian hurled his crust overboard, and it was swept away on a wave and out of sight in a moment.

Fiona collected the cups and took them below. She was just sloshing out the last one when a terrific gust hit *Fauna*, heeling her over and sent all the crockery flying. Fiona regained her balance and grabbed the edge of the sink. It had slopped over on the floor and two cups were broken. She heard Ninian shouting something and feet pounding on the deck. Then another gust hit *Fauna* and she plunged like a horse.

Gone was all thought of washing up. Fiona hung the wet cups on their hooks, wedged the Primus where it would not fall, and tore up on deck.

"Gosh," she said.

The sky was dark, the sea chill grey, whipped with white foam, the waves ever increasing in size and fury.

Hugh and Sandy were lashing the bucket and anchor to the capstan, Jean was struggling into her oily, while Ninian was doing his best to keep *Fauna* out of the greenest sea. Fiona ran to help him.

"Blasted squall," he said, as she came up. "Hope it doesn't get too bad."

"What had we better do, go on or run down to Erisort?"

"We don't know it well enough. It's stiff with rocks," said Ninian. "No, let's hope it gets dark, then we may see the light at the edge of the loch."

Fiona took over the wheel while he put on his oilskin. She was surprised to find how strong the sea was.

"What's the time?" she asked Hugh.

"Nearly seven."

Neither she nor Ninian answered.

Already the hills behind Faraway were blotted out and they could see a grey cloud of rain sweeping towards them across the Minch. Every minute the wind blew stronger, and the waves were becoming so large that it seemed certain that they would swamp *Fauna*. They were breaking all round in scudding masses of white spray.

Ninian hauled Jean into the shelter of the screen before she should get swept overboard.

"Will it be bad, Ninian?" she asked, leaning against him and peering out over the sea.

"Not worse than lots we've been in before," he said, smiling.

"Extraordinary how sudden it is," said Hugh, joining them.

"I should have guessed from those clouds," said Ninian. "But often these squalls get up out of nothing at all."

"Isn't this fun?" Sandy and James were in the highest of spirits.

"For goodness' sake put on your oilies," said Fiona, and as she spoke a spatter of rain hurled itself at them. She ran to close the hatch and found it difficult to keep her balance on the wet deck. From the look of things, whatever Ninian might say to Jean, this squall might turn into a nasty storm.

They stood by the wheel watching the waves come rolling in. The rain was pouring down now, and a sudden flash of lightning split the sky. Jamie counted ten before the thunder came, but there was such a noise of rain and wind and waves that they could hardly hear it.

"Hope the dinghy's safe," said Fiona suddenly, and then found she had to shout. She looked over the side at the water pouring past. At one moment it was almost on a level with the deck, the next it was far down beneath the streaming top-sides. Fronds of weed and scraps of broken wood were hurled past. Fiona suddenly wondered what would happen if they saw a man. Would they be able to pick him up in a sea as big as this? Better not to look. Instead, she glanced at Ninian. He was very pale, almost green, and was biting his bottom hp. Jean was too anxious to feel sick, but Hugh was looking a bit white as well. Ninian swallowed and cursed for the hundredth time. It was no good.

"Here, Fiona, you take it," he mumbled, pushing his sister towards the wheel. There comes a time during sea-sickness when nothing at all matters except that you should feel better. Ninian hung over the screen.

Presently Jean joined him, half in tears.

"Oh, Ninian, I do feel awful!"

"Go and lie down for a bit," suggested Ninian, who was feeling better. Gripping her arm, he struggled down the deck. The hatch had got stuck, but a savage kick pushed it back, and Ninian and Jean fell down the companion with the top of a wave that sloshed all over the floor.

Ninian slammed the hatch and wedged himself upright against the sink. It was practically dark in the cabin. Green seas were pouring past first one row of scuttles then the other. The water in the tanks was gurgling backwards and forwards and the door in the fo'c'sle kept banging.

Ninian groped for a match and lit the hurricane lamp. By its wildly swinging rays he helped Jean pull off her oily and boots and curl down into one of the bunks.

"Like me to leave the light?"

"Yes, please. I say, don't leave me in here if anything happens!"

"No, of course not." Ninian leant against the bulkhead, longing to be on deck. "If you want anything, bang on the skylight, we'll see you, but don't try and come along the deck alone."

"All right. I say, Ninian."

"Yes?" He paused, one foot on the ladder.

"I suppose we are all right?"

"Of course. Look, I'll tell you something; if it does get too bad we'll go back. It'll take some time, but with the wind behind us it won't be half so bad. Now, try and go to sleep." He reached up and heaved back the hatch.

A wave hit him full in the face, leaving him breathless

and gasping. It was dark and the rain had stopped. He looked up, but could see no stars. Lewis too, was invisible: only occasionally a light shone out some way in front of them.

"Faraway," thought Ninian.

He fought his way back along the deck and stood beside the others. Fiona was still steering. She looked white and rather worried.

"All right?" he shouted.

She nodded.

"We're still not making much headway. I wish it was

FIONA WAS STILL STEERING.

lighter, I can't see a thing, not even if we're steering straight."

"Where's that compass of yours, Sandy?" asked Hugh.

Sandy delved in a pocket somewhere miles beneath his oily, and produced it. He put it in the binnacle, where it looked ridiculous. Fiona peered down at it and moved the wheel a fraction.

"We should be steering north-west, shouldn't we?" she asked, without looking up.

"Yes. Want me to take over? I'm all right for a bit," said Ninian, with a grin.

Hugh was amused to see how neither of them considered he was capable of steering, even by compass. Still, he had to admit that what with keeping one eye on the binnacle and one on the sea it was a more difficult job than it looked.

"I'll go below and get a lantern," said Fiona. "And what about the lights, Ninian? There'll probably be other ships coming in to-night."

"Yes, of course, bring them up. They're in the fo'c'sle."

"Come on, James." Fiona went cautiously down the deck, one foot wedged against the cabin roof. The rain had started again, spasmodically. She felt she would be glad to get out of the tremendous buffeting for a little.

"Quietly, in case Jean's asleep," she shouted at James, as she pushed back the hatch.

It was indeed peaceful in the cabin after the wildness of the night above. Although the water was racing and slapping on the planking; although the lantern was rocking and drawing long shadows from first one corner and then another; although there was still the noise of wind and rain, it was muffled, and she had no longer to strain her eyes for a glimpse of that far distant light, nor to keep *Fauna* steady and away from the largest waves.

She pulled off her oily and sat on a corner of the table. Jean was asleep in the port bunk, the blankets drawn up to her chin. Her face looked small and white in the wavering light. She had not moved through all the noise James and Fiona had made on the ladder.

"Where are the lights?" whispered Jamie. Fiona slid off the table and opened the door to the fo'c'sle. Most of the lanterns were kept under the starboard bunk. She grovelled there and hauled out the red and green ones, and then a small one for the binnacle. They all had to be filled and cleaned.

"Let's hand them up through the skylight," suggested James. "We might drop them going along the deck. Gosh, it is rough!" An extra big lurch had thrown him off his balance and he followed Fiona's example and sat on the floor to fill the lanterns.

At last they were trimmed and lit.

James opened the skylight and Hugh's arm came down to take the lamps from him. They could see him, a black wet shape with wild hair against the grey sky.

"Would you like something hot? Bovril or cocoa or something?" asked Fiona.

"Bovril," said Hugh and Ninian together. Cocoa is all right on most occasions, but not in the middle of a storm when one is feeling none too good.

Fiona had put the kettle on when she came down, so it did not take long to boil, and Jamie handed up cups of Bovril and biscuits to those on deck.

"I'm going up too," he said.

"All right, but be careful," warned Fiona.

"As if you could do anything if I did fall in," said James.

Alone in the cabin Fiona tidied up the mess of wet oilies, cans of paraffin and the Bovril jar. Jean slept peacefully through it all, even when a huge wave broke right over the deck and made Fiona drop the empty kettle.

She pulled on her oily again and went back on deck. All she could see, apart from the port and starboard lights, were vague figures in the glow from the small binnacle. Otherwise it was pitch dark. All round was wind and water and flying spray. The gale had not abated, and as her eyes got used to the dark she could see huge white-capped waves pouring in towards *Fauna*, and, then miraculously, missing her. Suddenly a flash of light shone out from some way ahead and then away again.

"The lighthouse," shouted Hugh's voice, behind her. "It's getting nearer at last. We've been watching it for some time."

"Isn't the wind terrific?" she yelled back. "How's Ninian, still sick?"

"No, better, since the Bovril." They were nearly blown away on their way back to the screen, so strong was the wind behind them. Looking up, Fiona saw, for the first time that evening, the stars. Scudding clouds obscured them almost at once, but it was a sign that there must be a break somewhere soon.

"Look, another ship," cried Sandy, pointing.

On their starboard bow a red light bobbed into view and was lost again in a moment.

"On the same course as us, I expect," said Ninian. "I wonder what it is?"

"Jean's smugglers, perhaps," said Fiona, laughing. "I say, Ninian, can you remember the coast at all here? Are there any rocks?"

"I'm not sure," said Ninian. "I don't remember any, but we've always come in daylight before."

"What?" His words had been blown out of his mouth and away almost before he had spoken.

"There she is again," cried James, who had been keeping a watch for the other ship. "I say, let's follow her — they probably know the way."

"No, let's get in by ourselves," said Fiona, who, now they had so nearly reached the harbour, wanted to finish the journey alone.

"Here, Fiona, take over. I'll go and have a look at the chart — the rocks would be marked on that." Ninian handed over the wheel and disappeared along the black deck.

A few minutes later he was back.

"If we steer for the light we shall be all right," he said. "We're nearly in the loch, but there's still some way to go until we reach the town."

Fiona sighed contentedly. It was something to have got this far without mishap on one of the stormiest nights of the summer.

On and on into the wild dark. They could see the huge shape of Ben Barvas black against the sky and more gleams of light down the coast. It was much more sheltered here, as a big peninsula that jutted out before the harbour kept off most of the wind.

"Well," said Fiona, and found she was still shouting. "What a voyage. It has been fun. We might have guessed something would happen — Friday, 13th!"

"It's not over yet," said Ninian. "The harbour mouth is rather narrow and it's as dark as sin."

"Does any one feel hungry?" asked Sandy. "Because if not, I do. It must be late and we've had no dinner."

"It's eleven," announced Hugh. "D'you think we could face anything, Ninian?"

"Yes, just, in fact I'm ravenous. It'll take us about an hour to get in. What have you got, Fiona?"

"Scrambled eggs and bacon?" suggested Fiona. "Let's wait till we're right in, and eat them in comfort."

"All right. What sort of a place is Faraway?" asked Hugh.

"Oh, not very big, a cinema and a few shops, that's about all. We can fill up with petrol though, and get some stores."

"It'll be fun to wake up in a place, having no idea what it looks like," said Sandy.

They swung in past the lighthouse on a sea that was calm compared to the one outside. Once in the loch the wind dropped altogether, and it was still. Again the chugging of the engine was the loudest noise, and small waves slapped up against the planking in feeble imitation of the great rollers of the Minch, that had come thundering on them with such fury and determination.

"How long d'you suppose we shall have to stay here?" asked Hugh, his pipe alight once more.

"It'll probably be flat calm in the morning," Fiona said, unbuttoning the collar of her oily and shaking back her wet hair.

"Oh, don't let's go back in the morning," said Sandy. "There may be something good on at the cinema."

"You would think of that," said James.

"Well, why not?"

Presently more lights sprang into being as they rounded another corner. From the amount moving up and down they guessed the harbour to be full of ships. Somewhere behind them a trawler was coming in. They could see the gleam of her portholes on the waves.

It was pitch dark. Occasionally a star showed between the scurrying clouds and then was hidden. Every minute the wind was dropping. It would be fine in the morning, with nothing left of the storm but great rollers from the Atlantic, and piles of driftwood and floats and torn seaweed up on the rocks.

Another half-hour and they were in the harbour. There seemed to be hundreds of fishing boats tied up by the pier and many more on buoys.

"What'll we do?" asked James.

"Tie up to one of them," answered Ninian. "One against the pier if we can, otherwise we can't get ashore."

He went below to slow down, and Fiona followed to light the Primus and beat up the eggs. Jean was still asleep, the blankets round her ears, and Fiona left her and went on deck for the last bit of the voyage.

They were moving very slowly now. She took over the wheel from Sandy and he and the others went forward.

"Come alongside this one," said Ninian, as they neared a

row of herring boats.

Fauna edged slowly in.

"Ahoy, there!" called Sandy.

"Ahoy!" came back a gruff voice a moment or so later.

"Can we tie up alongside you?" called Fiona.

"Aye, ye can that. Who are ye and wheer d'ye come from?"

"The *Fauna* from Carrick," answered James, catching the rope that was thrown to them.

"When d'you want to be off, in the morning?" asked Ninian.

"Och, we'll be here for a bittie," answered the man. "We've got a casualty on board. Jock sprained his ankle, and I'm no juist cerrtain if oore dinghy is a' reet, so we won't be moving till the noon."

"That's all right," said Ninian, relieved.

The engine stopped, the ropes were made fast and a couple of big cork fenders dropped between them and *Hopeful Macduff* of Lochinver.

"Well," said Ninian, as he slid shut the hatch above the engine. "I can't help being glad that's over."

"Didn't you like it then?" asked Sandy, surprised. "I thought it was grand."

"Grand's not quite the word," said Hugh, who still felt as if the deck was heaving beneath him. "It was tremendous. Well done *Fauna,* and Stewarts."

"It was mostly luck," said Ninian. "In fact, I can't really imagine how we didn't lose our way. Hurry up with those eggs, Fiona."

"Coming." Fiona scraped them round in the saucepan. She turned the Primus low and dumped a handful of knives and forks on the table.

"Jamie," she called. "Come and help."

Protesting, he came down, leaving the others exchanging stories with the skipper of *Hopeful Macduff.*

The clatter of crockery woke Jean. Slowly she turned and

rubbed her eyes, not remembering what had happened. Then suddenly she did.

"Oh — oh, gosh!" she said, sitting up. "What's happened? It's all quiet."

"We're there," said James. "In Faraway. Fiona's cooking some supper."

"Oh, d'you mean I've missed it all? I do think you're beastly, letting me sleep through it."

"I can't think how you did," said Fiona. "There was enough noise to waken the dead. Hoy, come on down, supper's ready!"

There was the noise of wet boots on the companion and a shower of drips from oilies as they were wrenched off.

"I'm starving," announced Sandy. They all were. Now that the excitement of the voyage was over they felt ravenous. Bread and cheese followed the eggs and bacon, and then chocolate.

"Well," said Ninian at last, leaning back and regarding the still swaying lantern. "What are we going to do about to-night? There's not enough room for us all on board, and we need some sleep after this evening."

"The best thing," said Fiona, "is for two to go to the hotel: there may be room there."

"Or the skipper of *Macduff* might have a spare bunk," said Sandy.

"A bit smelly on a herring boat," said Jean. "But there may be a trawler or drifter. They generally have some room."

"Who'll go?" asked James, enchanted by the thought of spending the night in *Macduff*.

"You and Hugh," suggested Ninian. "I should try the hotel first, though."

Hugh agreed with him — a trawler was apt to be smelly.

They washed up the supper things and put them away. For a little while they sat about in the cabin, re-living their voyage and making Jean green with envy.

"We must put it all down in the log book," said Fiona, yawning.

"Yes, to-morrow." Ninian blinked, grown suddenly sleepy.

Jamie's head was nodding; Sandy was leaning back more asleep than awake.

"Bed-time," said Fiona firmly. No one disagreed.

Hugh and James collected a few night things and bundled them into a knapsack.

"If we don't come back, you'll know we've got into the hotel," said Hugh. "I hope they're still awake. It's after midnight."

Ninian followed them and helped them on to the deck of *Hopeful Macduff*. She was higher than they were, and it was difficult to climb in the dark.

"Good luck," said Ninian, and heard them stumble off across the deck.

He turned and drew in a deep breath before going below once more.

Nearly all the lights in Faraway had been put out, but now and then one flashed as a door was opened and shut. The great shoulders of the hills were dark against the sky, now scattered with stars. The moon was rising over the hills beyond the harbour. Lights still shone from the boats. There was an occasional shout from one of the men, and the noise of footsteps on the rough stones of the pier. Gently the fleet of herring boats creaked on their moorings as the tide went out, and ropes slapped the masts in the light wind. There was a distant roaring: some burn from the hills in spate, Ninian guessed, that came out in the harbour. He heard the splash of oars as a dinghy was rowed home, and a low murmur in Gaelic. A door opened and shut along the street by the quay. "The hotel," thought Ninian, "I hope they're all right there." He turned and went below and left *Fauna* alone with the creak of cables, the sleeping herring fleet, and the night.

Hugh and Jamie picked their way over half a dozen boats before they reached the pier. It was hard work in the dark, because of unseen ropes and coamings, and also none of the boats seemed to be the same height. As the tide was some way out they had difficulty in finding their way up the narrow iron ladder against the pier. Its rungs were encrusted with barnacles and seaweed and were very slippery. The moon was not yet high enough to be much help and several times they stumbled against bollards and over iron rings.

"Wonder where this blessed hotel is, if there is one?" grumbled Hugh, as he barked his shins for the third time.

"Somewhere along here," said Jamie, who, vaguely, remembered Faraway from his last visit.

They reached the end of the pier and continued up the street. Nearly all the houses were dark by now, although a few had a chink of light under the blinds.

"Ah, look at this," said Hugh, stopped to peer at a bigger house with a large board nailed all the length of it. There was a porch and another door farther along.

"The bar," suggested James.

Hugh pushed open the door and walked through into the hall. They were right. It was an hotel.

The hall was dimly lit by a lamp in a red silk shade. There were several stuffed fish in cases on the walls and the shadowy heads of deer. A passage led out into the back regions and another to the left. There were several doors in the walls and at the sound of their footsteps a woman opened one and came out.

"I say, I'm awfully sorry to come in so late, but can you put us up for the night?" said Hugh.

"We were caught in the squall: there isn't enough room for all of us in our boat," added James, yawning widely.

"Aye, there's a double room at the back, if ye'll no be minding that," said the woman, smiling.

"I expect you have a good few people here to-night in the

same state as us," said Hugh.

"Aye, but they mostly put up at the big hotels. Oors is juist a wee hoose, but we'll do our best tae make ye comfortable."

"I like this sort of place better than the large ones," said James, signing his name under Hugh's in the register. They followed Mrs. Macdonald along the passage and up a steep flight of stairs. She opened a door off the landing and switched on the light. It was a bare but clean room, with a big high double bed, a wardrobe, chest of drawers and a dressing-table.

"This is the best I can do," said Mrs. Macdonald. "I hope ye'll be a' reet."

"We'll be fine," said Hugh, wishing it had been two beds, but not minding much.

"Breakfast's at half-past eight," said their landlady. "The bathroom's opposite. Guid-night to ye. There's nothing I can get ye? Well, sleep well."

When she had gone Jamie ran to the bed and felt the springs.

"A bit odd," he said. "Gosh, I'm sleepy."

Hugh pulled off his shirt and in a few minutes had climbed into the big bed to an accompaniment of twangings and squealings and the rustle of brown paper that had been put under the mattress to prevent iron marks. He wriggled between the sheets and shifted his head on the hard pillow. James was left to put out the light and draw the curtains.

"Beast," he said, stumbling sleepily over a sea boot lying in the middle of the floor.

"Hurry up and open that window — and don't you dare kick me in bed," murmured Hugh.

James pulled the flimsy curtains and pushed up the window.

He could see the moon over the hills beyond the harbour mouth and the shapes of gently moving boats on the water. Somewhere out there was *Fauna*: he could not make out where.

"Oh, come on to bed," grunted Hugh, clanging as he turned over.

"Coming." Jamie took a last look at the bay, so still after the storm. He looked up for an instant and saw the stars, clear now of clouds.

"Thanks for the safe journey," he said.

CHAPTER IX

STEER BY THE STARS
Saturday, 14th August

JEAN woke first, and for a moment lay listening in surprise to the steady jabber of men's voices not far away. Then she remembered what had happened and stretched herself comfortably in the blankets, thinking of what they would do that day. The others were still asleep — she wondered what the time was. Resting her head on her crossed arms, she lay watching the reflection of the water through the portholes dancing in a motley pattern upon the ceiling. She could see it was a fine day outside: there were specks of dust floating in the shaft of sunlight coming from the port above her head.

There was a multitude of noises to listen to. The throb of engines as they were started up; herring boats chugging past *Fauna* on their way out to sea; the rock of their wash against her; the sound of hammering on both wood and iron; the squeak of a winch; the rattle of ropes, as a sail was hauled up; shouts and whistling; the splash as a bucket of refuse was thrown overboard; and in the background always the angry screaming jabber of gulls, fighting over scraps. Someone was whistling a tune she had heard before. It was a nice tune with a lilt to it, and another voice took it up and started singing, but she could not hear the words.

Jean could not bear to lie and listen to these noises any longer. Cautiously she crept from her bunk and dressed as silently as possible. With bare feet she tiptoed up the companion and out on deck.

It was a glorious sunny morning. Out beyond the breakwater there was still a big sea running, but inside it was calm. The bay was crowded with boats of every description, most of them under way now and heading for the loch. Almost all were trawlers or herring boats, but among them were a few dredgers and steamers, and Jean could see the graceful lines of a white sailing yacht moored out in the bay, as well as a couple of steam yachts, with yellow funnels.

She turned and looked inland. Faraway was not a big place. It was built at the head of the bay, and its waterfront was a high stone pier, against which every size of fishing boat was moored. The top of the pier continued into a wide street that seemed to run all round the harbour. This was bordered by houses, and the town ran back for some way until it met the hills up which a few buildings straggled. Jean was too near in to get a good view, but she could see all round and noticed white crofts scattered on the hills.

"Guid-morning," said a voice behind her, and she turned to see the skipper of *Hopeful Macduff* sitting on the edge of the low deckhouse, smoking.

"Oh, good-morning," said Jean. "I say, d'you know what the time is?"

"Aye, it's half-past seven, a bonny morning too," and he spat, cleverly missing her by the fraction of an inch.

"D'you think it's still rough out in the Minch?" asked Jean.

"Aye, there'll be a bit of a sea running, but no' too bad. Are ye thinking of crossing to-day?"

"Yes, some time. I don't know when." Jean turned and looked at the herring boats slipping out between the breakwater. "There are a lot in," she said.

"Aye," said the skipper. "Yon squall was a nasty one while it lasted. Are the others all asleep?" he added.

"Yes, they must be tired. I slept almost the whole afternoon. Two of them are ashore though, there's not room for us all on board."

They talked on amicably until Ninian poked his black head through the hatch to have a look at the morning. The others followed, much to the amusement of the skipper, who

FARAWAY.

thought they looked quite incapable of handling *Fauna* alone.

After breakfast they sat on the cabin roof watching the boats, and felt very weather-beaten, and as if they had accomplished a real voyage and were in a foreign port.

Presently two figures emerged from a house along the quay.

"Here they come," said Jean. "I wonder what sort of a night they had."

Hugh and Jamie sauntered along, looking into the shop windows that had been obscured last night. There were ships' chandlers and shops that sold postcards and souvenirs and sticks of Edinburgh rock. Jamie's eyes lit up when he saw the latter, and he made a mental note to call there again later in the day.

"Well?" called Jean, as they came within earshot.

"Lovely night," answered James. "We had to share a bed and Hugh kicked a bit and the springs were simply deafening, but otherwise it was all right."

"Had breakfast?" That was Fiona, who did not feel like cooking another at that moment.

"Yes, a huge one. Porridge and all sorts of things," said Hugh.

The tide was nearly out and the boys had to climb down a long slippery ladder, hung with seaweed like matted green hair. They scrambled across the trawlers and dropped down on *Fauna's* deck.

"She does look small." James looked at her proudly. She was their home for the present, and a very satisfactory one.

"Well, what are we doing to-day?" asked Hugh, pressing tobacco into his pipe.

"We must overhaul the engine," said Ninian. "Fill up with petrol and get some more milk and butter."

"And see the island a bit, and bathe."

"And look at the cinema."

"I'm glad we don't live here," said Fiona, after a moment or two. "I mean it's lovely to come here and see all the strange uncivilised things, but I'd rather live in Flatfish."

"I rather like this place," said Sandy. "I love these boats and all the different noises and excitement."

"Think how tired you'd get of them," argued Fiona. "You'd long for the peace of Flatfish."

"You'd get bored stiff with the gulls," said Sandy.

They argued in a friendly way while the sun climbed up over the hills and the tide reached its lowest ebb and all the cables and hawsers creaked as it ran out. At last, Hugh and Ninian disappeared below to the engine-room, and Fiona, stretching herself, remarked that it was getting late and set off with the others along the quay.

They got most of their purchases at the grocer's and then were lured on by Jamie to the sweet shop, where they spent a long time trying to decide what sort of rock or toffee was best.

Faraway had a fair sprinkling of trippers, and these stared at the Stewarts as if they were some different species altogether. They were certainly much browner and more untidy than any one else, and walked with a kind of swagger.

These other people had come comfortably to the island in a steamer, with suitcases and rooms ready booked. The Stewarts had sailed over on a stormy night with oilskins as almost their only luggage, and had slept in bunks in the cabin of their ship. The twins were moderately respectable in grey shorts and Aertex shirts. Their legs were long and brown and their feet were bare. Jamie needed a haircut. Fiona had blue trousers on, stained with sea-water and spotted with fish scales. Her shirt was clean but faded, with a hole in one sleeve. Sandy was the worst. His grey flannels barely reached his ankles and were covered with engine oil and various small holes. His sandshoes had once been white, more than a year ago, and his toes stuck through. A leather belt was round his waist with a big sheath-knife hanging from it, and a bag of provisions was slung from one shoulder.

"Why do people stare so?" asked Jean, as they passed yet another group of gaping trippers.

Fiona shrugged.

"They haven't any manners," she said. "They can't have ever seen any one civilised before."

"I say, do look at this blissful shop." Jean paused before a doorway lined with racks of knobbly sticks cut with every imaginable shape of handle. Shetland shawls and rugs were hanging beside them, and in the murky depths of the shop were inviting looking skeins of wool ranging from thinnest Shetland to great hanks of coarse undyed wool, still speckled with bits of dried heather and grass. This was a small dingy shop, not frequented by trippers and consequently had all the nicest things in it.

"We mustn't go in," said Fiona. "I know I couldn't resist a tweed, and I simply can't afford it."

"Hugh wants a stick, I know," said James. "Let's get him one, from all of us."

"All right," said Fiona, and followed him in.

They were the most lovely sticks, and so varied that it was

almost impossible to choose.

At last they decided on a firm plain stick, slightly taller than an ordinary walking stick, and with a crooked rounded grip.

"He will like this," said Jean, holding the smooth handle between her fingers.

"Come on, it's getting late. They will be raging if we don't hurry," said Fiona.

There was no sign of the boys when they did reach *Fauna*.

"Oh, well, let's put on the lunch." Fiona frowned, wondering where they were.

The skipper of *Hopeful Macduff* was still leaning against the deckhouse smoking. He nodded to them as they crossed the deck.

"When are you off?" asked Sandy.

"Och, not for a while yet." The skipper spat. "There's some trouble with the engine."

"Bother those boys, I wish they'd hurry up," said Fiona, after she had waited nearly half an hour. "What on earth can they be doing?"

"Fallen overboard?" suggested Sandy hopefully.

"Well, I'm getting hungry," said James. "What time is it?"

"Quarter-past one," said Fiona. "Let's start."

Half an hour later there was a burst of laughter from one of the trawlers, gradually growing nearer. There was something familiar about it.

Sandy and the others, who had finished lunch and were sitting, disconsolately, on the cabin roof, looked up.

"Well, I'm blest!" Sandy gaped.

Ninian and Hugh were emerging from the hatch on one of the trawlers. They were followed by a tall young fisherman, his cap over one eye.

"Hoy!" called Fiona. "What on earth?"

"Hallo!" called Ninian. "You remember Duncan from

"HOY!" CALLED FIONA.

Lochinver, don't you?"

The fisherman touched his cap, grinning still.

"Hallo," said Fiona. "What do you mean by leading my young brother astray?"

"Och, he does'na need so much leading," said Duncan. "But I'm sorry if I've kept them from their dinner."

"That's all right. Come and have some." Fiona got up.

"No, thank you, but I must go back, they have it waiting for me." Duncan smiled again and disappeared down the gangway.

"Well, I must say," said Fiona, as the two boys jumped down on deck. "A bit much. Going off and boozing and leaving us to do all the dirty work."

"I don't know what you call dirty work," said Ninian, inspecting his hands, still smeared with engine oil. "Anyway, you were so long yourself we gave you up for good." He tripped over a piece of rope as he spoke and nearly fell headlong.

"You are drunk!" said Jean, in horror-struck tones. "How disgusting."

"My dear child," her brother said scathingly. "I couldn't have drunk enough of anything in that short time to have made me the least little bit tiddley."

"I'm hungry," announced Hugh. "Any lunch left?"

"You don't deserve it," said Fiona. "Or this either," and she produced the stick.

"Oh, I say!" Hugh really was thrilled. "No, Fiona, I don't think I do."

"It's from all of us," said Fiona. "There was such a lovely shop, we couldn't resist one."

Hugh pressed it on the deck. It bent hardly at all, and yet was light and springy.

"It's just what I wanted," he said. "You are nice." He was feeling pleasantly full of beer, the sun was shining: it was a marvellous day.

After this second lunch, they dragged an unwilling Ninian to the cinema. This was in a dilapidated hall in the middle of the town, and to get up to the circle they had to climb flight after flight of narrow stone stairs, with unrecognisable photos on the wall, and a strange reek of disinfectant. There did not seem to be any attendants upstairs, so they went in and sat in the front row.

"Why you have to drag me to this beastly place I can't

imagine," grumbled Ninian. "I've never heard of the film or any of the stars."

"Shsh," hissed James. "It's going to be a cowboy one."

"Oh, blast." Ninian shut his eyes and sank down in his seat. But Fiona, watching him with amusement, noticed that he opened his eyes a minute or two later and forgot, at the end of the film, that he was supposed to have been sleeping. An attendant came round half-way through and they bought sweet sticky ices, almost too hard to eat.

They emerged, blinking like owls, an hour and a half later.

Fiona screwed up her eyes.

"They feel all hot," she said. "What an awful film too — why did we bother to stay?"

"It wasn't too bad," said Jean kindly.

"I laughed at all the wrong bits," said Sandy. "It's awful when you do, because you can't stop."

Fiona found herself humming the tune from the end of the film. She could still imagine she was in America, surrounded by newspaper men and gangsters and blonde secretaries. Funny how some kinds of film were always alike: she had seen this one countless times before.

Ninian brought her back to earth by pushing her into a tea shop, and for a little their voices were quenched by scones and jam.

From where they were sitting they could see out across the harbour. The water was glassy still and fishing boats were constantly passing each other, some coming home with the day's catch, others on their way out with the herring nets. The sun was reflected in bars of gold and pink that were mixed as a wash cut through them. It was so still that they could hear the chugging of engines and men shouting to one another, and the angry clamour of gulls. Ninian looked with satisfaction at the clear sky.

"It'll be a perfect night for crossing," he said. "The stars'll be bright as anything."

"When shall we start?" asked Fiona, trying vainly to catch the waitress's eye.

"Let's get out of the loch before it's pitch dark." Ninian counted in his mind the hours before the moon rose.

"That'll be about ten — or later," said Sandy. "If nothing awful happens we should get in by four."

"How marvellous: just as the dawn's coming." Jean wriggled with excitement. "We shall sleep all day."

"Some of us on the floor," grunted Hugh.

"Feigns," said every one.

"We could just fit in," said Fiona. "Jamie on the little seat, and Jean and I together."

"It's very small, the little seat," pointed out James.

"Well, you're the smallest," said Ninian reasonably.

"Oh, come on, waitress," murmured Fiona, as the girl passed again, apparently both blind and deaf.

At last she saw them and the bill was paid.

"Have we got everything we want for the journey?" asked Ninian, stopping in the street. "This is our last chance."

"Yes, I think so," said Fiona. "We've got some time before we need start, though. Let's walk over to those rocks and see what the country's like."

They wandered along the street and out of the town. For some way cottages straggled up the hillside, but they grew fewer and fewer, until at last it was bare brown grass and grey rocks: more rocks than grass really, and it seemed impossible that the small black cows, tethered here and there, could possibly find a living. The hills were much lower here than on the mainland, and altogether it was an arid looking place. Suddenly the bright blue of a loch showed like a slip of sky between the lulls, and a burn came charging down to it, foaming and tossing over the rocks.

They sat for a while playing ducks and drakes with the flattest stones they could find, and watching trout rise with a gentle swirl that made Jean's mouth water.

Softly, very softly, the hills began to blur and sounds

came more distinctly as the evening grew stiller. They walked back along the rocky road, down the hill and into the town. The harbour was distinctly emptier and they hurried on. It was already half-past nine.

Back on the quayside they jumped on to the first drifter and crossed to *Fauna*, saying good-bye to the crew of *Hopeful Macduff* on the way. Duncan poked his head out of the hatch as they passed and followed it by his long body.

"I'll come and gie you a hand," he said, evidently disbelieving that the Stewarts could take a boat to sea by themselves. "Are you crossing back to-night?"

"Yes," said Fiona. "At least we hope so."

"Where do you anchor?"

"Flatfish Bay."

"What? Oh aye, yon long bay by Melvaig."

"That's it." Ninian dropped down to the engine. "Stand by the moorings," he said. "And, Fiona, take the wheel."

The calm of the evening was shattered.

"Wonderful that it's actually started," murmured Sandy.

"Cast off," called Ninian.

Ropes snaked down on to the deck. James and Hugh grabbed them and hauled them on board.

"Good-bye," called Jean.

"Och, I'll be seeing you soon," said Duncan, lifting his hand. "And that Flatfish Bay of yours is a bad place in a storm. I'd advise you not to stay there."

"We like it," called Fiona across the widening strip of water between them.

"It's no' a guid place." Duncan's voice was firm. "It's no' guid at a'. There's fine places up the coast to Lochinver."

"We might try them," Sandy had almost to shout.

Fauna turned and settled down to an even throb as she crossed the harbour.

They waved a last farewell to Duncan, and looked ahead to the breakwater.

"Some time yet before we get to the sea," said Hugh.

The sun had turned the water to green shot with orange. Black gulls flapped home, and cormorants bobbed lazily on the waves, too tired to duck. Ahead of them were herring boats, setting out with their nets, and behind them were more. The hills were sharply black against the sky from which, at last, the sun had disappeared.

"Soon be dark." Fiona turned the wheel a fraction. "We've timed it pretty well, Hugh."

They passed the narrows and the lighthouse, flashing dimly in the half light.

"Here, you take over." Fiona handed the wheel to Hugh. "I'll go down and get some supper. Don't feel in the mood for anything elaborate, but I expect every one is as hungry as usual."

"They are," Sandy assured her.

Ninian came forward and sat on the cabin roof, frowning and whistling.

"What tune's that?" asked Jean.

"I don't know. Duncan was singing it."

"It's the one we heard on the cliff," said James, and they were silent.

"What's the matter?" asked Jean at last.

"Nothing. Why?"

"You're scowling."

Ninian sucked at his empty pipe. He had discarded his kilt for an old pair of grey flannels covered with engine oil and fish scales. He had on a faded blue shirt which had torn across the shoulder and his hair was extremely untidy and blown in all directions by the wind. He frowned again and leant back on his elbows.

"I'm scowling because I'm happy," he said. "One does sometimes. This is too good to be true; I think I must be dreaming, and yet I know I'm not."

"I feel like that too occasionally." Hugh peered ahead as they rounded the last corner. "This life at the moment seems as if it must go on for ever because it is much the best way of living, and yet in a week I shall have never been anything but a boring soldier."

Fiona was listening from the hatch.

"This is the only part that matters," she said. "This is the real part, the other just fills in."

"It's funny," Hugh was solemn. "It's funny that one should have so little of the real part and so much of the other."

"Good for your soul," said Ninian.

"I'm sure it's not good for mine," said Fiona firmly.

"You wouldn't enjoy it half as much if you had it all the time." Ninian did not seem sure all the same.

"I should," said Fiona. "That's just the point, I think we all should. I can never have enough of living here and doing this sort of thing."

"It's just life," said Hugh.

"That's what's all wrong, though," Ninian sat up. "Surely life shouldn't be doing what one does not want to do?"

"Yes, it should," said Fiona sadly. "Otherwise people would be too selfish, if they all did what they wanted and did not bother about the others."

"Bother the others," murmured Hugh.

"I agree, they don't help us," said Ninian.

"They do, really. If it wasn't for them we shouldn't have *Fauna*, because she wouldn't be built," said Fiona.

"We could build as good a one." Ninian knocked out his pipe.

"We couldn't. Others make the tools and the engines. Besides, we're in a minority. There are far more people who would rather live in crowds. And, I suppose in a way there's something to be said for that kind of civilisation."

"We've got a marvellous opinion of ourselves, haven't we?" said Hugh, and they all laughed.

They had reached the sea at last and big rollers were coming in, making *Fauna* pitch as she came out of the shelter of the loch and into the Minch.

"Come on, let's have supper before it gets any rougher," said Sandy.

"Or darker," added Jean.

Pin-pricks of light were showing from the surrounding hills, and the beam of the lighthouse shone dimly behind them. A white edge of foam showed where the hills ended in a rocky fringe by the sea. In front was darkness and no land, and a heaving mass of water, white tipped, and the first pale stars.

They ate in the cabin with the light switched on and left Hugh on deck. Sandy relieved him and the others sat for some time sprawling over the table and discussing Life and People and Themselves and all the other things people do discuss when they have the whole night before them and a big pot of coffee on the table. Jean got bored and went up to talk to Sandy, but James stayed and listened and occasionally made a remark. The talk drifted from subject to subject and wreathed round the cabin with the smoke from two pipes. There was a pleasant vibrant jingle from the cups and plates, the woodwork squeaked in rhythm with the engine, and *Fauna* climbed the rollers and slid down the other side, sometimes giving a wriggle as she reached the bottom. This was going to be a long night, a marvellous long night.

At last Ninian stretched and got up.

"It must be quite late," he said. "Time someone relieved Sandy and these babies got to bed."

"Here, I say," said James indignantly. "I'm not going to bed to-night."

"Well, go up and steer for a bit, but I'm not promising you can stay up."

Jamie pulled on a jersey and unhooked his oily from under the companion way. It was never any good arguing with Ninian, but Jean could sometimes persuade him.

He came out into the cool night and took a deep breath. It was cloudless and windless too, but for the rushing air they caused.

The stars were bright as diamonds, yellow diamonds, and as cold. They burned with a fierce strange light, and Jamie recognised several of Hugh's patterns sketched across the vaulted sky. He could see Jean and Sandy standing by the wheel, and went over to join them.

"Ninian says we've got to go to bed," he announced.

"What?" Sandy and Jean almost shrieked.

"He couldn't really mean it," added Jean.

"We'll, you go down and see," said her twin. "You know you can do what you want with Ninian."

"Not always, but I'll try." Jamie took the wheel, and Jean went back along the heaving deck and into the cabin.

Washing up was in progress, and a damp cloth was thrown at her and she was told to help.

"Bother," said Jean.

She dried for a few minutes in silence.

"I say, Hugh," she said. "It's a marvellous night for stars. It's like your map come alive."

"Oh, good," said Hugh. "Is Sandy managing all right? I ought really go up and see."

"So ought I." Ninian put down his cloth.

"That's right, make an excuse." Fiona rubbed at some mustard. "All right, you'd better go, there's hardly any more to do."

"I say, Ninian," said Jean, making a grab at him before he disappeared into the night. "We don't have to go to bed really, do we?" Her forehead wrinkled in her anxiety.

Ninian looked at her, unsmiling. "Well," he said slowly. "No, I don't think so."

"Oh, bliss," said Jean, and seized the last plate.

When the cabin was tidy she and Fiona joined the boys on deck. Indeed it was too fine to be below, with the cool wind and the crisp stars and the dark and friendly night.

"How far have we got?" asked Fiona, watching the green phosphorescence of the water where the waves broke.

Hugh peered at his watch and did some quick calculating.

"It's half-past twelve, nearly," he said. "That means we must have gone about twelve miles and a little more."

Fiona turned to get her bearings by her old friend the Great Bear. He was directly behind them and the Pole Star back to their left. It was too dark and too far to see the mainland or even the lighthouse.

"I suppose we're all right," said Fiona dubiously.

"Yes, we're fine," Sandy assured her. "This is much the best way of steering: the stars simply can't change."

And considering that they had been burning for more years than any one knew, Fiona thought he was probably right.

Right and left were the bobbing lights of fishing boats and there were more behind them.

Slowly into the vivid sky the moon crept up. The sea that had been green and orange, and then dark blue, turned to black and silver, silver that shifted and slid as the sea moved.

"Oh, what a glorious night," said Fiona. "We are lucky, you know, this is the most perfect night we could have had."

Beyond them, under the rising moon, was the far distant curve of the mainland, black like a snake.

Fiona felt a sudden ache of intolerable sadness. As time was measured these few hours were very short and would be over almost before they had begun, and she wanted them so much to go on for ever. As surely as the water moved, the moon would soon be behind them and a grey dawn creeping up over those silver hills. She was almost there in it, it was so real. It would be an especially cold and grey dawn because they would be tired, and a wind might have sprung up to make them shiver and wish for their bunks. Ninian's voice, telling her to steer, brought her back to the present and the warm night surrounded her once more.

There were such a host of stars that it was difficult to keep any particular ones in mind. Hugh's map had been easy to read, for he had only drawn the big constellations, but this was different, a tangled mass of gold like scattered coins.

Then the longest bit of the night began when mile after mile of spangled water flowed past, but the land never seemed to get any nearer. They talked at first but with longer silences between each sentence, until at last they were not talking at all. Jean nodded sleepily on the cabin roof, Ninian's arm round her.

"Go to bed," suggested Fiona, but she shook her head and Jamie was equally firm.

"Let's have some cocoa," suggested Hugh.

"Yes, do let's." Sandy sat up straight.

Fiona gave Hugh the wheel and went below.

"I'll shriek at you when it's ready," she said. "And Hugh can have his through the skylight."

Six cups of milk into the saucepan and the Primus turned up as high as it would go. Fiona mixed the powder with some milk at the bottom of each cup, and by the time she had finished the saucepan was almost boiling. She put the sugar basin on the table and a tin of biscuits, in case any one was hungry. Sandy was sure to be ravenous. She turned just as the milk was rising in a bubbly froth, ready to overflow, and filled each cup to the brim, stirring meanwhile.

"It's ready," she shouted up the skylight, and feet thundered on the deck and down the companion. Fiona handed Hugh's steaming mug up to him and smiled at his black silhouette. She could see a haze of stars beyond him and he looked larger than ever in his oilskins against the sky.

"Mind, it's hot," she said.

Hugh, himself, looking down the skylight, envied for a moment the warm and comfortable looking scene below him. He could hear voices and laughter above the engine, and could see the Stewarts grouped round the table, lantern light on their brown faces and bright eyes and silvering the

FIONA GAVE HUGH THE WHEEL.

twin's hair. But he was not long alone. Before he had finished half his cocoa and was warming his hands on the cup, Ninian and James appeared beside him and then the others.

They stayed on deck all the long night, watching the coast grow slowly nearer and taller. They had left most of the fishing boats behind now although one was still a dark shape of the waves a mile or so astern. They caught the glint of her lights sometimes and yet could not be sure it was not a reflected star.

For the last miles it was a job to keep awake, but they were on their mettle now, and meant to see the end of the voyage, whether it was night or not.

Suddenly Ninian spoke out of a long silence.

"I see where we are. There's the lighthouse right up to port, we've come too far south. Turn a bit, Sandy."

"Aye, aye, sir."

Hours later, it seemed, they saw the long white ridge of beach that was Flatfish Bay. The moon had crossed the sky and a faint grey light was coming over the hills. Fiona's dawn.

"Another half-hour and we'll be there," said Ninian, and suddenly the morning seemed less cold and dismal.

"The dinghy's still afloat anyway," remarked Sandy, a few minutes later, and they saw it bob, a black shape on the iron-grey water.

"It's almost light." James yawned and blinked.

Indeed the sky was paling and there was a thin wedge of light over the hills beyond Flatfish.

Fiona took the wheel for the last bit of the journey. There was no need of stars now: the old landmarks were already visible and the two stones. It was cold, in this hour between night and day, and Hugh was reminded of another dawn last summer when he had been the only human awake in the hills by the Carna Loch.

Now that the voyage was over, Fiona could hardly believe that at one time it had seemed endless. Nevertheless, here they were, and Jamie was even now leaning overboard with the boat hook to grab at the dinghy.

The engine slowed and stopped. The buoy was hauled on board and made fast. They were home again. Even Ninian was yawning unashamedly.

A few minutes later the sun rose, but there was no sound of voices, and *Fauna* rocked gently on the waves in the silent bay.

CHAPTER X

BEHIND THE STACK
Sunday, 15th August

JAMIE bumped his head against the end of Ninian's bunk for the third time and awoke, reluctantly. Bars of sun were lying across the cabin, and it was very hot. He tried vainly to stretch himself, but the little seat was at least a foot shorter than he was and consequently he was cramped.

Cautiously he sat up, trying not to wake the others. Their even breathing continued unabated, so he crept out and stole across to Hugh and peered at his watch.

Gosh, four o'clock, nine whole hours of sleep. He certainly had been tired. He yawned again and then stopped dead. Surely that was — yes, it was. An engine throbbing somewhere and getting nearer every minute.

He ran for the companion and pulled at the hatch. It had swollen slightly in the dew and would not open at once. Jamie swore under his breath and gave an enormous heave. It shot back and a flood of golden afternoon poured down on his head. Gulls' calls and the sound of waves came more clearly, so did the engine's beat. He looked round. There was no sign of any boat. The bay and the sea beyond was blue and empty, and still the engine throbbed. There must be a boat somewhere. He could swear it was only a few hundred yards away. Surely he was not still asleep. He shook himself hard and blinked — yes, it was still there. This was worth incurring even Ninian's wrath. He dropped back into the cabin and shook his brother hard. Ninian woke with a grunt.

"What's the matter? What time is it?" he said.

"Ninian, listen. D'you hear it?"

"Hear what?" His brother yawned and rubbed his eyes.

"A boat, an engine! Oh, do wake up!"

"A what, an engine? Don't be silly. Have you looked for it?"

"Yes, and it isn't there."

"Of course it isn't there. Jamie, you've been dreaming."

"I haven't, honestly. Oh, Gosh!"

"What?"

"It's stopped."

"It was never going, gump."

"Look here, Ninian, I promise it was. Quite close too, and I couldn't see anything."

By now they were all awake, grumbling at the noise.

"Can't you let us sleep in peace?" muttered Sandy, hauling the bedclothes over his head.

"You've slept long enough." For once Jamie was annoyed. He ran back on deck, but there was still no sign of the boat, though he knew that he had heard one, whatever Ninian might say. It had sounded so close that if it was still going he must be able to hear it. But there was no sound at all, save the gulls screaming round the Stack. They seemed to be more disturbed than usual, or perhaps it was that there were more of them now that the young ones would be hatched out.

Every one was awake and grumbling at Jamie for having been so noisy. He, too, was feeling bad-tempered about the mysterious engine. Suddenly, looking over the side, he thought that a quick dive into the sea would be just about perfect. He could hear Sandy coming up the companion.

"Bring up the bathing things," he called. "It's beautifully warm."

"Good idea," came Jean's voice. "I say, I feel all upside down, waking up in the middle of the afternoon."

"What will the next meal be?" asked Sandy. "Breakfast or supper?"

"Both." Ninian pushed past him and took a header over the side.

Hugh was still half asleep as he dived in, and the sudden cold shock woke and braced him. He swam vigorously in circles, and then crept up behind Fiona, just as she was shaking the water out of her eyes, and ducked her again.

A mad battle followed, and Flatfish rang with shrieks and yells and the noise of violent splashing. It was so warm that they stayed in hours, until they felt so hungry that they could not wait another moment.

"You all stay on deck, I'll get the food," said Fiona, having visions of the cabin with all its heaps of blankets and unmade bunks being covered with drips. She pushed firmly past the hungry mob and rooted some tins out of their store.

They sat on the boiling deck and let the salt water dry on their bodies and leave a white crust in their eyebrows. It was calm again, no wind whatever, just the long rollers breaking with slow rhythm on the sand. Ninian made a little boat out of an empty matchbox and fitted it with a paper sail on a match stick. Jean christened it with lemonade and they watched it bob slowly towards the shore. Sandy, inspired, began to carve a tiny dinghy out of a cork and that too was launched. It floated lob-sidedly, until its career was cut short by a hungry gull.

"What'll we do to-morrow?" asked Jean, spitting tomato skin into the sea.

"Sometime we must go up to the Green Laddie's Wood; we might almost fish in his loch," said Ninian.

"Oh, yes, do let's. How long ago was it that he was seen?" Sandy rolled over and sat up.

"A hundred years," said Fiona sadly. "I don't think there's much chance of him appearing, but still, it's a lovely lonely loch and a very spooky wood."

"Spooky?" Hugh raised his eyebrows.

"Yes, you know, ghostly and dark," said Jean.

"There may be trolls," suggested Ninian, thinking of last year.

"Thanks very much, but you can go and find them this

time," Jamie told him.

"What else can we do?" asked Sandy.

"How much more time have we got?" said Fiona slowly.

Ninian lay back and shut his eyes. He did not want to think of how few days they had left of their leave.

"Four days." Hugh's voice was low, and no one spoke for some time after that.

Then Sandy said cheerfully: "We can do stacks in four days."

"We've done nearly everything," said Jean. "I say, shall we go back a day early and get in some fishing?"

"No, don't let's; we can't end up like that," said Fiona quickly. "Besides, we haven't got the fishing, and anyway, it's too bright."

"May not be then."

"We must stay here. We couldn't go back, not possibly," said Fiona. "And, we'll have plenty of time for fishing when the others have gone," she added unkindly.

"Well, what shall we do now?" asked Jean, sitting up and looking across the bay. It was nearly six and would soon be evening. They must hurry up or it would be too late. It was flat calm, and the sea was gold with the sun. Out of the still water the everlasting mysterious rollers beat up on the sand. However calm the sea was there were always waves in Flatfish Bay.

Sandy was suddenly struck with an idea. The tide was nearly at its lowest ebb, and beyond the Stack was a long expanse of rocky shore, stretching on until a jut of cliff hid what was beyond.

"Let's land," he said, "and explore the coast. We've never been farther than the Stack, and there may be all sorts of exciting caves and things along there. The tide's not low yet, so we shall have plenty of time."

"Yes, do let's," said James, and Fiona got up too.

"I'm going to change," she said. "Those rocks look a bit spiky."

The others followed her example and pulled on shirts and trousers, and a few minutes later were rowing ashore.

They grounded some fifty yards out. It was too shallow to get any farther.

"You go on," said Ninian. "I'll come back and fetch you when you're ready."

"Don't you want to come?" asked James in surprise.

"Well, one of us has got to stay," said his brother. "I don't mind. Only if you find anything very super give a shout, and I'll come somehow."

"Sure you don't mind?" said Fiona, as Hugh jumped over the side and waded ashore with Jean on his shoulders.

"No, honestly, I don't. I'll get the supper ready and give you a surprise."

"Not too much of a surprise," said Fiona, laughing. She rolled up her trousers as high as they would go and waded after the others.

Ninian watched them splash ashore, then turned the dinghy and rowed slowly back to *Fauna*.

They had landed in the second bay and from where they were they could not see beyond the Stack.

"We'll have to go between the Stack and the land," said Fiona, as they walked along the beach. "The tide never goes out enough to let one walk round it."

"I hope we shall find a way along the cliff," said Hugh. "Otherwise we shall be stumped."

The wet sand was firm beneath them, and as they walked their feet felt the sudden knob of a half buried shell or the cold slime of seaweed. They splashed through small warm pools, making the minnows scuttle for safety and the crabs crawl under the nearest rocks.

At last they reached the Stack.

The cliff jutted out into the sea, and however low the tide went it never reached the foot of the cliff here. There was a deep gully between it and the Stack, about forty feet wide. Thick black strands of seaweed were perpetually washing to

BACK TO "FAUNA."

and fro as the water heaved and gurgled up the channel. It was a horribly dark and gloomy place, as the Stack itself leant slightly inland and overhung the gully. From where they stood they could see the length of the gully and no more as an outcrop of cliff hid the rest of the coast from them.

Looking up, they saw several ledges full of cormorants and shag, staring at them in fear, ready to flop down into the sea at the least provocation. Above them the Stack was splashed with white from the years-old nests of gulls.

"It's terribly sheer," said Jean at last, after they had stared silently at the cliff for some time.

"We can't wade either," said Hugh. "It's miles deep."

"There's got to be some way round," said Fiona. "Because we can't go back."

"We're idiots," said Sandy. "We should have kept on our bathing things. Then we could have swum along the gully."

"It looks a fairly fierce current."

"Well, we could have tried at least."

"Bother and blast," said Hugh, throwing a stone at the cormorants.

"No, listen a moment," said Fiona, crossing over to the cliff and staring up at it. "Surely if we climb up a little way there are enough bumps and ledges to crawl along, at least as far as we can see."

Certainly there seemed to be plenty of footholds along to the end of the gully, but what happened beyond that they could none of them tell.

"Let's try it anyway," said Sandy.

"Well, bags I go first." Fiona pushed past him and hauled herself up on to the first ledge.

"Careful, for goodness' sake," called Hugh.

"Careful yourself," said Fiona over her shoulder.

A piece of rock came away in her hand and she tossed it down into the gully where it fell with a sullen splash. The higher she got the worse became the footholds, for grass and thrift and sea campions had undermined most of the jutting rocks and at a touch they came away and went rattling in a shower of earth and pebbles to splash into the sea.

The others followed her, crab-wise, along the cliff.

Hugh, looking down, saw for one horrid moment the black sea rolling up the gully and long slimy strands of weed washing slowly up and down on the waves. He turned quickly, remembering last year when he had climbed the Stack and felt the same sick feeling on looking down.

> "The wrinkled sea beneath him crawls,
> Then like a thunderbolt he falls."

Hugh hoped that he would not.

Their progress along the cliff was disturbing myriads of gulls. The air was white with their wings and ringing with their cries. There was a subterranean cave somewhere below them and every now and then a long booming noise echoed up the cliff. It was one of the most eerie noises in the world, thought Hugh.

"I say," came Fiona's voice, "there's quite a good path here, at least it's a much wider ledge." She was some way above the others and Hugh, looking up, could see her standing against the cliff peering down at them. In front of her, across the Minch, the sun was sinking in a cloud of red and gold. It gilded the sea and turned Fiona's face to the colour of a Red Indian's.

She waited for them on the ledge and then led them along it.

"When we get round the corner we shall have to start coming down somehow," said James.

"Hope we can." Jean was dubious.

"Sure to be able to, somehow," said Sandy.

Fiona, in front, had reached the corner. The ledge came to an end here and she slithered on to a small jut of rock and pulled herself up.

"Gosh!" Her voice came in surprise.

"What is it?" cried James, dancing with excitement on the end of the ledge.

"Another gully, a deep one, running right back into the cliff."

"Can we get across?"

"Not possibly. We'll have to go round. It may not be very long."

She disappeared from view and the others followed her. Hugh, being last, had longest to wait and when he was able to see round the corner she was already some way ahead. From where he was he could see that the gully was some twenty feet wide at its entrance,

SHE WAITED FOR THEM ON THE LEDGE.

narrowing gradually until a sharp turn hid the far end. It ran back parallel with the cliff after about fifteen feet, so that it was invisible from the sea and the cliff seemed to have no break in it. This also made it completely calm and still like a miniature harbour. There was thrift and grass growing right down to the tide mark here and loose earth and rocks. Evidently a storm did not affect its stillness.

"What a marvellous place," came Sandy's voice, echoing in the silence. "What's the matter, Fiona?"

His cousin had reached the corner and was standing motionless, one hand against the cliff. She raised the other for silence and they half fell, half scrambled the last few yards. Hugh, peering over her shoulder, was also dumb with astonishment.

191

The gully ran back fifty yards or so, ending with a steeply shelving pebble beach. The cliffs remained as high as ever all round and at the far end was the black mouth of a cave. That was a find indeed, but far more so was the flat outcrop of rock against the left-hand cliff: It was made in the shape of a natural pier and moored to it was a fishing boat, tan sail furled, resting calmly on the still water.

Hugh let out a low whistle. The boat was deserted and so was the bay. There was no one about.

"There!" Jamie's voice was triumphant. "I told you I heard a boat this morning and no one would believe me! Here it is! What a marvellous little harbour, there must be a cottage up there somewhere."

"I can't see any path," said Jean.

"Oh, come on, quick," cried Sandy. "Gosh, this is exciting!"

"I bet this is the boat I saw when we first got here," said Jean, following him along the cliff. She looked down into the transparent water. It was very different to the outer gully; here one could see rocks on the bottom and the black shapes of fish flicking between them.

They ran across the last few yards and on to the narrow pier. It was worn smooth by men's feet and there were iron rings let in it which showed that it was used. The boat was the usual type of herring boat but smarter and in better repair than most of them. She had been newly painted blue and her decks were clean. But she was entirely deserted and they could hear no one moving about below.

"This is the best harbour I've ever seen in my life," said Fiona at last. "Isn't it perfect? No one could find it, no sea could ever make it rough, it could never go dry, for it's low tide now. I bet it's as calm as a mill pond in all the big gales."

"Let's see if there's a path up the cliff," said Hugh. "There must be a cottage about somewhere. I mean, people wouldn't just leave a boat."

"They must be pretty certain no one would find her," said Fiona, walking across the jetty and on to the large round stones that paved the bay. They wandered along looking in vain for a path up the cliff. There was nothing at all, nothing but some very rough and seldom used looking steps cut at ragged intervals to the top of the cliff, half-way towards the cave.

"Nothing doing," said Hugh at last. "Obviously those steps are hardly ever used, there must be some other way out."

"What about the cave?" suggested Sandy, sitting on a rock and unwrapping the end of a Crunchie bar. He bit into it noisily and the others looked at him in envy. They had forgotten theirs.

"Yes, let's explore the cave," said Fiona. "Any one got any matches?"

"Yes, a few." Hugh rattled a box in his pocket.

"Come on then. I say, there's almost a path worn in the rocks to the cave," said James.

Jean came close to Hugh. She never had been very fond of caves and Hugh looked the largest and strongest person present.

Fiona led the way, her hands in her pockets. There was something a little frightening about this place, though she would be the last to admit it. But that still and empty boat out there must mean something: she had a feeling it did.

A burn came pouring over the rocks out of the cave's mouth. It had worn itself a channel and was deep in places. There was a rough path beside it from which the boulders had been rolled back. Fiona walked up it into the cave.

The first strange thing she noticed was that there was no cloud of rock pigeons hurrying out as they came in. Also it was not a sea cave like most of the others along the coast and it was dry and airy. It was high with a stony floor, narrowing down to a tunnel at the far end. They walked half-way across and looked back at the entrance.

The harbour and the boat were framed in it as in a picture, with the tall cliff behind and the half dark of evening over them.

"We'd better go back along the top," said Fiona, half whispering in the silence. "We'll never find our way along the cliff in this light." As she finished speaking there was a loud drip from somewhere that made them all jump. In the silence of the cave it sounded extra loud, but it was only where one of the walls was sweating slowly on to the rocks. The burn made hardly any sound here, it was so deep and smooth.

"Come on," Fiona shivered. "Don't let's stand here, let's see what happens round the corner." She had never felt less like going round a corner into the blackness of the unknown than she did now. However, as usual, she would not show that she was afraid.

Jean took hold of Hugh's hand. She felt definitely creepy.

It was not pitch dark as they had expected. A thin shaft of light came through the ceiling and showed the vague shapes of rocks and the worn path between them. It was very high here, but it grew lower suddenly and plunged into an inky tunnel.

"Where are those matches, Hugh?" whispered Fiona. She took the box and was just going to advance into the gloom when she stopped.

"What is it?" hissed Sandy.

"Sh-sh-sh! Listen!" They stood like carved statues, their hearts thumping. Somewhere ahead of them they heard the rattle of a boot on the rocks.

"Somebody's coming," James's voice squeaked.

"Perhaps it's a troll," suggested Jean, in horror.

"Silly, trolls don't wear boots!"

"Hugh, I hate this!"

"You're all right."

The footsteps were coming nearer. Suddenly someone

started whistling.

"It's the tune Ninian was singing," said Jean. "Where did I hear it before?"

Whoever was coming was almost there. They saw a figure emerge from the gloom. Then it stopped dead at the sight of them and stood staring and silent.

Nobody spoke.

"Hallo," said Hugh at last.

The figure turned and gave three sharp whistles and at once more feet came running over the rocks. Before the Stewarts could turn, the narrow cave was full of men. The one that had appeared first came forward.

"I told ye Flatfish Bay was no a guid place to anchor," he said.

"Duncan!" gasped Fiona.

"What is this place? What are you doing here?" asked Sandy. Jean stopped, clutching Hugh's hand.

The men behind them started muttering in Gaelic, not loud enough for the Stewarts to hear what was being said. Duncan went over and joined them, effectively blocking their way out.

"Look here, Duncan, what is this?" Fiona was getting impatient. It was dark and cold in the cave and it must be late too. She wanted to see what happened farther up the path, but there were some more men there.

Duncan came over to them, his hands in his pockets, his cap still over one eye.

"What for did ye come prying in here?" he asked angrily. "Ye couldna' be content wi' the caves in the bay but ye must come in here."

"Well, we didn't know there was anything here," said Fiona indignantly. "Anyway, what is this? Are you smugglers or something?"

"No!" Duncan snapped. He looked worried and stared at them for some time, biting his lower lip.

"What happens at the end of this path?" asked Sandy,

unable to keep silent any longer. "Can't we go and see?"

"Ye'll do what you're told." This was one of the other men, a broad dark fisherman with a beard. Jean thought he looked awful, like a pirate. She was hating this: luckily Duncan was there. Duncan, however, did not seem very pleased about it. He turned back to the other men.

"What'll we do with them?" he asked in Gaelic. Their reply was too low to hear.

Hugh felt there had been just about enough of this. He wished Ninian had been there as he did not feel equal to tackling the five fishermen single-handed. There were probably more, too, in the back of the cave, whatever else there might be. He wished to goodness they had never stumbled on this gully. Fate had been against them finding it until Fiona had suggested that hair-raising climb along the cliff. He was certain that these men were smugglers but the question was what would they do with them? Nothing obviously — and yet?

Apart from the low murmur of voices and the pouring of the burn there was no sound in the cave. The steady long-spaced drip of water from the slit in the roof only accentuated the silence. The Stewarts shivered.

One of the men lit a cigarette and the sudden rasp of the match made them jump. They turned to see a dark scarred face under a peaked fisherman's cap lit red by the glow of the match. So far all they had seen of the gang looked horrid.

Fiona could bear it no longer.

"Look here, Hugh," she whispered, "what are we going to do? Are they smugglers? Won't they let us out?"

"Honestly, Fiona, I don't know. They won't do anything to us, but it's frightfully unlucky that we should have found this place. Heaven knows what they want. Can't you hear what they're saying?"

"No, something about a Chief. I can't really hear," said Jamie, straining his ears.

Meanwhile they seemed to have come to some decision, for Duncan was walking towards them.

"You're to come with me," he said abruptly, and started off towards the dark passage.

"Look here," Fiona was annoyed. "What is this? Why won't you say? You know we won't tell. You can't just lead us away, we won't go."

He looked round.

"I'm sorry but you canna help coming," he said. The men were advancing and one took hold of her arm.

She shook it off angrily and scowled at Duncan.

"You beast, you'll find you can't do this to us," she said.

"Come on, Fiona." Hugh dared not take her arm. "We are in their hands; it'll be all right."

"D'you think I'm afraid, then?" snapped Fiona.

"Yes!"

"What, of them? A miserable party of fishermen who dither about and can't make up their minds? Not likely!" She hunched up her shoulders and strode after Duncan. Hugh grinned in the dark.

Luckily the path was smooth as it was impossible to see anything but the vague shape of the person in front. Gradually the cave got lower and the burn beside them was down in a channel cut deep in the rocks.

"Mind the stepping stones," said Duncan, and the Stewarts had to pick their way in the gloom across the water. It was damp and smelly here and the air seemed stagnant. Jean had never hated anything more. Duncan might be leading them straight into a deep pit for all they knew. No one but Ninian knew where they were, and even he had only a rough idea. He would not have a chance against all these men.

At last the cave widened again and became large and roomy. There were several lanterns hanging from the ceiling and propped on ledges. The air was much better here and it seemed quite dry but there was a strange smell.

Hugh felt it was vaguely familiar but could not decide what it was. There seemed to be large things built against the walls and the glow of a fire came from the farthest corner. Someone was stoking it and an iron shutter slammed. The burn seemed to be coming in from the roof over their heads, but there was no time to peer about for Duncan was hurrying them on. A gap showed in the ceiling above the fire, but it was not large enough to light the cave.

Duncan stopped in a corner and Fiona behind him could see there was a rough wooden door in the wall. He knocked but there was no answer so he pushed it open.

There was a small low room inside with a hurricane lamp hanging from the ceiling. A table and chair were in the middle of the room, and an oil stove. Against the wall was a cupboard with several whisky bottles and glasses on the top. The table was covered with papers, a few books and a dirty plate and cup and half a loaf of bread. In the far corner was what looked like a bed.

"Chief's no' in," said Duncan to the men. "They'd better wait until he comes."

"Aye, they canna do any harm," said the bearded man. They filed out, leaving the Stewarts alone.

"Hoy," cried Fiona. "Duncan, come back, you can't leave us here, it's getting late!"

The young fisherman put his head round the door.

"Ye shouldna' hae come prying," was all he said. The door shut and a chain was rattled across it. The Stewarts looked at one another.

Ninian watched them walk off across the bay. Then he stood up and punted the dinghy into the deeper water. He whistled in time to his rowing and again it was that strange tilting tune; he still could not remember where he had heard it.

Half-past six: He hoped the others would not be long. He could see them standing by the Stack looking helplessly up at the cliff. Then he turned and saw *Fauna* over his right shoulder. He pulled on the port oar and bumped gently alongside. By the time he had climbed on board and made fast the only remaining figure in sight was Hugh, spread-eagled against the black rocks.

He dropped down into the cabin and stood looking at the Primus for a minute or two, wondering what he should cook. Perhaps, after all, something tinned would be easier. He went on into the cabin. The table was strewn with charts and the star map and some drawings of Jean's. Two letters, addressed and sealed up but forgotten, were shuffled in amongst them. He pulled out the log. Fiona had written up the last few days, but last night's journey was unrecorded. He had written the times down on a piece of paper and now copied them neatly in. This took some time and when it was done he picked up the chart and studied the coastline beyond the Stack. There were several small gullies drawn in, but nothing that looked very exciting. Surely the others would not be long. Ninian leant back and opened the cupboard behind him. Their larder was still well stocked and a row of tomato soup tins caught his eye. That and bully beef and the lettuce and tomatoes they had bought at Faraway would make a good dinner, especially if they finished up with raspberries and tinned Devonshire cream. He piled them up on the table on top of the papers. It looked an awful lot, but they were sure to be hungry after a long walk. Actually he had never known them not to be hungry. He peered through one of the scuttles: there was no sign of them on shore. It was after seven now, but he knew they would never think of the time. He might as well start opening the soup though and cutting up the lettuce. The evening dragged on.

A slight chill breeze sprang up and ruffled the sea. The sun had dipped beyond the Hebrides, but the sky still held the memory of pink and gold, and a slender cloud like a fish hung on the horizon. There was no sign of the others anywhere along the coast. Soon it would be dark and they had no means of signalling to Ninian, nor would they be able to climb back along the cliff.

"Bother them," he said, leaning on his elbows out of the hatch. He had exhausted all means of entertainment alone on *Fauna* and was getting distinctly bored. It was no use rowing ashore either, because he could not land anywhere except at the far end of the farthest bay. He tried a shout, but there was no answer, and he thought probably that his voice had not reached the shore.

At nine o'clock he became desperate.

Something must be wrong, because not even Fiona in her maddest moment would have left him so long without some sign. She would have sent one of the boys back with a message if they had found anything exciting. The tide was half-way in. He decided that he would row round to the far side of the Stack and tie the dinghy up there. Then he could set off along the coast and he was sure to meet them somewhere.

Ninian filled the hurricane lantern and lowered it into the dinghy. He pulled on a jersey and stuffed a new box of matches into his pocket. On second thoughts he threw down a coil of rope and jumped after it. Slowly he rowed ashore.

It was not yet dark, but the shore was an indistinct blur and looked nearer than it was. Luckily it was still calm and he rowed slowly along until he came to a place where he could tie the dinghy and leave it without it getting too bumped.

As far as he could see, the tide did not come in as far as the cliff, but left a narrow shelf of rocks above high-water mark. He slung the rope on his shoulder and took up the lantern. Might as well give a call before starting out.

"Fiona! Hoy, Fiona!" he shouted, but there was no sound but that of the sea against the rocks and the low rumble of it in the subterranean cave.

The lantern did not throw much light in the underground room. The rocky ceiling seemed to press down and great shadows loomed from every corner. The heap of bedding looked like a crouching animal, Jean was sure that a man was lying there, but she dared not go across to see. She and the two boys were standing round the table, Hugh was over by the door. Fiona crossed to him.

"Hugh," her voice was low, she put her hands on his arm. "Hugh, is it all right?"

He squeezed her hand.

"Yes, they can't do anything to us."

"No, but honestly, Hugh?"

"Honestly, Fiona. They wouldn't dare. Besides, you know Duncan. I wonder who their Chief is?"

"Perhaps we shall know him too. I didn't recognise any of the others, but it was pretty dark."

In the dim light he thought she looked pale.

"Fiona?"

"Yes?" His hand on hers was large and comforting.

"Don't worry, it really is all right."

"I'm not worrying — silly." She dropped her hand and wandered over to the cupboard. It was locked and the bottles on it were empty. One of the glasses had dregs of whisky in it. She tilted it round — it was white instead of amber and smelt very strong. As she tipped the glass an idea came to her. Hugh saw her frown and sniff the liquor again and then push back her hair in the same way that Ninian did.

She put down the glass and came across to the table.

"What are all these papers?" she asked, sliding her hand though a pile.

"Bills, mostly," said Sandy. "Bills for stores and petrol, and here's one for rope. Nothing much."

Fiona nodded and picked up a book. It was the same Pilot Book that they had. It opened at the part about their coastline and had several passages marked. She flicked over the pages, and again it opened, this time at the Hebrides. She picked up another book: Buchan, and under it a well-worn copy of *Wuthering Heights*. Fiona began to wonder what this Chief would be like. So far she approved of his choice of books. She pulled out one whose blue corner showed from under a pile of papers. *The Spirit of Man,* and an almost dirtier copy than her own. *Alice Through the Looking-Glass* came next and the last book of all was a thin old copy of some of Yeats's poems. Some she knew and, reading them, forgot where she was.

> "I went into the hazel wood
> Because a fire was in my head."

What kind of man was this smuggler who read Bronte, Buchan, Carroll and Yeats and the *Spirit of Man*?

Jamie rattled the door. It was firmly chained and no one came to shout at him.

"What will Ninian be thinking?" wondered Jean.

"Yes, Ninian; anyway, he knows vaguely where we are," said Sandy.

"He'll get caught just the same, though," objected Hugh.

"Perhaps he'll bring the rifle," suggested James.

"They'll be watching for him. Duncan knows he's with us. They won't give him the chance of going for help, they'll stop him." Jean sounded tearful.

"Never mind." Hugh put his arm round her. "You can take it from me that they won't hurt him."

"I say, I think this is pretty good fun." Sandy had recovered from his momentary fright and was ready for the next encounter. "I've never met real live smugglers before, not knowingly, anyway."

Fiona raised her head.

"They're not smugglers," she said.

"Well, what are they, then?" asked Hugh. "What are they doing here?"

"Making whisky," said Fiona slowly. "Making whisky and selling it in the Hebrides."

At that moment the door chain rattled.

CHAPTER XI

FERGUS
Sunday, 15th August

INSTINCTIVELY, as the chain fell back, the Stewarts drew closer together. Then the door swung open, inwards.

A man stood there, the light from the cave behind throwing him into silhouette. He was medium-sized and slim, with broad shoulders under a fisherman's jersey. He wore high boots and a cap like Duncan's, pulled over his eyes. He stood for a minute, hands in his pockets, watching them. Then he came into the room.

No one spoke.

He walked over to the cupboard, and as he passed the lantern they could see his face. It was thin and dark, no colour in it under the tan. A stubble of bristle over his cheek and jaw made him look almost swarthy. His nose was long and slightly arched and his chin too was long, with a cleft in it. The cap he wore was pulled down too far for them to be able to see his eyes, but his hair was dark and curly and needed cutting badly.

They stood watching him, waiting for him to speak. Fiona could feel her heart pounding and her mouth was dry. She wished he would say something so they could get it over and she would know their fate.

The other men stood silently in the doorway, gazing into the room. She could see Duncan amongst them and felt slightly reassured. He had been their friend for a long time and would not let anything awful happen. She turned to see what the others were doing. The man was tilting one bottle after another, but they were all empty. He pushed the last one aside and groped in his pocket for a key. Then he bent forward and unlocked the cupboard and brought out another bottle.

Still no one spoke.

The only sound was the far-away drip-drip of the sweating walls and the gurgle of liquid as the man poured it out. Fiona could hear the neck of the bottle rattle on the glass as he tipped it. He filled it half full, then drank and refilled it. Then he turned to them.

"What am I to do with you?" he said softly. He had only the faintest trace of Highland accent and his voice was stern and slow.

"There is only one thing to do," said Fiona, recovering slightly.

"Indeed there are more than one." The man raised his glass, looking appreciatively at the lantern through the liquid in it. Then he drank it, and they saw his throat move in one gulp. Fiona got the impression that he was not with them at all, so far away was his mind.

"What are you going to do?" she said, her voice shaking in spite of her.

"Keep you here until we have moved, or —" He paused, looking from one to the other. "There is one missing," he said, raising his voice to the men at the door.

"Not for long," they told him. "Murdo and Alec are outside."

"Good! We must wait for him."

"No!" It was Hugh who spoke. "No, you must let us go now, at once. You have kept us here long enough, as if this was some silly story. You can't keep us, you know that; you'd get found out."

"Who knows that you returned from Faraway? Your bodies, washed up on the shore, would look just the same if they were drowned to-day or yesterday."

Fiona stared, fascinated, at the man. She could not believe that this was real. No one could be saying such things in such a calm, slow voice, yet his mouth was very hard and she could not see his eyes. She watched him fill

"WHAT ARE YOU GOING TO DO?"

the glass again. Behind him, on the walls, a huge shadow moved as he moved. She heard Jean gulp and reached out a hand to take hers.

Hugh stepped forward. He was getting angry.

"Now, look here," he began.

The man was on his feet, the bottle and glass on the table and Hugh's wrist in his hand all in one movement.

"This is my cave," he said, and Hugh was powerless in his grip. "These are my men."

"And who are you?" that was Jamie, his hands tightly clenched in his pockets, outwardly calm.

"I am Fergus," said the man. "Where I am my word is law." Looking at that stern mouth they could believe it.

"And now go." He dropped Hugh's arm and his voice

was harsh suddenly. "Duncan, Rody, take them out and bring them back when you get the other one."

"Where are we going? I want to stay here," said Jean, nearly in tears.

"Get out, go!" Fergus leant over the table and banged it. Two men came out of the group and pushed them towards the door.

"Come on," said Duncan, "you're all right."

Fiona looked back.

Fergus was sitting down, filling his glass. She could just see his mouth set in a hard line, and his dark cleft chin below it. Then he tilted his head and drank.

Duncan led them through the main cave, across the burn and into a recess by the fire. There were benches here and a table scattered with mugs and plates.

"You can sit here, but dinna let me find you wandering about," said Duncan, and left them. He obviously did not want to get into conversation with them. It was a difficult position for him, being friends with both the Stewarts and Fergus.

Fiona sat on the edge of the table, her feet on a bench. The others sprawled round her.

"Who do you suppose he is?" asked Jamie at last. "I think he's awful," Jean shivered. "He's so fierce."

"How on earth can we get out of here?" Sandy peered out into the gloom of the cave. He could see the forms of men moving about in the half light there. It would be impossible to get past them.

Hugh was speaking.

"D'you really think this is a distillery?" he asked.

"Sure of it," said Fiona. "That big brick thing is the still: you can see the fire glowing underneath it. I'm not sure how these things work — Ninian would know — but I think the burn runs down into a tub to cool the whisky."

"What shall we do?" asked Jean anxiously. "We'll never

get out. I'm sure that man'll kill us."

"I do wonder who he is," said Hugh slowly. "Did you see him drink down that whisky? He must have a throat like leather."

"Fergus — Fergus." Fiona repeated the name, trying to think if she had heard it before. In spite of his stern mouth and jaw he looked sad, but as though he had an awful temper. What would he do with them? Who was he? And where was Ninian?

"I'm hungry," said Sandy. "I wish they'd hurry up and decide what to do. How late d'you suppose it is?"

"Nearly ten," said Hugh. "No wonder we're a bit hungry."

"Listen!" That was Jamie, and they all turned their heads in the direction that he was looking. Somewhere down the cave were the clatter of footsteps on the rocks and a murmur of voices. They stood in silence, waiting.

Three figures loomed into sight out of the murk of the cave.

"Ninian!" shouted Fiona. "Ninian, we're all right, are you?"

"Yes, where are you?" In another moment he was among them. Jean rushed to him and he put his arms round her. Over her head his eyes met Fiona's. He smiled.

"We've done it this time," he said.

The men went off to tell their Chief that they had caught the remaining Stewart.

"Have you found out anything?" asked Ninian.

"Yes, Fiona thinks it's a whisky distillery, and I'm beginning to think so too," said Hugh.

"I'm sure it is," said Fiona. "It's a perfect place for one."

"There's a creepy man called Fergus," said Jean. "He stares at one and one can't see his eyes because of his cap and he says things in a horrid slow voice. I'm sure he's beastly.'

"I'm not," said Fiona. "But the thing is, quick, before

they come back: what are we going to do?"

"There's only one thing to do," said Ninian. "Let's help him." Sandy and James breathed a sigh of relief. "Our ancestors used pot stills, so why shouldn't we? And whisky's outrageously expensive. You don't mind, do you, Hugh?"

"I'm not sure." Hugh spoke slowly. "There's a pretty severe penalty if we're caught, much more than for poaching. Why do you always have to do something against the law?"

"Oh, Hugh, don't be stoogy," said Fiona impatiently. "Think how thrilling it'd be, helping them."

"Thrilling if we're caught," said Hugh.

"Idiot," said Fiona, scowling at him.

Hugh turned to Ninian. "Are you set on this?" he asked.

"Yes, but there's not really much alternative," said Ninian, smiling.

"All right," said Hugh, and laughed. There was something about the Stewarts that made one want to join in with them whether one approved or not.

"Perhaps Fergus won't want us," he said, as an afterthought.

"Well, if we can't help at least we needn't tell," said Fiona, smiling at him again.

"Here they come," whispered Sandy, and two of the men came round the corner into their cave.

"Will ye come wi' us?" said the tallest, and they followed him out and across the burn.

Fergus was still at the table, his hands full of papers. He was looking through them despairingly, and when the Stewarts appeared in the doorway, put them down with a sigh of relief. He had taken off his cap and they saw that his hair was brown, lighter than Ninian's, and when he looked up in the dim light his eyes were dark under straight dark brows and the lids drooped over them. They stood staring at him and he stared back and nobody smiled or made a move. At last he raised his eyebrows.

"Well?" he said, in that same hard voice. "Hurry up, I'm busy," and he scowled at them.

"We're with you, of course," said Ninian. "You're distilling whisky, aren't you? You can trust us not to tell and we'd like to help if we can."

For a moment or two Fergus stared from one to the other, summing them up, and they stood very still.

Then he smiled, with one corner of his mouth, and his dark eyes were suddenly friendly.

"I hoped you would," he said, and stood up. Impatiently he brushed aside the pile of bills.

"I'm not really busy, not at all," and again his mouth went sideways. "I'm sorry to have been so rude, only you might not have come in with me. You must be ravenous, too. Duncan, Rody!" he shouted. "Get some supper, plenty of it, and bring it in here."

"You do distil whisky, don't you?" asked Fiona.

"Yes, you are the first people to have found this place for goodness knows how many years." He came from behind the table. "You know my name," he said, "but I don't know yours."

They introduced themselves.

"I must show you the still after supper," said Fergus. "It's rather ingenious the way the burn comes down in just the right place."

Standing among them, his hands in his pockets, he seemed some one quite different to the man they had first met. And yet when he was not smiling his mouth and jaw still had that hard line and the scowl came back between his eyebrows.

"I like your books," said Fiona.

"Do you?" Fergus turned to her, smiling. She saw that his eyes were very dark blue, under their drooping lids. Seeing her stare, he laughed and rubbed a hand across his chin.

"If I'd known you were coming I'd have shaved," he said.

"That's all right," said Fiona. "Ninian and Hugh were going to grow beards, but after a day or two they looked so awful they had to shave them off!"

Duncan and Rody appeared just now with a heap of plates and mugs and a big cauldron of stew. They laid the table by simply putting the plates on top of the papers and left the stew on the ground. Another man came in with a loaf and some butter and cheese and a big pot of tea.

"Come on, sit down," said Fergus, and they did not need telling twice.

Fiona pulled Yeats out from under her plate and as she ate, turned over the pages. Suddenly, she came to a very dirty page with a poem she had never seen before on it. She looked up at Fergus as she read and saw him watching her. He smiled.

> "Who will go with Fergus now,
> And pierce the deep wood's woven shade,
> And dance upon the level shore?" he said.

"It's nice," said Fiona, and thought, "He likes the same things as I do."

The stew was very good indeed, and they ate until they could eat no more.

"I suppose we ought to be getting back," said Fiona at last, looking at Jean whose eyes were becoming rather large.

"You haven't seen the cave yet," protested Fergus.

"We'll come back to-morrow," said Ninian, standing up. "I'm longing to see everything."

"Well, taste it before you go," said Fergus. "That's the next best thing."

He picked up the half-empty bottle and poured out three glasses full.

"D'you like it?" he asked Fiona.

"No, thanks."

Fergus picked up his glass and looked round.

"Slainte," he said, and Hugh and Ninian drank theirs down. It made them blink for a moment, but Fergus never turned a hair.

"I'll go with you to the end of the cave," he said. "Can you get back all right or would you like some of my men to take you?"

"No, I left the dinghy by the rocks. I hope she's still there," said Ninian. "Probably smashed up, but still."

Fergus led them through the cave and down the tunnel. They hurried after him, to keep in the dim patch of light that his lantern threw on the walls and rough floor. He walked too fast for them, knowing instinctively where to put his feet. Ninian and Hugh, their heads still singing from the whisky, had to concentrate to keep from tripping up.

At last they were out on the stony beach with the cool wind fresh in their faces after the close atmosphere of the cave. It was a perfect night: the stars seemed nearer than usual and twice as large. A light showed from the boat tied up against the quay and the water was shivered with gold as the wind blew the star's reflections into a thousand pieces. They could hear waves breaking on the rocks beyond the harbour, but in here it was still.

"You'd better take the lantern," said Fergus, handing it to Fiona. "You'll need it on the rocks and you can bring it back to-morrow."

"What about you, though?" asked Fiona. "The cave's pitch dark."

She could just see Fergus smile.

"I can find my way in there dark or light, drunk or sober," he said. "I think I know every stone."

"Come on," said Jean. "It's cold."

"All right." They crossed the beach and climbed on to the quay.

"Come early to-morrow," called Fergus.

"We will," answered Sandy. "Gosh," he added, "I am longing to see that cave."

"It is exciting, you know," said James. "We are lucky."

They called "Good-night," and climbed on in silence until they reached the corner. Then they looked back.

Fergus was a dark blob against the grey beach.

"He is a queer man," said Jean.

"Yes." Fiona lifted the lantern to pick the best way on. "Yes, he is."

"He seems rather a good chap," said Ninian.

"He looks awfully sad," said Fiona.

CHAPTER XII

WHISKY CAVE
Monday, 16th August

THEY woke early next morning, so much was the thought of Fergus and the cave in their minds.

At seven-thirty the tide was going out and breaking in calm smooth waves on the beach. It was another glorious day, no clouds in the unbroken blue sky. The sun was warm already and shone on the sea like molten gold.

"We'd better not go to the cave too soon," said Fiona, dishing out cornflakes. "Fergus doesn't look the sort of person who gets up early."

Ninian shook a large spoonful of brown sugar over his plate and stirred it in.

"I wonder what we'll do," he said. "I wonder if there's a cargo to run across to-night and whether we shall be allowed to go too?"

They had all been thinking and dreaming the same the whole night.

"Of course we will," said Sandy. "Why not? He ought to be glad of some extra hands."

The sun streamed in through the portholes in golden bars and specks of dust danced up and down in them. The cabin was in its usual early morning disorder; bunks piled high with blankets, pyjamas and clothes on the floor, the table a jumble of cups and plates, a loaf of bread, butter and coffee, on the ledge by the sink a packet of cornflakes and a large pink ham. This Ninian cut into slices, neither too thick nor too thin.

"Before we go," said Fiona firmly, folding over a piece and skewering it with her fork, "we simply must tidy up in here and sweep it out and dust it. We've left it for days."

"And the deck needs doing, too," added Ninian.

"What about the engine?" asked Jamie, knowing that the girls would do the cabin and he and Sandy the deck while the other two looked on.

"And the bilges," added Jean.

Ninian did not answer, but Fiona caught his eye and said: "Yes, you know perfectly well that they should be done."

"I know they should," said Ninian.

It was surprising how quickly everything was done. Down in the cabin the dust fairly flew as blankets were shaken out and bunks re-made. Fiona brushed the floor and Jean dusted and filled the lanterns and they both did the washing up. Water poured past the scuttles as James and Sandy scrubbed the deck and swearing and grunting came from the engine-room, and the rattle of tools on metal.

In the end Sandy and James had the best of it. No one could see what they were doing, so, having swilled water up and down for a bit they sat on the cabin roof, talking smugglers and watching the gulls clamouring round the Stack and a flock of sheep walking slowly along a tiny path on the cliff. The beach was white against the rocks and oyster-catchers were searching amongst the seaweed, whistling to each other and skimming low down along the water's edge, and then settling again. Sandy and James felt incredibly well and happy. They leant lazily on their elbows, and compared the brownness of their legs and arms. There was nothing in it.

About half an hour later the hot faces of Fiona and Jean appeared in the hatch, one with a pan full of dust, the other with the colander of scraps.

"Lazy beasts," said Jean, when she saw the boys. She flopped down beside them, wiping her face. Fiona threw the dust into the sea and watched it sink slowly.

"Wonder if the flat fish will like it?" she said to herself, and looked closely to see if she could spot one. But there was nothing but fronds of gently waving weed and flickering shoals of sand-eels. She looked over at the Stack, thinking of Fergus, that strange man, and his boat, so beautifully hidden in the gully. There was no sign of any one, no smoke, nothing to show that such a place as the Whisky Cave existed. Again she wondered who he was, where he came from, what he did when he was not smuggling: why he did it, only that she could guess. It was for the same reason that they had poached last year, not the obvious reason but the determination behind it to live in a way different to the ordinary humdrum way of getting up and eating and going to bed again. Fiona, looking up the cliff and not seeing it at all, knew there was so much more in life than that. She supposed that, like every one else, she would have to bow to it in the end, but for the moment grab, while she could, Fergus and the chance of escape that he offered.

"What are you thinking?" asked Hugh's voice behind her.

"Oh, nothing." Fiona started out of her day-dream.

"Fergus, wasn't it?" said Hugh.

"Well, yes, it was."

Hugh looked at her, wondering whether or not to be jealous. She turned and saw his face, serious and rather apprehensive, and smiled at him, but he was not reassured.

"What do you think of him?" he asked.

"I don't know. He's a queer person," said Fiona. "You couldn't tell what he was like until you knew him better."

"Look," cried Sandy, "there's someone on the cliff!" He pointed and they saw a figure standing above the Stack.

"Fergus," said Jean.

He waved his arm and they heard a faint shout across the water. "Come on, lazy bones!"

"Come on, then," cried Ninian, and slammed the engine hatch.

James pulled the dinghy alongside, and they jumped in.

"We can row right up the gully," said Jean, delightedly, "and tie up alongside their boat." She trailed her hand in the water — it was almost warm.

"WHAT DO YOU THINK OF HIM?" HE ASKED.

"If it gets any hotter we shall burst," said Sandy. "I should think this is the hottest day this summer."

"So should I." Ninian rested on the oars and wiped his forehead.

They were nearing the Stack and even on such a flat calm day as this, waves were breaking round it and the dinghy bobbed up and down on the swell.

Ninian rowed them round the corner and up the gully between the Stack and the cliff. It was always a gloomy place and the sun was not yet high enough to penetrate it. It was like rowing into a cool tunnel, and the birds peered down suspiciously at the boat from their ledges and the thick black

217

fronds of weed heaved in the water like octopus tentacles and seemed to want to hold the boat and suck her down.

"Think of the night we spent on the Stack," said Hugh, looking up at it. "We never guessed there was any one near."

"They were probably spying on us," said Fiona. "There are plenty of places among these rocks."

"I wonder if they did. How creepy," said Jean.

By this time Ninian had rowed them up to the second gully. They could see Fergus up on the cliff above them, and Jean waved to him. Jamie, up in the bows, was navigator and called directions to Ninian. The channel itself was deep but narrow and there were plenty of rocks on either side to run into.

"Fergus must be a pretty good pilot to get up here in the dark," grunted Ninian, as Jamie shouted to him, "Hard aport!" for the third time in quick succession.

They rounded the second corner and before them was the calm bay and the smugglers' boat tied up to the jetty. Fergus had run along the cliff and come down by some secret path and he was now standing ready to pull them alongside.

"It is a perfect place," thought Fiona, as she looked round at the high walls that sheltered the smugglers' harbour. It was so cut off from the sea that it might have been some inland loch, but for the bunches of yellow seaweed on the rocks and the everlasting clamour from the sea birds on the Stack. Also there is an indefinable smell about the sea and rocks, and there was always the hush-hush of waves beyond the gully.

The even creak and splash as Ninian rowed filled the harbour with noise, and Fergus, on the jetty, called to them to come alongside his boat.

"Careful of the paint," warned Jean. "He must have only just done it."

Hands were stretched out to prevent the dinghy

bumping, and Fergus himself took the painter and tied her up.

He was looking almost respectable this morning, for he had shaved and his hair was smoothed down. But he had the same old jersey on and stained trousers and sea boots. Without his cap he looked younger and his forehead was white from always having worn it.

"Good-morning," he said, when they were all on deck. "It is a good morning, too. Come on, because there's a lot to do."

"Oh, what?" asked Jean, who, now she could see Fergus in the broad light of day, was hardly afraid of him at all.

"Well," Fergus climbed up on to the jetty and brushed the dust off his hands, "well, there's the cave to show you, and how we make the whisky, and what we do with it, and then —" He stopped.

"Then what?" said Jamie.

Fergus looked at him with his queer twisted smile.

"I'll tell you later," he said, and they could not persuade him to say any more.

"How long has this cave been used?" asked Ninian, as they crossed the well-worn rocks by the burn. From the smooth deep groove in them it looked as if there had been smugglers here for ages.

"I don't really know how long," said Fergus. "My grandfather and his father used it, and probably their fathers too. It had been out of use for some time when I came here, but it didn't take long to put it right. No one had tampered with it at all."

"Where do you live?" asked Sandy. Fergus hesitated a moment before saying:

"I live in Lewis, opposite here. Either there or in the *Star*."

"The *Star*!" said Fiona, surprised. "What's that, an inn?"

Fergus laughed.

"No, it's not; it's my boat. That's not her full name, she's really called *Wandering Star*."

"What a lovely name for a boat," said James appreciatively. "How did you think of it?"

Fergus looked at Fiona, and quoted:

" ' For Fergus rides the brazen cars,
    And rules the shadows of the wood,
    And the white breast of the dim sea,
    And all dishevelled Wandering Stars,'

only she's not a bit dishevelled really, but very neat. I must show you when we get back."

They were in the cave by now, walking beside the burn that ran deep in the rocks.

"It's cold in here, after outside," said Jean, shivering.

"It'll be warmer by the vats," Fergus said. "There's a fire there."

Although he seemed perfectly friendly and pleasant, Jean kept close to Ninian. After all, Fergus might suddenly change his mind and kill them all, or take them out to sea in his blue ship and drop them overboard. She had not forgotten, either, the whisky he had had last night. He might suddenly become very drunk and think of some awful torture for them. She would rather stay near Ninian.

Fergus led them on, through the low passage and out again into the big main cave. Here some of the men were sitting, eating a late breakfast and talking. A delicious smell of bacon filled the air and wreaths of blue smoke curled upwards into the roof and out of the holes. To-day these were blinding patches of light and the sun was so strong that it almost lit the cave. The Stewarts could see far more clearly the shapes of the strange buildings in the corner where the fire was.

"Well, I suppose you know how whisky is made?" began Fergus, "because if not I'd better tell you roughly so that you will know what these things are, and what we do."

"We don't know," said Fiona. "At least, I don't. Do you, Ninian?"

"Only vaguely. I'd like to, though."

"All right, I won't go into details, I'll just give you an idea." He turned to the men and called to them to go out and tidy up the *Star*. "And look out for coastguards," he added, an unnecessary reminder which he gave them every time.

"Well, to start with," said Fergus, sitting on the end of the table, "whisky is made of barley. We get that by the bushel and ship it over in the *Star*. Before it can be distilled it has to be malted."

"D'you do that here, too?" asked Hugh.

"Yes, we do it all here. It's such soft water that it doesn't take so long as in most places. You see how lucky we are, having the burn running right through the distillery instead of having to have water laid on. Anyway, you soak the barley for three or four days and then leave it about ten days to germinate. That's on an open floor, of course, and then it has to be withered: that takes a day or two. By now it's called Green Malt and has one more stage to go through and that is the drying. We do it in a kiln over peat as that's the easiest thing to get, besides it gives it much the best flavour, at least I think so.

"Next comes the mashing." Fergus pulled out a packet of cigarettes and handed them round. He lit one himself and went on, "You grind the grain coarsely and put it into a mash tun with hot water. It has to be stirred for two or three hours and then left to settle. Then nearly half the water is drawn off, that's called the 'worts', which you keep to add later, and you add more hotter water and go through the same process twice more with the last lot of water almost boiling. It's then cooled and fermented with yeast and the foam is scooped off. This takes about sixty hours and at the end of the time you must keep the fermenting vessel covered up. After all that the mash is ready to be distilled."

"Isn't it whisky yet?" said Jean in surprise.

"Goodness, no," Fergus laughed. "It takes a long time."

"How much whisky does a bushel of barley make?" asked Ninian.

"And how big is a bushel?" added Fiona, who was vague on that subject.

"A bushel's fifty-six pounds," said Fergus, "and you get about two and a half gallons of proof spirit from it — that is, undiluted whisky.

"It's white when it comes out, isn't it?" said Jamie. "What makes it brown?"

"Caramel," said Fergus. "But we don't bother to colour ours; it tastes just as good without."

"What happens next?" Hugh wanted to know the end.

"Next comes the still." Fergus pointed to the glowing fire in the corner near the burn. "You heat the mash over the fire. The vapour runs down a long tube which goes through the tank where the burn comes in. The water cools it off and what drips out of the end of the tube is pure whisky, strong enough to blow your head off, or nearly.

He led them over to the fire which was burning in a big stone kiln.

"The still is inside," Fergus explained, and they could see the condenser attached to the head of the still and running down to a tank.

"The burn water is a marvellous cooler," said Fergus. "We never have to worry about turning off the tap or anything."

They watched for a moment or two the colourless liquor dripping out of a spout at the bottom of the tank.

"And that's the whisky," said Fiona slowly. "It's a perfect place for it here. Whoever made it was jolly clever. Don't you ever get found out?"

"No." Fergus shook his head. "No one ever thinks of looking behind the Stack."

"What about from the land," said Sandy. "The cove

would be quite easy to find. Any one walking along the cliff couldn't help it."

"Whoever would walk along the cliff just here?" asked Fergus. "No one ever comes here; it's too far for trippers, and the crofters, if they know about it, are all friendly."

"What about trawlers in Flatfish Bay? Don't you ever meet them?" Ninian rubbed his hand along the warm stones of the still.

"Yes, we have to keep an eye on them, but they don't come in very often. You were the worst trouble; no one ever came to Flatfish but you."

Hugh was still thinking of the whisky.

"Surely you don't sell it neat?" he said.

"No, we dilute it a bit," said Fergus. "And keep it, too, in barrels."

"Was that what you were drinking last night?" asked Hugh.

"Yes." Fergus's stern face was back, his brows drawn together, his mouth hard. "Yes, I was. Why not?"

"No reason," said Hugh quickly. "I just wondered."

Sometimes Fergus could be unbearable.

They walked over to the little room where they had been locked the day before:

"I can't believe it," said Fiona. "I can't believe that this has been going on and we never knew about it. Last year we might easily have seen you."

"We saw you," said Fergus. "We saw you and watched you and wondered when you would go."

"You might have told us," said Fiona. "Think what fun we could have had if only we'd known."

"You might not have been friendly," said Fergus, with his crooked smile. "We didn't know."

"No, I suppose not." Ninian looked up at the ceiling. "Did you carve this room out or was it here already?" he asked.

"It was here," said Fergus, pouring himself a drink. He

looked at Ninian and Hugh and raised his eyebrows, but they shook their heads. It was too early in the morning for whisky as strong as Fergus's.

"What'll we do to-day?" asked Sandy, looking round hopefully. Surely, now that they were friends with a real smuggler, something exciting was bound to happen.

"Yes, what?" asked Fiona, not looking at Ninian for fear he should squash her.

"When are you running your next cargo across?" said Jamie, and spoke the thought that was in all their minds.

Fergus looked at them and then at his glass. Slowly he tilted the liquid round and they could see his mouth half smiling. Someone's foot scraped on the rocky floor and a small stone, rattling down from the roof outside, sounded like an avalanche. Just as Fiona could hardly bear it another moment and was going to speak, Fergus lifted his head. "To-night," he said in the silence. "After dark and before the moon rises. We are taking it across to Lewis and coming back with barley."

Still no one spoke and Fergus grinned.

"Any of you like to come?" he asked.

"Yes, oh yes! May we? Oh, Fergus, what bliss! Are you sure you don't mind?" They all spoke at once.

"No, of course not. Providing you don't make a noise," said Fergus, standing up. "Now let's go and see the *Star*."

"Will there be room for all of us?" asked Sandy.

"And what about *Fauna*, will she be all right?" Fiona's conscience was suddenly pricked.

"Yes." Ninian frowned. "We can't leave her out in Flatfish alone; there's no shelter there."

"Bring her in here, then," suggested Fergus. "There's room for her to be tied up behind the *Star*."

"Oh, yes, do let's," cried Jean. "She'll be lovely and safe in here. But what happens in a storm?" She had been meaning to ask this for some time. "When there are really big waves, surely you can't get behind the Stack?"

224

"No, we can't," Fergus pushed the cork into the whisky bottle. "We have to be either inside or over in Lewis if there's a storm. But there won't be to-night, not with this sky."

They were out in the main cave by now and following Fergus down the tunnel. Already they were beginning to know their way and remember where not to step and where a rock tripped you up. They even remembered to duck their heads and had no need to advance with hands outstretched and one foot groping ahead. Fergus, of course, walked at his usual speed, or faster if anything. Sometimes Fiona thought he must be able to see in the dark like some kind of animal. He was queer, she thought, not really like an animal but more like a troll in disguise or the Green Laddie. He had strange eyes that made one feel creepy sometimes when one looked up and found him watching one. Thoughts of Dr. Jekyll and Mr. Hyde flashed through her brain. Or perhaps he was a ghost. More likely a troll, though. Then she remembered his eyes were blue, and surely no troll or half-human animal had blue eyes.

By now they were out of the tunnel and in the half-light of the outer cave. Through the entrance they could see the bay still wrapped in unruffled calm.

"Bother," said Fergus: "We want a bit of wind to-night."

"D'you sail across or use the engine?" asked Hugh, and when Fergus said, "Sail," Jamie's happiness was complete.

It was so hot and bright outside that it made them blink, coming out of the tomb-like cave. Gulls were crying from the cliff, and the burn, released from its journey in the deep channel, splashed and gurgled over the rocks on the beach. One of the men was whistling over on the jetty and two or three more of them were sitting with their backs against the cliff, talking and smoking and lazily mending a net. It was so calm and peaceful that for a moment Fiona wished they could sit in a row along the cliff, or better still climb up until they had found a ledge carpeted with thrift and grass, and there stay all day, talking and arguing and watching the gulls, and the tide creep in and out, and feel nothing but the sun on their backs and the scratching of grass on their bare legs. Indeed for a moment she stopped and looked up at the cliff, searching for a comfortable place, but Sandy called to her to hurry and she ran after them, determined to be first on board. Anyway, we might have lunch up there, she thought.

The tide was right up and the *Wandering Star* was almost level with the jetty. As they came up to her Duncan climbed out of the hold and vaulted on to the pier.

"Everything all right?" asked Fergus.

"Aye," said Duncan, "though I'm no' sure aboot yon engine. She was aye pig-headed."

"Well, we shan't need her," said Fergus. "At least, I hope not."

"Why not?" asked Jean.

"We only use it in an emergency," Fergus told her. "And that generally means —" and he raised his eyebrows.

"Oh!" said Jean.

Although the *Wandering Star* might be a smuggler's ship and run cargoes of whisky across the Minch at night, this morning in the sun she looked so clean and innocent that the Stewarts found it difficult to believe that to-night they would be sailing in her, silently, to land in Lewis.

Her decks were scrubbed white, her long tiller was clean and varnished as was the big hatch over the hold. The tan sails were furled and the ropes coiled as neatly as a battleship's. The name *Wandering Star* was painted in small black letters on her stern with her registered fishing boat number.

"Come on, let's go below," said Fergus; pushing back a hatch that ran smoothly, unlike *Fauna's*. A ladder led down into the fo'c'sle.

"Of course," Fergus told them, "to make the *Star* perfect I should do away with the hold and convert it into a big cabin. This one's terribly cramped. But that'll have to wait," and he sighed.

"Don't you like smuggling, then?" asked Sandy in surprise.

Fergus was silent a moment and then said:

"Sometimes I wish for a nice peaceful orderly life."

"Well, don't then," said Fiona firmly. "That's much too easy to get. Lots of people would envy you living like this. I do for one."

"Do you?" Fergus looked at her. "Do you really?" and although one corner of his mouth smiled his eyes did not. Then he turned.

"Well, this is where we live," he said.

The fo'c'sle was small and cramped for the living place of so many men. Two bunks, one above the other, were built each side and a table was fixed in the middle. A stove, sink, cups and plates were in one corner, while a cupboard and built-in drawers were in another.

"I'm the only one who really sleeps here," Fergus told them. "But if we want more space there's plenty for hammocks when the hold is empty."

"What happens aft?" said Hugh.

"There's a very small cabin with two bunks and then the engine," said Fergus. "This is the main living-room though."

"It's beautifully tidy," said Fiona, surprised.

Indeed the whole ship was spick and span, which was strange considering the mess of Fergus's room ashore.

"Who cleans it?" asked Jean.

"The men," said Fergus, with a glint of his old look, and Fiona was reminded of what he had said when he first met them. "Where I am my word is law."

He showed them the rest of the boat; the hold, so unfamiliar in its lack of fish scales; the "pig-headed" engine; the little cabin aft.

"Is it difficult steering with such a long tiller?" asked

227

Ninian. "I've never sailed anything bigger than *Black Swan.*"

"You can try to-night if you like," Fergus said. "If there's any wind," he added.

"She is lovely." Jamie had lost his heart to the *Wandering Star*. He ran his hand down the mast and Fergus, watching him, saw that here was someone who loved the boat as much as he did. Jamie, too, would be given a chance to steer to-night.

"It must be nearly lunch time," said Sandy at last.

"Yes, where shall we have it, here or in *Fauna?*" asked Ninian.

"You must come too," Jamie told Fergus.

"Let's go and have it on the cliff somewhere," said Fiona quickly. "Let's lie and bask in the sun. There's nothing to do till the evening, is there?"

Fergus shook his head.

"That's a good idea," he said. "I know a lovely place, too."

"Why not bring *Fauna* round now," said Hugh. "Then we shall be sure she's all right and not breaking loose or anything."

"Yes, and there're the lobsters. D'you like lobsters, Fergus?" asked Jean.

"Do I not?"

"Let some of us get them up and the rest bring *Fauna* round," suggested Sandy. "Can we cook the lobs quick enough for lunch, Fiona?"

"We can try, if we get any. Come on."

"I'd better come too: you'll need a pilot up the gully," Fergus said, and they dropped down into the dinghy.

On the way out to Flatfish they decided that Fergus, Ninian and Fiona should bring *Fauna* round while the other four hauled in the pots and rowed back to the harbour.

Luckily *Fauna's* engine was not as obstinate as the *Star's* and started straight away. Fiona went below to put on a pan for the lobsters, if there were any, and then returned to the deck to watch the course Fergus took and to try and memorise it. Ninian, too, stuck his head out of the engine-room to watch the way up the gully.

Over her shoulder Fiona could see the twins pull in the first pot, but they were too far away for her to see if there was anything in it.

Fergus, meanwhile, had called to Ninian to slow down, and was steering carefully up the first gully, the swell all but sweeping them on to the rocks. The noise of the engine sounded louder than ever in the narrow passage and drowned the roar of the subterranean cave, but nothing could overcome the noise of the birds.

With a calm, almost bored face, Fergus spun the wheel and *Fauna* wound her way along, sending waves splashing up on the rocks.

"The tide's so high that it's easy getting in," remarked Fergus. "If you ever have to do it yourselves, I advise you not to try at low water. There are all sorts of jagged rocks just under water, and none of them are marked."

At last they were out in the bay and Duncan came running to catch their rope. He dropped two fenders made of old tyres over the edge of the jetty to stop *Fauna* from getting scraped. Beside the *Star* she looked very shabby and Ninian decided then and there to buy some paint next time they came to a shop.

"Give me a shout when lunch is ready," said Fergus, climbing ashore. "I've got some things to see to in the cave."

"All right," said Ninian. "We won't be too long, I hope," and they laughed.

They watched him walk off across the rocks.

"Funny how fast he goes and yet he doesn't seem to stride," said Fiona.

"Umn." Ninian rubbed his forehead with an oily hand and left it black.

"I'll get some lettuce and tomatoes and things ready," said Fiona. "What shall we have for a sweet?"

"Peaches or something," suggested Ninian. "They're the easiest to eat out of a tin really."

Presently the silence was scattered by Sandy's well-known voice carrying on a fierce argument. Ninian turned and watched them come into sight round the corner. The bows of the dinghy were piled high with lobster pots and he could hardly see the crew.

"Did you get any?" he yelled, so loudly that Fiona below, not expecting it, nearly jumped out of her skin.

"Yes, three," Jean's voice shrilled across the water.

"Did they?" called Fiona, who had not heard the answer.

"Yes, three," repeated Ninian. "Hurry along that Primus."

"It's nearly boiling," protested Fiona, giving the stove another pump and making it roar.

The lobsters were the first on board. Their stay was very short, for hardly had they been put down than the water boiled and they were plunged in it.

"How long will they take?" asked Jamie, piling the pots up on the deck.

"Twenty minutes to cook," said Fiona, "but they should be cold. Perhaps we can dip them in the sea."

"It'd take too long to get them absolutely cold," said Ninian, "but still, I expect they'll be delicious."

"I know, I'll put some eggs in on top." Fiona disappeared into the cabin. "As long as they don't crack they won't taste lobstery."

She hunted and found seven. There was not much room in the pan, but she dropped them in hopefully. Already the shells of the lobsters were red. They would not take much longer.

Jean came down to help her pack the knapsacks and Sandy shouted to them to throw up his bathing things.

"I'm so hot and a bathe would be just right before lunch," he said.

It was such a good idea that the remainder of the food

was hurriedly stuffed in, the pan was left bubbling, and all six were over the side as soon as possible.

"Gosh, it's cold!" gasped Jean, spluttering after her dive.

"Lovely!" Sandy and James were having a splashing competition and nearly drowning every one else as well. The harbour was churned up like soda water. Fiona swam out of reach and found that, by putting her face under water, she could see the bottom, miles below, and fish and fronds of weed. Turning on to her back, she floated lazily, her hair washing round her like a mermaid's. The sun was so bright that she shut her eyes against it and nearly fell asleep while waves splashed on to her face and all sounds were deadened by the water over her ears. Eventually her feet were tweaked by Hugh and, struggling back to wakefulness, she just managed to avoid being ducked.

They swam back and climbed on board. Sandy, who had dressed first, was sent along the rocks to give Fergus a shout. The others slung knapsacks stuffed with food and books over their shoulders and walked slowly ashore.

Fergus joined them at the mouth of the cave.

"This way," he said, and they followed him along the rocks to the right. Presently he began to climb up what looked like the sheer cliff, but as they got nearer they could see small ledges of rock that formed steps up to the top.

When Hugh reached the summit he turned to look back at the bay. It lay below them, perfectly smooth, the two boats moored to the jetty. The gully was completely hidden from him by the high cliffs round it, so that the harbour did not look at all like the sea but like an inland loch.

Ahead of them the ground stretched on towards the villages — hummocky ground, rising slowly to a few hills behind Inverasdale. It was bleak and desolate looking land, no trees or any break in the thin brown grass.

"Beyond that hill is the Green Laddie's Loch," Jean whispered to Hugh. She whispered in case Fergus should hear and laugh at her, but without turning he said:

"The Green Laddie has been dead for more than a hundred years."

"Not dead," said James, "only disappeared."

"Where do we go now?" asked Ninian.

"Down here." Fergus led them on towards the sea. The cliff line wound along, black against the water, and from where they stood they could see the lighthouse sticking up like a white pencil. There were two or three hundred yards of ground between them and the cliff, the same rough boggy ground with tufts of bog cotton and sun-dews and occasionally a yellow bog-asphodel. Lumps of grey rock stuck up through the peat and became more and more frequent as they neared the edge.

"Not a particularly nice place for a picnic," thought Jean, and felt disappointed in Fergus.

However, he had not stopped but was climbing down over the cliff. They watched him slither on to a narrow ledge.

"Goodness," said Jean. "It looks most unsafe to me."

"It's all right," Fergus called up. "Slide down and I'll catch you."

Obediently they dropped over to find a strong arm behind them to prevent them falling backwards into the sea. The ledge continued along the cliff for about thirty yards and then broadened out into a wide platform cushioned with grass and thrift.

This was big enough to hold them all comfortably, being about twenty feet by fifteen. The sides were smooth, rising out of a fringe of boulders that had by degrees broken off the cliff and rolled down. There was no way out but that by which they had come in, and below them was a sheer drop to the sea.

"Oh, what a super place," cried Fiona. "You do know of wonderful places, Fergus. How do you find them?"

Fergus laughed. "I just do," he said.

They flopped down on the grass and lay watching the sky

and the white wings of gulls. It was absolutely still and peaceful, and if they had not been so hungry they would have gone to sleep.

Sandy, of course, was the first to sit up and demand food. The lobsters were produced, much to Fergus's surprise, and the hard-boiled eggs were excellent and did not taste at all of fish. They sat in a circle and dipped the lobster into a bag of salt.

"It's delicious, even if it is warm," said Hugh, with his mouth full.

"It's hardly warm at all," protested Fiona. "Not warm enough to notice, anyhow."

"Lovely convenient pig-bucket," said Sandy, throwing lobster and egg-shells into the sea. "You don't even have to get up."

They lay on the ledge all afternoon talking and reading and lying back, half asleep. The sun seeped into them, half intoxicating them, and the sea played a lullaby on the rocks, softly but without ceasing.

Fergus told them more about himself; how he lived on an island off Uist; how his brothers, the Black Maclouds, lived on Lewis and distributed the whisky.

"Have you always lived on your island?" asked Jean.

"No, not for long."

"Where did you live before?" Sandy rolled on to his back and shut his eyes.

"Oh, different places. With my brothers or wherever I wanted to."

"Who looks after your island when you're not there?" asked James.

"I get someone, or else leave it to look after itself."

"D'you live alone there, then?" said Hugh.

"Yes."

"What's it called?"

"Hanga, the Island of Hanga. And now tell me something about yourselves."

At about four o'clock a trawler passed close in to Flatfish Bay. For a few minutes they thought she was going to stay and fish, but she went on down the coast. They lay prone on their ledge, pressed into the grass and, although they could see the men on her decks plainly, no one thought of looking at the cliff, and when she was out of sight they sat up again.

An hour or two later Fergus opened his eyes and yawned. For a while he lay watching the sleeping Stewarts and wondering whether he had done a mad thing in asking them to come with him. He had not much experience of children like Jean and Jamie — they might shriek at the wrong minute or talk or fall overboard. They looked so very young asleep. He turned to look at the others and found Fiona watching him.

"Shall we wake them?" she whispered.

He did not answer, but said: "Will they be all right to-night?"

"Who, the twins? Yes, they're all right, even Jean, though she is young."

He nodded and, turning, tickled Jean's nose with a piece of grass. It had the result of waking them all, as Jean sprang at Fergus in revenge and they rolled on to Sandy.

"Don't fall over the edge," called Fiona, retreating to a safer position.

Fergus sat up and brushed the grass off himself.

"It's time we were going," he said, "and I'm getting hungry, too."

They gathered up the remains of the picnic and followed him up the cliff.

Only the flattened grass and a half-gnawn crust of bread showed that the smugglers had lain there all afternoon.

CHAPTER XIII

TARANSAY
Monday Night, 16th August

IT WAS quite dark. The Stewarts, waiting in the mouth of the cave, could just make out the line of the cliff against the sky. Even the stars were hidden by clouds which had come up with the darkness, as had a light wind from the south-west.

It was silent too, in the bay, for waves did not break here, but only rippled on the rocks and occasionally splashed a little.

Fergus had told them to wait and they were doing so, but it seemed hours since he had left them and they began to think that perhaps he had changed his mind about to-night or else that something had happened and they could not go. They dared not talk except in the lowest of whispers. Fergus had told them not to make a sound. They were glad they had brought thick jerseys and oilskins for they could not move about to keep warm.

Sandy suddenly gave a stifled sneeze which made them all jump, and before they had recovered from that a voice behind them said:

"Not much longer, sorry to be such an age."

It was Fergus, but they had not heard him approaching and neither did they hear him go. The smugglers could move as silently as deer and it was creepy, never knowing whether they were just behind you or not.

Fiona strained her eyes into the darkness of the cave but she might as well have been looking at a black wall. She could hear the others breathing beside her and shifting their feet on the rocks. Someone opened the hatch on the *Star* and for a moment a light shone out and was gone again. It was so still she could hear her heart beating, so dark that the sea, the cliffs and the sky were one and the two boats were not seen at all. "After dark and before the moon rises," Fergus had said. He would have to come soon.

"Someone's coming," whispered James, so low that if their ears had not been keyed to catch the lowest murmur they would never have heard him.

A faint glow of light was visible at the far end of the cave. As it came nearer they saw it was a lantern, heavily shaded.

"Ready at last," said Fergus, putting it down on a ledge. He stood with them while the men filed past, each with a keg on his shoulder. They were only visible as they passed the lantern, and in the dim light looked sinister, like pirates, with their dark stern faces and caps pulled down. Again Fiona had to remind herself that this was not a dream. They really were passing her, these silent men, and soon she was going out with them to sail across to Lewis on a sea as black as ink.

Faintly they heard the bumps as the kegs were lowered into the hold. The men came back for a second load, and then a third, while Fergus watched and counted to see that nothing was left behind.

It was impossible in the bay to tell how strong the wind was. Duncan was sent up the cliff to find out and came down saying it was fine and steady, blowing from the south-west.

"I shouldn't like to climb up there in the dark," Hugh whispered to Fiona, and she agreed.

Fergus, who had vanished out of the cave, was back again.

"Come on," he said, "we must be as quick as we can. I don't know how long these clouds will last and I want to be as far out as possible before the moon comes through."

The Stewarts stumbled across the rocks after the dim lantern. They could faintly see the outlines of what they were stepping on and so managed to keep their balance. The jetty felt like tarmac, although Sandy managed to trip up on it.

A creak of ropes told them they were near the *Star*. The tide was coming in, so there was only a short drop on to her deck.

"Don't fall down the gap," hissed Fergus, as Jean nearly disappeared into the sea between the boat and the jetty.

Once on board they could hear the low voices of the men, the creak of warps as the tide rose and the lap of water between the *Star* and the rocks.

"This way," whispered Fergus, shepherding them aft. "Stay here until we get outside."

"How do we get out? There's no wind in here." asked Fiona.

"They tow us." Fergus jerked his head in the direction of a splashing of oars and squeak of rowlocks astern of them.

"Why don't you use the engine?" asked Sandy.

"Too much noise suddenly in a still place," said Fergus.

The ropes were thrown down on deck. With a jerk the dinghy took the strain and slowly the *Wandering Star* moved off into the night.

They could see the figures of men standing on the jetty. "Don't they come with us?" asked James.

"Not to-night. I've got my crew." In the darkness they could not see him smile.

"D'you mean us?" said Ninian.

"Yes, of course. You can sail a boat like this, can't you?" asked Fergus.

"Yes." They could not say any more. An adventure like this exceeded all their dreams.

"The twins stay here: the rest of you go forward to haul up the mainsail directly we get clear of the Stack," said Fergus. They vanished into the darkness, feeling their way by the hatch over the hold.

They were in the gully now: the tall sides loomed black above them, leaving a thin channel of blue that was the sky. Already they could hear the waves much louder on the rocks outside, and phosphorescent beads of spray were splashed up by the men as they rowed. The wind came coldly round the last corner of the gully, and the Stewarts grasped the mainsheet ready to haul directly they were past the Stack. Waves came racing in and splashed up on deck. Already they could feel the *Star* beginning to dance slightly. In another minute they were out and Fergus was shouting to them to haul up the mainsail. It was hard work, for the *Star* had a long gaff and the great sail creaked and flapped as it crept up. The men in the dinghy tossed the rope back on deck, the sail filled, Fergus put the tiller down and the *Star* heeled over.

"We shall have to tack," said Fiona, joining the others in the stern.

"Yes, but it's a good wind," Fergus said. "We couldn't have a better one really. Any one like to steer?"

Every one wanted to, so he gave Ninian the tiller first.

"Keep her like this with the wind on your left cheek," he said, "and I'll send one of them to relieve you."

Hugh and Sandy were sent to coil up the ropes and the others went below. "There's no point in us all staying on deck," said Fergus. "We shall have enough of it by to-morrow and some of you had better try and get some sleep."

"Why?" asked Jean.

"Well, we shall be up all night," Fergus told her. "We go straight to Lewis, unload, and get back before morning."

"You'll have to be up all night, though," said Fiona.

"I always am," said Fergus.

The two boys came clattering down the ladder.

"Gosh, it's light down here," said Sandy. "It's the blackest night I've ever seen — perfect for us, of course."

"Yes, we're lucky." Fiona balanced on the end of the table.

"What about some supper? We didn't have any." suggested Fergus.

"Oh yes, let's," said Jean. "What is there?"

"Eggs and bacon. Who's the cook?"

"Fiona," said James. "I say, can't I go back on deck?"

"Yes, if you want to."

Jamie scuttled up the ladder and out into the night. He shut the hatch behind him and stood for a moment in the blackness, trying to get his bearings.

The wind rushed past. Over his head the sail curved farther than he could see and he groped his way along to Ninian.

"Hallo," said Ninian, "is that a twin? This is a super boat to steer, James. I wish *Fauna* had a sail."

"What's that big tiller like?" asked Jamie.

"All right. She is a beauty, this boat. It's pretty decent of Fergus to trust us alone with her. He thinks she's marvellous, too."

"I wonder what he'd have done if he hadn't taken us on his side. D'you think he really would have killed us?"

"No, not really. But goodness knows what he would have done, probably thought of something awful."

"I wonder how fast we're going?" said James, after they had sailed for some time in silence.

"You never can tell at night," said Ninian. "Probably simply licking along."

"It feels like it anyway."

Down in the cabin Fiona was making scrambled eggs. Everything was so neat and clean that she felt afraid of dirtying it. How Fergus must have looked with horror at *Fauna's* cabin which, however much it was tidied and scrubbed, always seemed to look the same. However, she cracked the eggs into a basin and beat them with a fork, while Jean fried some bacon.

"This is very grand. Two Primus's," said Sandy. "We can make tea at the same time."

"And I'll cut some bread," said Hugh.

Fergus said nothing, but leant against the bulkhead watching them and smiling.

The supper was delicious, and when he had finished, Fergus went up on deck to relieve the two boys. He took Sandy with him and left him there after a minute or two. All the Stewarts had been used to boats for as long as they could remember, and although the *Star* might be larger than their own she was no more difficult to steer.

"Where do you keep your drying-up cloths?" asked Fiona, as Fergus came down the ladder. "And also, d'you want any more tea?"

"Yes, please," said Fergus, and he showed her the cloths in a drawer.

He sat on the end of the table, the hot cup between his hands, watching the others dry the cups and plates and put them back in their places. Now they had got used to him the Stewarts thought he looked much younger — when they were talking to him anyway. Sometimes Fiona would look at him and he was miles away, his face so stern and sad that she hardly recognised him. He was a very changeable person and would flare into one of his tempers for no reason that they could see. That kept them a bit in awe of him: they never knew what he was going to do next. He was laughing at the moment at Jean, trying to hang a cup on to a high hook.

"Let me do it," said Fiona. "You'll only break it."

"I wouldn't have — but still," said Jean.

"Who wants to go to bed?" asked Fergus, finishing his tea. "We've got another five hours at least, as well as the way back. We shall never get back in the dark unless the wind freshens, which is a bore."

"There's room for four of us," said Jean.

"Two can go in one if necessary," Fergus told her. "They're terribly wide."

"Jamie and Ninian have had their spell," said Hugh, "so they could go."

"And Jean," added Fergus. "She looks a bit sleepy."

"That leaves one bunk," said Ninian.

"I'm not in the least tired," said Hugh and Fiona together.

"Well, there's no need to go if you don't want to." Fergus threw his cigarette end out of the hatch and overboard in a way that showed he had done it hundreds of times before.

"Let's stay up a bit then," said Fiona.

The others took off their sea-boots and jerseys and climbed into bed in shirt and trousers. Jean and James were one side, Ninian at the bottom on the other.

For a little while Jean lay with her eyes shut, snuggling into the coarse blankets. She could hear Ninian grumbling that they scratched him, and wondered whose bunk she was in. Probably some filthy smuggler, and she started to itch at the thought.

"Whose is this bunk?" she asked.

Fergus looked up. "Duncan's," he said, and smiled.

"Oh," said Jean, feeling comforted. Duncan was fairly clean as fishermen go.

She lay awake, listening to the others talking, although she could not hear what they said. The lantern hardly lit her bunk, but in the gloom she could see that Duncan had pasted pictures on the boards all round. They were mostly of film stars in varying stages of undress. She tried to make out who they were but could not recognise any. She turned over and pulled the blankets up. Facing her was the photograph of an ordinary girl — not a film star at all. Sleepily Jean thought she looked nice and wondered if she was Duncan's wife.

"I wonder if he wakes up or goes to sleep on this side," she thought, and decided that he went to sleep on it.

Fergus and Fiona and Hugh sat round the table, talking. The *Star* was heeling over and Fergus, sitting on the port side, had to brace his feet against the table leg. The lantern hung crookedly and anything that was put on the table immediately rolled on to Hugh and Fiona. The smoke from a pipe and cigarette wreathed up and round the lantern and three flies buzzed round it, burning their feet whenever they landed.

Fiona, leaning back, listened to the others arguing and decided that this night was one of the special ones that must be remembered afterwards. There were times like that, times that you could keep and look back on as something more than usually good. She was sure there would never be another time like this, at sea in a smuggler's boat with a cargo aboard. Soon she would be on deck, alone in the night, steering the *Wandering Star* in a black sea to an unknown port. She could imagine it so clearly that she did not hear Fergus talking to her.

"Fiona, hoy, Fiona! Wake up," he said.

"Sorry." Fiona came back to the cabin.

"Look, if you go to bed now I'll wake you when Sandy comes down."

"All right, then I go on deck next?"

"Yes."

Hugh boosted her up to the bunk above Ninian.

"Whose is this?" she asked, like Jean had.

"Mine," said Fergus, and she slid down between the blankets.

There were no pictures pinned round this bunk, although there looked as if there had been one that you would see as you turned over. There was something pencilled there too, but it was not light enough to read it. Fiona fell asleep quickly, still wondering who Fergus was and what made him seem different to other people.

Fergus woke her much later.

"It seemed a pity to wake you so soon," he whispered. "So Sandy got in with James, and Hugh's on deck now. Come on, it's a lovely night."

"Has the moon come out yet?" asked Fiona, struggling with sleep and sea-boots.

"It's still cloudy, but she comes through occasionally."

She pulled on her oilskin and followed him up on deck. It was cold after the warmth of the blankets, but it was worth it.

The moon was hidden behind a bank of clouds that moved fast and allowed her to shine between them as they passed.

They had gone about in the night and were sailing on the port tack. Fiona could see Lewis close to them and the lighthouse at the entrance to Faraway shining away on their right.

"All right, Hugh?" said Fergus.

"Yes," he yawned. "A warm bunk seems bliss at this moment, but wake me when we get there."

Fiona took the tiller and he disappeared down the deck.

"We shall be there quite soon," said Fergus. "Would you like me to take over then?"

"Perhaps you'd better. What sort of place is it?"

"A bay. We don't come alongside but have to anchor. You see, if we built a jetty people would wonder why in such a wild place."

"Do we row the cargo ashore?"

"Yes." Fergus seemed uncommunicative so Fiona did not bother. She offered him some chocolate out of her oily pocket and they shared it. He lit a cigarette afterwards and it made a tiny point of light in the pitch blackness. When he drew on it she could just see his lips and chin and his nose jutting out. He could see nothing of her but the dim oval of a face.

"I have loved to-night," said Fiona.

"Have you? It's not over yet."

"No, thank goodness. It's funny: this must be an ordinary night to you, but it's a super one for us."

"Is it? I'm glad. What a pity you didn't find the cave last year."

"We shouldn't have had time to come often: we were too busy."

"I might have come and helped."

"Yes, you might." Somehow she could not picture him in anything else but thigh-boots and fisherman's clothes.

Guessing her thoughts, he said: "I'm quite a good shot with a rifle."

They were sailing close to the shore now and he peered forward into the darkness. A cloud sailed past the moon and she shone clear for a moment, lighting up the coast. Fiona saw the water stretch on ahead into a narrow bay.

"We're here," said Fergus abruptly. He put his arm behind her and leant on the tiller. The *Star* turned slightly.

"Shall I go and fetch the others?" asked Fiona, over her shoulder.

"Yes, do. Be quick, and mind your head, I'm going about."

Ducking, Fiona ran forward along the deck. The boom swung, creaking, over her head and the sail flapped and struggled for a moment before filling. She dived down the hatch, shook the others violently and rushed back on deck.

"Fetch the lantern," called Fergus. The *Star* was gradually losing way on the sheltered water of the bay. They were slipping along quietly, the water rippling under the forefoot. After its brief glimpse the moon was hidden again and it was very dark.

"Light it," Fergus told Fiona, as she stood beside him, "and hide it under your oilskin. Ninian and Hugh, stand by the main sheet, twins and Sandy go forward and keep your eyes skinned for a buoy: the boathook's on the deck."

There was a patter of feet as they ran forward. Fiona stood by him, her oily wrapped round the lantern. She felt like the Spartan boy with the fox and wondered how soon it would start to burn her. Anxiously Fergus looked at the sky. The moon was hidden but the edges of the clouds were pale gold and presently she came into sight again. In the short moment Sandy saw the buoy.

"On the starboard bow, Fergus!"

"Down the mainsail!" Fergus's voice was urgent, and it came down with a clatter and a rush. He put the tiller hard a-starboard. The *Star*, scarcely moving, turned slightly and Sandy, hanging over the bows with James sitting on his legs, was just able to reach the buoy.

"Well done," said Fergus, as it was hauled on board. "Be as quiet as you can, every one." This to Ninian and Hugh who were struggling with the mainsail. They waited breathlessly but the loch was silent. Fergus lifted his head and gave the cry of a gull three times, but there was no answer.

"What's happened?" whispered Fiona.

"They're late, or we are," said Fergus. "Show the lantern once or twice."

Fiona lifted her oily and left it fall three times and at the third there was an answering flash from the shore.

"Show it again," said Fergus, and when she had done so the lantern on shore answered.

"It's them all right." Fergus sounded relieved. "Got that mainsail stowed? Good. Then open the hatch."

The hatch over the hold came off in sections and by the feeble light of Fiona's lantern the boys soon had them off.

"One of you in the hold pass the kegs up to the others," said Fergus. There was such authority in his voice that they did not think of questioning him. As Hugh dropped down into the darkness there was the sound of oars in the water and a voice said:

"*Wandering Star?*"

"Yes, is that you, Rory? I've got a new crew to-night, the Stewarts from Carrick and young Murray from Corriedon."

"You're mad, Fergus," said the voice. "They're all children. We'll have the coastguards here in a day or two."

"Oh no, you won't," said Fiona furiously.

"And girls too," said Rory, grabbing at the gunwale.

"They're all right." Fergus lifted the lantern and held it above Hugh who was groping in the pitch darkness of the hold.

Rory Macloud jumped lightly on to the deck. In the darkness he looked huge, taller than either Ninian or Hugh and very broad. He bent down to pick up a keg from the pile beside the hold and tossed it to someone in the dinghy as if it weighed nothing at all.

"That's my young brother," Fergus told Fiona. "I'll introduce you when we get ashore: there's not time now."

They worked like slaves to get the whisky unloaded. Jamie and Jean between them could carry a keg and they staggered across the deck with them to drop them into the dinghy. Sandy joined Hugh in the hold and the giant-like Rory took a cask under each arm and did the work of two men. When the dinghy was loaded he and Ninian took a pair of oars each and rowed her ashore.

"How many trips?" asked Fiona, rubbing her hands, which felt sore after handling the rough kegs.

"Three, I think. Why, are you tired?"

"No, of course not," said Fiona scathingly. She was determined to show Rory Macloud that girls were not to be as despised as he seemed to think.

Brief flashes of moonlight showed for an instant the bay ringed by tall hills. Clouds still raced across the sky, but it was sheltered where they were, and anyway they were working too hard to get cold.

The dinghy had to be loaded three times as Fergus had said before all the kegs were ashore. Then Rory came back for the crew.

"You must be hungry," Fergus said, as they waited for the dinghy.

"We are, and thirsty," said James.

"We'll remedy that ashore," said Fergus. "I say, d'you want very much to get home to-day, because it's after three o'clock. I think we'd better stay here and go back to-night." He looked at Fiona, who said:

"Where should we stay?"

"Oh, with us, there's room enough. I'd start back now, only I don't want to get in by daylight."

"We don't have to get back." Ninian loomed out of the shadows, his hair standing on end. "As long as *Fauna's* all right."

"Do let's stay," added James.

"Good." Fergus spoke as if it was decided. The squeak of rowlocks announced the return of the dinghy. "Hurry along there, Rory," he called. "We're hungry."

The boat bumped alongside and Hugh, who had taken turns with Ninian at the oars, grabbed the gunwale.

"Do we leave the *Star* alone?" asked James.

"Yes, but I'll be back to stay the night in her," said Fergus.

"Oh, can't we?" cried Jamie.

"You'd be more comfortable ashore."

Jamie was silent.

"You can if you like," said Fergus.

"I would like, if you don't mind."

"I'll be glad to have your company."

"Come on," urged Rory from the dinghy, and they jumped down.

They were about one hundred yards from the shore and the boat fairly flew along with the load so much lighter than the piled kegs of whisky. Rory seemed to know where to go in the dark, although, of course, his back was towards the shore. Afterwards he said he could see the hills against the sky across the loch and he knew just how many strokes to row, having done it more times than he could count.

The keel grated on the rocks and Sandy, in the bows, jumped ashore. He wondered, in the air, what he would land on, and slipped a bit on the seaweed. The tide was coming in but the loose stones were still wet, and they slithered about as they landed.

"This way," said Fergus.

It was still dark but a group of men were vaguely visible.

They were carrying the last of the kegs up the beach on to the dry rocks. To the Stewarts' surprise they heard the scrape of a horse's shoe and the snort as one blew its nose.

"Ponies!" whispered Jean.

"Yes, of course," said Fergus. "All proper smugglers have ponies."

Although they could not see him they knew he was grinning.

They had reached the end of the rocks and now stood on

"PONIES!" WHISPERED JEAN.

grass and heather. There were several ponies to the south of them, some of them breathing heavily after their climb up the cliff. Fergus was speaking.

"We've got six of them."

"Seven," interrupted Rory.

"Shut up. They carry four kegs each up the cliff and along the moor until they get to the lorry."

"Lorry?" said Jamie, in horror.

"Yes, it is a bit of a come down," said Fergus apologetically. "They really should go miles over the moors in single file with masked men with muskets on either side, but they don't."

"A lorry's much more convenient," said Rory, "as well as not being so conspicuous as a whole string of ponies."

The darkness was full of their snortings and the clink of bits and creak of leather. Hoofs stamped in the grass and occasionally grated on a scrap of rock, but they were wonderfully silent on the whole.

Looking back over the bay, Fiona saw the sky was gradually lightening. She yawned, suddenly tired after the strenuous night and began to wish for a bed even if it was in a croft and probably on the floor.

"Look! The dawn!" she said, and Fergus swung round.

"We must hurry. You've been slow to-night," he said to the men. "Is this the last load?"

"Aye, we'll be gone in a moment," said a small fisherman. He limped and Jean was convinced he must have been wounded in a brush with excisemen.

They started off up the cliff. It was too dark to see the path clearly and the Stewarts were constantly tripping over rocks. Jean nearly fell at one place and before she knew what was happening Rory had swung her up on to his shoulder.

"This can't be real," thought Fiona. "I'm not really doing this. I must have gone back a century or I'm asleep or something." She stubbed her toe hard on a rock but she did not wake up: it was real.

The path up the cliff seemed very long and steep. Goodness knows how far it was until they reached wherever these strange Maclouds lived. What sort of a house would it be? Probably a croft, black with peat smoke, and she would get half a box-bed with Jean.

Gradually it grew lighter and when at last they reached the top Fiona, looking back, could see the Minch beyond the hills and the black shape of the *Wandering Star* in the bay. Ahead of them, dimly, the line of ponies wound their way along the track, the click of hoofs on stone and the creak of leather betraying their whereabouts. Rory put Jean down and went off with them to superintend the loading of the lorry.

"Come on," said Fergus. "It's only a little way now."

The ponies were going inland, but they turned along the top of the hill and walked towards the sea. The ground sloped down and presently they found themselves on a rough track which was a relief after the thick bracken and heather. Below them in the water a peninsula jutted into the sea, a high one with sheer sides and a craggy top. As they came closer they saw that it was not a peninsula at all.

"Goodness, is that where you live?" said Fiona, in astonishment.

"Yes, that's my home, or used to be," said Fergus. His voice sounded sad. The sight of the Castle of Taransay always made him feel homesick.

They were on the beach now and crossing the narrow neck of land that joined the castle to the mainland. It was built on a peninsula and was so huge that it covered all the ground except for a few narrow strips of green that ran down to the water.

"Whose is it?" asked Ninian.

"My brother's," said Fergus, in his sternest voice.

It was too dark to see any details, but they could tell it was immensely old and strong as they passed under an arch into the courtyard. Fergus led them across it and pushed open a huge door. Far away there was the sound of barking and a rush of dogs' feet on a stone floor.

"Be quiet! Down!" shouted Fergus, and his voice echoed round the hall they were standing in.

Suddenly Fiona felt this was the creepiest house she had ever been in. There was a fierce, wild feeling about it as if there was much hate in it and no friendliness. There was a light shining through a door at the far end of the hall and by that she could see the three huge dogs, still rumbling with suppressed fury, that cowered under Fergus's anger. The hall was high and very cold and seemed to be bare of furniture. Fergus muttered something and led them quickly through the lit door and along a passage. The walls and floor were of bare stone and a single oil lamp gave the only light. Fiona wished that she, like James, was going to spend the night in the *Star*. Thank goodness Hugh and Ninian were here.

Fergus pushed open a small door and they entered a sitting-room furnished in moderate comfort and with a large peat and log fire burning. This gave sufficient light to show that the room was empty. It seemed to be both sitting and dining-room, as a table was laid in one corner and a sideboard covered with bottles stood against one wall. Above the fireplace was the portrait of a dark man in red velvet, a Macloud by his face. Fergus crossed to the fireplace and pulled a long bell rope. The Stewarts could hear it jangling in the silence of the castle. He bent down and lit a spill and from it two lamps. Fiona walked over to the window, which was small and set in such a thick wall that it was rather like looking down the wrong end of a telescope. The sky over the water was faintly grey but it was not light enough yet to see the hills of the mainland. She did not want to turn round and face the creepy atmosphere of the castle. Almost she wished they had never found the smugglers but were sleeping peacefully in *Fauna* at Flatfish Bay. It had been such a marvellous adventure too, and now she was hating it.

Fergus came and stood beside her. The others were at the far side of the room clustering round the fire.

"What are you thinking?" he asked.

"I was wondering why you don't live here." She turned to look at him and saw in the grey light that his stern face was back.

"My brother lives here," said Fergus softly. "He doesn't like Taransay: he wouldn't care whether he lived here or not, and I would give my soul for it."

"I'm sorry," said Fiona. "It must be beastly."

"Where I am my word is law." Fergus had said that and he could never live in a place with someone he did not like: one of them would have to go, and his brother could not go. Taransay belonged to him.

The door behind them opened and an old man came in. Fergus turned.

"We're all hungry, Murdoch," he said. "Bring lots of food and be quick."

"Yes." The old man shuffled out.

There were more footsteps outside and Fiona, watching him, saw his face turn to ice again. He moved away from her and a tall man came through the doorway. He was so tall he had to bend his head; he was big too, but not so big as Rory.

"My brother Colin," said Fergus. "And these are the Stewarts and Hugh Murray."

"How do you do? Have you joined our smugglers also?" The man smiled patronisingly, not looking at Fergus.

Fiona felt inclined to say, "You don't seem to do much," but instead she said: "Yes, we're the new crew."

"I hope Murdoch's bringing something to eat?"

"Yes, he is," said Fergus.

Colin came nearer the fire. Fiona could see in his face a resemblance to Fergus, but he was softer looking and lazy and his mouth was weak. There was nothing weak in Fergus's face. Colin lounged against the mantelpiece, his black head resting on the frame of the picture. He was one of the largest men and the darkest that she had ever seen. She could feel the hate like a bar between the two brothers and she spoke to break the spell.

"This is a lovely castle," she said.

"It could be," Colin said. "It's cold and damp and old-fashioned. There's nothing comfortable in it and it's far too large to be used and there's no money to make it any better." He sounded so sorry for himself that Fiona murmured, "Sissy!"

"I've seen it sometimes from the sea," said Ninian, "but I never knew who lived here. Has it always belonged to the Maclouds?"

"Yes, always, and no one knows how old it is."

Murdoch and a younger man entered at that moment with trays heaped with ham and cold grouse and venison.

"Come on," said Fergus, "let's start."

"I notice you don't include me," said Colin.

"You can't be hungry." Fergus carved a slice off the ham and handed it to Jean, whose eyes were as large as saucers.

"Did you get up when you heard us or hadn't you been to bed?" asked Jamie.

"I was asleep but not in bed," said Colin, pouring himself out a whisky. "We're night-birds, we Maclouds, we always sleep better by day."

Loud footsteps announced the arrival of Rory.

Fiona was glad. He was a sane and even-tempered person. The atmosphere was noticeably less tense when he came in. She had not seen him in the light before and as he was introduced she saw he was very like Colin, but with a much more childish face. He could hardly be as old as she was but he was far larger than Ninian and his hair was as dark as his brother's. They were well named the Black Maclouds, those two.

He grinned at them.

"Hallo," he said, crossing to the sideboard and carving an

enormous slice of ham. "I must say I think this crew is an improvement on the other, Fergus, although I can't think what made you do it." He filled his mouth to bursting point with ham and while he was chewing poured himself out a glass of beer. They were all too busy eating to talk, all except Colin. Fiona glanced at him. He was slouched back in his chair at the head of the table, an ornate carved chair with a high back, his lower lip pouting, his ill-contented eyes on Fergus. Fiona noticed with surprise that he was dressed in a shabby suit of tweeds. She had half thought he was wearing a kilt and velvet coat like the man in the picture, so much was the atmosphere of Taransay that of centuries ago.

The fire hissed as it caught a new piece of wood and a cake of peat crumbled into glowing red ash. The room was so silent, the atmosphere between the two brothers so tense, that the food seemed to choke Fiona. Rory and the others were unaware of it, or Rory, if not unaware of it, was so used to it that he took no notice. Colin sat still in his chair, a glass of whisky in front of him, his chin resting on one white hand, the other, a heavy gold ring on the third finger, ceaselessly sliding a knife round and round. Always his eyes were fixed on his brother, black and brooding in his white face. Fergus ate on, apparently unmoved by this scrutiny, but once Fiona saw him look up and give back a glance of such hatred she had not thought even he, with his fierce temper, could have given. There was something greater than Colin's loathing and Fergus's love for Taransay between them.

Then mercifully Rory started to talk of smugglers, of narrow escapes they had had, boasting slightly and very boyishly about his own part in the affairs. Fiona felt a glow of affection towards him for breaking the silence. He caught her eye and grinned at her and she could not help smiling back. He had such a cheerful face and was so large and yet so young despite his size.

They were soon, with the exception of the elder

Maclouds, talking and laughing, while the dawn crept up over the Minch and lit the room with a grey ghostly light. One by one they stifled yawns and laid down their knives and forks. Fergus stood up suddenly and turned to the window.

"I'm going down to the *Star*. Coming, Jamie?"

"Yes." James pushed back his chair.

"What about us?" asked Fiona, not wanting to be left with Colin.

"Rory will show you your rooms," said Fergus, looking at her. "You'll be all right."

"Aren't you staying?" asked Colin, with a sarcastic smile. Fergus did not answer, but crossed to the door as if eager to be gone.

"Sleep as long as you like," he said. "I'll be in the *Star* until the evening, then I'll come for you," and he was gone.

"Fergus," cried Fiona. She followed him into the passage. He stopped and turned.

"What is it?" he asked.

"I don't know." She felt rather foolish. "Colin — he seems so — so angry."

"You'll be all right. I said you would," Fergus took her hand. "Colin wouldn't dare do anything to any of my friends, I promise you. Good-night, sleep well, I envy you." He left her standing in the doorway and she turned back into the grey room.

"Come on," said Rory. "You must be tired. I am, anyway."

"Good-night," said Colin, still in his chair. "The beds will probably be damp, the windows are probably broken, there are no lamps and no hot water, but good-night."

"Good-night," said the Stewarts.

Rory led them along the passage, away from the hall, down another long passage to the right and up a narrow winding stair.

"We don't use the main part of the castle," he said, over

his shoulder. "It is jolly uncomfortable, as Col says, because most of it hasn't ever been touched. It's still a stronghold, not a house. But this part's all right."

At the top of the stairs a passage led back along the length of the castle. Stairs went winding up into the gloom and grey light filtered through small barred windows on the right. Left were doors of different shapes and sizes, and ahead the passage curved and dipped and ended in a flight of stairs.

"That's my room." Rory pointed to the first door. "You two had better be in here," and he ushered Fiona and Jean into a small room chiefly furnished with an immense double bed.

"You don't mind sharing it, do you?" he asked.

"No, of course not. I say, what a huge one, it's more quadruple than double," said Jean.

"The one next door is even larger," said Rory. "D'you think you three would mind all sleeping in it? It's easily large enough."

"Feigns be in the middle," said Ninian and Hugh.

"Hell," said Sandy.

They inspected the bed and agreed that it certainly was large enough for more than three.

"Good-night, every one," said Rory, and went back along the passage.

Fiona and Jean shut their door. The room was lit by the dawn and Fiona, crossing to the window, found herself looking down a sheer wall southwards across the Minch. There was such a deep embrasure that she had to crawl along it before she could see out.

"Lovely comfy bed after a bunk," said Jean sleepily. "Hurry up."

"Coming." Below the window, thirty feet down, was a narrow strip of green ending in the water. It was very still and there was no sound.

As she undressed she looked round the room. The walls

ran into odd angles and corners and even the ceiling was not level.   Furniture loomed out of the darkness: an old-fashioned washstand, a wardrobe, a dressing-table with a huge glass. She slid between the sheets: linen ones, very fine and smelling of heather. Something scratched her bare arm and, groping, she found it was a head of thrift. Sleepily, she smiled and held it in her hand: she had often found the same thing at home. The Maclouds, too, dried their linen on the hill.

A little while later she heard steps coming up the spiral stairs and passing her door. They receded up the passage, unevenly. Colin of Taransay was on his way to bed.

CHAPTER XIV

THE BLACK MACLOUDS
Tuesday, 17th August and Wednesday, 18th August

FIONA woke slowly, the sound of shouting and splashing in her ears. Drowsily she lay in the great bed with Jean still asleep beside her. She did not want to wake; she was too comfortable, but gradually sleep left her and she became aware of things; the sun, bright in the room; the sound of the boys bathing outside; the distant jangling of a bell somewhere in the castle and lastly the ticking of her watch under her ear. She lifted herself on one elbow and looked at the time. Nearly four — she had certainly slept long enough.

She jumped down from the high bed and crossed to the window. The sun was half-way down and gilding the water of the Minch, flat calm to-day like a great pond. The boys were bathing off the rocks. Jamie had joined them, and she recognised Rory's huge figure among them. Fergus was not there, nor Colin. From his white face and hands it did not look as if he ever went out, much less bathe in the sun.

Jean woke while she was dressing and together they went down the stairs and along the corridors, wondering if they were losing their way or not.

"We're all right, here's the hall," said Jean.

It looked smaller by daylight but was still immensely high and bare, its great roof hidden in shadows. They opened the door into the courtyard. There was no one about. The place seemed deserted.

"Isn't it old and huge?" Jean whispered, because everything was so still.

The great walls towered up all round them and small shuttered windows peered down with dead eyes. A good many panes of glass were broken; tufts of weed, ragwort, thistles and thrift, grew out of crannies in the walls, and the floor of the courtyard was paved with cracked and broken flags. Fiona and Jean hurried out under the arch and were greeted by shouts.

"I brought your bathing things," called Jamie, and in a few seconds they too were in the sea.

"Sleep well?" asked Rory, his black hair sleeked smooth by the water.

"Beautifully. What a change from a bunk and blankets," said Fiona.

"Where's Fergus?" asked Jean.

"In the *Star*. You don't catch him coming up to Taransay if he can help it," said Rory.

"Why not?" asked Sandy, who had apparently noticed nothing last night.

"He and Colin fight; they always have," said their brother.

"Do they?" Sandy sounded surprised. He had never thought of grown-ups fighting like children and to him Fergus and Colin were quite old.

They swam and basked in the sun until they were dry and then walked back to the castle. They were all ravenous.

"I've lost my place with meals," said Ninian. "What's the next one, tea or breakfast?"

"Who cares?" said Rory. "Our meals are always in a muddle, and generally I'm the only one there."

It was a sort of high tea when they got to it — boiled eggs and scones and baps and a variety of jam and honey. Hungry though she was, Fiona was half sorry to go back into the castle again: it had such a cold and chilling atmosphere. The other half of her was longing to see it all: the great rooms, the battlements and the dungeons. She sat next to Hugh and asked him in an undertone whether he too did not feel Taransay to be a creepy place.

"Yes," Hugh whispered back. "It's Colin mostly, Colin

and Fergus, and I'm sure the place is stiff with ghosts."

That made her laugh, and, looking up, she saw Rory's cheerful face as he teased the twins about something and knew that there was nothing to be afraid of at Taransay in daylight.

"Who's that?" Jamie was asking.

Rory looked over his shoulder at the portrait of the man in velvet.

"My great-great-grandfather," he said, and made a face at the picture. "Black Colin, and he was black too, in his deeds as well as his face."

"Will you show us the Castle?" asked Sandy. "Are there any dungeons?"

"Yes, but we don't use them now," said Rory solemnly.

"What day is to-day, by the way?" asked Ninian. "We're all upside down: I've lost my place."

"I don't know," said Hugh, and turned to Fiona. She shrugged her shoulders and they looked at Rory. "Search me," Rory grinned, "I never do know."

"I'm not sure if it's to-day or to-morrow," said Jean, and they had to laugh.

"Murdoch'll know," said Rory, and crossing the room in a couple of strides, he pulled the bell. When the old man appeared he told them it was Tuesday. Tuesday, the seventeenth.

The Stewarts looked at one another, disbelief in their eyes.

"It can't be," said Fiona.

"Murdoch generally knows." Rory looked at them inquiringly.

"But that means we've only got till the day after to-morrow," Hugh said in horror.

"What d'you mean?" asked Rory.

"We have to go back on Friday," said Ninian miserably.

"Back where?"

"Back to England."

"What, all of you?"

"No, Hugh and I, but the others are going back to Carrick."

"Why bother? Stay here." invited Rory.

"Can't, we have to go back: we're in the Army."

Rory shrugged his shoulders. To live a life you did not like, to have to leave the places you loved and go back to work was more than he could understand.

The discovery of the date made the Stewarts sit in silent gloom until Rory, finishing an immense meal, got up and said:

"Coming?"

The Castle of Taransay was so huge that it would have taken them hours to see everything: the great banqueting hall, the kitchens larger than any the Stewarts had ever seen, dungeons cut deep in the rock under the sea, damp and dark with the ceaseless drip of water in them. Rory had a lantern and by its light they could see old chains and fetters still bolted into the walls.

"Lots of people died down here," said the youngest Macloud cheerfully, as he led them along a narrow passage. He stopped beside a large hole and held the lantern above it.

"People were just flung down there to die," he said. "It's rock below, and lots of bones. I shouldn't look in."

"No, don't let's," said Jean, feeling rather sick.

They seemed to have walked miles when at last Rory pushed open a small door and they found themselves on the battlements.

The sun was behind them, half-way down beyond the hills. A lovely cool wind was blowing off the water into their faces. Fiona went to the edge of the wall and rested her arms on it. The stones were warm from the sun and she leant over, looking down at the sea. The rough wall below her jutted and curved and then fell away straight. A great bunch of yellow ragwort was growing out of a cranny half-

"NO, DON'T LET'S."

way down and beyond that she could see white splashes showing that some bird had its nest there. Looking up, she saw the mainland like a distant black snake crawl across the horizon. It was lovely up here in the sun and wind after the damp and musty smell of the castle. It had been so long shut and the rooms without fires to warm and air them that it smelt like a ruin already. As they had passed through many of the rooms lit dimly by Rory's lantern, she had seen pictures on the walls and tapestries. They were furnished too, and carpeted and looking down at her hands she saw they were black with dust and grime. The walls she had touched as she passed had been damp; in some rooms the pictures had rotted on their cords and had fallen; there were bats almost everywhere, scurrying from the light, and an owl had swooped through one doorway ahead of them. Several of the windows were broken and open to rain and sun. Out here on the battlements Fiona could feel some of Fergus's hatred for his brother who could let Taransay fall into ruins before his eyes. Most of those pictures and tapestries must be rotten now with damp. She could imagine in winter the never-ceasing rain sweeping against the castle, in at the windows and chimneys, chilling the old rooms and passages, dripping down the stone walls. No wonder Fergus would not live there, he who would have given his soul for it.

The others had gone farther on round the top of the walls and she followed them. It was like walking down a narrow lane, for the battlements were so high either side she could only see over them if she stood on tiptoe. Left was the sea and right the ridged uneven roof of the castle. As she hurried after the others she thought it was probably the most uncivilised castle in Britain.

As she caught the others up Sandy was saying:

"There must be hundreds of creepy stories about this place."

"Are there any ghosts?" asked Hugh.

"Yes, it's seething with them," Rory said. "There are so many that they bump into each other and we can't sleep for the noise of them quarrelling."

"Idiot," said Jean, throwing a chip of rock at him.

"Careful!" warned Rory, and pounced at her. He picked her up by the back of her shorts and held her over the roofs.

"Rory, please put me down!" shrieked Jean. "Rory, I'm sorry. My shorts will bust, beast!"

"Put her down," said Fiona, laughing. "They probably will tear."

Jean was returned to her feet, scarlet and breathless but careful not to tease Rory any more. He was so strong and large that he did not realise he might be frightening to someone smaller than himself.

Gradually it was growing dark. In fact until they looked back over the sea they had not realised how dark it was.

"Getting late," said Rory, hurrying them along the battlements. He took them in by a different way.

"I'm hopelessly lost," said Ninian, after a minute or two. "I just haven't one idea which way we're going or where we are."

"Did it take you ages to find all these places?" asked Fiona.

"Yes — Col and Fergus showed me mostly, but I always used to get lost. Fergus has got some places of his own that he never shows any one. I've often tried to follow him, but I never can."

"I bet there are all kinds of secret passages and things," said James, as they ran down a narrow spiral stair, balancing themselves with one hand on the wall.

"Yes, there are, if you can find them. Come on," said Rory, hurrying on ahead.

They ran up and down stairs, along passages; round corners.

"I could disappear at any minute," Rory called over his shoulder. "Then you would be in a mess. You'd probably be here for days, wandering about and starving until you fell through a rotten bit of the floor!"

"We couldn't," said Sandy incredulously. "Don't be silly."

"Look out," said Jean, "or he will."

Rounding a corner, Jamie, who was leading, stopped.

"Which way did he go?"

"He has done it," said Fiona.

It was dark in the passage. A faint grey light came through the windows high up in the wall. There was silence too, but for the creak and rustle of a house at night, the quick breathing of the Stewarts and the far-away slam of a door. They looked at each other.

"Have you any idea where we are?" asked Hugh.

"No, none." Ninian looked round. "Come out, Rory. You've certainly done it."

There was no reply.

"Perhaps they're all mad," whispered Jean. "Perhaps they lured us up here and will leave us here to die. It's just a trick of Fergus."

"Don't be so silly," snapped Fiona. "It's only Rory being an idiot."

Ninian went to look round the corner. Passages stretched on both in front of him and to the left. They were dimly lit and dipped and twisted in the castle walls. Behind them was the way they had just come, ending in a flight of stairs.

"It's no good going back," said Fiona. "I haven't the least idea where we came from."

"Let's try one of these doors," suggested Sandy.

They walked back along the passage and Hugh carefully turned the handle. The door opened with a loud squeak and immediately there was the hurried scatter of mice and rats across the carpet. The glass in one of the windows was broken and the draught as the door opened blew out the curtains which knocked over a spindly chair standing in front of them. They could not see much of the room as it was so dark, but on the walls were shadowy portraits of past Maclouds and a great mirror reflected the moving curtains like fronds of black weed. The sudden slam of the door behind them made them jump.

"Gosh, this is ghostly," half-whispered James. "I'm glad I'm not alone."

"Come on," said Rory, "I'm tired of waiting."

They whirled round

"I must say you did it well," admitted Ninian. "Where were you all the time?"

"Not far," said Rory. "I could hear what you were saying."

Jean blushed in the darkness.

"Well, we didn't look for you far," said Sandy.

"We still wouldn't have found you," said Jamie.

"Come on," said Rory again. "Fergus'll be fuming if we're late."

They hurried after him, for miles it seemed, until at last they heard voices and found themselves in the passage outside the sitting-room.

"They're at it again," said Rory gloomily.

They heard Fergus's voice, low and angry, and Colin's, much higher, laughing and sneering. However, directly they heard the Stewarts' footsteps they stopped, and Fiona, coming into the room behind Rory, saw Colin leaning against the mantelpiece and Fergus, his hands in his pockets, sitting on the back of a chair. He sprang up as they entered.

"Time we were off," he said. "You're late, too."

"Sorry," said Fiona. "It was our fault."

"Mine, you mean," said Rory.

"Ours."

"Stop being magnanimous and come on," snapped Fergus. They could see he was in a fury.

Colin rocked himself on his heels and grinned.

"Good-bye," he said. "I hope you've enjoyed your stay. I'd have come over with you, only —" He stopped and looked at the window which was still uncurtained. The night was black outside. "Only I've got other things to do."

Rory gave a stifled laugh which made his brother glare.

"TIME WE WERE OFF."

"Good-bye," said Fiona. "And thank you for having us," she added, as gracefully as she could.

Fergus was out of sight by this time and Rory took them as far as the courtyard.

"Come back soon," he said. "It has been fun."

"We will come back," they promised. "We're always at Carrick if you ever come across."

He shook his head and they left him standing under the arch, seeming, in the dusk, to be far taller than a human man.

Already Fergus was across the rocks and climbing the hill the other side. They caught up with him and climbed beside him, not daring to speak. They were so queer and wild, these Maclouds, and in a real fury there was no knowing what they might do.

Presently Fergus gave a sigh and looked up at the stars. There were very few as yet: Venus low down and the dim outline of the Bear. "Sorry if I hurried you," he said, "but we don't want to be late." It was the best apology that he could make and they realised that.

"We had been exploring the castle," said James. "We nearly got lost. It is a huge place."

"Rory said you had secret places that only you knew," said Jean. "Is that true?"

"Rory talks too much," said Fergus, hurrying up the hill.

Fiona kicked her sister on the ankle and Jean was silent although she did not know why she should be.

"How long will it take us getting over?" asked Ninian, at last.

"Till dawn," said Fergus abruptly. He stopped for a moment at the summit and looked back at Taransay, a dark bulk against the shifting sea. Several pricks of light shone out in the black walls, the only sign that it was a castle and not a peninsula, as the Stewarts had first thought it.

Fergus turned quickly, hurrying along the cliff top, and they followed him, leaving the strange castle asleep in the night.

Fergus was uncommunicative on the way over. He still seemed to be brooding over Taransay, and though they tried hard to make him talk he would do nothing but answer in monosyllables, and sat on deck staring over the dark sea, his mind thousands of miles away, thinking of things they did not know.

It was a fine starry night with a wind from the west, the right wind for them, and the *Wandering Star* flew on, singing a little to herself and creaking in a friendly way. The Stewarts spent most of the night on deck, watching the racing water that looked in the dark to be moving so much faster than it really was, and the great spread of stars that seemed so near to-night. Though none of them said so, they were all thinking that this was one of their last nights and that it would be a pity to waste it in sleep below in however comfortable a cabin.

At about two in the morning Fiona was steering. Hugh and Sandy had fetched up blankets and were lying, half asleep, on the hatch, opening their eyes every now and then to watch the stars sliding past the sails and the spangled heaving waves. The others were below and Fergus was standing in the stern, rocking on his heels as the boat rocked, whistling under his breath. They had been silent for some time when Fiona spoke softly:

"What *are* you thinking?"

He stopped his whistling but did not speak for a time. Fiona was relieved because she thought he would probably be livid at being disturbed. Then he sighed and said:

"Having you all at Taransay made me remember what it used to be like. Hearing people laugh there and not quarrel. Hearing the boys whistling and stamping about. Taransay must have liked it too: it is so long since it has heard anything but Colin and me swearing at each other."

"Why do you fight so much?" asked Fiona, moving her hand slightly on the tiller.

"I don't know," said Fergus slowly. From his voice it sounded as if he did.

"Surely he needn't live at Taransay," continued Fiona. "Surely he could live where he liked and leave you there.

Don't you love the castle more than you hate him? Wouldn't you rather be there?"

"Fiona — don't! You don't understand." Fergus swung round towards her, his face hard with misery. "I'll tell you some time. I can't now. And don't go about imagining that I'm miserable all the time, because I'm not. It's only when I go there that I get like this, and I go there as seldom as possible." He was silent for a minute watching the sea. When he spoke it was over his shoulder. "I've enjoyed this trip more than you would imagine," he said. "You've made me feel as if I belong among people again: one is apt to forget that when one comes of my family."

Again Fiona had that feeling that he was more lonely than any one she had ever met. She put out her hand to touch his arm when Hugh yawned loudly and sat up, rubbing his eyes. Fiona clasped her two hands over the tiller and Fergus remained as alone and distant as before.

"It's about my watch, isn't it?" said Hugh sleepily.

"Yes, it is," Fiona felt suddenly tired. "We've not much farther to go."

They changed places and she took off her sandshoes before sliding down between the blankets. She was tired too. Her eyes shut almost at once, and she forgot to look up and watch the sail against the sky as Sandy and Hugh had done. Before she slept she had one wakeful moment and opened her eyes with an effort.

Fergus was still standing where she had left him, a black figure against the gleaming sea and the sky, pin-pointed with light. She guessed he would be whistling his song under his breath and his eyes would be fixed on a horizon beyond any she knew. And he would be more lonely than a gull, lost in the darkness, knowing only where the stars lay and which way the wind blew.

The sudden splutter of the engine woke her, hours later. Quickly she rolled over and sat up. The Stack was almost on top of them, or so it looked in the dim light. Fergus was at the tiller and called to her to hurry up.

"They're lowering the sail," he said.

She rolled on to the deck as Sandy and Hugh let the big sail down, covering the hatch with flapping red canvas.

Fergus kept his eyes fixed on the cliff; it was too dark to see the rocks and the channel was very narrow. The noise of the engine woke the others below and they came hurrying up and stood on the deck, yawning and admiring Fergus's skill in steering up the gully in the dark.

As they rounded the last bend they could see a lantern gleaming on the quay.

"Duncan, I expect," said Fergus, and yawned in spite of himself.

"*Fauna's* still here anyway," said Jean, as they got nearer. Not that she had really expected anything else. They were half awake, too sleepy to talk.

"What's the time?" asked Sandy, as they stumbled ashore.

"About five," said Fergus. "Come and have some breakfast in the cave: you must be hungry."

In the grey chill of dawn breakfast sounded most cheering. They followed him, still sleepily, across the rocks and along the black tunnel.

"It seems ages since we were here," said James.

"That's because such a lot has happened," Hugh told him.

"Yes, we have done masses," said Ninian, ducking quickly before he bumped his head on a low bit of the roof.

A delicious smell of sausages and bacon drifted down the cave to meet them.

"Gosh, I *am* hungry," said Sandy, suddenly realising it.

They sat down at the long table that the men used, and Fergus sat with them though it was not his custom. Duncan brought them heaped plates of sausages, bacon and mash, thick slices of bread and butter and large, strong mugs of tea. They enjoyed that meal more than any they had had for ages.

"Well," said Ninian, leaning back when at last he was full, "we'd better be getting some sleep."

"Back in the *Fauna*?" asked Jean.

"Two of you can come in the *Star*," offered Fergus.

"Thanks very much," said Hugh. "We really haven't room for six."

"You'd better take *Fauna* back into the bay when you wake up," said Fergus. "You don't want to get caught in here." He led the way back down the cave.

"What'll we do after that?" asked Jean.

"We must go to the Green Laddie's Loch some time," said Fiona.

"Let's go this afternoon," said Ninian. "Like to come, Fergus?"

"No thanks. I shall be busy. I mean I should like to come, but I really can't. But come here to dinner when you get back."

"We shall have to come to say good-bye," said Jean gloomily.

"Jean, you beast," muttered Fiona.

"Why, when are you going?" asked Fergus.

There was a pause.

"To-morrow morning, first thing," said Ninian eventually.

"I see," said Fergus.

It was light outside.

"Don't let's sleep too long," said James, who with Sandy, was going over to the *Star*.

"You'll probably be first awake, so wake us," said Fiona. "We only want about four hours' sleep."

"I'll wake them," Fergus promised.

Jean and Fiona shared the fo'c'sle. They felt they had rather deserted their boat the last few days and it was nice to be home in her again.

"I wish it wasn't to-morrow already," grumbled Jean

sleepily. And Fiona, her nose deep in the blankets, knew what she meant.

CHAPTER XV

INQUISITION
Wednesday, 18th August

THEY were wakened by the bumping of a dinghy alongside and by footsteps walking noisily above their heads. Then Fergus's voice came shouting down the hatch:

"Hoy! Any one awake?"

"Yes," Ninian grunted sleepily. "What's the time? Anything wrong?"

"Nothing exactly wrong," said Fergus, coming right into the cabin followed by Sandy and James. He sat on the end of the table. Fiona and Jean woke up in the fo'c'sle and hung out of their bunks to hear what was happening. "Not exactly wrong, but I've got some pretty vital letters that simply must be posted, and as I can't take the *Star* out in daylight I was wondering...?" He paused.

"If we would take them," finished Fiona.

"Yes," Fergus grinned back at her.

"Right back to Beanault?" said James gloomily. "Can't they wait till to-morrow?"

"No, they must go."

"Let's go to Melvaig," suggested Sandy. "We've never been there and it isn't as far as Beanault."

"We needn't even all go," said Hugh. "If any one wants to stay and laze they can."

"Meaning you, I suppose?" said Fiona.

"It'd be a good opportunity to get some more petrol." Ninian propped himself on one elbow. He could not sit up in his bunk as he banged his head. "In fact, it's absolutely essential to get some more. I doubt if we've got enough to get us there and back."

"Who wants to go?" said Jean.

Nobody did, much, except Ninian and James. Sandy said he would too.

"But don't go and do anything exciting without us," he said.

"We won't," promised Fiona.

"Well, I'll leave you to get up," said Fergus, taking a lump of sugar out of the bag Fiona had left out. "You seem a bit crowded in here." He went back up the companion, scrunching the sugar, and sat on the cabin roof, watching the waves run towards the shore before a light west wind. He thought of the cave and of the *Star*, caged like a bird in the hidden harbour, of the Stewarts and of the black castle of Taransay, on the far blue hills of the Hebrides.

Looking up at the sun he guessed it was about eight o'clock. If Ninian started soon he should be back in five hours. Fergus thought Melvaig was about ten miles away. But then, of course, they had had no breakfast.

Suddenly he got bored. He jumped up.

"I'm going ashore," he called.

Fiona's head appeared out of the hatch.

"Don't you want any breakfast?" she asked.

"No." Fergus was in his dinghy.

Fiona looked at him in surprise and wondered what had happened and why he had got furious when there was no one to annoy him.

"I'll come and fetch you, shout when you're ready," said Fergus, over his shoulder, and Fiona, feeling angry herself, did not answer. She went back into the cabin wondering whether she would not go to Melvaig after all.

They had a hurried sort of breakfast and then tried to tidy the cabin. This had to be done as otherwise it was impossible to move down there. Anyway, a ship looked horrid in a mess, and there were hardly any protests when Fiona told them to make the bunks.

She got out some tins for the boys' lunch and cut sandwiches and slices of cold ham for herself, Jean and

Hugh. Then thinking of Fergus and his thoughtlessness, cut a few extra.

Ninian meanwhile was crouching beside the engine. This was being more obstinate than usual. The more he wound and primed and tested the plugs, the more dead it became. He grew oilier and hotter, he dropped things into the bilges and banged his head on the bulkhead. After he had dropped the spanner for the fourth time into the black slime that slid to and fro below the engine, he swore, got to his feet and looked out of the hatch, leaning his arms on the deck either side. He sighed and sniffed in a breath of air, feeling ill-used. Sandy and twins were chasing each other on the deck, dodging round Hugh and Fiona, who were sitting on the cabin roof, talking. Nobody was bothering about anything except himself, thought Ninian, ducking as a lump of seaweed came whistling over his head. As Sandy flew past he caught hold of him by the ankle, nearly breaking his leg, and told him to start pumping out the bilges. Sandy swore slightly, but knew that Ninian would probably torture him if he did not. So he collected Jamie to help.

"Hugh," said Ninian, "the engine won't start."

Hugh turned slowly and looked at him.

"You know I don't know anything about engines," he said.

"You might think of something," said Ninian.

Fiona laughed. "Go on, Hugh, don't be lazy," she said.

"Well, I like that! Why don't you do something?" Hugh was indignant.

Fiona leant back. "Nobody's mad enough to think that I should do anything except break an engine," she said.

Grumbling, Hugh got up and pushed Ninian back into the engine-room, dropping down after him.

Fiona lay back on the cabin roof and smiled. Below her she could hear the noise of tinkering and the vain swinging of the starting handle and occasional bursts of oaths and muttering. She looked at the green slopes of the bay and wondered what Fergus was doing. He was probably lying up there in the heather, planning his next voyage, or else brooding over his strange secret Taransay. How wise he was not to bother with engines; the *Star* would run like a bird before this light west wind. Fiona tried to imagine what sort of a bird she was. A stormy petrel perhaps, with her brown sails, but there was no dark sea-bird graceful enough; guillemots and razor-bills were too stumpy, more like *Fauna*.

Sandy and James were steadily pumping jets of foul water into the sea. A film of oil spread over the surface and little bits of twig and stuff floated amongst wisps of cotton waste and match-ends. Fiona could not imagine how twigs got into the bilges and remarked to Sandy and James that the pump would be choked in a minute.

"No, it won't," said Sandy, but he spoke too soon, and for the next few minutes he and James grappled with lengths of tubing and valves and horrible matted lumps of oil.

Eventually the engine started.

Fergus must have been listening from the cliffs because directly the engine roared across the bay a small dinghy shot out from among the rocks and came towards them.

Fiona went down into the cabin and collected the lunch and bathing things. On second thoughts she grabbed a book, in case Fergus was still in an unpleasant mood.

When she appeared on deck Hugh and Jean were already in the dinghy sitting in the stern. Fergus, holding with one hand to *Fauna's* low bulwarks, noticed her looking inquiringly at him, and he smiled with his sideways smile. Fiona knew that he had finished his sudden burst of temper. Sandy held a packet of letters in his hand."

"Sure there's nothing else you want?" he asked.

Fergus shook his head.

"I've left some tins and things in the cabin," called Fiona, perched in the bows. "I'm afraid there's not much selection now, we've nearly come to an end of the stores."

"If we see anything specially nice in Melvaig we'll get it," said Sandy.

Fergus, meanwhile, had let go of *Fauna* and they were drifting away. "See you about four," called Hugh, and ducked to avoid the spray as Jamie flung the buoy overboard.

"What are we going to do?" asked Jean, watching Fergus's dark stern face as he rowed them towards the bay.

"What would you like to do?" He glanced over his shoulder and pulled with the port oar.

"Oh, well," said Jean, who had not thought but had imagined Fergus would have some plan. "What do you generally do in the afternoons?"

"Nothing much." Fergus tried to remember what he did do. He seemed to spend most of the time in the cave, or else sleeping, since so much of his work was done at night. Sometimes on a long hot afternoon he would take a book and lie on the cliffs, and read and sleep and think and watch the clouds over Lewis and the lines of each well known hill. He tried to explain this to the Stewarts.

"Don't you ever bathe?" asked Jean.

"It's not much fun by oneself." Fergus tried to make an excuse and indeed that was hardly an excuse.

He rowed them close to the foot of the Stack and then across the end of the gully to the rocks where there was a secret place to tie a boat. The Stewarts had never found it, but it was much better to leave it there than getting it bumped in the usual place.

They wandered aimlessly up the beach.

"Don't let's do anything special," said Fiona.

So Fergus led them up a narrow path like a flight of irregular steps on the cliff's face. When they reached the top they lay for some time in the heather, watching *Fauna* get smaller and smaller as she travelled down the coast to Melvaig.

"Hope she doesn't break down again," said Hugh, chewing the juicy end of a grass stem.

"Perhaps they'll have to stop the night there," suggested Jean. "Then where would we sleep?"

"In the *Star*, I suppose," said Fergus. "Or else up here on the cliffs."

"Be a bit cold," objected Fiona lazily.

"I'd lend you some blankets," said Fergus.

They talked and drowsed till Jean suggested a bathe or lunch. Fergus bathed with them, his body surprisingly white against his brown face. But he could swim faster than any of them and beat them all at diving.

They had lunch on the beach and ate sandwiches, full of grit, and warm, half-melted bread and butter.

"Have you ever been on the Stack, Fergus?" asked Jean.

He shook his head.

"Never been on the Stack?" Fiona and Jean could hardly believe their ears. "We must go up after lunch."

The boys arrived at Melvaig in good time, and brought *Fauna* alongside the high stone pier that looked much too large for such a small village.

"There's the post box," said Jamie, pointing to a splash of red in the white-washed wall of a cottage. They walked up the rocky road towards it. From the state of this track it did not look as if cars ever came to the village; there was a ridge of grass and rushes between two stony ruts.

"Almost as bad as the road to the Carna Loch," said Sandy.

He took Fergus's packet of letters, by now rather crumpled and dirty, out of his pocket and dropped them into the post-box.

"I'm sure no one ever collects letters from here," he said, as they listened to them clanging into the depths of the box.

"On the contrary," said Ninian, "we've arrived just at the right moment."

He pointed to a tiny speck on the road which slowly turned into the pedalling figure of the postman, a very old man who looked like Mr. Chips.

He greeted the boys, who knew him well as he was brother to their own "post."

"Ye've come a long way to post a letter," he said, as he unlocked the box and took out Fergus's three envelopes.

They explained to him and asked him about petrol.

He shook his head at this. There was no pump in the village. Mr. McVarish at the shop might have a spare gallon. He was the only person with a car.

"Well," said Ninian, as they walked back along the road to the cottage that was a shop, "if Mr. McVarish hasn't got any, we're sunk."

"Is Fairloch too far?"

"Yes, much," Ninian scowled. "If we can't get any you'll have to row to Beanault for some on Monday, and I shall have to walk back. I can't miss the early bus."

"What a horrid ending," said James.

"All endings are horrid," said Sandy.

By now they had reached the shop and pushed open the door. A little bell rang as they stepped from the warm, windy out-of-doors into the cool and many scented atmosphere inside. The usual jumble of goods met their eyes, and Ninian, ducking under a large pair of sea-boots that were hanging from a line with several oilskins, advanced to the counter.

Mr. McVarish shuffled forwards and they asked him about the petrol.

He shook his head.

"There's only a wee bittie in the car," he said. "Juist enough to get me to Fairloch to fill up. I'm awfu' sorry."

"I suppose there's no one else in the village who has a car?" asked Jamie, hoping that Mr. Chips might have been wrong.

Again McVarish shook his head.

"No. I've juist got the van," he said. "That's all there is here. The other folk walk or cycle."

Sandy's expert eye had meanwhile been scanning the

shelves for cartons of chocolate. This shop seemed to be particularly well stocked with Terry's and he nudged Ninian, who had the money.

They left the shop carrying several bars, both milk and bitter, and James had a box of eggs. They were silent and depressed.

"This would happen," said Ninian, kicking a stone, and then wishing he had not as it was firmly embedded in the ground.

"If only *Fauna* had a sail," said Jamie.

"Well, she hasn't," snapped Ninian. "You might as well wish we could discover a petrol pump in Flatfish Bay."

"Well, I wish we could," said Jamie, unabashed.

"I don't," said Sandy. "It would look horrid amongst the rocks." He broke off a piece of chocolate and handed it round. They ate it in silence and it made them feel better.

"Let's have lunch here," suggested James. "We could find a place in the rocks."

They left their purchases on the cabin table and took the tins Fiona had put out for them and a loaf and butter and climbed a little way up into the heather. There they lay and ate, and the warm smell of the heather and the whistling of the wind in the grass reminded them of lunches eaten out stalking or by the side of a loch.

"I suppose we ought to be going back," said Ninian, at last.

"Yes," said Sandy, not moving but lying still and watching faint wisps of cloud over his head.

Ninian ran his fingers up a spray of ling and let the small hard flowers drift slowly down on his kilt. They had had a useless morning and the posting of Fergus's beastly letters did not seem at all worth the long tramp back to Carrick that he would have to make early to-morrow morning.

"Come on," he said, and got up, picking fronds of heather out of his hair.

They wandered back to *Fauna*. Two white-headed

children and a black collie stood watching them on the pier. Ninian went down to the engine, which started beautifully. Sandy took the wheel and Jamie cast off. The children and the dog stood motionless, minute figures that grew smaller and smaller as *Fauna* sailed back to Flatfish.

They did not hurry on the return journey and rounded the last point into the bay at about half-past four.

"Gosh!" cried Sandy and James together.

Ninian stuck his head through the hatch.

"Snakes!" he said.

Anchored some way out in the bay was a squat black fishing boat. There were men on her deck and a dinghy tied alongside.

The boys looked at each other. Suppose she had come in while Fergus and the others were bathing and picnicking on the beach? How could they explain him? Had they come especially to find him? No fishing boats or drifters ever came into Flatfish Bay. In a few minutes they had picked up the buoy and stopped the engine.

"Where are the others?" asked Sandy, looking round for the dinghy.

"There's Fiona," said James, pointing, "and Jean." There was no sign of Fergus or Hugh.

The girls were signalling madly for the dinghy to come and fetch them.

"Obviously they'll have hidden Fergus's dinghy," said Ninian, in answer to Sandy's question. "We'd hardly have brought two with us."

"D'you think they've caught Hugh and Fergus?" asked Jamie.

"How could I know?" said Ninian impatiently. "You two wait here while I fetch the others."

He jumped into the dinghy, rocking it violently, and rowed quickly ashore.

Sandy and James waited on board, hardly able to bear the suspense. It seemed to them as if Ninian was taking longer than ever, and once he did get there he waited for hours. Stamping with impatience, they watched Fiona grab the dinghy from the rocks and start talking to Ninian, pointing and gesticulating. Eventually Hugh appeared down the cliff and they started back for *Fauna*.

"What! Tell us what happened," cried Sandy, as the dinghy bumped alongside.

"We'd better all go below," said Ninian. "Jean, you stay on deck and warn us if there's any one coming."

Jean's eyes were large and her face, under its brownness, a little pale. However, she nodded and sat down on the cabin roof while the others disappeared below.

"Now tell us," said Sandy.,

"They're suspicious of Fergus," began Fiona, perched on the end of the table and pushing back a strand of hair. "They think we know something about him, but they're not certain of anything. They don't know about the secret harbour, they don't know where the still is, they don't even know who Fergus is, in fact they are not certain of anything."

"They just think there's a secret still in the hills here somewhere," said Hugh, "and as we've been anchored in here they're sure we know something about it."

"But where is Fergus?" asked James. "Have they caught him?"

"No!" Hugh and Fiona looked at one another. "Fergus is still on the Stack!"

"Gosh!" Sandy let out a whistle. "But why, exactly?"

"Well, we were all up there when the boat came in. She's called the *Rose of Clyde*," explained Fiona. "Of course the only way down was in full view of everybody so we had to leave him, up there."

"Couldn't you have all stayed?" suggested James.

"They'd seen us," objected Hugh. "We had to come down. Now they want to see you, Ninian: they think you might tell them something."

"Who are 'They'?" asked Ninian.

"Sort of coastguards. Apparently they police the coast as there is such a lot of this distilling going on. But someone must have given them a hint about Flatfish and us. We might have been here for a day's fishing, and anyway, *Fauna* wasn't even in when they came along."

"It's all most odd and creepy," said Fiona. "Who could have spied on us?"

"D'you think Fergus has got a traitor in his gang?" suggested Sandy.

Ninian shrugged. "That's his business, not ours," he said. "The next thing to do is to get him off the Stack."

"Yes, that's more difficult than it sounds." Fiona clasped her knees in her arms and leant back. "You see, he doesn't know the way down, not really. He might do it by daylight, but he'd never do it in the dark."

"He's pretty good on rocks," James reminded her.

"He didn't seem to relish the idea of coming down at night," Hugh said. "I dare say he could do it but there wouldn't be much left of him if he slipped."

"No-o-o," said Ninian slowly. "I don't know if I should like to do it much myself."

"We shall have to do it by night," said James. "How long is this boat in for?"

"They didn't say." Hugh pulled out his pipe.

"Well, we can't just leave Fergus up there with no food or anything," said Sandy. "I don't mind going up."

"You don't know it well enough," objected Ninian.

"I'll go then," said James.

Fiona slid to her feet.

"I'll go," she said firmly. "I know those rocks backwards."

The others looked at her. She was the obvious person. None of them were as good on a cliff as she was.

"It's terribly dangerous," began Hugh, but Fiona gave him a pitying look.

"Nonsense," she said.

Hugh raised his eyebrows and looked at Ninian, who

shook his head.

"She's right," he said. "She'll have to go. But Fiona," he added, "it's no use thinking that the climb's an easy one. Don't go charging up there as if it was broad daylight or a full moon. Remember you've got to come down."

At this Hugh's frown increased, but Fiona laughed and said:

"Strange to say, I had thought of that. But anyway, when one's climbing down a cliff one can never see where one's stepping, so it might just as well be dark!"

"That's not the point," said Ninian, but she only laughed at him.

Hugh did not think Fergus was worth such a perilous ascent. Surely it would not hurt him to be cold and hungry for one night, but he said nothing, seeing that the Stewarts had made up their minds.

"How will you get there?" he asked.

"Directly it gets pitch dark," said Fiona. "Ninian," she said, thinking suddenly, "I can't take the dinghy. I shall have to swim."

"Gosh, yes, I suppose you will."

"With your clothes on your head like we did last year," interrupted Jamie.

"And the food on my head too," added Fiona. "I shall probably be drowned."

"If we had a sort of tub you could push it in front of you," suggested Sandy.

Yes, but as we haven't that isn't very helpful," said Ninian.

"I'm hungry," said Fiona suddenly. "Let's have supper."

"Let's go on deck," said James. "We needn't look as if we were discussing anything."

Jean was delighted to see them and they explained their plan to her while Fiona broke and scrambled the eggs Ninian had bought in Melvaig.

"I say." Sandy was struck with a sudden brilliant idea.

"The coastguards may have some petrol."

"So they may. Anyway they might fetch some for us," said Ninian.

"I expect they'll be coming to see us soon." Jean looked over towards the ugly, black boat. She ruined the beauty of Flatfish Bay.

"I wish they'd go," said James.

It was nine o'clock before the coastguards made any move. Already outlines were blurring, and if there was more clamour than usual round the Stack only the Stewarts realised it. They were sitting on deck discussing who could have given Fergus's hidden harbour away when a man appeared on the deck of the fishing boat.

"Can you come over and see us?" he called.

"Shall we?" asked Ninian quickly, and the others nodded. "All right," he shouted.

"Shall we all go?" asked Hugh.

Nobody much wanted to stay behind. Sandy and James flatly refused to, Ninian obviously had to go and Fiona was already in the dinghy. Hugh and Jean looked at one another.

"It'll have to be us, I suppose," said Hugh.

"Get some sandwiches ready for Fergus," suggested Fiona.

They had not dared cut any before in case the coastguards had arrived unexpectedly. Fiona and Ninian each took an oar and pulled away towards the black boat.

"I wonder what they'll say," said Fiona softly to Ninian, in front of her.

He only grunted, but he, too, was wondering. If the men had any proof that they had been helping or even approving of the distillery there would be an awful row. He could not quite imagine how any one would know that they were in any way connected with the smugglers; perhaps they were not really suspicious, just curious.

At that moment the dinghy bumped the *Rose of Clyde* and

Ninian, turning, grabbed a short ladder that was hanging over the side.

Directly they were on board they realised that even if she had once been a fishing boat she was now converted into a kind of official yacht, clean and newly painted. She was larger than the *Star* and not nearly so pretty, having a tiny wheel-house aft and a long expanse of deck forward with an unshipped mast resting on the wheel-house. She had a small sail aft of that to steady her. Ninian's spirits rose slightly: she must have a motor and probably some spare petrol.

"Good-evening," said the man who had hailed them. He seemed quite polite and an Englishman. "Sorry to bother you so late but we wanted to ask you some questions."

"That's all right," said Ninian. "I want to ask you one, too."

"Go ahead," said the man.

"Have you got any spare petrol?" Ninian came straight to the point"

"Oh." The man looked at Fiona.

She shook her head.

"They couldn't get any," she said.

"We could spare you a couple of gallons. That be enough?"

"Yes, just enough to get us into Carrick."

"Come over with the tins in the morning," said the man. "We'll be going out early, about eight."

"Thanks very much," said Ninian, glad that, after all their forebodings about walking back to Carrick, they should have got the petrol so easily.

"Will you come below?" The man showed them an open hatch aft and offered to lead the way.

Fiona followed him, feeling as if she was going to an unknown doom. However, the three boys were close behind her.

They entered a large cabin rather like Fergus's in the

Wandering Star, only not so nice. It was far bigger to start with and was only a sleeping and living-room, no stove or sink in the corner. The table was piled with papers and official-looking books and two men were sitting there writing. They looked up as the Stewarts filed into the cabin. Sandy, as usual, tripped on the last rung of the companion and Fiona was glad. She thought these men looked too prim.

The objects of her scorn looked up. They obviously had been expecting them but chose to look surprised. The Stewarts scowled back.

"Ah, yes, sit down," said one of the men.

There were seats round the table, but not enough. Jamie perched on a bunk. Fiona, at the table, tried her best to read the papers nearest to her, but they were all upside down and one of the men quickly gathered them up when he saw her looking.

There was a little silence. The coastguards looked uneasy. The Stewarts took in every detail of their faces and of the cabin so as to relate everything to Fergus.

"Well." The elder of the two men spoke. He was from Glasgow by his accent and had a round red face. He looked at Ninian. "Can you give me any information at all about these smugglers? I dare say your sister has told you what we asked her."

"Yes," said Ninian. It was going to be awkward if the men were nice, so much easier if they were rude. "I don't think I know of anything," he said. "This is a very deserted place, you know. We never see anybody here, that's the chief reason we come."

"We have definite information" — Fiona caught Ninian's eye — "that there is an illegal distillery in the hills here somewhere," said the man, MacAndrew. "As you say, it's a deserted place, but you would be the most likely people to notice anything going on. No mysterious noises at night? No footmarks in the sand? No boats appearing and disappearing?"

"No," said Ninian. He hated lying, but he could say "No" quite truthfully to all that. Jamie had heard the boat and Jean had seen her, ages ago, it seemed.

"I know you'd like to help if you could," said MacAndrew, "being in your position at Carrick you have to uphold the law."

Sandy, thinking of last year, choked suddenly.

The man went on: "I'm sure you understand my position," he said. "It is impossible to get anything out of the crofters here. If they're not mixed up in it themselves, half their friends are, so you are just the people to help us."

Fiona was livid. Accusing them of being less loyal than their own crofters! Her eyes flashed. "I'm afraid you'll find loyalty a very strong quality up here," she said.

Ninian kicked her under the table. If she lost her temper she was liable to say anything, and he noticed the other man, Donaldson, sharp and thin-faced, looking at her suspiciously.

"Is that so?" he said quietly. He had not spoken yet, and he did so now in a calm even voice. "Perhaps you can give us details of what you have been doing since you got here?"

"I'm sorry, we can't give you details," said Ninian.

"Why not?" flashed Donaldson.

"We don't keep a diary," said Ninian coolly.

Fiona had to admit he was doing well: she would have flamed up long ago.

"A rough outline perhaps," suggested MacAndrew.

"Well. . ." Ninian began a long rambling story, calculated to muddle any one who heard it.

Donaldson was listening with half an ear but mostly he was thinking.

"They know something," he thought. "They're much too clever with their innocent answers. Wild young devils: I've heard stories about them over at Carrick. They don't care a toss for the law — in fact they'd rather be without it than within. But they'd better watch their step or they'll find themselves being too clever."

"Then we went to Melvaig to-day," Ninian was saying. "And to Faraway, let me see, was it two days ago or three?"

"Three or four," said Fiona, adding to the muddle her brother was creating. "I think it was four because I can remember…"

"Never mind," interrupted Donaldson, and Jamie suddenly thought he must be rather like Chauvelin in *The Scarlet Pimpernel*. Then to his horror Donaldson was speaking to him.

"You've seen nothing either, youngster?"

If there was anything Jamie loathed it was being called youngster. "I haven't exactly seen nothing," he said. "I mean ships pass and there are gulls and sheep and there was a seal the day before yesterday over by…"

"That'll do." Donaldson turned to Sandy.

"Sorry," said Sandy, before he could speak. "I've been with my cousins all the time."

The two men looked at one another.

"Well," said MacAndrew, "thank you for your help. Don't forget if you see anything suspicious to inform the police at once. Any one in the least way connected is severely dealt with. It is as well to be within the law on these occasions." He looked at Ninian. "Especially when children get involved."

Ninian would have given anything not to have blushed, but he could feel himself getting red.

"I'll remember that," he said lightly, "in case I ever get tempted." He got up. "Is that all?" he asked.

"Yes, thank you." Although provoked, MacAndrew was still polite.

The Stewarts rose to their feet. "Good-night," they said.

"Good-night," said MacAndrew, while Donaldson nodded and went back to his papers.

Up on deck it was half light.

Fiona, looking instinctively towards the Stack, could see nothing but its canopy of birds.

"You're sure it's all right about the petrol?" Ninian was saying to the young coastguard who had met them first.

"Yes, of course. Come in the morning," he said, and helped them over the side.

They rowed back to *Fauna*, bursting with speech. However, they managed to contain it until they got below and had left Jamie, protesting, on deck. Hugh and Jean were told every detail.

"They were jolly suspicious," said Ninian. "Only they couldn't prove anything. But someone must have spied and told them. I mean they knew something definitely, but not enough to accuse us."

"I wonder what they'll do next?" said Hugh.

"I don't know, but they're going early to-morrow morning or so they said. Ninian looked a little worried. "D'you think they'll stay and spy?"

"They know we're going back the day after to-morrow," said Fiona.

Just then Jamie banged on the hatch.

"They've put up a riding-light, hadn't we better?" he said.

"Yes, coming." Ninian grovelled in the fo'c'sle, wishing they had put theirs up first.

He went on deck with it. He could still see a vague outline of the *Rose of Clyde*, but it was nearly dark. Not much longer for Fiona to wait.

"You go below," he told James, "and send Jean up for the first watch. The rest of you had better go to bed."

The two lights made the night more dark.

Jean came up with Fiona and they all three sat and waited till they could see nothing but the waves directly below the boat and the bright starry sky.

CHAPTER XVI

FIONA ALONE
Wednesday, 18th August and Thursday, 19th August

IT WAS nearly midnight when at last Fiona slipped over the side *of Fauna* into the black water.

"Gosh, it's cold," she gasped.

"Good luck," said Ninian and Jean, and Hugh who was not asleep, looked out of the hatch and wished her good luck as well.

In a few seconds she was out of sight.

She was in a bathing costume and had her clothes on her head. On top of them was Fergus's food wrapped in a sou'wester. She swam steadily and gradually the water grew warmer. It was a good long way to the Stack, several hundred yards, and Fiona felt she would have given anything to be back in *Fauna*, in bed, with this perilous journey over. She was dreading her climb more than she would admit. She could not see the Stack; all that was visible was the dark line of the cliff against the sky. She had to guess her position and hope she was swimming straight.

She had got about half-way when, above the noise she made, swimming breast-stroke, she heard the muffled splash of oars.

This was something none of them had thought of.

They were behind her, coming from the *Rose of Clyde*. For an instant she could think of nothing but swimming as fast as possible in the opposite direction, then her presence of mind returned.

She sank herself as low as she could in the water, cursing her clothes and Fergus's food that prevented her from going entirely underneath. She turned her back on the oncoming boat, hoping that her wet hair would act as a kind of cloak over her shoulders. Then she trod water, keeping her arms, which would show white under-water, in front of her.

They were so near now that Fiona could hear the murmur of voices, very low. She thought she could recognise MacAndrew's voice and then, suddenly, Donaldson's, raised slightly in anger.

"It's hopeless," he said. "We'll get nothing out of them, though Colin Macloud told me definitely that they were helping his brother. Between Carrick and Melvaig he said, in a big bay. There is another one farther down. We'll watch that to-morrow..." his voice faded.

Fiona nearly sank with surprise, but she just remembered the food in time. So it was Colin who was the traitor, Fergus's own brother. No wonder he loathed him.

Where were they going now, the coastguards? Not into the harbour surely? Not into that hidden place that was Fergus and their secret? She swam quicker and quicker, hoping that she could reach the Stack before them. Then she realised that from the scrap of conversation she had overheard it did not sound as if they even knew if this was the right bay. Probably they were on the look-out for suspicious lights. The thing to do was to tell Fergus as soon as possible. He would think of something.

Presently she could feel the swell carrying her in towards the rocks. Away to the right was the swish and rumble of the gully. "Please don't let me be sucked in," prayed Fiona, paddling gently in the shadow of the cliffs. Looking up, she thought she could see the white-splashed rocks of the Stack and its tufted crown. "Ouch." She had bumped her knee very violently on a barnacley rock. It didn't hurt much now, but it would out of the water. She must be close in. Her hands groped in front of her and eventually found sheer rock. If she went right a bit more there was a shelf to pull herself up on to. Careful now, careful, her knee was sore enough already.

By the time she was crouched on the narrow platform at

the foot of the Stack the other knee and both elbows had suffered. However, she had got there. The first part of the ordeal was over.

She rested a few minutes before peeling off her bathing dress and putting on the slightly damp clothes she had been carrying. She felt the sandwiches anxiously. They were quite dry. She stayed on the ledge until her heart had stopped pounding. It was no use climbing the Stack in that

THE FIRST PART OF THE ORDEAL WAS OVER.

condition. Presently she stood up, the great cliff wall looming above her. She was only just able to stand on the narrow ledge. It tried to push her back into the sea. Above her head the gulls had started to wake. She hoped desperately that the coastguards would not notice. After all they quite often went on crying far into the night.

She turned and grasped the first ledge. The food, tied into the so'wester, hung from her belt and bumped about as she moved. But she mustn't think of that, nor of the black sea beneath and the jagged rocks round the base of the Stack. She must look up at the steady stars and the uneven line above her. She would have liked to call out to Fergus but the coastguards were not far off. All she must think of now was of the next ledge and the one above that and the diagonal crack some way to the left, a good rest for a toe and finger. She got that far and hung there a minute. Where next? A reach up to the right and a snag to step on, level with her knee, then a small even shelf, wide enough for both feet but with a nasty overhang. Would she ever get Fergus down in the dark?

Suddenly she put her hand on the warm feathery body of a gull and almost fell off with fright. Luckily she had a good grip with the other hand, but a cloud of birds seemed to rise out of the rock all round her and beat at her with their wings. She clung there until they had subsided and then went grimly on.

For a little the going was easier, big jutting rocks for foot-holds and hand-grips but at the end, a nasty moment. Was the next grip right or left?

First with one hand, then with another she groped over the smooth bare rock: she was so nearly there, only another foot or so to climb. But there was nothing to hold on to: she had gone wrong somewhere.

There was nothing for it but to go back. Until then she had not quite realised the full horror of what was to come. This descent where there were large rocks was easy

compared with the stretches below. Then, too, she would
have Fergus depending on her. They would both be spread-
eagled in this incredible pitch darkness, a darkness so black
that it pressed on one. Better not think of that now. Ah!
there was the grip that had eluded her.

Two minutes later she had her elbows over the edge and
was worming her way on to the flat tufted crown of the Stack.

Just for a second she lay still, revelling in the sense of
safety that the flat ground gave her. Then, crouching, she
called softly:

"Fergus! Fergus!"

There was no answer.

The top of the Stack was deserted except for Fiona and
the gulls. That long and agonising ascent had been for
nothing. Fergus had gone by a way of his own and there was
nobody there but her.

Against her will two tears trickled slowly down her cheeks.

"Fergus!" she called again, louder.

"Who is it? Fiona!" His voice came from the other side of
the Stack. Then she saw him lying in a slight hollow between
tufts of thrift.

"Fiona!" He got to his feet. "What on earth are you
doing up here?"

"Better keep down: they'll see you against the sky." She
crawled over to him and crouched beside him.

"What on earth possessed you to come up here in the
dark?" His voice was stern: she could imagine the
expression that went with it.

"I... we thought you would be hungry," she said. "Look,
I've brought you some food." She undid the sou'wester and
took out the treasured sandwiches.

"Fiona!" She had never heard his voice like that before.
"I could have waited."

"How would you have got down in daylight?" she asked,
giving him the packages. He took them.

"Have one yourself," he said, and she took one to steady

her nerves after that horrid moment when she thought he had left.

"They couldn't have stayed for long," said Fergus, munching hungrily.

"As it happens, I'm jolly glad I did come up," said Fiona. "I'll tell you when you've finished."

They lay in silence amongst the sleeping gulls, watching the great arch of stars above them and the two riding lights down in the bay.

"Does Colin know of this place?" she asked suddenly.

"Colin?" Fergus's voice was hard. "No, why should he? He knows I've got a still, but he doesn't know where. Do you think I'd tell him?"

"No, I don't. But..."

"But what?"

"Fergus." Fiona's voice was desperate. She turned to him in the darkness but he did not move. That terrible rage at the mention of Colin's name had possessed him. "Listen, Fergus, I know you and Colin hate each other, and I don't want to make it worse, but there's something I must tell you. Don't revenge yourself on Colin too much, will you, please?"

"You mean — Colin sent those men here?" said Fergus. "You mean Colin's a traitor, that he betrayed me, or would have done if I'd trusted him? That's what you mean, isn't it?"

"Yes," said Fiona softly.

Fergus lay still and silent. After a bit he turned and looked out across the sea to Taransay. Still he did not speak.

At last he said:

"Fiona, I am very ashamed of my family. I had guessed for a long time that Colin would betray me if he could. I am sorry that you should know people like us, but you need never see us again."

"It's all right." Fiona did not know what to say. "I don't mind. I mean Colin and you, you're so different. I don't like him either. Don't mind, Fergus, he isn't worth it."

Fergus, his head on his arms, said so low that she could hardly hear: "And Taransay belongs to him."

She could find no answer to that. Presently she said:

"We ought to be going. The moon'll be up soon."

"We?"

"I think I can get down, if you can trust me."

"Yes, I can trust you," Fergus laughed. "Fiona, are you sure?"

"No, but we can try." She told him how she had overheard the conversation in the dinghy and how it was essential for Fergus to get back.

"All right. Come on then."

They crawled to the edge of the Stack.

"Come down after me and I'll put your feet right. Don't move unless I say," whispered Fiona.

"All right," said Fergus again. Then, as she was lowering herself over the edge, he grasped her wrist.

"Fiona. Don't tell the others."

"I wouldn't anyway," said Fiona.

Inch by inch, foot by foot, they descended the cliff. Fergus never moved until Fiona touched his ankle and lowered his foot to the right place. It must have been nerve-racking for him to have to climb downwards, trusting blindly that the girl below him would not make one mistake or slip. It was just as bad for Fiona, having Fergus's life in her hands.

Very slowly, with infinite care, they reached the ledge at the bottom. Here they sat to regain their breath and relax.

"How are you going to get back?" whispered Fiona.

"Swim down the gully — how are you?"

"Swim back to *Fauna* — I left my bathing dress here. Swim in all your clothes?"

"Yes, it's darker like that. I wonder where that beastly boat is?"

"We must hurry or the moon will be up. Do have a care, Fergus, and don't walk into a trap. They may be waiting for you in the harbour."

"I don't think they'll catch me." He grinned and got to his feet. "See you to-morrow." For an instant he held both her hands in his. "Good-night, Cat's-eyes," he said. "No one could have done what you did to-night. Thank you." He turned, and dived into the dark sea.

Fiona hardly heard the splash. She watched for him to come up and saw for a minute the paleness of his face against the water. She sighed and shivered. She had a warm bunk waiting for her, and a hot cup of cocoa. And maybe Fergus would have nothing but a long cold night in the heather until the distant dawn.

CHAPTER XVII

THE FAIRY LOCH
Thursday, 19th August

"FLATFISH looks complete again," said Jamie, gazing down at it from the top of the cliff. The others turned too, panting, and looked back the way they had come.

Once more *Fauna* alone lay in that still half-circle of blue, looking, as they had thought before, so like a little ark. It was twelve o'clock, an hour yet to go before high tide. The triple line of breakers creamed up the sand while beyond them the water was flat and shining, like a guinea under the sun. The rocks on the left of the bay were almost covered, but from where they were standing they could not see the second beach nor the Stack. There was no throb of engine or gurgle of water over the rocks to betray the harbour. It was a still and perfect day, the wind had dropped and the sun, at its height, poured down on the dry country.

The Stewarts shouldered their knapsacks and turned their faces inland. For a long way the cries of gulls down by the Stack and the steady hush of the sea followed them across the moor.

Ninian had fetched the petrol and seen all three men, so there did not seem much chance that any of them were left lurking in the rocks to spy. The *Rose of Clyde* had gone just after eight, sailing south for Fairloch.

"Don't talk about them to Fergus," said Fiona. "It makes him furious. Don't ask me why because I don't really know."

They guessed she knew more than she would say, and they could also imagine what sort of thing it was. So they left the unpleasant subject of the coastguards alone.

Hugh pushed back a piece of hair that was tickling his forehead and looked up. The ground rose slowly in front of them, a barren-looking expanse of brown grass, patched green where there was a bog, dark hollows of peat hags and lumps of grey rock. Ninian had said it was about two miles to the Fairy Loch and Hugh hoped he would not hurry too much as it was terribly hot. Already he was getting thirsty. The knapsack of beer and lemonade bottles that he was carrying bumped irritatingly on his shoulder, and as he stepped on to what looked like a dried piece of earth, peaty water squirted up all over his shoe and made it most uncomfortable.

"Bother," said Hugh, and looked up at the sky. This was so tranquil and blue that he forgot to be irritated and started to whistle instead.

"What's it like, this loch?" Sandy was asking.

"Very small, half in the wood and black and deep," said Ninian. "That's where the Green Laddie is. There's a bigger loch this side of it."

"I wonder if we shall see him?" said Jean.

"Not very likely," said Ninian, "as he's been gone for hundreds of years." He looked instinctively over his shoulder as he spoke, in case clouds were piling up by the islands, in which case they would have to hurry back to *Fauna*. But the sky was un-touched and the sea was still as glassy calm.

"Gosh, it is hot," said Sandy, wiping his forehead.

"We shall be eaten alive by midges," said Jean.

"Perhaps a wind'll get up, just a small one," suggested Jamie hopefully.

"We can always light a fire," said Fiona.

"Don't speak to me of fires on a day like this," groaned Sandy.

"How much farther is it?" asked Jean.

"About a mile and a half. Honestly, the fuss you all make. I'll race you there," said Ninian, hoping inwardly that none of them would accept the challenge.

"Oh, go and race yourself," said Sandy.

"Well, since you're all so weak, let's have a rest." Ninian

subsided on to a long grey rock and the others dropped down into the grass beside him.

Fiona lay back and stretched. It was a glorious day, the hottest they had had since their voyage back from Corriedon.

"I wish Fergus and Rory could have come," said Jamie, plaiting three pieces of dried grass together.

"Rory anyway — Fergus is so odd," said Jean.

"Yes, he is queer: you never know if he's going to fly into a livid bait or not," said Sandy. "It's rather putting off."

"It's rather fun to be just us for once," said Hugh, watching through half-shut eyes the glitter of the sea beyond the rim of the cliff.

"Yes, it seems ages since we were alone," said Ninian, and they were silent, thinking of how short a time was left to them.

"Come on!" Fiona sprang up, unable to bear that any longer.

They went on up the hill. Right and left of them were small intensely blue lochs.

"Much too weedy for fishing," said Jean.

"Much too small, anyway," said Sandy.

They walked on through the dry grass, through a patch of heather that covered the toes of their shoes with pollen. A covey of grouse flopped up in front of Ninian, making them all jump.

"Wish we had a gun," grumbled Sandy.

"When we get to the top of this hill we shall see the loch," said Ninian, impatiently curbing his long strides to match the others.

They pushed on.

"We shall be able to bathe when we get there. I shouldn't think the Green Laddie would mind," said Jean.

"It'll be lovely and cool in the wood," said Fiona.

"What sort of a wood is it?" asked Hugh.

"Hazel and birch and oak," said Ninian. "And there are

a lot of big pine trees, very old ones."

"The kind they say, Scotland was covered in, in the olden days," explained Jean.

"I'll take your word for it," said Hugh.

They were nearly at the top. Already they could see the lower slopes of the high hills beyond the loch, cloaked with a thick green wood that stretched on and on inland, down towards Inverasdale.

"But it's a huge wood," cried Hugh.

"The loch's right in it, all except one side," Ninian told him.

"Is this it?" said Sandy, as they reached the summit.

Below them lay a long loch, Loch an Draing, peaceful and smooth in the sun. At its farthest end the woods touched the shore, black impenetrable woods they looked from where the Stewarts were standing. The hills rose suddenly behind the trees out of the moor and ran in a ridge down towards the villages some six miles to the south-east.

They walked slowly down to the water.

"What sort of fishing d'you get here?" asked Hugh.

"Nice trout of about half a pound," said Jean. "Sometimes a bit bigger, but generally not."

"If you can get fish out of that mill-pond you're more of a genius than I thought," said Ninian.

"Yes, I suppose it is a bit calm, but it may be better in the evening," said Jean, undaunted.

"Look, there's a boat all ready," said Sandy, pointing to a heavy grey dinghy pulled high up on a small shingle beach. They raced down to it.

"We could row across instead of walking round," said Ninian.

"Yes, we could, if there were any rowlocks," said Fiona, who had guessed they would be gone.

"That's a pity," said Sandy. "Anyway," he added, looking at Jean, "there's no cork in the bottom," and they both laughed, remembering last year.

"Where shall we have lunch, here or in the wood?" asked Hugh, longing to be rid of the bottles.

"Oh, in the wood," said Fiona. "We must go right up to the Fairy Loch."

"How much farther?" said Sandy resignedly.

"Just round the loch and through that first lot of trees," Ninian told him.

They walked on along the edge of the water, the heather swishing round their feet, and reminisced of last summer.

"This one's been just as good," said Jamie decidedly.

"Better really," said Sandy.

A burn came tumbling into the loch from one of the smaller ones that lay round it.

"Let's have a drink?" suggested Sandy, stopping on a rock half-way across.

"I'm going to wait," said Fiona, "and drink out of the Fairy Burn. It's not much farther."

There was still no sign of wind. Even so Ninian kept glancing behind him just in case. He wished Fergus would have let them keep *Fauna* in the harbour but it was for their own good that he had not. He had not wanted them to get mixed up with the smugglers if anything had happened.

"I wonder what father would think of all this," thought Ninian. "Would he have a fit or not? Probably be livid. It's just as well he's still abroad."

As they passed the small loch a couple of teal flew up out of the reeds and again Sandy longed for the gun.

"Think what a delicious dinner we could have had," he grumbled. "Roast grouse, roast duck — we shall probably see some snipe too."

"There's one now," said Jean, as a small brown bird darted away over the boggy ground at the head of Loch an Draing.

They were nearly in the wood now. Birch, oak, rowan and hazel trees with an occasional tall pine rearing up its dark head were scattered between the two lochs, and as they got amongst them it was suddenly cool. The trees grew thicker and thicker shouldering each other over the moss-covered boulders and forcing the Stewarts to fight their way through.

"You can see that no one ever comes here," said Hugh, crawling on all fours after Ninian under a bent birch tree.

"The crofters think it's haunted," said James. "I'm not surprised either: it is a bit creepy-feeling, being so thick and tangly."

"It's getting better," said Ninian, who was in front. "There are more pine trees here."

He was able to stand soon, and waited for the others to come up, brushing dead leaves and grass off his kilt.

"Listen a minute," said Fiona, when they were standing under a thick oak tree.

They stood motionless, peering into the leaves.

"What is it?" whispered James.

"It's nothing, just the silence. Have you ever heard anything so still, and especially in a wood?" said Fiona.

Indeed there was no sound, no crack of breaking twigs, no whisper of leaf against leaf, no rustle of falling acorn or cone. It was still and cool and quiet.

"Like a church," whispered Jean.

"A cathedral," said Hugh.

"An abbey," said Fiona. She shivered. "Come on," she said, "it is a bit creepy."

They pushed on between oak and pine, their feet rustling over generations of dead leaves and small broken twigs. Gradually the trees grew thinner although the bulk of wood in front made it no lighter.

"I can hear a burn," said Jean presently.

"The Fairy Burn," said Ninian, hurrying on. The silent gloom of the wood was depressing them all.

Suddenly they emerged through the last of the oaks into a glade of tall rugged Scotch firs. Between their rough trunks lay the water of the Fairy Loch, as dark as a sapphire.

It was wedge-shaped and two of its sides lay among the trees while the third was out in the sunshine of the moor.

"The Fairy Loch," whispered Jean, her eyes as large as saucers, looking as if she expected the Green Laddie to come walking between the trees at any minute.

At this corner of the wedge the trees grew so tall that they met overhead, darkening the water until it looked like jet.

"It's funny that there should only be pines growing here,' said Hugh. "I wonder why it is?"

Fiona shrugged. "It's lovely, isn't it?" she said. "And it's not nearly so creepy here either."

"Shall we go out on the moor to have lunch, or have it in here?" asked James.

"Oh, here," said Fiona. "It isn't too creepy, is it?"

For an answer Ninian sat down and heaved off the knapsack of sandwiches that he had been carrying.

"After all," said Jean, half to herself, "the Green Laddie was a friendly fairy."

They sat among the pine-needles on a little bluff above the water, their backs resting against huge gnarled trunks of trees that had been there for hundreds of years. Looking across the loch was rather like looking down a tunnel, so dark were the trees on either side, so bright was the sun outside.

Fiona lay on her back while she chewed and looked up at the thick entwined branches above her, black and twisted like serpents. A darker patch showed that a squirrel had its nest up there.

"A real red squirrel," thought Fiona. "Not one of those horrid grey rats!"

The hot sun beating on the pines gave forth a most delicious smell, and, looking up, myriads of pin-points of light between the needles made the whole ceiling look as if fire-flies were up there or that the Milky Way had come much closer. The tree trunks certainly did look like the pillars in a church, thought Fiona, although beech trees were really the best for that. But there was something about the cool quiet of a wood like this that was like the stillness that is felt on entering a church after the glare of summer outside.

"I wonder how deep this loch is?" said Hugh, peering at the black water. "It looks unfathomable."

"I don't know," said Ninian, "but this end looks pretty grim. There's no beach at all — the ground seems to fall straight away."

A sudden clatter of wings in the branches over their heads made them look up. Bits of twig and bark scattered down amongst them.

"Some clumsy old wood pigeon," said Jamie. "I suppose it's suddenly seen us."

"I'd begun to think that this wood was really haunted and that no animals lived in it," said Hugh. "I suppose they are all asleep or something."

Jamie crawled to the edge of the bluff with his ham sandwich and hung over, munching and staring down into the loch. Although it grew deep so suddenly, where the water touched the shore it was pale amber quickly darkening into a rich brown peaty liquid that looked very much like stout, especially in one corner under an overhanging rock where creamy yellow froth had gathered. Peer as he might Jamie could see nothing of the bottom of the loch, no boulder, no frond of weed, no fin of trout. He rested his chin on his folded arms and gazed along the length of the loch, chewing slowly. Flashes of sunlight, breaking through the pine branches, lay on the still water like scattered coins, while beyond the tunnel of the trees the moor sloped slowly down to the crofts of Inverasdale. They were too far away to be visible, but Jamie could see the thin blue spirals of peat smoke rising slowly in the still air. He was too low down to see the white sand of Fienn Mor and Loch Carrick beyond it. The trees arching above the end of the Fairy Loch framed the view like a picture. Jamie envied the Green Laddie living in the shelter and peace of this wood.

Thoughtfully, he dropped a crumb into the water and watched it enlarge and then sink slowly as it became waterlogged. Fiona was kicking his leg.

"Cake, Jamie?"

He rolled over and took a piece. It was fruit cake, thick with currants and sultanas and an occasional red cherry.

"I say," said Jean, "we've got some sandwiches left. Let's cut them up small and leave them for the Green Laddie."

"That's an idea," said Hugh. "We could wrap them in a leaf and put them somewhere where he's likely to look."

"How tall d'you suppose he is?" asked Sandy.

"Oh, tallish, about three foot," said Ninian.

Hugh pulled out his knife and cut the remaining sandwiches in half.

"D'you think he likes crusts?" he asked.

"No, he may be very old and toothless," said Fiona. "Better cut them off."

The crusts were removed and broken up for the birds. Jean returned from the thick part of the wood with the largest leaf she could find to wrap the food in. Jamie climbed up a pine and broke off a new green needle for a fastening. Fiona hunted about until she found a dry hollow in one of the trees at a convenient height from the ground.

"He'll be able to reach it all right in here," she said. "It's nice and dry, too."

Slowly they tidied up the mess from lunch and put the paper back in the knapsacks.

"What shall we do now?" asked Jean. "Can we fish?"

"Not in this loch." Ninian yawned and stretched his arms behind his head. "You'd only get frightfully tangled up. Go and try in the big loch, although it's much too bright."

"Aren't you coming?" asked Jean, in surprise.

"Yes, presently," Ninian's eyes were almost shut. The warm silence of the wood, the knowledge of the boiling heat outside, and the fullness after the meal he had just eaten were making him feel incredibly sleepy.

Jean shrugged her shoulders at the peculiarity of older people who could waste an afternoon in sleep. She supposed that some time she probably would too, but at the moment it was enough to be in an unexplored bit of country with a rod and fly-book and large glittering loch at one's disposal. James and Sandy were of the same frame of mind, and they left the others prostrate and went out through the wood by the way they had come.

Hugh, Ninian and Fiona lay comfortably on the pine-needles, listening to the footsteps and the crackling of twigs grow fainter until again there was complete silence.

Fiona lay on her back watching, through half-closed eyes, the points of sunlight flickering in the dense blackness of the branches. The silence, which had been so deep when all of them were there laughing and talking and eating, was, now that there was no human noise, filled with tiny indistinguishable sounds. Somewhere, far in the woods where no one ever penetrated, was the summer noise of doves, more languorous than the sea on a hot day. In the tree above her head something was scratching and a tiny shower of bark and twigs scattered down beside her. She opened her eyes and looked up but there was no sign of a squirrel: the branches were much too dense. Something splashed in the loch, a trout probably, after a midge, and beyond on the moor, two grouse were calling, and so still was it that she could hear the whistling of twites as they flitted from rock to rock amongst the grass and heather. The sound of the burn, too, that ran out of the loch at the far end, came distinctly every so often and then faded. The other burn, running into the loch through the wood was nearly silent. It had cut itself a deep channel and, although it was noisy farther back in the hazel wood where rocks and tree trunks provided water-falls, down here on the level ground it made no sound. It would be fun, thought Fiona, to follow it up through the wood, crawling in it under the branches that wove themselves into a canopy above, climbing up the black slippery falls in a shower of spray. There would be big falls, too, when it reached the hills, for they rose steeply and the wood covered them half-way to the top. She was so taken with the idea that she half thought of waking Ninian and Hugh and getting them to accompany her. One glance at them, however, showed that they were very fast asleep.

"Shall I stay here or not?" she wondered. Certainly it was comfortable beneath the trees and it would take no time before she too was asleep, yet it was their last day and it seemed a waste to spend it in oblivion of such surroundings. The twins and Sandy were not doing so. Even if they caught no fish they would at least have not wasted so perfect an afternoon.

Softly she got to her feet. If they had wakened she would have taken them with her, but they slept on. "Lazy hogs," she thought. It seemed a pity not to wake them, but it would be fun to be alone for once, to explore and find a place of one's own.

Her feet made no sound on the pine needles. She reached the burn and stood looking at it. The first part of the journey would be easy, for the trees were not too dense, but as they grew closer it would be simplest to climb along the rocks in the water. At the beginning of the hazel wood she rolled up her trousers as far as they would go. She had sandshoes on and it would not hurt them to get wet. There were plenty of rocks to use as stepping-stones and she pushed on among the branches. It was hot work, continually stooping and trying to keep one's balance. Half of the stones were just beneath the water and very slippery. Before she had gone far both Fiona's feet were wet and then it did not matter walking in the burn itself, where it was shallow-enough. The water was icy cold, not surprising, thought Fiona, seeing that it comes down from the hills. In front of her a rowan grew right over the burn and she had to crawl under it, hands on one lot of rocks, feet on another. Shafts of light slanted between the boughs and lit the sherry-coloured water. Fiona, upright for a moment and pushing back the hair that would flop over her face, stood still, listening. The roar of the burn was growing louder: she must be up to the hills at last. She wriggled her shoulders where a piece of bark had fallen down her back and was scratching, then she ducked under the next branch.

The roar grew louder and louder. Then suddenly she was standing upright and a great sheet of water was pouring down in front of her. There was a gap in the trees here and the sun was full on the fall. The myriad drops of spray that flew off the water were like a golden halo. There was a big pool under the fall, a deep one, and Fiona climbed on to the bank and walked round it. The cliff in front of her was fairly steep and the trees pressing in on the narrow channel made the climb most difficult. Some of their leaves dangled in the water and one tall delicate birch reached out farther than the rest and drooped a fragile branch of black and pale green into the middle of the fall.

Fiona hauled herself up by the trees that clung somehow from crevices in the dank black rock. It was like climbing a living ladder with rungs of birch and rowan and hazel.

At the top of the fall was a little plateau of grass right on the cliff's edge. Fiona lay there for a few minutes, her chin on her elbows, looking over the tops of the trees in the Fairy Wood. She was not high enough yet to see the moor and the loch beyond it, but another climb like the one she had just done should bring her near the top. She turned and went on through the wood, jumping from rock to rock along the burn. It was fairly racing down here and the trees grew taller so that it was like walking down a tunnel.

"In a cool curving world he lies," said Fiona to herself, and felt rather like the fish, for the light through the leaves lit the world she stood in with a translucent green.

After a few hundred yards of uphill climbing along the burn, the noise of water grew louder and in a few minutes she stood again in front of a fall. This time there were rocks projecting out of it all the way down, and Fiona skirted the pool at its foot and started climbing in a shower of spray. Handfuls of grass, that hung over the rocks like wet hair, came away in her hands and every foothold was as slippery as ice. Her fingers and feet got numb even though the sun on her back was hot. As she was reaching for the trunk of small birch growing out of a tiny island, the rock she was standing on slipped. She grabbed the tree and hung there while a shower of stones and pebbles rattled down the cliff and splashed dully into the pool below. The icy water trickled down her body and she looked wildly for a ledge to put her feet. By hauling herself up an inch or two she could reach one, and a few moments later stood at the top of the fall, panting and pretending that her heart was not really pounding so much. The pool at the bottom looked a long way away and the rocks in it would have made a horrid mess of her. She shivered, partly with cold from her wet clothes, and hurried on into the wood. Presently, the trees thinned and the hot moor was before her. She was thankful for it because her clothes were clammy. Resolutely, she did not look back when she was out of the wood. She would wait until she reached the summit and could drink in the whole view. The hill she was climbing was not really high, but all the ground in front of it sloped down to the sea.

Coming out from the cool of the wood to the moor was like stepping suddenly into a boiler-house. It was incredibly, blazingly hot. She could feel it baking up through her shoes from the ground and after a few minutes her shirt was almost dry. The earth in the peat hags was cracked: she could hardly bear her hand on the rocks. Flies buzzed about her; twites flickered across the heather like bats; a speck high above the horizon was a buzzard, soaring effortlessly above the hot toiling creatures on earth. She was going much too fast but she would not stop now. The top was nearly in reach: she would fling herself on the ground and watch the sky swing above her as she recovered her breath. Even as she thought it she was there and flung herself panting on the warm turf. For a while she lay with eyes closed, listening to her heart knocking on her ribs, then she rolled over and looked out towards the Hebrides.

It was a wonderful view and it was all hers, for ever. There was no one who had shared it with her.

Directly below lay the Fairy Wood like a green patchwork, dark pines, pale birches, and a splash of red from a bunch of rowan berries. All that showed of the Fairy Loch was a small slip of blue in its farthest corner, but the big loch was there and Fiona, screwing up her eyes, could see three small figures on its far shore. They seemed to be paddling more than fishing and she did not blame them. The sea was intensely blue beyond the rim of the cliff, and so was Loch

IT WAS A WONDERFUL VIEW.

Carrick, with a black spider of a boat crawling in to Inverasdale. The small white crofts looked asleep in the sun and there was only an occasional spiral of blue smoke ascending from them. Black Aberdeen Angus were grazing on the hills near the village and the telephone booth at Naast looked startlingly red in the sun. Turning, she found she could look up the loch towards Carrick itself and saw the black patch of pines round Camas Glas and a small speck that was *Black Swan*. Ben Carrick was huge and blue in the heat haze and so were the far peaks of Cam More and the hills of Corriedon. She lay there, her mind ranging over the country that she knew and out to the Hebrides.

The slow dipping of the sun and a faint shout from the wood brought her back to reality. There were some slim clouds on the horizon: she hoped it did not mean wind. She jumped up and glanced round, suddenly remembering that she had never followed the burn to its source. It went on along the top of the hill and there was not time now — it would have to be explored another day. She decided to go down by the edge of the wood and started to run downhill. It was impossible to stop once she had started and on she charged faster and faster — no time to pick which tuft to step on next — they were flying beneath her. She ended up by catching her foot in a hole and rolling over and over until she grabbed a bunch of heather and so stopped herself. From then on she proceeded more sedately, scaring the rabbits that were sunning themselves on the edge of the wood and sending a covey of grouse swinging up the hillside. A little roe-deer leaped into the wood and disappeared and she was glad, for it showed that animals did really live in it, it was not haunted.

At last she rounded the corner of the wood and went back towards the loch. She could hear the boys' voices and came upon the water suddenly, round a huge pine. It was as black and still as ever and Fiona felt as though she was looking into a cave, so arched were the trees above it. Across the dark water were Ninian and Hugh sitting by a wood fire. Midges, of course. She had escaped them, being on the top of the hill.

Hugh looked up at that moment and saw her.

"Come on," he called. "Where have you been?"

She walked slowly round the edge of the loch between the pine-trunks.

"What have you been doing?" said Ninian, when she got closer. "You look as if you'd come through a hedge backwards."

"And you two lazy hogs look as if you'd just wakened up, which I suppose you have," retorted Fiona.

"No, but you are in a mess, really," said Hugh.

"Well, I've been up the burn to the top of the hill," said Fiona. "You'd look like this too after climbing waterfalls and nearly being hurled to your death."

"You might have wakened us," grumbled Hugh.

"You needn't have gone to sleep." Fiona kicked a flaming branch. The smell of burning pine wood was delicious.

"What was it like up there?" asked Ninian.

"Bliss," said Fiona. "You could see for miles. And it's grilling out, too."

As she spoke she stood still to listen.

"What is it?" Ninian looked at her.

"You can hear it too, you're not deaf."

"Hear what?"

"Shsh!"

"Yes," said Hugh. "It's the trees. The wind must have got up."

All through the wood there was a soft sighing and a faint far rustling as the leaves gently moved. It seemed as if the wood had come to life and was breathing.

"It sounds like the sea, far away," said Hugh.

"It'll be lovely going back," said Fiona. "Not so hot."

"I suppose we'd better start." Ninian slung a couple of knapsacks on his shoulder.

315

Hugh stamped on the burning branches and sparks caught and flared among the needles.

"Careful, put it all out," said Fiona, stamping. "We don't want the Green Laddie to lose his home."

Soon a blackened round was the only sign of the fire. Fiona scattered the pine-needles over it.

"Then he won't know we've been here at all," she said.

"Except for the sandwiches," Ninian reminded her.

Regretfully, they left the cool glade, their church, their cathedral, their abbey. They hurried out through the thick trees, and across to the loch where the twins and Sandy were still playing.

They had given up all pretence of fishing and were wading out to a tiny heather-covered island some fifty yards from the far shore. Sandy was there already, but Jean and James were getting extremely wet.

"Come on, you three," shouted Ninian, when they came nearer.

"Caught anything?" called Fiona.

"No," came back a chorus.

By the time they had reached the grey boat Sandy and the twins had waded ashore and were wringing the water out of the legs of their shorts.

"No fish?" Ninian raised a scathing eyebrow.

"It's much too hot," said Sandy. "Anyway, it was dull with only one rod."

Jean untied the cast and wound in the reel. Jamie took the rod to pieces and slid them into their case.

The cool south-west wind stirred the heather and whistled in the long grasses. It blew a lock of white hair into Jean's eyes and she tossed it back, looking enviously at the ripple spreading over the loch.

"It's too late," said Fiona.

"Anyway, the sun's as bright as ever," said Hugh.

"I suppose so." Jean sounded extremely doubtful.

"It must be nearly six," said Ninian, looking at the sun.

"I'm getting hungry, too."

"I should think so, after all the exercise you've had this afternoon," said Fiona.

Ninian ignored her.

They climbed the short hill up from the loch and then started on their long descent to the sea. Once out of the shelter of the hills the wind came rushing at them, not cold but infinitely refreshing, as it moved the heavy hot air that had lain on the hills all day.

They looked up at a rush of wings over their heads. It was duck flying home to rest on the loch behind them.

"Four, five, six," counted James. "I wonder if they go to the Fairy Loch or the other one?"

"The Fairy Loch's too dark and creepy," said Jean, thinking how much she would hate to sleep there even if she was a duck and had five comrades to nestle up against.

"I wonder what Fergus has been doing all day?" said Sandy.

"I wish Rory could come over." Jean had liked this large young Macloud although he had held her over the battlements of Taransay by the seat of her trousers.

"Perhaps he will somehow. They do very unexpected things," said Hugh.

"I don't see how he could. The *Star's* this side," said Fiona.

Ninian said nothing. He was feeling too aware of the fact that this was his last evening, that this time to-morrow he would be in a hot and airless train, watching the hills flash past, knowing he could do nothing to stay with them.

The cool wind came sweeping in from the sea, bringing a tang of salt to the hot heather and scented hills. As she walked, Fiona felt it blow right through her. It did not make her cold, but she felt as though she was transparent. She hardly walked; her feet did not seem to touch the ground; she felt greater than ordinary humans, as if she belonged to another sphere. All the time her eyes were fixed on the dim blue band of the Hebrides that bordered every view she could remember, looking to the west. She wished this evening did not have to end: perhaps it would not but would remain however far on they went themselves. The sky was flaming from beyond Slaggan all along the Minch, such shades of pink and gold that would not be believed unless they had been seen. The thin clouds, dark against the sunset, were, if you looked long enough, exactly like headlands reaching into an orange loch, reflected from an orange sky.

"This mustn't stop, it mustn't!" cried Fiona to herself, and so that the others would not see or hear she went flying on down the hill, her body feeling so light and cool that if she half closed her eyes she could imagine she was flying. The others found her at the top of the last slope down to the cliff. She was lying flat, looking over the sea and plaiting three rushes.

"Hurry up, slow coaches!" One of the rushes broke and she flung them away.

"You do look wild," said Ninian, grinning. "Your hair's full of twigs, your face is black, your —"

"Who cares?" Fiona jumped up. "Anyway you've got pine needles all over you."

"Come on, I'm hungry," protested Sandy.

"You'll have to wait," Fiona said. "We're having dinner with Fergus, remember, and he may not be ready."

"Well, a biscuit would fill up a corner," said Sandy.

They went on down the last of the hill, tired enough and hungry enough to find the thought of *Fauna* very welcome.

The magic of the evening was still there and the whole of Flatfish Bay was filled with colour. The breakers of the outgoing tide were pink and gold, the gulls' wings were pink, two black-faced ewes on the slopes above the bay were tinged with the same colour.

"The dinghy's still there," said Sandy, breaking the spell.

"Thank goodness," added Ninian. It had been in the

back of his mind all day.

They hurried across the sand and along the rocks.

"She's not bumped at all," said Jean.

Ninian rowed them out to *Fauna*.

"What's that stuck in the hatch?" cried Jamie.

"Where?" he craned over his shoulder.

"It's a letter," said Sandy.

"From Fergus, I expect," said Jean.

Standing on deck, Fiona read it. "It only says, 'Dinner to-night in the bay by the Stack at midnight.' "

"Midnight!" shrieked Sandy. "We can't wait till then!"

"No, we'll have something first."

She looked round at the gulls and the Stack and the flaming sky, at the line of the cliff against the blue mist of night, creeping up beyond it, at the empty beach and slow-moving tide, at the faint flash of the light over the headland and a first dim star and wished she was not seeing it for the last time.

CHAPTER XVIII

"WHO WILL GO?"
Thursday, 19th August and Friday, 20th August

MIDNIGHT. It had seemed so long when they had been waiting and now at last they could see by moonlight the hands of Hugh's watch, together at the top.

They talked in whispers as they climbed along the rocks by the Stack. There was no sign of Fergus on the beach; perhaps something had detained him; perhaps he was not coming.

There was a bright half-moon in the sky, a sky as full of stars as a lawn is scattered with daisies. The tide was nearly full. Black and silver waves rolled up on a black and silver beach. So bright was the moon that each rock and lump of sea-weed was clearly shown, as was the cliff and black caverns of caves.

"I wish he'd come," said Jamie, as they walked slowly up the sand.

"Isn't it a super night?" said Fiona. "It's so warm."

"And so light," added Ninian. "I can't remember such a bright moon for ages."

"I wonder where he'll come from?" wondered Jean, looking up at the cliffs.

"Here," said a voice, and Fergus was beside them.

"Hallo — where have you been?" asked Fiona.

"I've been waiting for you," said Fergus.

"We didn't see you, though," said Sandy.

"I know you didn't. You never do if I don't want you to."

"Where are we going?" asked Jean, as they followed Fergus towards the cliff.

"There's a good place among the rocks here," he said, "out of the wind."

"Not that there is much, but still," put in Fiona.

"I'm hot," said Sandy. "I could bathe, easily."

"Well, why don't you?" asked Fergus.

"Yes, let's," said Jean. "By moonlight. It'd be bliss."

"I'll dash back and get the things." Ninian threw the knapsack he was carrying at Hugh, and in a few moments they heard the quick splash of oars as he hurried back to *Fauna*.

"What have you brought for dinner?" asked Fergus, stopping in the shelter of a tall rock.

"Eggs and bacon, tinned peaches, cake and fruit, and chocolate of course."

"And beer." Hugh, as usual, was carrying it.

"What have you brought?" asked Jean.

"Some whisky," said Fergus. "And my squeeze-box."

"Oh, good. You can sing the seal song this time," said Jamie, laughing.

"I didn't know you had a squeeze-box," said Fiona.

"I don't play it very often," Fergus told her. "I prefer the pipes."

They scattered along the high-water mark searching for wood and anything that would burn. By the time Ninian returned with the bathing things a fire was blazing.

"I'll do the cooking while you bathe," said Fergus.

"Don't you want to?" said Jean in surprise.

"No. I'll stay and guard your things from the trolls. Only don't be too long because I'm ravenous."

A few seconds later they were flying over the firm wet sand and out through the first line of breakers.

"Why haven't we bathed at night before?" cried Fiona. "It's much the best time."

The sea was almost warm. They plunged through the moonlit waves and out into the calm deep water beyond. Fergus, watching them from the shore, thought they looked like a family of seals, except that seals did not make so much noise. He bent down and put on the pan of bacon, screwing up his face as the wood-smoke blew into his eyes. At once the fat began to splatter and smelt delicious.

"Hurry up," he called.

The seals turned in towards the shore and, splashing like fountains in the silver water, raced each other back.

"I'm cold," cried Jean, running up the beach.

Fergus picked up his box and started to play a reel.

"Come on," shouted Sandy.

"There's two missing!" cried James.

"Doesn't matter." Fiona seized his hand and they danced

FERGUS PICKED UP HIS BOX AND STARTED TO PLAY.

a wild eightsome on the sand. Half-way through Fergus changed to Strip the Willow, and while the Stewarts were whirling down the line he suddenly remembered the bacon. The music stopped abruptly. Fergus scraped madly with a knife. It was hardly burnt at all.

"What happened?" asked Ninian, as they came up, breathless and laughing.

"Any one hungry?" Fergus cracked an egg on the side of the pan and dropped it in amongst the bacon and small pieces of twig and seaweed that had got in somehow.

"Hungry?" said Sandy, pulling his jersey on. "Hurry up, Fergus."

The eggs were done. Bread and butter was cut. Beer bottles opened. There was silence but for the scrape of a knife on a tin plate, the gurgle as someone drank from a bottle, somebody asking for the salt. At last, full and content, they lay back on the sand, lazily sucking chocolate.

"What a night," said Hugh, looking up at the blazing sky. They listened in silence to the shsh-shsh of the waves, the crackle of the dying fire, the lapping of water on the rocks. A curlew called from somewhere in the other bay, and then again. A ghostly cry at night. Fiona, listening, remembered how Ninian used to call them sea nightingales. He was right too. If a nightingale's heart was broken, a curlew's was lost, and he was for ever searching for something he could not find. Again it came, a bubbling, haunting cry. She moved uneasily, it was too sad a sound at night, this night especially.

Sandy swallowed his chocolate and reached out to break off another piece. "What a lot we've done this time," he said.

"Yes", said Fiona, glad of a chance to talk. "We've found the Whisky Cave."

"And Fergus," added Jean.

"The best harbour on this coast," said Jamie.

"We've sailed by night with no compass." Ninian, on his back, looked up at the stars.

"Explored Faraway."

"And the Fairy Loch."

"Fairloch and Corriedon."

"And the lighthouse."

"And Taransay," said Fergus, in his deep voice.

"When are you going back?" asked Hugh.

"To-night."

"To-night?" said Jean in horror.

"Yes, the *Star* should be out any minute."

"Must you go to-night?" asked James.

"Yes, I must."

"Why?" began Jean, but Fiona kicked her. She knew that if Fergus said he must go he would, and that he would not like any of them to ask why.

Seeing how gloomy they looked, Fergus picked up his accordion and started to play. He played all the songs they knew and could sing, a good many reels and even Jamie's seal song.

Then he played his own.

"Who will go with Fergus now,"

"We did," said Jamie.

"And pierce the deep wood's woven shade,"

"Us, this afternoon." Sandy rubbed a scratch on his arm.

"And dance upon the level shore?"

"We just have." Fiona sat up.

"Young man, lift up your russet brow,"

Ninian looked up.

"And lift your tender eyelids, maid,"

Fiona smiled at him.

"   And brood on hopes and fears no more.

    .   .   .   .

    And no more turn aside and brood
    Upon Love's bitter mystery;
    For Fergus rides the brazen cars,"

His voice ran out.

"He means the sun as well," said Hugh.

"And rules the shadows of the wood,"

"D'you think he's the Green Laddie?" whispered Jean.

"And the white breast of the dim sea,"

"It's more silver really, to-night," said James.

"And all dishevelled Wandering Stars."

There was silence as he finished. Fiona, turning to look out to sea, saw that the *Star* was already in the bay. Her sail was down and she drifted easily between the wind and the tide.

"I must go," said Fergus, jumping up. "They're waiting for me. Do any of you want to come too?"

"We can't," said Fiona miserably.

"Never mind," Fergus smiled. "No, don't get up, stay here!" He turned as he spoke and started off across the beach.

"Good-bye!" cried the Stewarts.

"Good-bye," he called back over his shoulder.

He reached the rocks and dropped into his dinghy, which he had left moored there. They watched him row across to the *Star*. She looked so graceful in the moonlight with her mast and shrouds moving slowly against the sky. Beyond her lay *Fauna*, small solid ark, and Fiona felt a sudden longing for her warm and friendly cabin. Very soon the *Star* would be sailing out of the bay, as *Fauna* would too, next morning. But instead of going west towards the moon with the silence of a sailing ship, she would be going home, chugging back into the loch to her old moorings.

They heard the bump of the dinghy alongside and saw Fergus climbing on board. He called something and the *Star*'s big sail crept up. She turned, with Fergus at the tiller, and moved slowly out along the moon's path over the dim sea.

Fergus did not look back though they watched until they could no longer distinguish him, and the *Wandering Star* might have been any ship upon any moonlit sea.

Then the curlew called again from the edge of the tide and Fiona came back to earth and shivered.

"I wonder if we shall ever see him again?" said Jamie.

THE END

fidra*books*

We are a small publishing company, specialising in reprinting some of the best children's fiction from the 20th century. By reissuing these books, we are enabling collectors to acquire the books that they have been searching for and also bringing the books to a new generation of readers.

Authors whose work is being published by Fidra Books include Mabel Esther Allan, Joanna Cannan, Primrose Cumming, Anne Digby, Elinor Lyon, K M Peyton, Josephine Pullein-Thompson and Victoria Walker.

Details of titles already published and forthcoming can be found on our website or by contacting us at the address below.

Fidra Books Ltd
60 Craigcrook Road
Edinburgh
EH4 3PJ

www.fidrabooks.com

The House in Hiding

by Elinor Lyon

Ian and Sovra are thrilled when their father, Dr Kennedy, buys them a boat of their own. Exploring the loch, they discover a stone stairway hidden behind a waterfall and an abandoned shieling – the perfect place to camp. The arrival of the awful Mrs Paget and her irritating daughter, Ann, interferes with their plans to a degree, but Ian and Sovra still manage to explore the abandoned village of Kindrachill on the isolated Fionn-ard peninsula. There is a legend that when the village is left empty, the heir of Kindrachill will only return when a fire is kindled in the hearth of his own house. But the last heir, Alistair, was reported killed in the Far East some years before...

We Met Our Cousins

by Joanna Cannan

First published in 1937, *We Met Our Cousins* concerns John and Antonia who are sent from London to spend the holidays with their Scottish cousins and their grandfather at Roid House in the Scottish Highlands. The children are initially incompatible, with John and Antonia (from whose perspective the book is written) cosseted and rather precious whilst Angus and Morag and the younger Hamish are wild and scruffy and spend their time riding and sailing. Despite a prickly start, when John saves wee Hamish from a maddened bull, friendships are firmly cemented, especially when they manage to discover the truth of the MacTavish and MacAlister feud.

Fly-By-Night

by KM Peyton

Fly-by-Night was not the best choice for an eleven-year-old girl who had never ridden before; but as soon as Ruth Hollis saw the sturdy, lively pony, she knew that he was the one she wanted. All her life Ruth had longed to own a pony and now that her family had moved from London to a new housing estate in East Anglia, she had persuaded her father to let her spend her savings on a pony. But having taken possesion of Fly-by-Night, Ruth found that her troubles had only just begun.

The Winter of Enchantment

by Victoria Walker

A magic mirror enables Sebastian to travel from his Victorian world to that of Melissa, Mantari, a wicked Enchanter and many other exciting people. Melissa has been imprisoned in a large house by the Enchanter who intends to keep her there for ever and ever. Sebastian first meets Melissa through the magic mirror and resolves to do everything in his power (and with the help of a little magic) to free her. This involves collecting together all the wicked Enchanter's 'Power Objects': the mirror, a teapot, a silver fish, an emerald and a green rose, throwing them into a magic well and so destroying the Enchanter's power. An iconic and elusive book written by the author when she was just 21, *The Winter of Enchantment* has been out of print for thirty years and its reissue has been clamoured for by many.